VALOR'S WORTH

THE WINDRIDER SAGA:BOOK 3

REBECCA P. MINOR

REALM MAKERS

Published by Realm Makers Media

939 N Washington St

Pottstown, PA 19464

ISBN:978-0-9962718-7-5 (print)

978-0-9962718-6-8 (ebook)

Cover art by Kirk DouPonce, DogEared Design

Editing by Catherine Jones Payne/Quill Pen Editorial

For Scott, who bears with me with the patience of Majestrin, even when I am as stubborn as Vinyanel.

PROLOGUE

First blood, then bones in circle cast,
Forthwith to fill each darkling cleft.
Ne'er tarry till moondeath is past,
Lest grinding toil leave ye bereft
The legion ye be due.
Queldurik's reign ensue

NAGHAX PUSHED ASIDE THE NEAREST BOUGHS OF AN EVERGREEN and settled a glare upon the rough stucco of the cottage just beyond the forest's edge. The tidy structure stood at the western boundary of a little village composed of a score of similar single-story dwellings. Windows stood dark or shuttered. No human activity stirred along the dirt byways between the buildings. For the moment, utter peace reigned amidst cricket songs and dapples of moonlight that filtered between dry autumn oak leaves overhead.

He twitched the tip of his ridged tail. The fire of urgency surged through his veins, and he flexed his clawed fingers against the itch to draw his sword and make an end of the silent suspense.

His companion's voice rumbled from behind him. "Sit still, would you? Standing on a fire anthill?"

Naghax cracked his knuckles. "You know the softbellies' patrols won't bother to ask questions of any dragon-kin they find on their outskirts. Every delay threatens to undo our stealth."

"Your nervous prattle will undo us faster." Hanash pushed back his hood to reveal his reptilian head and disapproving glare. "Shut up."

A flare of light arced across the ebony sky above, and Naghax looked to trace the path of the flaming ball of catapult shot that streamed on a ruinous path toward the village center. A grin creased his cheeks when the shot crashed into the wood-shingled roof of the council building.

"There, see?" Hanash slid his scimitar free of its scabbard. "It won't be long now."

A mechanical *ka-chunk* from somewhere in the deep cover of the woods rang out, and a streaking comet sailed into view. This one smashed through the front window of the building with a satisfying tinkle of shattered glass. A bell pealed in a stout fieldstone tower, far across town from where Naghax and Hanash crouched.

Naghax's focus settled back upon the nearest home. Surely the lout inside must hear the bell. Who could miss the shrill of its desperate alarm? Finally, some of the other little dwellings surrounding the council building flared to life, the yellow glow of candle and lantern swelling in their windows. As if to join their ranks, slivers of light lanced through the chinks in the shutters just feet away.

Despite his long anticipation, Naghax still jumped when the front door to the dwelling burst open. A long-legged man in a hastily wrapped toga and unevenly laced sandals marched out. He reached under his arm and tightened a final buckle on his leather breastplate. A woman in a pale dressing gown trailed behind him, a beaten bronze helmet in hand. They halted a few paces from the house. The man turned his face to the spreading flames a furlong away. His eyes hardened, and his jaw muscles bulged.

"What could this mean?" the woman asked.

"Perhaps we are compromised," the man replied.

Perhaps. Naghax suppressed a snort.

Another figure, lankier and a hand span shorter than the first male softbelly, dashed from the home. He, too, buckled a breastplate. "Father, what should we do?"

So many of the problematic members of the household were now outside. Naghax looked to his comrade and raised an eyebrow.

"They'll go," Hanash whispered. "You'll see."

Finally, a clamor arose somewhere in the shadows beyond the growing flames in the distance. The clash of steel and the shouts of both softbellies and Naghax's own kinsman cut through the crackle of flame. The harsh scent of smoke stung his nostrils.

The woman handed the elder softbelly his helm. "Creo shield you, beloved."

He looked to the youth. "Ready, Son?"

The youth swept a sword from the scabbard at his hip with a clear ring. "Lead on, Father."

"Praesidio, please," The woman stepped toward the youth and straightened his armor. Her voice was tight. "Stay close to your father."

The three softbellies embraced, and Naghax writhed as though his scales were too confining. *Get on with it—so much ceremony!*

At last, the two men, the young and the mature, dashed for the fire. The woman watched after for a long moment that stretched into an opportunity Naghax could not have orchestrated more perfectly.

With a leap that released all the tension of the wait, Naghax and Hanash sprang from the cover of the shadows. Naghax bared blackened steel and filled the gap between the woman and her front door. Just as planned, Hanash intercepted her while Naghax lunged through the entry.

Guttering candlelight cast a dance of hard, black shadows around the first floor of the dwelling. At the foot of a rough wood ladder to a loft, there *they* huddled. Could anyone have made the task simpler? Three softbelly maidens, none yet old enough for the blossom of womanhood to cast doubt upon her purity, clung to one another. The youngest shrieked—and well she should.

Another sharp, feminine cry from outside the door implied that Naghax's partner had cleared the way. He descended upon the maidens, his webbed wings spread for dramatic effect, and grabbed at the eldest.

"Cassia! Marilla! Run!" Naghax's target screamed. She writhed and kicked against his grasp, but he wrestled her behind his forearm and clamped his opposite hand over her mouth.

Naghax swallowed a cry as his prisoner's teeth found their way between some of his palm scales and cut flesh. Blood squeezed from his veins. *Serves her right.* She could live with a bloodied face and whatever mouthful she got of the acidic stuff.

Still, she wrenched her crimson-smeared mouth free. "Find Father!"

The other two girls, in a stream of tears and panic, bolted around the roughly-crafted dining table and toward the door, only to be met by Hanash, who pounced upon them and caught the two smaller maidens under his arms.

"Mama! Papa, help!" the smallest girl squealed.

"It's no good, my lambs," Hanash said. "Papa can't hear you. And Mama's busy trying to tuck her innards back where they belong."

With a swift kick, Naghax swept the eldest maiden's feet from beneath her. He shouldered the door wider and dragged his flailing prisoner through. At the sight of her mother sprawled in a spreading pool of her own blood, the girl shuddered and fell silent.

The chaos in the distance had reached just the right, fevered, distracting pitch. Naghax and Hanash, along with their cargo of maidens undefiled, vanished into the embrace of the darkness.

Finally, the Chalice of Gherag-Tal would awake.

1
_____

THE PHOENIX

We sailed high over the dense pine forests of northeastern Kelmirith, our only companions winging birds, clouds, and wind. The westering sun warmed my cheeks, although its dip below the horizon would soon usher in the frosty chill of a mid-autumn night. Far below, the winding river Nuruhain flashed, a strip of amber glass set alight by the sun's inevitable slumber.

The rhythmic whoosh of Majestrin's silver wings thrust us forward with both ease and speed, and I grinned. His lithe neck pumped in a slow rhythm with each wing beat, and the topaz glow of the sun played off the reflective surface of his scales. Astride this beast, I became part of both breeze and setting sun.

Our smaller companions, the griffon Erynir and the winged lion Llewethan, flew slightly behind Majestrin and out to his sides, taking full advantage of the path he cut through the force of the headwind. Even so, he drifted almost lazily along, while the griffon and the lion flapped with focus. I called back to their riders.

"This seems as good a region as any to make camp tonight. Agreed?"

From Erynir's back, the dark-skinned North Deklian rider, Hridayesh, leaned around Galdurith, who guided the mount. He shouted back, "Can't you find a village with a decent bed? You'd think elves preferred sleeping on pine needles and moss to a civilized mattress."

I guffawed. "I find there are fewer bugs on the ground than in the beds of most inns."

Behind me, my passenger shuddered. "What a disgusting observation."

"True, nonetheless. I would think of any of us, you would have the deepest objection to sharing your sleeping quarters with fleas, Veranna."

Veranna sighed. "But now that you've brought it up, I'll spend the whole night imagining phantom legs crawling all over me."

"Is an over-active imagination a typical half-elven trait?" I asked.

Veranna stuck her nose in the air.

Squeamish prophetess. I dismissed my irritation. "Major Galdurith, Sergeant Althoron," I yelled to the soldiers guiding the lion and griffon. "We shall make our descent."

A shiver seized Veranna. "It's growing cold quickly. A fire would be best, don't you think, Galdurith?"

I twisted in my saddle and frowned at the prophetess. "It is not worth the time to search for terrain that will shelter a fire enough to mask it."

Galdurith huffed. "With all due respect, sir . . . we're in the middle of nowhere." He threw an arm out to his side. "I don't think anyone will see a fire. Or care about one, anyway." He raked his fingers through his thick shock of blond locks.

I scowled. Though he had opened his remark in a manner befitting an elf of subordinate rank, his tone hardly carried it through. "You can be warm when we have made it safely inside Delsinon's walls."

We circled and wove down to the forest floor, where birds chattered in their raucous end-of-day conversations. The aromas of sap, rich earth, and mouldering leaf litter hung thick in the woodland air. When Majestrin settled to a stop, I cast my glance around the canopy. Only a small gap in the towering sentinels left a view of the pale blue sky.

A streak of fire lanced across it.

I started. "What was that?"

Galdurith swung down from his saddle and quirked an eyebrow at me. "What was what?"

"None of you saw it? Something just streaked across the sky. In flames."

He stepped to Veranna's side and grasped her hands, upon which she slid from behind me to the ground. She and Galdurith exchanged a glance, a sigh, and a shake of the head.

I gritted my teeth. "'Vinyanel's one stirrup short of a saddle,' eh? Would you two stop?"

"Then cease your jumping at shadows," Veranna replied. She smoothed the rumpled layers of her tiered skirt, setting the bells a-jingle. "You're due for furlough soon, correct? I may suggest to Lerendir an early leave."

I sucked a long breath through my nose. "You would not dare—"

A flash just beyond my peripheral vision cut my words short. I twisted in my saddle.

"You see?" Galdurith said. "She's right."

"One moment," Majestrin rumbled, his voice vibrating through my legs. "I just saw something too. An orange light between the trees."

At least I had one advocate amidst of a passel of doubters.

"Thank you, my friend." In a silent maneuver, I pulled my shield from my back and loosened my sword in its scabbard.

Hridayesh dismounted and landed in a crouch. He scanned the woods where I directed my attention. Althoron followed suit, sliding twin blades from the scabbards on his back and holding them at guard. He licked his lips.

The flash zipped between trees again, now in an erratic zigzag none could deny. It closed the distance between itself and us, and once it had drawn within a hundred paces, Galdurith pulled his crossbow from his back.

I dismounted and landed with a creak of armor plates. My gaze fixed on the fireball.

The bright bolt hesitated, hovered, and pulsed with crackling flames. How could a soldier defend against a fireball, even a small one like this? It lanced straight for me, and I threw my shield up in front of my face. A waft of heat swelled over me, but no impact rocked my shield. No flames licked around it. I peered from behind the barrier.

The fireball stopped about six paces from me, then settled to the ground. Just when I worried it would kindle the mulch covering the forest floor, the flames darkened to deep red. They took form. A long neck sprouted from the fiery center, topped by a small round head and the point of a petite beak. A trail of long feathers grew at the anomaly's posterior. Spindly legs with clawed toes emerged beneath it all.

The last of the flames dimmed until only a smoldering remnant clung along the tips of the creature's cascading tail and on plumage that crowned its head. Within a curl of smoke at the creature's chest, a scroll tube attached to a cord around the fowl's neck coalesced. The fire-turned-bird angled one golden eye to me. After seeming to study me for a moment, it bobbed its way up to my feet in a high-stepping strut. The glow that retreated from its body revealed an array of copper, orange, and vermillion feathers.

"Adramalech's nails!" Hridayesh whispered. "What's this about?"

The bird bent its head to the ground and shimmied until the scroll slid from its neck and landed on the ground. It pushed the tube toward me.

With a slow, deliberate motion, I crouched and placed my hand on the tube. Once I had determined it was cool enough to cause no warming to my gauntleted hand, I closed my fingers around it. I stood again.

The bird watched me while I claimed the item, but after I grasped the scroll, it meandered away and pecked at the ground around it.

I weighed the scroll in my hand. The tube's caps were bronze and pictured a bird in flight, wreathed in flame. I narrowed my eyes and dredged what knowledge of heraldry I possessed.

Veranna eased to my side. "What do you make of it, Vinyanel?"

"Peculiar." I scratched my cheek. "Unless some other group has adopted the image, I would say the scroll comes from the Elgadrim."

Althoron's eyes widened, and he marched straight to my side. "May I?" He extended a hand to me. I placed the case in his palm. After furrowing his brow at the item for a short moment, the light of recognition kindled in his eyes. "From their knighthood—the protectors of their king. But that only makes it more peculiar, since they have no king and there's been no true knighthood in six hundred years."

"That we know of," I said.

I took the alabaster cylinder back from Althoron, twisted one of the caps from it, and tipped it. A roll of vellum slid out. After handing the tube to Althoron, I unrolled the vellum, and my glance lit upon cleanly-penned calligraphy.

"'To the great and enduring Delsin, a missive from a

remnant of the Elgadrim, whom Creo has preserved,'" I read aloud. *If by 'preserved,' they mean 'has driven into hiding and out of casual knowledge.'*

While I read, the bird hopped a few more strides away from the group. With a great thrust of its wings, it leapt into the air, and after only a half-dozen wing beats, erupted into sudden ball of flame that streaked away to the south.

Hridayesh frowned. "And here I was hoping I wouldn't have to bother with the flint and tinder to get a fire going."

"The issue of the fire was settled, assassin," I said without lifting my eyes from the scroll.

"Well?" Galdurith tugged his tooled leather breastplate to straighten it. "Does it seem authentic? That the Elgadrim still exist?"

"It would appear the Elgadrim still exist, Major, if only in pockets," I replied. "And one such pocket has invited the dragon-kin's ire. They request aid from our people."

A realization struck my insides with palpable force. If the dragon-kin were harassing Elgadrim, the beasts still lingered on the mainland. The time I had spent hunting the elven talismans of passage, lost due to their mischief, had not granted them sufficient time to retreat to the Isle of Desolation. Unless their aim was never to make that return journey. My mind began to churn from one thought to the next. My pulse quickened.

"Then we best get this message back home and present it to the Ambassador's Council," Galdurith said. "They can decide if there is any call to heed it."

I shook my head. "We are only a few days' flight from the rendezvous point the Elgadrim have requested. I can see no reason to tie this up in a bureaucratic debate while there is a threat so close that we should investigate. The message came to us—it makes perfect sense for us to gather all the information we can. *That*, we can present to the council and save weeks, at least."

"I would not snap to a decision to embroil ourselves in a human conflict." Galdurith folded his arms.

Veranna narrowed her eyes. "The Elgadrim have historically been the Delsin's staunchest allies. I thought your attitude toward humankind was less, well, elven, Galdurith."

Galdurith straightened his back. "That is not exactly what I meant. I meant on a personal scale. Our party. And besides, those alliances are so old that not even the most aged of our people recall a time when they were in effect. It seems a fluke to me that this message came to us at all."

"I do not believe in flukes, Major," I replied. "It is folly to dismiss this. We would be fools to harbor the delusion the storm does not already amass upon the horizon.

"I seriously doubt the dragon-kin have the numbers to make a noteworthy attack against us."

I groaned. "What hammer hits the Elgadrim will likely deflect into the elf as well. Clearly, the dragon-kin are already making moves. What we need now is decisive action, not debate."

"Moves? Action?" Galdurith spread his hands. "What signs can you point to that make it apparent the dragon-kin have a fight brewing for us?"

"Who can tell how it appears—with all the years we as a people have spent behind our walls and our illusions?" I wrenched my pack down from Majestrin's back. "If nothing else, wisdom demands we at least investigate the threat, if not help a noble but vulnerable people. No workable tactics were ever devised from behind a blindfold."

Galdurith clenched and unclenched his black-gloved fists. "With all due respect, *sir*, I worry that you assume too much authority on the matter."

I took a firm step toward Galdurith, my eyes narrowed.

"And so your true protest finally comes out. Just because you lead with protocol does not give you license to spout whatever you want afterward."

Althoron took a halting step forward. "Begging your pardon, sir, but surely you intend to rest the mounts for the night, no matter what you deem our next step to be, correct? Eyrnir is weary." He indicated his griffon mount. "As is Llewethan." He lashed his tangle of chestnut waves into a tail at the base of his neck and tightened his jaw against a yawn.

I shot a frustrated glare around the group. But Althoron was correct. The griffon and the lion's shoulders hung heavy upon their frames, and their half-lidded eyes rumored they lingered on the threshold of dozing. "You are correct that the smaller mounts do require the sleep. Unsaddle them and set up camp. I will inform you all of our plans in the morning."

*A*t dawn's first blush, Galdurith emerged from his tent and cut a straight path to where I stood on the edge of the camp. He stopped beside me and rubbed his arms. His breath steamed from his lips in crystalline clouds.

"Another six days' flight will place us at Delsinon's gate, correct? Perhaps five if we press harder?" he said.

"I know what you are thinking." I stared straight ahead. "Still too long. I could hope to reach the Elgadrim rendezvous point in three weeks, minimum—and that is *only* if the council decides quickly to allow me to return. 'Quickly' does not fit their history."

"This is the job of an ambassador." Galdurith shook his head. "Something you are definitely not."

A dozen paces to my left, Althoron bundled his bedroll, but his eyes stretched wide. He glanced sidelong at Galdurith.

"The information that needs gathering is military." I said.

"One might even venture intelligence, which would make you a fair candidate to come along."

"We have one mission incomplete already."

I drew a deep breath. "I will send you and Althoron back to Delsinon to deliver the talismans."

Galdurith snorted. "What, and have you miss the accolades for saving the world again?"

I turned a frown upon the major. "Let them throw the parade for you. The pomp turns my stomach. There are far more important issues that I will give my attention."

Rustling and soft words drifted from behind us as the rest of our group began their day. Veranna drew near. She pulled a wool mantle tight around her shoulders.

"It looks to me as though you two have started the day on a sour note," she said. "Such curdled expressions."

It was far too early for her singsong commentary.

Galdurith turned his chin toward her but kept his eyes trained on me. "The lieutenant commander proposes we divide the group so that he can go play envoy while the rest of us tie up his loose ends."

I wheeled on him. "Care to rephrase that, Major?"

Our gazes locked in icy contention.

"I will learn of this Elgadrim remnant what they require of us, and I will glean from them what movements of the dragon-kin army they can report." I swept my glare to each member of the group. "All that information, I shall report to the Council. Yes, our detachment has a duty to 'tie up loose ends.' What remains hardly requires all of us to do so. I assign that task to the Major and Sergeant Althoron."

Althoron shouldered his backpack. "Sir, what of the civilians? One is still technically a prisoner of the crown." He eyed the tent pitched beside his.

"I assume responsibility for Hridayesh," I said. "As for

Veranna, she is under no compulsion to do anything other than her own will."

Hridayesh yawned. "Do you intend to drag me all over the continent until I grow so weary of it that I beg you to put me back in jail?"

"If I send you back now, a decision about your fate might be made before I can return and make my testimony on your behalf. If you want to leave that to chance . . ." I shrugged.

Veranna sighed. "You and Hridayesh cannot meet with the Elgadrim by yourselves."

"Yes," Galdurith said. "Listen to your mentor for once. Let us all stop wasting time, since that is your chief worry, and—"

Slender palm raised, Veranna arrested Galdurith's thought. "What I was implying is that I will accompany the young Windrider and make sure he doesn't miss any of the subtleties in the humans' requests."

Galdurith coughed. His features tightened as he searched her face. "You're supporting him in this?"

"It's more a matter of offering to work as a potential buffer. Vinyanel may be Creo's servant, however rough-edged, but the Elgadrim are the Maker's chosen among men. In this, my having some human parentage is a small advantage." She stepped up to Galdurith, took the strap of his backpack in one hand and smoothed his hair away from his face with the other. "It will be good for the Blackwatch to have the primary hand in returning the talismans. And better for you if many people are not reminded of me when you are standing in public sight." Her eyes lowered.

Galdurith clenched his teeth. "What I choose in my personal dealings will not impact my career as a soldier. Why can you not trust me in that?"

Sorrow creased Veranna's brow, and her glance flicked to his face, then back to the earth. "Even though it is your province to know much, you do not hear everything . . ." Her dark curls fell in a curtain alongside her face and masked her expression.

I left Veranna's conversation with the major to continue unobserved. After collapsing and stowing my tent, I made my way to the glade where Majestrin and the other mounts rested. I approached the silver dragon with my bundle. "Say, friend, how familiar are you with the location of Bilearne's ruins?"

"It's no secret, though I have not flown that way in several years," the silver dragon replied. "It doesn't bother you that your subordinates think you wayward to head there?"

I scrunched my brows. "What makes you say that?"

"Big ears and a distinct lack of white noise out here in the wilderness." He smirked a hint of apology.

"No, I will not heed the Major's complaint this time. I am prepared to face whatever consequences that invites when I return to Delsinon. Dalliance has created the very situation I mean to investigate."

"And what situation is that?" Majestrin asked. "Your urgency belies the idea that the Elgadrim's safety is your primary concern. You're after something closer to your heart."

Leave it to Majestrin to sense the cry of my inmost thoughts. I glanced back toward the camp. I lowered my voice. "The matter of the Chalice of Gherag-Tal being lost to us again has gone unmanaged long enough." Besides Majestrin, only a willful eavesdropper might have caught my words.

The dragon sighed. "As your ordained mount, I am at your service, Lieutenant Commander. But as your friend, I recommend you examine why you feel a need to whisper."

I was not wrong about this. Urgency clutched at my core.

"And I implore that you weigh Veranna's point of view on the excursion."

I draped an arm over Majestrin's neck, between two of his dorsal plates. "You strike a hard bargain, but I heed you, my friend."

. . .

*I*n less than an hour, we all sat mounted, Hridayesh upon the griffon Eyrnir, Veranna behind me on Majestrin, Galdurith and Althoron upon Llewethan.

"Fly safe, officers, and convey the talismans to the chancellor." I tightened a strap on my left gauntlet. "I thank you for your service on this endeavor and wish you Creo's speed and protection as you journey homeward."

Veranna pulled a jade ring from her finger and reached over to hand it to Galdurith. "Convey this to Lerendir as well, and tell him to place it in the Basin of Seeing."

Galdurith raised a brow. "The basin of what?"

"Seeing. Lerendir will know what I mean," she replied.

"Very well." Galdurith clasped her fingers when she passed the ring into his keeping. "Be safe. Don't allow any insanity." He narrowed his eyes at me.

My lips tightened. "Officers, move out."

Llewethan leapt forward, and after a few long, sinuous strides, thrust his deep chestnut wings. He sped skyward, southward, and beyond sight.

I drew a long breath. "Majestrin, on to Bilearne. May we discover what pieces of the puzzle the Elgadrim hold."

2

"*W*here is the baby?"

Raen dashed to the far side of the rough stone cavern, crouched, and took Mythrenese's indigo-scaled face in her hands. The dragonling's long neck was stiff, and he stared, unblinking. A stab of terror lanced Raen's chest. Was he . . .? No, his flanks still rose and fell with breath. But what made the young dragon as unyielding as a block of wood?

"Mythrenese, can you hear me? What's happened?"

Mythrenese managed a throaty groan, but no more.

Raen released his cheeks and dashed back to the narrow cleft in the rock that led to the cavern exit. She clutched the skirt of her heavy gown in one tight fist. "Little one," she called in a faltering voice. "Iriscendra, please. Come out if you're hiding." The drone of the falls beyond the cavern's outlet offered the only response. She paced. *I was a fool to let her out of my sight. Curse my lack of vigilance.* Her breath came in shorter gasps.

Mythrenese moaned again. "Mmmshrm . . . hmmf."

A brisk spin turned Raen back to his still form. He blinked. His pupils dilated, contracted, then settled upon a steady diameter.

"Mythrenese, where is she?"

The dragonling shifted his jaw, if only a little. "M'shrry, Raen."

She crouched at his side again. "Please, try very hard. Do you know what's happened to the hatchling? Do you remember?"

After a few labored blinks, Mythrenese scarcely shook his head back and forth, the motion only perceivable due to the way the low light of the cavern shimmered over the purple cast of his scales. "Rrrnn uh-ey."

"What?"

Tears welled in Mythrenese's eyes, and Raen bit her lip. "I'm sorry. I don't mean to be short with you. You seem like you're improving—a little. I'll gather the others, and maybe once we have everyone, you'll be able to talk." *I hope. How can I even guess when I have no idea what could be wrong?* She gathered the long skirt of her gown in one hand and swept from the cavern, through the narrow cleft that led to the falls.

From the threshold of the cavern, Raen stared across the wide, bowl-shaped valley she called home as the rising sun cast long shadows across the bluegrass carpeting the floor of the expanse. High above the sheer stone walls that rimmed the vale, the silhouette of a lithe, winged creature circled and dove through a mottled pink and gold sky. She pulled a crystal on a thin chain from inside the neckline of her azure gown. Time after time, she angled the charm into the dawn's glow until a shaft of light reflected from the crystal in a bright flash. The flier in the distance jerked suddenly toward her, then dove into the dense autumnal canopy beyond the cliffs.

Pacing failed to sooth Raen's tremulous nerves, but it was

better than sitting to wait. Return visits to Mythrenese only revealed continued immobility, to which Raen seemed to be adding mounting guilt. She hovered in the cavern entrance.

Finally, after no less than a half hour, they came. The vibrant, orange-scaled Fiernoth led the copper twins from the southern distance. They winged their way over the lake at the base of the falls, and the reflection of their flying forms danced on the water's surface, mingled with the play of pure morning sunlight. When they neared Raen's position on the narrow shelf that ran behind the falls, they spread wide wings to slow their approach. Their majesty stirred in Raen's heart. So young, but already so amazing. Why could the world not see them as she did?

The three young dragons settled onto the gravel-strewn path that led up to her.

Fiernoth's green eyes searched her. "What's amiss, mistress? The signal looked urgent."

Raen took a shuddering breath. "Follow me."

She led the dragons back into the chamber where Mythrenese lay, but at least now he held his head up on a curved neck.

"Praise the Maker!" Raen cried. "You can move now?"

"Shome," Mythrenese slurred. "Can't use my legsh or tail yet."

"Has someone stolen Iriscendra?"

The indigo dragonling shook his head, then let it hang until the tip of his snout touched the floor. "No," he whispered. "She ran away."

Fiernoth reared his horned head. "Ran away? How is that possible?" He fired a deadly glare at Mythrenese.

Mythrenese's shoulders heaved and his wings trembled. "I'm sh-sh-sorry. I shwear, mistress Raen, I didn't lose her. Not on purpose. She came up to me, sneezed, and my whole body went sh-stiff..."

A gasp hissed through Raen's teeth, and she clapped a hand

over her mouth. *Why would Iriscendra...? No, it must have been a mistake.* A lock of carmine hair slipped over Raen's eye, and she shoved it back into place behind her ear point. *Slick as satin, confounded hair.* "Any idea how long ago?"

Mythrenese's chin quivered. "It's so hard to tell here in the nesh..." He gulped. "Nesting culvert."

"But it was your turn to know such things," Fiernoth growled. Smoke trailed from his nostrils.

"None of that!" Raen snapped. She smoothed a crease in the bodice of her gown. "We won't find her by bickering and blaming. Fiernoth, Cuprinir, Pyrien—search every inch of this valley for signs of the hatchling. Bring even rumors of her whereabouts to me immediately."

"Yes, mistress," the dragons replied in chorus. They bustled from the cavern.

Raen walked the perimeter of the circular chamber, passing by the nesting niches she herself had labored to carve into the walls. She scrutinized the two waiting eggs that sat nestled in soft grasses, milkweed, and cattail fluff. Both eggs' shells remained smooth and flawless, each with their own delicate sheen of gold or pale green. The final culvert contained the remnants of a breached shell.

Though the hatchling had emerged weeks ago, Raen had yet to find the heart to clear away the lovely, pearlescent fragments. She reached into the culvert, and the radiant heat from the falls that ran on the other side of the rock warmed her hand. Tracing a finger over a fragile shard, Raen sighed at the likeness between its sheen and Iriscendra's own hide. What fury Raen would visit upon anyone who dared so much as scratch one of the hatchling's pliant new scales.

. . .

he last rays of the sun retracted their waning fingers over the western horizon, and a chill wind blew across the summit of Madivitra Falls, stirring Raen's skirts. Clouds of steam billowed from the water's surface as cooling air swirled over the lake heated by subterranean wonders.

With tears walled behind a show of competence, the elf maiden stood firm before Cuprinir, Pyrien, and Fiernoth. The copper twins' eyes brimmed wet, and the muscles around Fiernoth's jaw tightened, relaxed, and tightened again.

"She would have enough sense to seek shelter as the sun sets." Raen surveyed the water and the mountainside for the hundredth time.

"If she wants it," the fiery orange dragon replied.

"How could she not?"

"She's been trying to bolt from the nursery from the moment she shook the shell free," Pyrien replied. "Though why she has such an objection to the place, who knows?"

"There's certainly no trace of her now," Fiernoth grumbled.

"Now, no jumping to conclusions," Raen said. "Mythrenese may yet bring us hopeful news."

"He is the best at detecting signatures, no doubt of that." Cuprinir shifted his weight, and he swallowed audibly. "Mistress, do you think it's possible Iriscendra meant to use her abomination on Mythrenese?"

Raen's clenched her fists. "Impossible. How could she have even known about it?"

Cuprinir cringed. "I saw her blowing little puffs of breath on beetles the other day and giggling about it when they stiffened up. I told her to stop—that it wasn't nice."

"But why would she want to escape? Where would she even think to go?" Fiernoth's yellow-tipped scales along his spine lifted like hackles.

Raen pressed her forehead into her hand. "Few compulsions would take one so little away from the nest. Only the dragonsbond or the hatching—" A brick of dread plummeted to the pit of her stomach.

The stares from the crew of dragon youths bored into her.

"Did any of you touch Iriscendra's egg during the weaving time?" Raen began to pace.

They all shook their heads.

"Well I know I didn't, so she wouldn't have been looking for me, and besides . . ." Raen's breath caught. "Oh no." She sunk to her knees as sudden crash of realization bowled into her. "But he said he didn't touch it." Fire surged in Raen's gut. *The lying brute. How dare he?*

"Mistress?" Fiernoth raised a brow. "What is troubling you?"

Raen pressed her lips together. "No use speculating. For now, our only focus must be finding our lost little one." She rose and retreated on slow steps for the steep descent from the pinnacle to the cavern behind the waterfall, her fists clenching tighter all the while. "Inform me immediately when Mythrenese gets back."

She passed through the entry cleft and across the hatching chamber. Increasingly hesitant strides carried her to a battered trunk against the wall. With trembling hands, she dug to the bottom of the few dresses, handful of scrolls, and hairbrush within, until her grasp closed on a chain. She lifted it.

Raen ran her index finger over the smooth curve of a silver talisman. The sword and the quill. Could she again face a city she had worked so long to drive from her mind? If it meant finding Iriscendra, she would thrust away her own misgivings, however insistent. She clutched the chain in her hand until the links bit the skin of her palm.

"Mistress?"

Raen jumped and her heart thundered. She turned to find Mythrenese and Fiernoth sidling through the nesting culvert entry. She clasped her hands behind her, talisman concealed by tight fingers. She drew a silent breath and steadied her quavering spirit.

"You're back! Any news?"

Mythrenese nodded. "On the northwestern edge of the vale." He panted for breath. "Her signature leads that way. It's a little faint, but I could follow it without trouble for several leagues."

The twin dragons joined the group.

Raen surveyed the clutch of magnificent creatures before her, and her stomach tightened. She glanced again at the eggs, and her pulse pounded in her temples.

"She is small, and still very vulnerable," Fiernoth whispered. "We're safe here. You must go after the one who's lost."

Raen looked full in the face of her dragon companions, the only company she had known in . . . how long? "But what if the eggs . . ."

"We have minded hatchlings before," Cuprinir said. "And we know you. You won't be a moment longer than needed."

After a deep breath, Raen closed her eyes for a long moment. She re-opened them to the earnest but confident faces of her charges. "Fiernoth, I place you watcher over the nursery. And I want the twins to spend every day scouring the vale's perimeter in case our little daughter makes her way back."

Mythrenese hung his head. "I don't blame you for not giving me a job, since I bungled the last one."

Raen stepped to Mythrenese's side, placed a gentle hand under his chin, and lifted his face. "Not at all! I will never have a hope of finding her without you, my talented tracker." She grabbed a satchel and stuffed a cloak from the trunk inside it. "We may have a long way to go, my friend." *And if I'm right, woe to Ecleriast when we get there.*

3

HATCHLING

*W*ith Veranna riding double behind me, and Hridayesh upon the griffon, we set out into the gloom of a leaden sky. We allowed the course of the Nuruhain to lead us southward into the heart of Kelmirith, and when it branched to the southeast and became the turbulent Celerrio, we followed the river's lead, officially turning aside from the path that would have led into the elflands. The eastern arm of the Triastead Mountains dwindled from towering crags to softer, tree-covered heights, within whose terminus we would find the remains of the once-great Kelmiri capitol.

On the third overcast morning since we had parted ways with Galdurith and Althoron, when the chill spray of light rain soaked our clothes and set us shivering, the crumbling towers of Bilearne finally rose from the mist below like battered soldiers struggling to stand at attention despite grievous wounds. On both sides of the river, the city's remains clung to the hillsides and hugged the riverbank. The warfare of a faded era scattered chunks of her wall about the valley. Columns lay on their sides, wearing a tangled web of ivy and creeper vines. The city was at once wild and dead, and the wind blew through the derelict stone edifices with a tomb's breath. I pulled my cloak tighter around me. More than the damp wind seeped raw into my bones.

And despite all the disrepair that plagued the ruins, majesty clung to the Bilearne remained. We made our descent and skimmed the remnants of old, square foundations that marked the outskirts of the toppled metropolis, and then we sailed over its wall.

Deep inscriptions of valor, of honor, of knowledge and wisdom, engraved the lintels of so many doorframes. Noble statues of toga-clad men stood sentinel over the squares and the plazas. Their stone eyes focused far off, upon times whose memories were lost to all but the stalwart few lore-keepers of the world. An uncanny mix of decay and hope hung over the ruins, drifting with the windswept rain through the bowls of fountains and over the tiers of the amphitheater.

We landed within the city wall at the north-most building, one of the few structures in the city that remained intact. It dominated an entire side of the plaza it overlooked. My squinting scrutiny of the arched openings at the tower's top revealed a cluster of silent bells. This must have been Bilearne's legendary temple of Creo: an architectural wonder that outstripped even the temple in Delsinon for size and splendor. It towered over us, silent. The drizzle wept down its pale stone face in green-edged streams.

Two-story sculptures of the twenty-one patrons upheld the side walls of the temple. Intricate relief sculptures of the Vareinor's proud service to Creo, before history renamed them Elgadrim, graced every door and window frame. Aromen, king of the sunrise, bowed before his Maker in vibrant stained glass. A dozen other stories whose details I failed to recall filled other portals. I slid from Majestrin's back in mute reverence.

Hridayesh dismounted as well and stretched. "We look pretty alone, Vinyanel. We're supposed to meet the note-senders here?"

"We have likely arrived before they expected or hoped," I replied. "But the message made clear their intent to send emissaries here right after they dispatched the phoenix."

Veranna scowled. "You seemed awfully insistent time was short before."

"Are you here to help me or to second-guess and challenge me on every breath I take?"

A laugh broke loose from Hridayesh's lips. "If you wanted obedience, you chose the wrong half of the group to bring with you. You've forgotten what it's like to work with normal people instead of scared soldiers."

I huffed. "The Elgadrim will be here within the next couple of days, barring disaster. In the meantime, we ought to hunt for some reasonably intact quarters for the wait. I would not hold to the hope that we are as alone here as it appears. When people move out, other *things* move in."

Veranna pushed a wet raven curl from her eyes and shivered. "A usable fireplace is my only requirement at this point."

I surveyed the plaza. "Then let us see if we cannot find a way out of the damp."

Across the plaza from the temple, a long structure with a half-collapsed colonnade stretching along its front presented a possibility. The temple looked in better condition, but somehow, turning such a place into an encampment seemed inappropriate. We navigated the fallen chunks of marble and sandstone within the colonnade to find the ten-foot double doors to the building behind it. One of the paneled bronze doors hung askew. The gap it left was just wide enough to duck through without moving either door. I feared they would come crashing down if we tried to open them the customary way.

Inside the foyer of the place, a line of a dozen doors faced us. Perhaps the building had served as a governmental meeting place—it was hard to tell, for despite the rubble and the dust, it was clear not a tapestry, a sign, or an article of defining clutter remained. My feet crunched across the rubble-strewn floor. Once magnificent with large, inlaid stone of multiple colors, it was now chipped in some places and smashed in others. I peered beyond the first cherry door.

A flutter somewhere behind me caught my ear. I wheeled and caught my hilt with my right hand. "What was that?" I whispered.

Hridayesh glanced behind us. "That?"

"I heard flapping."

"Probably just a pigeon roosting in all this disarray."

"It sounded bigger than that to me." I searched the corners and the shadows.

Veranna rolled her eyes.

"Be wary, both of you. You may think I am crazy, but you will thank my madness if it prevents you from being eaten or shot."

I turned back to the room beyond the first interior door, which held a small desk, devoid of the usual heralds of work. No paper, no ledger, not even a dry quill. A dust-laden chaise sat against one wall, facing an empty fireplace on the other.

"So long as we can find some dry wood, this might not be awful." Veranna stepped over to the chaise and plunked her pack down upon it. It kicked up a cloud of dust that the prophetess fanned away from her face. She coughed. "Maybe."

Clearly the Elgadrim had not left Bilearne in a hurry, as the emptiness in each room we searched indicated. Furniture remained, but none of the other evidence people had once lived and worked in the rooms. I selected the office that shared the fireplace wall with Veranna's chosen quarters as the place where Hridayesh and I would wait out the Elgadrim emissaries' arrival.

"It's not like we're lacking in space, Vinyanel," Hridayesh grumbled. "I could very easily take the next room down."

I lowered an eyebrow. "Despite our exchange of saving one another's lives, I would be remiss to ignore all the protocols of the prisoner-guard relationship."

The North Deklian pulled his headscarf off with an exasperated huff. "You still don't trust me?"

I swallowed the chuckle goaded by Hridayesh's short ebony hair, sticking in all directions after the removal of his ever-present scarf. "If you want the best chance of a pardon when we do get back to Delsinon, do this my way."

We eased into the ancient office, and I scanned the coffered ceiling, the corners, the mahogany desk at its center. Cabinetry covered the entirety of the rear wall. Hridayesh approached the first raised-paneled door at once and placed his ear against it. He listened for a moment, his eyes focused far off. After a quick shrug and a frown, he threw the door wide. It groaned on hinges that probably had not moved in centuries, and I was surprised the dry and cracking wood of the door did not split with the sudden movement.

I retreated a step and stared at the opening, my hand tight on my hilt.

The cupboard interior offered nothing but empty shelves. My North Deklian roommate moved on to the next set. More of the same. All the way down the room he progressed with the repetition of the listen-then-look routine, and each time he was rewarded with emptiness. I sat on a couch in the corner and coughed at the dust cloud I stirred with the act.

He proceeded to the long desk and pulled open one of the drawers. He frowned and pushed it shut.

I shook my head. "It seems clear the Elgadrim left not even an empty ink bottle behind."

"So say those who never persist." Hridayesh pulled the next drawer open, scowled, and thrust it shut.

I drummed my palms and fingertips absentmindedly on the arm of the couch.

"Do you mind?" Hridayesh said. "I don't search by sight alone, and you're making that difficult."

I folded my arms.

More wood slid against wood, when Hridayesh laughed. "Now here's something."

I craned my neck to catch a glimpse of the low drawer before which he squatted.

"This drawer doesn't go as far back as the others." He knocked on the rear of the drawer's interior and cocked his ear to it. He knocked again.

I rose from my seat and joined him at the desk.

A few taps and touches later, and Hridayesh slid a panel up from what looked like the rear of the drawer, but having moved the panel away, he revealed another small compartment, lined in dark fabric.

"Here! See? I'm rewarded." He reached into the compartment and produced a metallic flask. The metal of the container was a deep gray with a slightly blue cast to it.

"Good for you," I said. "Now you can appear to have a drinking problem instead of just using a skin like the rest of us."

Hridayesh squinted at the flask. "Only an idiot would waste this on toting swill. Don't you realize what this is made of?"

I raked my fingers through my wet hair. "Apparently not. And apparently you shall give me no peace until you tell me, so out with it."

A dagger slid from Hridayesh's belt, and he tapped its blade against the flask. The vessel rang with a clear, deep note that sent swarm of gooseflesh over my arms. "That, soldier, is the voice of adamantine."

My eyes widened. "There is a tidy sum tied up in that flask then. Looks like you could retire from the assassin's trade if you know how to handle a windfall."

A flapping and scrabbling clatter broke out in the hall. My head snapped to the doorway. "That's no pigeon," I whispered.

I drew my sword and shield, then advanced on swift strides to the door. I stopped, put my back to the wall on the latch side of the doorway, and peered into the hall. "We're not alone."

Hridayesh laughed. "No, we're not. You insisted on bringing Veranna too, though I can't fathom why. Do yourself a favor. Once we've met with this emissary, take a trip to the hot springs—"

A bright blue eye set in a pale face peeked around the corner of a side hallway at the end of the foyer, but withdrew so quickly that I failed to catch what sort of person did the peering. "No! Look." I pointed. "Something is there."

Hridayesh grabbed my arm. "Hold on, Captain Conspiracy. Why don't you let me take a look? I'm a tad quieter than you with all that black carapace."

"Lieutenant Commander." I glanced down at my lacquered breastplate. "It really is very quiet compared to other suits of plate."

"That's like saying the river isn't cold as compared to the snow on the bank." Hridayesh frowned. "Whatever you think you see or hear clearly isn't too interested in being seen, so let me see if I can steal up on it before you follow. I'll yell if there's a problem."

I gestured ahead. "It ducked into the hall at the far end."

Hridayesh glided off, skulking in a low crouch that I had to admit was nearly silent, despite the debris in his path and underfoot. He slowed as he drew within a dozen paces of the turn, his every motion deliberate and fluid. My teeth clenched. My pulse raced. My muscles tensed, combat-ready.

Shoulder pressed to the wall, Hridayesh eased his head forward to sneak a glance around the corner. He at once stood up straight and cocked his head. "Would you look at that?"

I marched to his position, scarcely able to restrain my strides from breaking into a run. "What?"

"Well, not what I expected, which was nothing," Hridayesh called over his shoulder.

When I reached my black-clad companion's side, I still adjusted my shield on my arm and readied my sword, but glanced around the corner as well.

Backed against the dead end of the hall crouched a little, pearly-scaled creature with nubby horns, dorsal plates that reminded me of newly-sprouted baby teeth, a short snout, and wide, fearful blue eyes. Little translucent wings trembled down at its sides. It pressed its belly to the ground and stared up at me.

We locked gazes, and in that moment, the creature's terror melted into bright glee. It let out a high-pitched squeal, sat up, and clapped its little foretalons together.

I nearly dropped my sword. What in the Maker's dominion?

The visitor, a hatchling dragon as best I could guess, sprang my direction and circled me like a puppy whose master had just returned home from a long journey. All the while, it gazed up at me, eyes alight with unfounded admiration.

"Do I . . . know you?" I scratched my head.

The hatchling sunk back onto its hindquarters and cocked its head.

Hridayesh clapped my shoulder. "I hope Majestrin isn't the jealous type. This little pet seems to have quite a fondness for you. Which just goes to show, it couldn't possibly know you very well."

4

WOVEN

"*W*ell, not exactly what I suspected," I said to the baby dragon. "Where did you come from?"

I reached out a palm to the hatchling, and it sprang toward me as though it had only been waiting upon the insinuation of my interest to thrust its head into my hand and rub its cheek against me like a cat. I patted the hatchling's neck. "I hope we are not crowding your lair."

The creature made a low thrumming noise in its throat and continued to smile at me.

The jingle of faint bells grew behind me. The hatchling's smile dissolved, its eyes went wide, and it scrambled for the cover of the side hall again.

I laughed. "Smart for a baby."

"What have you run into out here, Vinyanel?" Veranna swept up beside me.

"A hatchling dragon, so it would seem," I replied.

Hridayesh cleared his throat. "A baby dragon? Am I the only

one who's concerned a baby dragon might also mean there's a *mother* dragon nearby? I doubt she'd be open to a lot of explanation she finds us messing with her hatchling."

"You have a point." I scratched my cheek. "Perhaps we should inquire with Majestrin on his thoughts or experience."

I headed for the foyer exit, and the hatchling scampered after me in a flurry of clumsy limbs and flapping wings. I leaned down to glance out the gap beside the crooked door. Both Majestrin and the griffon had settled down beneath the colonnade, which kept them out of the worst of the rain. The damp ground in front of Majestrin's snout wore a semicircular layer of ice crystals.

One of his leaf-green eyes snapped open the moment I emerged from the building with the hatchling close on my heels. The silver dragon's gaze locked onto the hatchling, and his eyes narrowed just enough to betray the tension in his face.

"So there's the source of the signature that was prickling at me all this time," the silver dragon said. His attempt at nonchalance was foiled, if only subtly, by the furrow in his brow.

"Why did you not mention it?" I said.

"If I told you about every flutter of signature I felt, we'd have no time to speak of anything else." Majestrin yawned, exposing his scores of piercing teeth.

"Veranna can sense them too, correct?" I cast a suspicious glance back over my shoulder. "I am surprised she did not say anything."

"I suspect the hatchling kept enough distance that she hadn't picked up on it yet. Especially with the way she needs to stay shielded against your signature."

I grimaced. My discomfiture at Veranna's ability to feel my presence rattled in my gut.

"While that little hatchling's signature is still a bit faint, I started sensing it while you were hunting around here for a place to bed down. At first, I thought it might be yours, for some reason picking at me although I've mostly mastered my shielding against you. But the more I focused on it, the more it became clear it was distinct and separate."

"Dragons are Thaumaturgists, then?" I said.

"More innately magical than conduits of Creo's Utterances," Majestrin said. "Though there have been some scholar dragons who have mastered Thaumaturgy. And curse-bearing." He shuddered. Anyway, while you were sight-seeing, I noticed the trail of her signature leads steadily east from here, straight over the wall and into the wilderness."

"Her, eh?" I drew my hood against the soggy weather. "So you are saying this creature likely came here from somewhere else. Tell me, friend, how high is the risk that her mother will come looking for her?"

Majestrin frowned. "That's the part that makes no sense. No hatchling properly woven with either a mother or father would stray from the sight of that parent, not at so young an age. She cannot be much more than a month old."

Woven? What did that mean?

Veranna cast a wary eye into the distance. "Would you know if there was another adult dragon in the vicinity?"

"Absolutely," Majestrin replied. "And I can say with certainty there is not."

I crouched down and looked the hatchling in the eye. "Where is your family, little one?"

She began thrumming again, and she placed her chin upon my knee.

Majestrin drew his head back on his serpentine neck. "Curious, indeed."

"An orphan, perhaps?" Veranna said.

"Possible," Majestrin replied. "But this gravitation toward Vinyanel..." He clenched his jaw.

I waited, but Majestrin fell silent and turned his snout toward the rainy plaza.

The long-term potential of an orphaned dragon crept into the back of my mind. If such a creature could be raised to maturity by the Delsin, how much more ready might she be to become a mount for another officer of the future Windrider battalion, once she was big enough? Very interesting indeed.

"Well then," I said. "Should she stay here with you?" I turned to the hatchling. "You want to stay, correct?"

The little dragon paid me little heed, too preoccupied with pouncing on a blowing leaf the wind stirred from a corner near the building.

"I'm not inclined to babysit," Majestrin said, his tone snappish. "If this little one wants to linger, you can play caregiver."

I took half a step back. No matter how close Majestrin and I had become, I was still not so rash as to argue with a dragon. "Very well, friend." I cleared my throat. "We shall see if this creature is just paying us a quick investigative visit, then decide."

Majestrin rustled his wings. "In the meantime, Lieutenant Commander, might I request your leave to hunt?"

"Absolutely. Eyrnir, would you care to do so as well?" I took hold of the wet leather straps that held my pack to Majestrin's harness. It took a few firm yanks pulled the satchel free of his back.

The griffon bobbed his hawkish head. "Yes. Thank you."

"And you do not think this little one should come with you? She could be hungry as well."

The silver dragon turned a glare upon me. "No, Vinyanel. Let that be the end of it."

I swallowed. Never since I had met him had I seen Majestrin so clearly rankled with one of my suggestions. "All right. No offense intended. Just you and Eyrnir then. You've both more than earned a full belly."

After Hridayesh had removed the gear from his mount, the beasts loped a few strides down the weed-strewn street and launched skyward. I squinted after them until the haze of mist obscured them from sight.

What had soured Majestrin's disposition so, I could not begin to guess. I looked down at the hatchling, who met my gaze with shining eyes as soon as my attention lingered upon her. Could Hridayesh have guessed closer to the truth than perhaps even he thought? Majestrin struck me as wiser than to fall prey to something as petty as jealousy. But somehow, this little, seemingly innocuous creature had found a way to flap the unflappable.

_____

5

SANDS THROUGH THE GLASS

*T*he caravan of dragon-kin lumbered along the overgrown forest road, trampling under boot, claw, and hoof all that had grown in the forgotten thoroughfare. The harness of thick-shouldered oxen creaked as they hauled crudely-fashioned wagons through ruts, around mossy rocks, and over rotting tree trunks that had fallen across the span. Armored dragon-kin warriors held bows or spears at the ready while they marched the perimeter of the phalanx.

Naghax walked beside one of the carts and gnawed the last shards of bread from the hard rind of a crust. A week had passed since the raid where Naghax's kin had procured the loaf. Stretching the meager plunder that long had rendered the food items inedible. But the rations never stretched as long as any excursion, so he scraped at it with his teeth anyway. Worthless. As he reached back to hurl the stale scrap, the distinct prickle of a stare chittered across his flesh.

His sidelong glance caught the eldest of his prisoners

eyeing the remnants in his hand. From behind the bars of her wheeled cage, the softbelly female watched with eyes set in dark circles. The other two abductees, her younger sisters, huddled in a tight ball behind her, perhaps sleeping. At the very least, sealing the world out with closed lids, despite the fact that dusk had scarcely fallen. All their faces had lost much of the rounding fat they carried at the time of their capture.

"No good having you waste away before we get there," Naghax muttered. He tossed the crust through the bars, and the girl lunged at it as though he had cast off the crown jewels. She scooped it up in dirty hands. Clutching the scrap to her breast, she scuttled back to the others.

"Wake up!" she whispered. "I have something for you."

Naghax maintained a veiled attention toward the girls—though likely too feeble to conspire, desperation could breed uncharacteristic boldness.

The youngest prisoner's eyes fluttered open first. "What is it, Helena? Can we go home?"

The eldest shook her head. "Not yet. But I have some bread for you." She broke off a section of the crust with a crumbly snap.

Tears welled in the small one's eyes. As usual. Would she never tire of sniveling? "Oh. It's ... um ..."

"It's not much. But you must keep up your strength, Cassia dear." Helena extended the scrap. "Here."

Cassia took a small nibble. "It's a little hard . . . to . . . swallow."

"I think we still have a little to drink in the skin."

A grimace overtook Cassia's features. "That awful stuff they give us to drink is no help. I don't like how it makes me so tired and confused. It's worse than being thirsty."

Naghax clanged his club against the bars. "Enough of your griping! Things can get worse, little lambs. Much worse."

The last of the three prisoners jumped at the clatter. "What's going on?"

"Don't you worry," Helena said. She faced Naghax. "Thank you for the bread, sir. I know you could have cast it away, but you gave it to us. I appreciate your kindness."

The middle prisoner huffed. "Bread? Kindness? You have to be joking. And I wish you would give it up already. These beasts don't care how cute you try to act."

"I'm not trying to be cute. But snapping and snarling all the time likely don't—"

"You might as well try nothing and save your breath," Naghax said. *You are far too essential to talk your way back home. And once we're done with you, home and kin will be the next to fall.*

6

GUARDIANS

*E*mptiness. At every turn, Bilearne offered a complete lack of human warmth, as though her stone edifices had cast the memory of their makers into the bleak nothingness of the gnawing wind.

"I hope Majestrin or the griffon manage to track down enough game to bring a bit back." Hridayesh's stomach rumbled audibly, as if to underscore the cavernous vacuity of the city around us.

I peered in the window of the barren residence on the right side of the narrow street. Nothing more remarkable than sheets of cobwebs occupied the place. "If there is anything to catch, they will remember us."

The hatchling dragon reared up on her hind legs and squinted at the window I was examining. She pointed her nose up at me and raised her scaly brows, if they could be called that.

After patting her head, I said, "I know. But it does not hurt for us to investigate a bit while we wait for those who have summoned us." Truthfully, even having only been in the city for six or seven hours had already begun to wear on my ability to tolerate idleness. My muscles wound tighter with each passing hour of quiet, and my wandering thoughts too often turned to memories. My inner monologue prodded—slow down too much and your failures will strangle you. I thrust away the squeezing in my chest with a focused examination of the city's every feature.

The cracked streets, the overgrown beds, the trees rooted in the most unlikely places, all owing to generations of dereliction, wrapped my soul in a profound sense of sadness. How fleeting were the lives of men, even Elgadrim, who lived five times the lifespan of other ethnicities. And how decay had ravaged a place of legendary splendor in the time the Elgadrim had spent in scattered exile. The failing light of evening cast the cityscape in a gloomy pall. Deepening shadows and the half-light around me made my vision murky, the irksome product of too much light for darkvision, yet not enough for daytime sight. My shoulders tensed. I pressed onward.

The drab surroundings did not seem to trouble the hatchling in the least. She scrabbled from empty planter to set of stairs, across the street to sniff at tufts of weeds, and around in circles for the seeming delight of running. At times, she bounded sideways with her back arched, in a reptilian version of a weasel war dance. A smirk tugged at the corner of my mouth despite the gloom that hung on my shoulders like a leaden mantle.

I felt Hridayesh's eyes on me. My glance flicked his way, and I wiped the mirth from my face.

A patter of drops began to speckle the pavement before us. Hridayesh frowned at the sky and tugged his hood up over his headscarf. "Maybe we should go back."

"Pfah. Not for this," I said. "The more we laze around that

administration building, the more it tempts Veranna to find 'useful' ways for us to spend our time."

Hridayesh's expression soured, and inwardly, I counted my victory. Despite whatever verbal truce he and the prophetess had called, it was no secret he still found her distasteful at best. How long did it take to undo a lifetime of indoctrination that women existed as possessions, prizes to be gathered or cast off at will? Clearly more than a few weeks' exposure to another perspective.

The rain fell more heavily, until I also felt compelled to draw my hood to keep the cold droplets from sliding down my neck and under my armor. The growing puddles delighted the hatchling, for she leapt in any collection of water she could find, which brought a smile to my face. Her antics warmed me, despite the foul weather.

She circled the streets as we investigated, until one of her gleeful charges brought her back toward me. She skidded in a puddle to my right. Gritty spray spattered across my legs.

"Enough." I scowled at her. "I need no extra work in cleaning this suit of plate when we go in."

She shrank down. Her wings drooped, and her tail dragged on the ground.

I chose not to soften my admonition. If there was any chance this creature might one day be a member of the Windrider battalion, it did not hurt her to get an early sense of who was in command.

We reached the end of the street, and through the haze of the rain, beheld a conical tower, mostly crumbled on its north side and leaning perilously because of it, all enclosed in a wall of stone blocks. Perched all along the wall at regular intervals were gargoyles of myriad designs. Some brooded as though in thought, others bared rows of jagged teeth. A deep stone overhang in the wall closest to us sheltered the iron gate to the complex.

Hridayesh tilted his head. "That looks important. Something worth checking in the morning."

"Why not now?" I said. "You have a pressing social engagement?"

"I didn't bring a lantern, and I doubt I could keep a torch lit for long if this weather keeps deteriorating."

Ah, yes. As the dusk around us deepened, while my vision actually improved, I had nearly forgotten that Hridayesh would soon be stumbling blind without a light.

"I will just take a quick look through the gate, and then we can head back." I took a stride toward the gate, when a weight snared my leg. I looked down with a start.

The hatchling clutched my greaves, her blue eyes flitting back and forth between my face and the wall.

I shook my leg free. "Come now. We will not be long." I only accomplished another pair of steps before she lunged and grappled both my legs this time.

"What has gotten into you?" I barked. "Unhand me." I grabbed onto the hatchling's scaled foretalon and sought to pry it loose.

A bright flash made all three of us jump, and the peal of thunder to follow came too soon for my comfort.

"It appears you win this time," I grumbled at the hatchling. "We head back to Veranna."

We retreated the way we had come. Along the route, the steady rain strengthened to a torrential downpour in a matter of moments. Wind buffeted us and rattled the browning leaves of oaks along the street. The flashes of lightning came more frequently with each block we covered, and the thunder boomed its authority.

We turned the last corner to approach the plaza again, when a shriek cut through the drone of the rain.

Veranna.

I swept my sword from the scabbard and broke into a run.

My shoulder caught the edge of the crooked door with a solid whack, but I gritted my teeth and barreled through. Veranna stood in the hall with a torch in hand, and she waved it to and fro, her eyes wild. The crazy dance of light on the walls confounded my vision for a moment. I blinked and shook my head.

A dozen shelled monstrosities circled the prophetess, none shorter than my arm. Many at least half my height. They scrabbled over rubble on segmented legs. Their shells were deep rust domes, reflective, and made a clatter as they scuttled about. Pincers dripped and antennae groped before them.

I swung my blade, and its edge caught the closest massive beetle. The force of my blow cut a gash halfway through the creature and flung it to the side, where it crashed into the wall with a crunch like pottery. It wheezed and thrashed in a repulsive, convulsive dance.

"Vinyanel, get her out of here," Hridayesh roared. "They're everywhere!"

I spared only a brief glance around the hall, and indeed, from beneath every pile, from within every crevice, more beetles issued. In a tight space, we would be swarmed—and the torch Veranna wielded did not seem to inspire much hesitation in the horde.

"Surprise. This place is not empty," I yelled.

Veranna thrust her torch at the closest beetle. "Gloat later."

I slashed another beetle and sent it flying, which opened a small gap in their circle around Veranna. "Come on!"

The prophetess grimaced and lunged for the gap. The beetles chattered and hissed, wheeling in pursuit. I thrust Veranna behind me and toward the door, brandished my sword, and fixed a snarling glare on the growing crowd of creatures that assembled in haphazard ranks.

What they lacked in hardiness they made up for in numbers. I backed while I hewed. Yellow-green slime flung from the wounds I inflicted, and the more of it I spilled, the ranker the air became with a thick, earthy stench. When I finally emerged from the building, I welcomed the cleansing smell of the autumn downpour. It cleared the gag from my throat. The moment I stepped into the avenue, the hatchling dashed to my side and whimpered.

Clambering over a swath of their slain hive members did not deter the beetles. They gushed into the street like an oily flood.

"How well do you think they climb?" Hridayesh called over the clatter of their armored legs and the chatter of the pelting rain.

"How should I know? They are heavy, so perhaps not well?" I cleaved two more of the beasts only an instant before their mandibles reached my middle.

"Maybe we could get behind that gate—"

"Right. Can you find your way back in the dark?"

Hridayesh nodded.

I pulled my shield from my back and swept my next assailant aside. "Veranna, follow Hridayesh."

They turned and ran.

"Let us hope these foul insects are not quick," I said to the hatchling. "Come."

Another sword stroke deflected the lunge of what seemed like the hundredth beetle. The hatchling tore after Hridayesh, and I pounded my way behind as well.

The rain slackened as we charged, and the sound of clattering bug legs lessened. A glance over my shoulder revealed their continued pursuit, but we were outpacing them.

Hridayesh barreled straight for the gate that blocked the crumbling tower complex. He throttled the metalwork, but it did not so much as clang. It remained fixed in place, firmly locked, though without a keyhole or latch I could see.

I stopped about twenty paces from the wall and faced the

way we had come. The swarm of beetles boiled around the corner.

The grate of stone-on-stone met my ears.

Our pursuers skidded to a halt in a glossy front.

Grinding rock sounded again, and the swarm scuttled back. For a confused moment, they climbed over one another. Every last one skittered into the nearest crevice, under cover, or otherwise out of sight.

I might have sighed in relief, if it were not for the hatchling's trumpeting sounds. She clamped her maw on my cloak and tugged like a petulant toddler.

"Now what?" I snapped. "No distractions." My glance swept the streets, now empty of beetles.

She fixated on the walls to the tower complex behind me. I looked over my shoulder.

My first glance landed upon Hridayesh. He rubbed his chin and ran a finger along the tight seam between the gates. The grinding sound repeated, this time from multiple sources. I raised my eyes to the summit of the wall. Veranna contemplated the gates with him, but the grating stone intercepted her attention and she peered from beneath the arch.

The gargoyles were moving.

Every figure I could see, no fewer than two dozen, turned faces both animalistic and mannish toward the gate. Some dropped to all fours, while others walked on hind legs, but all threaded their way along the top of the wall toward Hridayesh and Veranna. The golems' eyes glowed with a pale blue light. Though their bodies still had a mottled granite look, they moved in a sinuous prowl.

"Get out of there!" I bellowed.

Hridayesh turned a glare my way.

"Listen to me! Get out of the archway. You will be trapped against the gate!"

The gargoyle closest to the gate leapt from the wall,

spread marbled wings, and landed upon the ground with a thunderous crack. Hridayesh's scowl snapped to wide-eyed shock. Veranna screamed. Rearing its bestial head back, the gargoyle paused. I was at once reminded of Majestrin's body language when he was about to douse an enemy in a blast of cold.

"Look out!" I cried.

Just as the gargoyle's head thrust forward, Hridayesh tumbled to the side. Veranna leapt. Steaming liquid shot from the stone guardian's mouth, and it roiled across the stone of the street.

At once, the remaining gargoyles launched from the wall. I wrenched my sword from the scabbard. "Little one, let me go! Get into a building." I thrashed, and the hatchling released my cloak, but she did not dash away as I instructed. She lingered at my side.

There was no time to give the order a second time. I raced between my companions. Hridayesh was just regaining his feet, and he groped for the hilt of his khanda.

"What now?" Veranna cheeks went pale, her hair hung in limp waves in the slackening rain.

Stony *thunk* after stony *thunk* announced the landing of the gargoyles, and to my dismay, the sounds came from every direction. I cast my glance back and forth between the prophetess and the North Deklian.

"Looks the beetles have more sense than some warriors." I groaned.

"Certain death has a way of spawning humility," Hridayesh replied.

The hatchling fell in behind me, but the crunch of stone from that direction told me she was hardly safer there. She growled like a tomcat guarding its territory.

I scanned our perimeter. The gargoyles were closing in, slow and ponderous. It was only then that I noticed how pitted and uneven the stone underfoot was, like partially melted ice that had refrozen again.

"Look sharp!" Hridayesh cried. He barreled his shoulder into me, just in time to knock me out of the path of another stream of steaming, bubbling liquid that issued from the mouth of one of the guardians behind me.

The hatching yelped and launched straight up. Her leathery wings fought against the thunderstorm wind to draw her higher. She cradled a foretalon against her chest, but in my short glance, I could not ascertain the reason.

Veranna spun out of the path of the assault.

Rage flooded through me and wound my muscles tight. An attack upon me, I could brook, but injury to the hatchling? "Veranna, try to find some cover."

These statues *would* halt—after all, was that not the proper behavior for such objects? I pointed my sword straight ahead. Would an Utterance meant to halt a living creature work on whatever these were? Could I ensnare more than one at a time?

"Creo restrain you!" I yelled.

No surge of power glowed around my blade or streamed for the gargoyles. How was that possible? How could it be Creo's will that we should be melted in this forsaken ruin?

With his free hand, Hridayesh hurled a throwing star. It ricocheted with a spark from the scaly chest of the gargoyle that had just spewed its wrath at us. Somewhere behind me, Veranna's voice murmured in an unintelligible chant, which I could only hope would produce some advantage in our circumstances.

In a sudden clatter, stone feet thundered toward us. I put my back to Hridayesh's. "If I notch my sword today, these curs will all become whetstones."

Hridayesh swung his khanda. "And you never seem to have a dragon when you need one." His blade clanged against stone, but I would have to wait to learn the result.

I had troubles of my own.

Two gargoyles lunged at me with granite claws, which I deflected in a pair of swift strokes. In my peripheral vision, it seemed to me that a few of the larger guardians hung back, while the smaller, four legged types led the offensive for now. Lighting flashed and thunder answered in resounding booms. Our swords flew in arcs and cuts. I could not speak for Hridayesh, but my strokes served solely to parry the rake of claws and diving bites.

Hridayesh cried out and hissed.

"You OK?" I yelled over the din of battle and weather. I swept my sword in an uppercut that knocked my nearest gargoyle sprawling. Unscratched. My heart palpitated.

"For now," Hridayesh answered. His words came through his teeth by the sound of them.

The hatchling plummeted from the sky and lashed with her tail to catch one of the oncoming gargoyles closing on my position. Chips of stone flew from the curving horn and rounded ear she had assaulted. She flapped and sped higher again.

The crowd of rocky opponents thickened around us, and every golem that could reach me in the jumbled fray made attack after attack, until a mob of swinging claws and snapping stone teeth flooded me. For every enemy I deterred, even temporarily, another was more than ready to assume its place.

Rainwater mingled with sweat ran into my eyes, forcing me to swipe at the intrusion with my shield arm. My unguarded flank left an opening for one of the beasts' clawed hands to swing in, and the plate on that thigh split open, as did my flesh. Instinctual self-preservation welled within me and spurred my heart to a thunderous gallop. I swung my blade, and it gashed deep into the offending assailant. It took all my strength to wrench it free, but at least the gargoyle staggered away.

My leg throbbed and threatened to give out. Spots danced before my vision, and the heat of my exertion roasted me inside my armor. I performed parry after parry, and too few slashes that made any difference. The crowd around us became a wall of living rock. It began to seem only like a matter of time. The hatchling dove in and out of my peripheral vision, distracting her targets with swipes of her tail.

"I don't understand," Veranna said. "No ward I've tried has helped. Something very strange—"

"Strange?" I guffawed. "Try hopeless."

No matter what we tried, whether sword stroke, or dragon strike, or divine supplication, the gargoyles all pressed closer until a sea of stone interposed between ourselves and any prayer of escape.

7

EXILES

𝒜 gargoyle at least Veranna's height and resembling a muscle-bound satyr shouldered through our circle of foes. It met me with eyes both featureless in their glow and full of unswerving focus. No hatred, no surging battle rage like that I was so accustomed to facing in toe-to-toe opponents—just a unfaltering clarity of purpose. It reared its head back and opened its fang-lined maw. What flight I might have had within my limbs drained away. A bitter, hopeless cackle welled up from my gut.

"Restrirrenen, chalagne sen Creo!" The words rang out from somewhere behind me. A male voice, one I did not know, in a language or dialect that prevented my understanding. Or perhaps the roar of my pulse in my ears muddied my comprehension.

The gargoyles in the horde around me slowed, as though they strove against a worsening paralysis.

What in the Maker's dominion? My laugher dropped off. A glimmer of hope swirled through my bafflement.

"*Concusario!*"

The ground beneath my feet jolted, and a loud boom rocked the air. The gargoyles closest to me launched backward, colliding with those behind them just before they too were flung as though buffeted. At the same time, I lost my footing and crashed to the pavers just beside Veranna. The death-spewer crunched to the ground, motionless. As did the rest. All landed at least ten paces from where they had stood when the foreign words rang out. Each creature locked into the threatening postures of combat, a sudden sculpture garden of malice lay disheveled all around. The glow in their eyes winked out. Only the patter of rain and the sizzle of lingering gargoyle vomit remained within hearing.

I righted myself, which awoke a flaming pain in my injured leg, but nonetheless extended a hand to the prophetess. While she pulled to her feet, I swept a glance skyward. No hatchling. Though given the circumstances, I could not say I would fault her avoidance of the area.

"Lieutenant Commander, look." She pointed up the street.

I raised my sword to guard. I squinted through the swirling clouds of fog that drifted along to behold a trio of men marching up the dark street. Rather, two men and a youth it seemed. A squire, perhaps? They all wore helms of beaten copper, the two adults with brush-like plumes running along the crests of their helmets, tunics dyed deep burgundy, crème linen togas, leg wrappings, and tightly-woven sandals whose thongs cross-gartered to the knee. Woolen cloaks that shed rainwater in droplets hung over their shoulders. Each member of the trio wore a sword at his hip and leather bracers on his forearms, and the two adults also bore glowing lanterns of glass and iron.

I clasped my fist over my heart and bowed, albeit clumsily

owing to my reluctance to rest my full weight on my bleeding leg. "Hail, newcomers," I said in the Western tongue. Such a rough, uncouth language, but hopefully one we might hold in common. As I straightened, I gritted my teeth against the fiery spasm that lanced from my thigh up and down the length of my limb.

"Hail, friend Delsin," the tallest of the men returned in my own tongue.

I was not sure whether I ought to hang my head in shame or heave a sigh of relief. I fixed a blank façade over both inclinations. "Was it you who repelled these golems?" I gestured to the tumbled army of gargoyle statues around me. The answer, while obvious, at least offered a conversation starter.

"Indeed." The leader studied me with narrowed eyes. "Did you try to gain entrance to the complex?" He nodded toward the wall enclosing the dilapidated tower and its outbuildings.

"We sought refuge from a swarm of attacking beetles, and apparently found worse trouble instead of safety."

"Beetles?" he said, his face quizzical.

"Really, horribly big beetles." Veranna shuddered.

The second man stepped forward and examined the stone over the archway. "Alas, brother Aulus," he said. "It does seem the inscription of warning is all but worn away." He eyed Hridayesh, who rose from a crouch about fifteen paces off to my left and behind me. "Though if any among you harbored malicious intent, that would have stirred them to action regardless."

Hridayesh snorted. "My reputation precedes me, then." He splinted a hand against his chest, where a red smear fouled his right side.

Aulus raised a hand. "Forgive us, but our people have seen little favor in the eyes of the North Deklians. And yet, this elf calls you friend, and that does not go unnoticed." He reached into his toga and held a talisman forward on a chain. A phoenix wreathed in flame.

I nodded. "So you are the Elgadrim emissaries named in the missive. Fortuitous timing."

The second man's eyes widened. "I should say so. We never guessed an envoy from Delsinon would arrive here before we did."

"We were unsure when to expect you," Veranna said. "But we are glad of your coming. I did not recognize the utterance you intoned."

"I suspect not," Aulus replied. "There are many mysteries we Elgadrim keep unto ourselves." He clapped his hands. "*Decapit.*"

The gargoyles ground into motion again, lumbered with stony strides over to the wall, and climbed into place along its summit. They all settled back into their frozen poses once again, just as they had looked before our near-disaster.

A scraping on the tile roof to my left drew my sudden notice. I spun.

Only the hatchling alighting upon the single-story building. She licked at her left foretalon and winced.

So, she had not gone far. A troubling mix of relief and concern churned in my middle. Or perhaps that was just the nausea of battle ebbing from my veins and wounded weariness creeping in.

"If you do not mind," I said, pressing the bottom of my cloak to the sticky openness of my gash, "if we could converse somewhere we can clean and dress our wounds, that would be best. My provisions are back, well . . . back there a few blocks." My gesture indicated a vague northward distance.

"I'm not that interested in offering myself up to the bugs again." Hridayesh swallowed.

"Perhaps we should try the temple instead—get our supplies during the daylight hours?" Veranna said.

"That might be wise—there are quarters within the temple. I have bindings and medicine." Aulus regarded me. "Do you need assistance?"

I took a limping step forward. While I might have appreciated a shoulder to lean on, my desire to make the best possible impression overrode my discomfort. "No, it is not debilitating."

"As you wish." Aulus turned to the youth. "Praesidio, please get the horses and bring them behind us."

"Yes, father." The Elgadrim boy sprang ahead of us and down a side street.

I led the way, albeit slowly, back to the temple plaza. The hatchling followed at a wary distance, ground-level once again, and she limped on three legs. The flutter of her undersized wings offered occasional stability if she stumbled.

I scrutinized the foretalon she cradled against her chest and bit my cheek. Hridayesh clenched his teeth as he went. The splotch of dark wetness on his black tunic had not grown with any significance over the last few minutes—one mercy amidst an evening of troubles. Veranna appeared unscathed, if a little pale.

Outside the temple, the young Praesidio tethered the horses and then sat in the shelter of the entrance's overhang. Aulus pulled a roll of gear from behind one of the horses' saddles, nodded to the boy, and led the way through the entry.

The Elgadrim's flickering lanterns revealed the temple's cavernous interior, with high-domed ceilings inset with octagonal coffers that ran in countless rows. Mosaics whose colors eluded me in the low light encrusted every arched doorway. Seating for no fewer than two thousand worshipers filled the main temple sanctuary. Numerous wings branched from the main chamber where pillars topped with leafy embellishments marked the halls' entrances.

I strained my ears through the silence. Would I hear a clatter of predatory feet? Had some other vagabond species also made this place its lair, just waiting for the unwary to provide its next meal? A growing smattering of black spots popped across my vision.

"I fear our predicament has forced us to do things all out of order, gentlemen," Veranna said. She curtsied. "Since Vinyanel doesn't seem to be planning to get to it, please allow me to introduce myself: I am Veranna, prophetess of Creo."

Aulus bowed and removed his helmet to reveal short-cropped, sandy hair shot with gray at the temples. "My lady, please accept our apologies that some of the safeguards my people left in place here in Bilearne have proven dangerously zealous in their duty this afternoon. I do regret our introduction must be amidst such upheaval, but I am Aulus of the Elgadrim, and this is Cnaeus." He gestured to his companion.

Veranna ducked her head and smiled. "I fear I am at a loss as to whether I might say 'welcome' or 'thank you for having us.'"

Cnaeus grinned back. "Both and either would do. May I have the pleasure of knowing whom the Delsin send as ambassador?"

"You may. Though I would use the word 'ambassador' loosely if I were you," Veranna gestured to me. "This is Lieutenant Commander Vinyanel Ecleriast, cavalry soldier of the Delsin. And we are joined by Hridayesh Al'Mamuduri."

Cnaeus's grin crumpled back to a frown. He eyed Hridayesh and folded his arms. "This is a strange company."

I chuckled, despite the leaden weight of my limbs. "I will not argue that point. If you desire an explanation . . ." The room rocked, and I gripped the doorframe of the main chamber for balance.

Everyone else in the room stood firm. I swept my free hand across a clammy brow.

Aulus rushed to my side. "Perhaps I might address your

wounds before we attempt a focus on more challenging business. I am a surgeon."

I lowered my weight onto the floor and pried at the fasteners on my cuisses. The rent across the front plate inspired curses I refrained from uttering. "Those gargoyles have some claws."

"Better the claws than the venom." Aulus took the damaged armor from me.

The hatchling edged toward me, her brow furrowed. She sniffed at my hand, then nudged my arm in an attempt to stroke it with her snout. Had she not been so insistent I stay back from the gate, who knows how we might have fared?

Creo, permit whatever wound she has taken be minimal. I brushed my fingertips over her snout.

She curled up beside me, plopped her head on the floor, and sighed.

After producing an array of bandages, bottles, and tools from his pack, Aulus wet a wad of gauze, knelt, and squeezed the fluid over my gash.

A swarm of hot needling flooded through my wound. "Gah!" I clutched the stone molding of the doorframe.

"The best anti-infection agent you will find," Aulus said. "Mind this wound. It is rather deep."

"Perhaps we could discuss the Elgadrim's need while you work." I panted. "If you feel you can do both."

He laughed. "If *I* can do both? I might wonder if you are somewhat . . . distracted."

I licked the sweat from my upper lip. "Distraction is something I could use at the moment."

Aulus shrugged. "Cnaeus is the spokesperson more than I, so I am amenable to that request. Someone ought to get at least a blanket over your shoulders. I have one in my pack."

Aulus found thread and needles among his supplies, and

while he squinted at the eye of the probe, Cnaeus grabbed a chair from beside the entry and plunked it beside us.

"Have you any experience with the dragon-kin, Vinyanel?" he asked.

I snorted. "Much. At least of late."

Cnaeus froze, hovering just above seated. His brow folded into a half-dozen creases. "Truly? Why would that be? That is, if you are at liberty to tell."

"There seems to be some debate between their kind and mine what the limits of decency allow," I said. "Especially regarding an object the dragon-kin and I seem to have made a habit of exchanging—against one another's will, that is."

He settled into his seat. "So, perhaps your people know something of how they are focusing their movements here on the mainland?"

Aulus prodded lightly at the edges of my sliced flesh. "How is this feeling?"

I frowned. "A little numb. Should I be concerned?"

"Not at all," he replied. "That is just what I hoped." He stabbed his threaded needle through one side of the rent and out the other.

My breath came in shallower draughts. I had endured stitching without the benefit of numbing agent enough times to consider this session of treatment comparatively luxurious.

"As for the dragon-kin's movements, they dared forge as far south as the branching of the Nuruhain and Arin. The last I heard was they were withdrawing a host of about five-hundred to the northwest." *Unchallenged.* I clenched the bitter thought behind tight lips. "But I have been away from Delsinon for a few months, so I fear my information is not current. Your missive made it seem they had not gotten as far as I thought they might by this time. Frankly, it was from you I had hoped to update my knowledge."

"The group we encountered could not have been as many

as five-hundred, unless they withheld some of their number beyond our sight," Aulus said. "But yes, at least a remnant remains between the southern arms of the Triasteads."

I tensed my leg against the repeated prick-and-tug of Aulus's stitching.

"Try not to do that," Aulus said. "It's too soon to put that sort of strain on the thread."

I blew a breath through my mouth and loosened my muscle as much as discomfort allowed. "And thus, you come to the elves to learn why the dragon-kin have breached the sanctions? Why they have left the Isle of Desolation?"

Aulus paused and met my eye. His deep grey glance brimmed with nameless pain. "Oh, no. We have long known the sole reason their kind would act rashly. We do wonder, however, why the Delsin have not enforced the penalty more in accord with our understanding of the terms."

Cnaeus scowled. "Brother, perhaps it would be best if you focused on surgery and I rhetoric." He removed his helm and swept his palm over a bald pate.

"If your meaning is that we have done too little, master Aulus," I said, "know that you and I are in agreement."

"Vinyanel!" Veranna shook out a blanket and tucked it roughly around my shoulders. "And here is why you would never make an ambassador. Would you really cut down your own people?"

"I am not 'cutting anyone down,' Prophetess." Heat crept into my neck. "But I will speak freely my belief that we have sat upon knowledge that might have prevented a litany of grief. Our peoples set the terms of the sanctions long enough ago that even the elves grow forgetful of their necessity. We grow complacent during what was once a hard-won peace." My glance shifted back to Cnaeus. "Besides the dragon-kin being ancestrally significant to your people, do you have a further concern about them?"

Cnaeus nodded. "We fear that they have located at least half of our settlements, if not more. However, what they are doing with this knowledge, or plan to do, is a puzzlement. Their actions so far have amounted to little more than harassment."

Aulus choked on a gasp. He fired a glare at his countryman. "Harassment? How dare you!"

"You fail to maintain the air of calm you assured me you could," Cnaeus said.

Aulus's balled fists provided only a portion of his response —the creases in his face and the tightening of his lip spoke more to contained woe than fury.

Veranna took a step closer to him. "You have lost something. *You* came for more than information, even if that is all your people request."

Aulus drew a tremulous breath. "Indeed I have, Prophetess, and if an ambassador's even sensibilities will not request it, you shall hear the crux from me." He laid a folded strip of gauze across my newly-stitched skin. "You are familiar with the political state of the Elgadrim, Vinyanel?"

"Your current state?" I lifted a brow. "Has something changed from your being scattered around the western third of Argent?"

"No," Cnaeus interjected. "That is still the arrangement of our people. But if the locations of our settlements have been uncovered by dragon-kin spies, we must take strides to amend the peril that puts us in. Centuries of separation have made us weak in repelling a threat when it finds us. We believe the dragon-kin have determined themselves equipped enough to embark upon our extermination."

Aulus put pressure under my knee, which I interpreted as a request to lift my leg. He nodded and rolled a bandage around it, which held the padding in place over my stitches. "What exactly has changed to embolden them now, we cannot be certain. But they have proven their willingness to strike with their attack on our village."

Cnaeus sighed. "*Attack* is overly-strong wording."

The surgeon drew a deep breath, and his cheeks reddened in a flash-flood.

Veranna knelt beside Aulus and locked onto his face with her amber eyes. "Pardon my asking, but did they cause a great deal of loss?"

He clapped his mouth shut and swallowed. "The amount of loss is relative in the heart of the loser." Tears welled in his eyes. "There were only a half-dozen deaths, but one of them was my wife. And my three daughters. . ." He rolled his glance to the ceiling and blinked, but the tears still spilled down his cheeks. ". . .they went missing while my son and I fought the raiding party."

Veranna reached out and placed a palm on Aulus's cheek. While I found it awkward, Aulus seemed to draw some peace from the gesture. His creases softened. Another tear spilled.

In a voice scarcely above a whisper, the prophetess breathed, "I'm so sorry—"

Running footfalls increased in volume outside the door. "Father!" a male voice flipped in the pitch of panic.

Aulus sprang to his feet. The door to the chamber flew open.

"Father!" Praesidio panted. "Come quickly."

"Are you all right?" Aulus swiped a forearm across his wet cheek.

"Yes," Praesidio replied. "But there may be a problem." He turned back for the exterior.

I hauled myself back onto my feet and hobbled along after the youth and two older Elgadrim, back into the street.

Praesidio pointed across the plaza. "Something's out there. Something big."

We all stared the direction the Aulus's son pointed. Aulus and Cnaeus drew a simultaneous gasp.

"I cannot see very well, but is that . . .is that another dragon?" Cnaeus asked.

"Creo help us," Aulus breathed.

I grinned. Perched on the rooftop of the administration building sat Majestrin, who rustled the rainwater from his wings. Glints of moonlight that fought its way through breaking clouds outlined his silhouette in a cold glimmer. "Yes, it is." I shouldered my way through the men.

"Are you mad?" Cnaeus blurted. He grabbed my upper arm.

"Not to worry," I replied. I stepped into the open of the street and waved.

With a heave of his wings I could hear across the blocks that separated us, Majestrin took to the air. The horses tied behind me whinnied, and their hooves scraped across the stone. I turned to them—their eyes were white-rimmed and their heads strained against their bonds. I took a few slow strides toward the horses, hands raised.

"Easy, friends," I said in a low croon. "Old Majestrin will not eat you if I do not let him. Easy now." My fingers slipped around their tethers and gently lowered their heads. I continued to mutter in Elvish until the animals resumed a normal posture, though their ears remained pricked in Majestrin's direction. I stroked each horse's neck from the poll to the withers.

Praesidio's wide-eyed stare snapped from the distance to the horses. "What in the Great Patron's name?"

"He is with us," I said.

Cnaeus gaped. "He . . .?"

"The dragon, yes."

Aulus cleared his throat. "You are certain? Who, or perhaps I should ask what, is he carrying?"

I glanced back to Majestrin. From this closer vantage point,

I saw he carried a limp figure in his mouth. Further inspection revealed a scaly tail hanging from beneath the bottom hem of the figure's cloak.

Majestrin landed in the street about a hundred paces away, and the gust of his wings sent raindrops spattering across us. The horses threw their heads up again.

"Not to worry lads." I sniffed. An acrid scent burned the lining of my nose. "Not about the dragon, anyway."

After a final pat on the horses' necks, I advanced toward the dragon.

"It must have been poor hunting indeed, Majestrin," I said. "I hear dragon-kin is awfully tough, no matter how you cook it."

The silver dragon laid his limp captive on the ground. "Very funny." He smacked his lips and grimaced. "How it's even possible, I don't know, but they taste worse than they smell."

"Should we burn the body?" I asked. "Or do you think that would create some kind of worse fetor?"

Majestrin tilted his head. "Certainly not yet. Look closely, Lieutenant Commander. He's not dead."

8

RELIGION

"The dragon's wearing barding?" Cnaeus whispered somewhere behind me. "The elves have grown more powerful over the years."

I smirked and looked back. "Just some of us."

A snort rang out from Majestrin's direction.

I cleared my throat. "I jest. The arrangement is not of my own making, but rather part of an agreement between Majestrin and Creo, as I understand it."

"He's your mount?" Praesidio asked.

"Vinyanel is my rider," Majestrin replied. He padded toward us on great talons that made loose gravel chatter with the weight of his steps.

The Elgadrim men blanched but stood firm. They trained their glazes upon me, as though waiting upon the admission this was a colossal joke and that we should all run.

"Banter aside, we seem to have a complication on our hands." I approached the prone dragon-kin and nudged him with my foot. Dead weight. But his chest did indeed expand with shallow breaths. "What is the tale behind this, friend?"

Majestrin eyed the three Elgadrim who huddled in the entry of the temple and out of the rain. "While I was hunting this afternoon, I caught sight of a staggering figure fumbling his way along the edge of a clearing." He turned a glare on the dragon-kin. "And once I drew within a few furlongs, *that* stink filled my nostrils."

Aulus stood straighter. "This afternoon?"

Majestrin nodded.

The Elgadrim exchanged a tense glance.

"I told you we were being followed," Cnaeus said in a low voice.

"If that's so, he must have been desperate to keep up with you. He marched under light of day, poor though it was with the weather." Majestrin shook his head, and a shower of droplets sprayed across my face. "His steps wove like those of a drunkard."

"The sun sickness," I said.

"That makes sense. I bade Eyrnir to continue the hunt for meat, while I tailed this beast at a distance. His bumbling clatter made my task easy, and when he finally collapsed, I simply collected him. My first thought was to question him, but once I wearied of waiting upon him to regain consciousness, I opted to bring him here." An enormous digestive rumble echoed in Majestrin's gut, and a sheepish smirk tugged at the corner of his lip. "Without resuming my dinner search."

"We are in your debt." I bowed lightly. "While part of me would enjoy watching you question a prisoner, I know it has been long since you ate. If you are still inclined to hunt, please go right ahead."

Majestrin grimaced and smacked his lips. "I certainly have to find something to get this awful film out of my mouth. A deep drink if nothing else." He bowed his head to Aulus, Cnaeus, and Praesidio. "Gentlemen."

And with a thrust of his wings that bent every tree within sight, he launched skyward again.

My focus hung on Majestrin for a moment, until his silver form vanished into the shroud of nighttime clouds. A scowl overtook my features, and I aimed it at the limp form of the dragon-kin. "I cannot imagine what mischief this oath-breaker had in mind, but I will find out. For now, we need rope and a strong place to bind him."

Veranna and Hridayesh emerged from the building behind me. The hatchling also peered through the doorway, but after a furrowed look at the dragon-kin, she shrank back out of sight.

"Oh, no." Veranna rubbed her temple with her fingertips. She kept her distance.

Hridayesh laughed. "Somehow your friends always find you, eh, Vinny?"

A huffed. "For once, I think this beast's interest may have centered upon someone else. Help me lash him to one of the columns. I prefer he has no use of his limbs or teeth when he wakes up."

Praesidio reached into one of the horses' saddlebags. "I have rope here." He brought it to me with long strides and chin high. Though still a boy, his proud bearing and assured stride rumored a lofty future.

I took the rope from him and nodded.

Cnaeus and I hauled the dragon-kin to the furthest column down the line from the horses, which were already tense enough. The dragon-kin's horned head lolled on a limp neck as we forced him upright and bound him that way. While not entirely closed, his eyes rolled back and a filmy third eyelid obscured most of his red iris. Moss-green scales bit into my hands when I gripped his arms to move him. An occasional moan rumbled from his throat, but he made no further indications of lucidity.

I removed his pack and rifled through it. Dried meat, a few maps in poor condition, flint and steel. The usual -- except for a corked bottle a little smaller than my palm. I opened it and sniffed it. It was empty, but putrid-smelling. I grimaced and re-corked it.

"May I?" Aulus held out his hand.

I pressed the bottle into his palm. He, too, uncorked it, but was wiser in keeping his nose further from the neck of the container. A frown creased his cheeks. "Looks like someone doesn't plan very well. Ran out of his tonic."

I wrapped the prisoner's wrists with the rope Praesidio had brought, while Hridayesh bound the creature's feet. "Ran out of what?"

"The tonic they use to stave off the sun sickness."

"I never knew there was such a thing," I said.

Aulus nodded. "It is precious, and notoriously difficult to brew. Between the tonic and heavy cloaks that keep the sun off their skin, they can usually withstand some activity during the daylight hours."

Some of the tension that had crept into my shoulders eased. At least the tonic's limited availability might keep some of them from making chase were I to prod the proverbial hive of horrors.

I stepped back once we had lashed the prisoner to the pillar. This particular creature baffled me. He was largely unarmed, aside from a knife of which we relieved him. He wore no armor, unlike the warrior-types I had seen in the past, just a hooded robe with a gargoyle pin on one shoulder, and a row of three leather-covered buttons on the other. It was to this pin Cnaeus paid particular attention.

His brow creased. "Something runs further afoul here than we understand, I think."

"What gives you that impression?" I asked.

"We have not known the dragon-kin to wear the Tebalese Theocracy's symbol."

Hridayesh laughed. "Well, it's not like you Elgadrim have been the most in-touch group of people in the world. How would you know what heraldry the dragon-kin employ?"

Cnaeus glared. "Perhaps we have remained out of the public eye, but that does not mean our own eyes have not been trained upon the goings-on of the world. When the dragon-kin began appearing in increasing numbers on the mainland of Argent, we employed what vigilance we could."

"There have been no reports that I have heard," Aulus added, "that speak to Queldurik's symbol upon these oath-breakers."

"If the myths are to be believed, it is a marriage of convenience," I said.

"Cryptic, to say the least." Cnaeus's expression hardened.

The spark of suspicion in the man's eye set my instincts buzzing. "Our scholars hold a theory that the reason the original generation of dragon-kin did not simply die out, being all male, is by some arrangement with Queldurik himself. Nonetheless, I have experienced division among their people as to who they worship."

Both Cnaeus and Aulus chewed on this for a silent stretch.

I prodded our prisoner again. "Can we get him awake enough to question?"

"Now that the sun is down, I suspect he will regain consciousness fairly soon," Cnaeus said. "And when that happens, we may find we all need to be on our guard, for who knows how crafty he might become, or what the measure of his strength might be?"

Veranna approached me and placed a hand on my shoulder. "What are you going to ask him, Vinyanel?"

I shrugged and squinted at the sky. The clouds were thinning, the rain had ceased, and the sickle moon fought its way through the occasional gaps. "To start, wisdom dictates we determine if he was really alone. I have never known the creatures to employ a lone tracker." I cracked my knuckles. "I am certain I can develop a suitably damning series of questions by the time the creature wakes."

The dragon-kin still hung heavy against the ropes.

"It appears that will not be immediately," Aulus said.

"Good. Perhaps in that amount of time, Vinyanel will make sure he avoids the swift current of vengeance." She turned and swished her way out of the rain and out of sight.

I narrowed my eyes. *Vengeance.* It appeared Veranna, for all her visions, failed to see how we might serve the Elgadrim and the fallen both.

9

TRACKING

"Are you sure you're still following the right signature?" Raen asked. She rubbed her arms against the raw air of an afternoon that had gone from drizzly to blustery and punctuated with scattered downpours. She glanced down at the river that flowed easterly far below. Her legs tightened around Mythrenese's middle.

The indigo dragon craned his lithe neck to glance back at her. "Yes, mistress, I'm sure. We're gaining on her, so it's getting stronger."

Raen chewed her lip. *So far north? I thought for sure . . .*

Mythrenese's sudden dive to the right snapped her thought off at the root. She grappled his neck and leaned close to his body, into the thrust of his maneuver in order to stay seated.

"What are you doing?"

"Shhh!" Mythrenese replied. "Someone's up ahead, skulking around the edge of the clearing."

"What kind of person is it?"

"Can't tell, so it's probably better if it can't see us either." Mythrenese slowed his course within the treetops, dodging from one cluster of cover to the next. He settled into a giant sycamore, close to the clearing, but still with plenty of cover between themselves and the open space.

Raen squinted through the brown, gold, and green foliage. There it was—a person in black, vanishing, albeit clumsily, into the forest on the due north side of the glade. The dark figure followed an overgrown path, arguably wide enough to have once been a road before its makers forgot it. She held her breath. Only after all rumor of the traveler had vanished, did she dare speak. "I'm afraid to ask . . ."

Mythrenese smiled. "Iriscendra's trail crosses this space, still heading east-northeast. Looks like we won't need to worry about whoever that was."

Raen strained her ear after any footfall or further sign of the traveler. Nothing. "Well, that's a relief. Let's stay low for a bit, just in case."

They perched in the tree for a few long moments. Raen blinked away the bead of rainwater that ran off her brow. Darker clouds beyond the hills rumored worse weather to the northwest. Raen pulled her hood closer and waited.

Just as Mythrenese stretched his wings to lift off, he quailed, collapsed his pinions, and cringed against the bole of the tree. He squeezed his eyes shut and shook his head, as though biting flies swarmed him.

"Now what?" Raen asked.

A whoosh and a flap met Raen's ears, somewhere to the south, but difficult to pinpoint amidst the chatter of rain and wind through the trees. Still, she heard it, so it could not have been as far as she'd like. She peered that way.

"I'll continue on this mystery, friend," said a voice as deep as rolling thunder. "You see if you can't claim yourself a meal this evening, and meet us back at the colonnade."

The whooshing drew nearer, when overhead, not forty paces off, a flash of silver approached. Mythrenese flattened himself against the tree trunk, and Raen pressed to him as close as she was able. Mythrenese trembled.

The huge silver shape passed overhead, across the glade, and on north, lithe, broad-winged, and reflective. And wearing an empty burgundy saddle. Was it possible? It drifted onward, focused intently on the northern distance. Only when it was beyond sight did Mythrenese relax and cease quaking.

"I've felt that signature before," Mythrenese said. "How strange for us to encounter *that* particular dragon again when we're looking for Iriscendra."

Raen clenched her fists. "Not strange at all. It bolsters my suspicions. If that particular dragon is nearby, his rider likely is too. Which would explain why Iriscendra's trail is leading up here instead of to the elven capitol of Delsinon." *Appears I might not be needing my old talisman after all.*

"Why would she have gone to Del . . .what did you call it?"

After a deep breath, Raen patted Mythrenese's neck. "Delsinon. You might as well know what I'm thinking now that we've seen the silver dragon again. I think Iriscendra is looking for that elf soldier who chased you down for the talismans you took last season. What I don't know is why he's out here and not home with his kindred."

Mythrenese's eyes widened. "But why would she want to find him?"

"I'll save my accusations for the offender. For now, hurry, Mythrenese. The sooner we find the hatchling and take her back home, the better."

~

he more the night deepened, the less the dragon kin's head lolled on his fat, scaly neck, and the more periods of seeming clarity he had. He strained against his bonds at intervals, but the effort seemed too great for him. He would begin to breathe heavily, sometimes even to retch, and resume his slump in front of the pillar where we bound him.

I stood at a distance, beneath the portico of a narrow residence across the street from the temple. Aulus, Praesidio, and Cnaeus had withdrawn to their own set of rooms at the rear of the temple—apparently quarters provided for clergy and visitors, which had proven blessedly predator-free. Hridayesh and Veranna retired with the agreement they would take watches after they had slept. For now, the prisoner remained too groggy to offer challenge.

The quiet hours of the deep night crept on. My stomach rumbled. Even over the growing ache in my leg, my hunger managed to emerge. Alas, my few rations remained in the beetle lair. Just when I thought perhaps I would give up the watch to Hridayesh and instead figure out how to recover my gear, the dragon-kin hauled himself to a straighter posture.

"You wanna know what's good for you, elf?" the beast rasped in the common tongue. "Stay outta what don't concern you."

"You follow my allies," I called back, "I consider that concerning."

He began to laugh, but the outburst transformed into a hacking cough. "What's between Elgadrim and dragon-kin won't touch elves. Not if you don't poke your nose in and catch a stray blow."

I limped over to the prisoner. "Well, our noses are in it, so you had best use care in where you swing." I lowered my voice. "Now this can be quick, or you can make it as miserable as you choose. What are your people planning on doing . . ." I glanced toward the temple. The doorway contained no hint of motion. I leaned in and said, " . . .with the chalice?"

The beast eyed me and huffed. "It's an object of worship. We have rights to worship who we like. Our god'll favor us for enshrining it."

"You went to all the trouble of stealing it from my people in order to put it on a shelf in a nice light?" I leaned back and guffawed. "You did not invite the ire of the entire military machine of the Delsin for a trinket."

The dragon kin wagged his long snout. "Pfah. Your military don't care about this. Your primitive church, maybe. Your people've already proven they'll only commit the bare minimum to the hunt. Your superiors are smarter than you. Make like them and go home."

I sucked raw night air through my nose. The creature was more right than I was interested in admitting aloud, at least about the level of concern the Delsin leadership had shown about the chalice. Now that the king was safely home from his abduction—and in a matter of days, the talismans would be as well—I could just hear Lerendir ordering me to let the issue of the chalice drop. But something in my gut insisted the dragon-kin had not risked so much over a religious practice this beast depicted as trivial. There was more. But how to get to it?

I pulled my sword and leveled it at the dragon-kin's throat. "I know what the chalice does. I cannot assume that in your hands you will fail to avail yourselves of the power it offers."

The beast cocked his head. "Power? It's just a cup, elf."

"You expect me to believe that? The least you could have done is show up here with an interesting story." I pushed my blade against the notch between his collar bones.

He leered. "I'm not afraid of death. And you elves have always been too spineless to utilize pain."

I clenched my fist harder around my hilt. "You might find

me distressingly unlike your impression of elves. It is overly simplistic, like your story."

"Vinyanel, what are you doing?" Veranna emerged from the temple with the two Elgadrim emissaries behind her.

"Stop!" Cnaeus bellowed.

I rolled my eyes and lowered my sword.

"Creo may offer a way to free up this fellow's tongue," Veranna said. "You should have told us he was awake."

The dragon-kin's attention snapped to the newcomers, and his eyes widened. He dipped his snout and bit one of the buttons that fastened the left shoulder of his robe. He ripped the button free and clamped his jaw with a snap.

"No!" Aulus cried. He dove for the dragon-kin.

Greenish foam seeped through the thicket of the beast's teeth, and his eyes glazed over. He thrashed against his bonds for a brief moment, then went still.

"Just like the raiders and other spies." Aulus stamped a foot and turned away. "They're getting cleverer in how they hide the poison."

"You knew there was a risk he would poison himself and did not search him for the means to suicide?" I gaped.

Cnaeus glared. "Calm down, Lieutenant Commander. The other prisoner had the capsule tied to his wrist. That, I looked for. And prior to that, they wore vials around their necks."

I conceded the point. After all, I too had failed to recognize the disguised means of escape, however grim. "Veranna, you say I may never make a diplomat, but you will certainly never make an interrogator."

Veranna folded her arms. "I cannot say that displeases me."

"But it leaves us with no way to glean why the dragon-kin might be shadowing the Elgadrim's movements, or how much they know about the location of their villages."

"And I'm sure you were getting right to that," Veranna

snapped. "Right after you obsessed over that confounded chalice."

I slammed my sword back into the scabbard. How did she know? How did she *always* know? "It is key. I am sure of it. I need to learn more about the application of the thing."

Aulus cast a sidelong glance to Cnaeus. "Chalice? What chalice?"

"The tale is longer in the telling than I want to undertake standing in the street," I said. Not that the growing ache in my leg had any influence on my opinion. Now that Aulus's pain remedy had worn off, every beat of my heart throbbed in the wound.

Aulus looked back at the limp form of the dragon-kin. "Very well. Let us move indoors so we can get to the center of things. Today's interruptions have slowed what I had hoped would be quick and simple talks."

I stalked past Veranna and toward the temple entry.

After drawing a deep breath, Aulus followed me back inside, and Cnaeus shadowed us.

I led the group into the room they had chosen for Hridayesh and me. It was a snug pair of square chambers—one a sort of sitting room, and one with two cots and an ink-stained writing desk below one deep window. Wrapped in his cloak, Hridayesh lay on his side, facing the wall.

I pulled the chair from under the desk, took a seat, then released a loud breath inspired by the protest in my thigh. So bothersome for a single wound. "If I may be direct, what is it you believe the Delsin are equipped to do for your circumstances?"

Cnaeus licked his lips and tapped his fingertips on the desk. "There is a matter of some territory the elves hold, unpopulated land, that we mean to petition your people for its use. If we can just gather our remnant in an unknown place, one that is especially defensible if need be—"

"A human settlement, within our borders?" I frowned. "Even if it were temporary, I am not optimistic that would sit well with my father's generation."

Aulus rubbed his neck. "Would it make any difference if the territory were not on the mainland?"

"Not on the mainland?" I pursed my lips in thought. Well, there was that . . . "There is only one island I am aware of that belongs to us, though why we maintain ownership over it is a great mystery to me. We do not even value it enough to name the cursed thing."

"Precisely," Cnaeus said. "Such a place would be far more defensible should the dragon-kin threat mount."

"Have your people been to the island in question?" I leaned back and raised a skeptical brow.

"We have no navy." Aulus sighed.

"The eastern shore is crawling with harpies."

Cnaeus scratched his temple. "So it is not just a rumor. Even so, we believe that we stand a better chance of protecting ourselves from them than we do the dragon-kin. While appetite is a strong motivator, centuries of hatred forge a more tempered tenacity."

I rubbed the creases from the tension in my forehead. "The idea is an interesting one, gentlemen, but I have neither the jurisdiction nor the resources to make this determination for you."

Cnaeus took a few steps away from me. "What if we said we could lead you to abundant documentation about this chalice Veranna speaks of being so important to you?"

My pulse quickened. "I can probably gain you audience with better elves to address your request, though."

A rustle from Hridayesh's cot told me he stirred. "I know this is none of my business, but what has changed that makes the dragon-kin more likely to move against you now than during all the ages that have passed?"

"That is what we want to determine," Aulus said. "Some key component to their aggression must have fallen into place to push them from a place of watchfulness to skirmishing. We fear what skirmishing might build into."

The North Deklian rose and approached us. "You said there is a matter of an artifact between you, right, Vinyanel? That wouldn't be a certain cup that disappeared from the Elven treasury?"

I faced him. "Just how much did the bounty posters tell you before you botched your chance to relieve me of my head?"

"They try to make sure we hunters know at least what our targets might be peeved about."

Cnaeus straightened and cast a hard glare at Hridayesh. "Bounties? What sort of company are you keeping, Vinyanel? I begin to doubt our request is in entirely savory hands, given the hints about the past of one you call 'friend.'"

I sighed. "I cannot make you trust those whom I trust. But in your position, options seem to be in short supply." I turned to Hridayesh. "The lingering point of contention between the dragon-kin and the elves is over the Chalice of Gherag-Tal."

Veranna folded her arms. "You mean between the dragon-kin and you, young Windrider."

I clenched my jaw, but before I could assemble any kind of retort, Hridayesh asked, "What does it do?"

"Oh, not much." I circled my hand in the air in a dismissive gesture. "It just summons fiends by the score and binds them to a curse-bearer, who can then command them." My eyes flicked to Aulus and Cnaeus. "I am sure that will not cause any trouble in the dragon-kin's hands."

They had both grown deathly pale.

"Gherag-Tal? Are you sure?" Aulus breathed.

Veranna clenched her skirts in her fists. "The question is: do they intend to actually use this thing? It sounds as dangerous to the wielder as to the target."

Hridayesh blew a long whistle. "More likely, how long will it be before they do? Or have they already?"

Veranna met his eye with a stern countenance. "Don't let Vinyanel's obsession infect you, Hridayesh." She shifted the glare to me. "Be careful you do not assume too much in your desire to vindicate your friends. You could be dead wrong about this."

Something in the core of my being told me I was not. *Laermelion and Veryan did not die for me to turn a blind eye. Nor Beriadhan.* My throat tightened at the thought.

Hridayesh guffawed. "Veranna, even *you're* not this naïve. Of course they're going to use it. You had just better pray to that god of yours that half-elves aren't first on their list of people to exterminate."

I rose and took a few strides clear of both of them and their clamoring. "We need to know more about the chalice. How it works. What they need to be able to utilize it."

"Well then," Veranna said, "let's go back to Delsinon and talk to the professors of arcana. Then we can present the actual findings to the correct authorities, who will decide what to do."

"You sound just like Galdurith. What a phenomenal waste of time! A committee is the last thing we need right now." I cracked my knuckles with a resounding series of pops.

"You have a better idea of where to learn this information?" Veranna propped her fist on her hip.

"I need to think." A few strides into pacing a track across the room, I slowed and instead leaned on the back of a chair. Apparently my stitches were not going to leave much room for my usual thinking habits. I drummed on the wood with my fingertips.

Aulus and Cnaeus whispered amongst themselves in their deeply-inflected tongue. "We are willing to lead you to more information on the chalice if you will expedite our request, Vinyanel," Cnaeus said.

"How far would we need to go?" I asked.

After an exchange of tense glances, Aulus and Cnaeus both settled gazes upon me. "Merely across town," Aulus replied.

"Information? Here?" Hridayesh said. "Where, under the biggest pile of rubble?"

Cnaeus grabbed his hilt, but Aulus in turn clasped Cnaeus's wrist.

"Bilearne is not as empty as it appears," Aulus said.

"Splendid." I brought my hands together in a single, booming clap. "Get me a piece of parchment. I shall pen the writ for your admittance to Delsinon this moment."

10

PACT

The last of the dragon-kin caravan's supply carts rolled into place in the circle of camp, and in a copse of walnut trees down the hill from their position, a songbird trilled in the stillness. Naghax hauled a heavy canvas bundle from the cargo area of the barred cart he followed and dropped it with a solid *whump.*

"Finally," Naghax groaned. "I was beginning to wonder how far past sunrise we were going to plod." He marched up beside the driver's seat of the cart, where Hanash held the reins. "We cannot expect to maintain this pace and not risk vulnerability. I'm nearly reeling."

"You're the one who keeps whining you won't have enough time to study the texts. You should be happy we're pushing onward." Hanash stretched his brass-gauntleted arms high to the brightening sky.

"We should have captured more sacrifices." Naghax glanced back at the three softbelly females sleeping with puckered brows on the floor of their cage on wheels. "I don't like having only one shot at this."

"Any more would have provoked pursuit."

A scoff hissed through Naghax's teeth. "I'm not confident these few haven't earned us a tail anyway. Any word from the scout about the movements of that party of Elgadrim?" He unbundled his tent and craned his glance toward the bright eastern sky. More birds joined the first singer's lilt, chattering their welcome of the sun's return. Naghax scowled.

"None back yet." Hanash shook his head. "It's too soon to expect anything anyway. Your paranoia is really beginning to get between my scales. Focus on learning the ritual—or stop whining about how complicated it is."

"Complicated or not, I am sure you have well in hand, correct, Naghax?" someone asked from the opposite side of the cart from where Naghax stood. The voice struck Naghax as too buttery in tone to belong to one of his kin.

A broad, gray-skinned man rounded the cart. The long, gray moustache that he wore in thin braids dangled nearly to the banded mail of his breastplate. He brushed at the rectangular plate that jutted from his left shoulder. The red cloak that hung around his neck boasted a jewel-encrusted triangle, set with a gargoyle's head with ruby eyes that glinted in the sunrise. He reached out a scarred hand to Naghax.

Dragon-kin claw met Tebalese hand in a shake of greeting. Naghax forced a smile. *When did he join the caravan?* "I thank you for your confidence, Inquisitor . . . Ezio, if I'm not mistaken?"

The Inquisitor nodded. His flat-featured face offered only a practiced impassivity.

Hanash straightened his sash. "Indeed, I believe Naghax has almost every nuance committed to memory, thanks to the excellent documents your people have provided. The sacrifice, the theurgic circle, and the summoning that the pact hangs upon will go so beautifully it will bring a tear to Queldurik's eye —won't they, my friend?"

Friend. Naghax contained his guffaw. Hanash only claimed friends when his aim was to appear magnanimous and well-liked to someone who did not know better. But so newly elevated as Scitherias's successor, Hanash did need to surround himself with as many allies as he could buy or bully. Was the approval of a politically insignificant culture of any benefit, though?

As brutal as Scitherias's rule had been, a portion of Naghax's inmost being felt the lack of his leadership and the clear respect he had enjoyed as the now-deceased lord's chief scribe.

"I don't doubt the ceremony will be a decadent fragrance to Almighty Queldurik's liking," the Inquisitor replied. "And in that case, you will have yourself to congratulate for an unstoppable alliance, ready to obliterate our common enemies." He leveled a hard stare at Naghax. "But I expect all will come to pass on *this* moondeath. None of this talk of hesitating until the next. Or else maybe Hanash will second-guess keeping remnants of the old regime in his employ."

Naghax rubbed his burning eyes, then pulled his hood lower to his snout. "Surely you understand the intricacy—"

"I did not march a legion of Tebal's best warriors to your stinking hole in the mountains to be contradicted by . . . what? A scribe? You lizards have no hope of victory in this plan of yours without us, so I advise you spend less energy whimpering like a cur and more on covering ground."

Naghax clenched his fists. Had there not been an apparent formation of an alliance, he might have proven to this mouthy Inquisitor how much warrior this scribe had in him. For now, he could play along, a means to an end. Almost any level of temporary insult was worth enduring if it meant no more craven hiding on the cursed isle to which his people had been banished, where the wind always howled its torment in the ears of his kin. Once their army was summoned, neither pathetic Elgadrim nor troublesome elf could withhold any territory the dragon-kin sought to conquer.

But if at any moment this Tebalese cock-of-the-walk proved more mouth than might, Naghax's previous liege-lord had taught him plenty of ways of managing pests. Whether Hanash liked it or not.

11

THE UNDERKEEP

*A*ulus and Cnaeus led us back to the gated complex with the crumbling, conical tower as soon as the morning sun brightened the eastern horizon. Gone were the rainclouds of the day before, torn to tatters by a stiff westerly wind that wielded winter's keen edge, despite the fact that autumn should still by rights linger another six weeks.

When we neared the outer fortification of the tower complex, I cast a quick glance about the wall's summit and swallowed. The gargoyles all *seemed* very still. The ground beneath my feet often threw me off balance, pitted and uneven as it was—in the places the gargoyles had erupted venom at us. Stone blocks had lost their shape and looked more like slag, as I imagined cooled lava would appear. The hatchling pressed close to my side.

Fortunately, the Elgadrim saw no harm in her accompanying me wherever they wanted to go this morning, since she had proven an unwillingness to allow me from sight. And to my relief, she walked on all four legs today, appearing much more whole than I felt, for certain.

The attendance of Hridayesh had required further negotiation, but while he had grown to more of a comrade than prisoner, I still did not feel it prudent to leave him unattended for potentially long stretches. It had taken Veranna only a few bats of her eyelashes to earn her a place in the entourage.

"We could probably find something to fashion into a crutch for you, Vinyanel," Aulus said. He eyed my leg.

A crutch. The concept rankled me, but at the same time, the wound felt just awful enough to holler above the clamor of my pride. I sighed. "Perhaps. But let us finish what we have set out to do this morning first." How strenuous could research be, anyway?

We reached the gate, which a masterful craftsman had wrought of cast iron. The center of the scrolling design depicted a symbol I had come to know well—the spreading oak of Creo—and the curls of metalwork that spiraled out from it formed clouds and a mountainous horizon. Cnaeus stepped up to the gate.

A grind of stone sent my heart plummeting back into my stomach. My attention shot to the wall, where every gargoyle's head had turned and now faced us. I grabbed for my sword and shield. The hatchling scuttled behind me. Hridayesh clasped his hilt and bent his knees in a spring-ready stance.

Aulus raised a palm. "No need."

I was not entirely inclined to believe him until we had passed the gate with no advance from the gargoyles.

After placing his palm on the trunk of the iron tree, Cnaeus uttered a few quiet words, and the gate swung open. The hatchling bounded through. The gargoyles turned their heads back to the front, and I followed the Elgadrim through the archway, close on their heels. A groan of iron hinges and a solid clang announced the gate closed behind Hridayesh and Veranna.

Within the walls, the crumbling tower inspired further tightening around my thundering heart. "Do we have to go inside?" I nodded to the leaning turret.

Cnaeus shook his head. "This way."

Within the walls, a series of stone structures lined the complex. Some of the structures stood several stories tall, while others stretched long and low. In the rear-center of it all stood a strange, sloped building—like a tiled roof that rose from the pavement, as though someone had erected half a gable in the middle of everything but never troubled to complete the symmetrical slope. We rounded this to find the roof sheltered a downward slope, and at the base of the ramp stood another gate.

Cnaeus opened this barrier much in the same manner as he had the last, and we stepped into the cold vacancy of the darkness.

"I fear we shall need to light lanterns," Aulus said.

Just when my eyes had adjusted. I shrugged off the inconvenience. "Thank you for the warning."

I averted my gaze to prevent the painful flare in my vision that was inevitable when the Elgadrim men lit the wicks. When the warm swell of light grew behind me, I turned and blinked a few times as my eyesight adjusted again. Wonderful. Half light. The hairs on the back of my neck lifted in a tingle.

The first chamber we entered, wide and rectangular, was even more barren than the topside buildings we had investigated. Four corridors branched from this room, two on the long wall ahead and one on each end of the chamber. The hatchling sniffed around the entrances to each hall.

"Where to, gentlemen?" I asked. My voice echoed through the quiet emptiness.

Cnaeus led us to the left, his swinging lantern casting a dance of light across the stone blocks of the walls and low ceiling. Upon the lintel and posts of the doorway I caught a glimpse of deep, runic carvings, and when we reached the threshold, Cnaeus stepped forward and placed his hand upon a cluster of these runes. Starting at his hand, the characters graven in the stone lit up, as though kindled from within with lavender light, and the effect spread over the lintel of the door and ran down the opposite post.

He turned and nodded at me. "Go through."

I did as he bade, just behind Aulus. The hatchling lingered in the doorway and breathed deep, a broad smile on her lips. It was as if she drank in the glow of the runes as one breathes the fragrance of new blooms or fresh bread. I waved her on.

She fluttered her wings and bounded onward. Last came the prophetess and the assassin.

Hridayesh hesitated. "The passages don't get any narrower as we go, do they?"

Aulus looked back across the threshold . "Are you unwell? Perhaps you should stay in the first chamber."

Hridayesh licked his lips. "I'll be fine." He passed through the doorway, stopped at my side, and whispered, "Not a lot of room to swing a sword down here."

I tried not to think about it.

"What would happen if we turned around and stepped through that doorway again?" Hridayesh asked.

"Without me?" Cnaeus cocked an eyebrow. "I don't recommend you try it."

"Would you indulge a more specific answer for one who is young in the craft of Utterances?" I whispered. Why I lowered my voice so, I hardly knew, but somehow it seemed appropriate.

Aulus replied, "Ever seen a victim of lighting strike?"

I grimaced. Needless to say, none of us would be heading to the surface on our own. Not unless we fancied nasty burns or heart failure.

The hall we entered sloped steadily downward, making

square turns to the left after every hundred feet or so, as best I could guess. Foot-thick posts of silvery wood buttressed the walls and ceiling at regular intervals. We passed no fewer than a dozen doors, crafted of the same wood, all banded with iron, and similarly carven with runes.

We rounded yet another left-turning corner to find the hall before us piled floor-to-ceiling with rubble. My Elgadrim leaders halted. Cnaeus scratched his head.

"Well, this complicates matters." Aulus folded his arms.

Overhead, where the rubble piled, the hallway was rough and earthen. The hatchling scrambled up the mound, sniffing again. She clawed her way to the summit, and the smaller chunks of rubble rolled from beneath her talons as she went.

"Little one," I said. "Come down. This is no time for antics."

She turned her head back toward me and cocked it. After that short moment of regard, she continued her ascent. Here and there, she tapped the hook on the end of her snout, something like an egg tooth, on the stones. One area she knocked upon several times. The hatchling flashed me a smile.

"What?" I said.

She reared back and gave the rock she had tapped a shove with all her body weight. It shifted. She repeated the assault. The stone ground, creaked, and then tumbled away from her thrust. It crunched down what I guessed must be the opposite side of the pile and out of sight. The movement of the stone created a gap between the ceiling and the top of the cave-in, roughly the breadth of my shoulders.

"Interesting," Cnaeus said. "I had heard some dragons have a talent for finding passages and the like. Handy you should have one such creature with you."

I shrugged. "Creo provides, I suppose."

Veranna nodded and the corner of her lip curled in a satisfied way.

We all labored up the pile, and after clearing a few more

stones, opened a gap between the rough top of the passage and the rubble large enough to squeeze through. We all came out on the far side rather dusty and disheveled, but better that than turned back by the obstacle.

Two more doors down the hallway beyond the cave-in, Cnaeus approached a set of double doors. "*Gasthenerri*," he said in a droning voice that drew out each syllable on a single pitch. Light spread across not only the doorjamb, but over the doors themselves. It shimmered like a quick frost, but dimmed in the next instant.

He grasped the curving iron handle of the door. Our eyes met.

"Vinyanel, Veranna . . . you are bound to secrecy with regards to the existence of this chamber," Aulus said. "The route this place will leave your minds the moment we depart, but I permit you to retain the information we gather, upon your oath to use it only in actions friendly to the Elgadrim."

I nodded. "Of course."

Veranna bowed her head. "Your people's arcana will remain safe, as far as it is up to me."

"The North Deklian, however," Cnaeus said, "will remain in this antechamber. The wards along the route to the surface will keep you from losing him to mischief.

Hridayesh huffed. "Doesn't much matter what kind of company you keep, I see. Always mistrust." He put his back to the wall and slid to a seated posture on the floor.

Cnaeus pushed the door open to reveal a domed cavern supported with an ornate grid of vaults. Orderly stacks, rows, shelves, and cubbyholes containing tomes, scrolls, tablets— any manner of ways written word could be chronicled— stretched as far as I could see in the failing light. Tapestries depicting maps not only of Argent, but of Tilanet over the sea and even more distant Gharanna, hung from the stone arches. The collection of knowledge made the central library of

Delsinon appear but a private store of a few fancies. My eyes widened.

"I could spend the lifetimes of several elves hunting what I need to know in such a place," I said.

Cnaeus chuckled. "We would not be so cruel. I know what records we need, and it should not take me more than a few minutes to find them."

He ushered Veranna, the hatchling, and me inside, and once Aulus had crossed the threshold as well, closed the door behind us.

I clasped my hands behind my back and waited while Cnaeus vanished around a mountain of books. The hatchling eyed some of the scrolls and eventually nudged a nearby volume open. She scanned its pages.

"Can dragons read?" I asked.

Aulus shrugged. "I thought you would know better than I. It certainly appears so."

"Well, if she can read, why does she say nothing?"

"I imagine we could possibly find something to answer that question somewhere down here as well, though I suspect we would do better to focus our efforts on the chalice. One question at a time, I think."

The hatchling's attention did not linger very long on the book, or anything else, for that matter. She scuttled from one stack to the next, spun a globe on a stand for a moment, but after only a few minutes, yawned and curled up in a crevice between two pyramids of scrolls.

Veranna drifted about the room with a reverent awe setting her features aglow. She reached her slender fingers to the pile of the tapestries and traced the subtle contours of sculptures with a ginger touch.

As promised, Cnaeus soon returned with a fat tome with a thick leather cover and pages whose edges gleamed with gold leaf. Intricate embossing of interwoven geometric patterns edged the cover, and a gold double circle enclosing runes filled the center. Several words ran above and below the circle, but the characters were wholly unfamiliar to me. Cnaeus handed me the book.

I eased the book's cover open, and found each page bore not just words, but intricate diagrams, illustrations, and perfectly-penned text. All beautiful to behold, but incomprehensible. My brows knit.

Aulus reached toward my head. "If you will permit me, Vinyanel? I suspect you may have some difficulty interpreting the text?"

My lip curled. "Well, yes. Is this your language?"

"A form of it," Cnaeus said. "It's actually the dialect particular to those who worship Queldurik, which is a bit of a hybrid between the Vareinorean tongue and Tebalese. Aulus should be able to convey upon you the ability to translate it for all of us."

My glance flicked to Aulus's extended hand. "You two are pretty free with the Utterances, it seems."

"Does that bother you?" Aulus closed his fingers and lowered his arm part way.

"No," I said. "You just seem to have a lot at your disposal. Of what little I know, the Utterances seem to work only about half the time."

"To be fair, the passage of the gates and doors here does not fall under the same type of power as an Utterance. Cnaeus's area of expertise is in enchanted objects and wards, a few of which you have seen here. Stopping the gargoyles, however, required a quicker, direct request to the Maker. But I think you would agree those were dire circumstances to which Creo was likely to respond." Aulus hesitated. "May I be so bold as to ask how long you have been a Thaumaturgist?"

I pursed my lips. How long had it been since my encounter with Lord Scitherias? "Not yet half a year."

Cnaeus laughed. "Well, there stands your answer. It takes a lot longer to develop an ear trained to the Maker's voice than that. You being an elf, I had just assumed . . ."

"I suppose one might call me a late bloomer. I had no idea I had the talent until Veranna informed me."

"And he's terminally impatient," Veranna chimed in from across the room.

"I see," Aulus said. "Is it safe to assume, then, that you do not yet know the Utterance of Tongues?"

I shook my head. "I suppose you had better open my eyes, then."

I focused on the calligraphy within the book while Aulus laid a weathered hand on my head. A tingling wave spread through my scalp, and as it did, the words on the page shifted, merged, broke into fragments, and reformed into clear Elvish. Fascinating.

Over the next couple of hours, I ransacked the tome, as well as a half dozen scrolls and a tablet Cnaeus brought to me. I filtered through the many words that detailed the process of summoning. The precise day of the moon's cycle, even the position the moon should hold in the sky during that night appeared in a long list of convoluted preparations the ceremony conductor must adhere to for the summoning to proceed safely. The words he must speak. The gestures of his hands. The position of each finger, even. After that, the text explained the summoning circle needed for the ceremony.

I turned a page to behold careful draftsmanship that depicted the exact dimensions of the theurgic circle. My gaze locked upon the artwork, and a cold fist clenched around my heart. I had seen this circle before. The sacrifice chamber, illustrated in a smaller inset on the next page, was all too familiar. Every rune within the circle mocked me. The dark doorway at the rear of the chamber, in my mind's eye, filled with a menacing shadow. A shadow that once erupted with fire that consumed . . .

My gut performed a flip. I squeezed my eyes shut and shook the memory from my mind. *Focus, Ecleriast.* I swallowed hard. Forced my concentration back to the pages.

Could the dragon-kin utilize the chalice in another location, so long as they replicated the circle and the chamber? Or would they take the accursed thing directly back to the place from which I had once wrested it? Could they already be there? Of course, they must be, with all the time I had spent hunting the talismans.

My vision darkened.

"My dragon-kin can learn much of sorcery, given a month or two for unharried study of . . . say, a demon-blood chalice." The old man's face turned stonily serious. *"But instead of going with your instinct, you follow orders. Thank your superiors when you see them."*

I began to shake. Fists clenched, I spun back to Queldurik, the weaver of lies. "For what?"

He grinned. "For taking my bait."

More memories—unbidden and unwelcome. I shoved the recollection of my final encounter in the immaterial plane back into the mental cask where it belonged.

A legion of fiends might already be poised for the right moment. My hands trembled as I turned the next page in the tome. A bead of sweat ran down my nose.

"Vinyanel, are you all right?" Aulus asked.

Blast. Of course he had to have seen.

"You have gone awfully pale all of the sudden," Cnaeus put in. "Perhaps you need to step back out on the surface for some air?"

I swept a hand across my damp brow. "No. I am fine. I am just getting to the information that really matters." I scanned the next page, which detailed the exact ingredients the fiend binder would need to sprinkle into the carvings of the theurgic circle in order to complete the summoning. Lime, ashes, and powdered bone, preferably from sacrifices in some way related to the binder's preferred target. The more innocent the victim, the better.

"Aulus," I said. "Did you not indicate you lost some family members in the attack on your village? That little else seemed affected?"

Aulus cleared his throat. "Alas. My daughters, all three of them, went missing, and my wife . . ."

Slain. I nodded. "If I am properly understanding what I see here, the good news is: your daughters may still yet live."

12
_____

Vows

*E*verything I read in the Elgadrim's library of arcane texts confirmed what I already suspected. "We need to set out after the chalice in the morning," I said

"For mercy's sake, Vinyanel, you're freshly wounded. Can you not give yourself a moment's rest? What are you running from?" Veranna shook her head.

"From? Nothing. But something about the wording of the chalice ritual's timing—an act that must be completed on the eve of 'moondeath'—speaks to a limited horizon. But when exactly is this, I wonder?" I stretched my arms behind my back until the joints in my spine popped and crackled.

Veranna chuckled. "Oh, that's simple. The eve of the new moon."

I froze mid-stretch. "You are certain? How?"

"My mother was a Thelenese caravaner. It's a matter of ethnic pride to keep track of such things." She huffed. "Superstition and occultism are central to the tribe's way of life, I fear."

"Has anyone noticed what phase the moon is in currently?" I asked.

Cnaeus nodded. "Waxing crescent, I believe."

A few smooth strides carried Veranna to my side. She squinted at the page in front of me, but upside-down or not, without the benefit of the Utterance of Tongues, I supposed all she saw was worse than gibberish. "What happens at the new moon?"

"They sacrifice Aulus's daughters and grind up their bones for use in drawing a summoning circle." I delivered the concept impassively, despite the fact that the very thought turned my stomach.

Her jaw slackened. "Please tell me you're not sure of that."

"Only if you prefer I lie to you."

Aulus stared at his folded hands, elbows propped on his knees and lips tight. "And so your assertion that they still live is only a notice of death forestalled. Our confirmation that the dragon-kin do indeed have a sect of Queldurik worshippers underscores the peril. I fear I'm a fool to cling to my last tatters of hope."

I rubbed the back of my neck. "There may yet be time." The question I did not voice, however—how much time? Could the abductors make it back to their hive in the mountains before the coming new moon? I would need to operate on the assumption they could.

"But it leaves me with a terrible choice," Aulus whispered. "If my daughters can be saved, it foils this current abominable plot. For a time. But it does not change the dragon-kin's knowledge of my people's locations. They will continue to whittle us away if we remain in our settlements. We are weak flocks, scattered, shepherdless and in the wild. Do I honor my pledge as a member of this delegation, or do I pursue my children?"

Cnaeus paced the floor. "You see why I advised against your

participation in this envoy. Your conflictedness is understandable, but—""

"Peace, Cnaeus," Aulus said. He crossed the room on slow
strides, palms pressed together and fingertips resting on his
lips. "I must also think of Praesidio, whose sense of honor
outstrips his might. He would rush at my side to save his sisters.
But do I lead the last of my kin into peril?"

Veranna swept across the archive chamber to Aulus. "Fear
not, master Aulus The Lieutenant Commander will rescue your
children. I promise."

I choked on my breath. "*You* . . . what?"

"There is no other acceptable course of action here."
Veranna lifted her chin and surveyed us all in a lofty manner.
"You cannot leave those poor girls in the clutches of those who
also hold the chalice."

I slammed my hands on the table and my chair clattered
backward from the force that brought me to my feet. "Who in
this room, save me, has been where the dragon-kin have taken
both?" My voice boomed in the echoing expanse. "You do not
know what you presume to pledge on my behalf."

I rounded the table with ponderous steps, and stopped with
scarcely more than a hand span between the prophetess's face
and my own. While the volume of my words diminished to a
near whisper, I focused their intensity. "It is easy to make senti-
mental vows in a quiet vault, where civility surrounds you. But
we shall see how many promises *you* think you can keep in that
hive, where even the best warriors' courage melts in the flames
of malice."

Veranna's eyes rounded until a thin rim of white
surrounded her amber iris. She took a step back, then another.
Her jaw tightened as she forced a swallow. "But surely you see . .
. you—you must—"

"I must." I spat the words, but those that followed escalated
back into a bellow. "Creo may have ordained you a guide,

Prophetess. But commander? How dare you? At Majestrin's behest I weigh your opinion, but if you for one moment presume to steer me according to your sentimentalities . . . you must earn such trust."

I held Veranna's astonished stare until her gaze faltered. She drew a breath and faced me again, but as my glare dared her to risk her poised words, she choked them back.

I blew out a long stream of air. It failed to steady my heart's disjointed rhythm.

A flash of fire. The shriek of agony.

I clenched my fists and dragged my mind back to the present. "To extract able-bodied soldiers from such a place is one matter. Children present a cascade of more complicated circumstances. But nonetheless, some measure of intervention is imperative, for if the dragon-kin accomplish the task behind the abduction, it will unleash devastation few will withstand."

Aulus placed a trembling hand on my shoulder. "I will not ask of you any bond, though I will say this: your experience is the stoutest weapon any of us carries against this peril."

The prophetess had crept several paces from the discussion and stood with her back to me, her arms wrapped around her middle.

After returning to the tome and its diagrams, I stared at them in silence. My own assertions of knowledge and experi-ence, which I had wielded before with pride, now threatened to swamp me in churning emotion. There really was no question. I had chosen this path, and in my heart, I had always known the risk of it leading back to the dragon-kin stronghold. At least this time, Scitherias was dead.

"I will minimize whatever further loss it is in my power to prevent," I said.

Aulus heaved an exhale. He collapsed into a dusty chair.

"In the meantime, I recommend both of you to travel to Delsinon with the writ I promised," I continued. "So many

Elgadrim are counting on you to provide them a shield against what you now suffer. Unless my people have grown utterly blind, they *should* agree to an alliance."

Cnaeus narrowed his eyes. "You are aware that it is an alliance that will likely bring more trouble than strength?"

"Compassion for the vital is no kind of compassion at all," I said. "If my people care to truly be what we say we are, they will either grant your request or propose a better solution I cannot see from my limited perspective." After retaking my seat, I added, "If you do not mind, I will transcribe a last few notes, and then we had best be back to camp. We have an early start in the morning."

Veranna withdrew to a niche in the chamber beyond my sight, but not my hearing, though I do not think she realized that fact. Aulus pursued her.

"When you endeavor to tame lions, maiden," Aulus's smooth voice soothed, "you must expect them to roar from time to time."

Her words of response were both low and garbled by what sounded like snivels.

Aulus continued. "Sometimes the subtle hand is the one for which Creo calls . . ."

I smiled. Their discussion lowered beyond what I could hear from that point, and I buried myself in the manuscripts for the details I wanted to be sure to take with me. It felt good to know even sometimes the mentor could use a little mentoring.

～

The gates in the outer wall of the underkeep complex clanged shut behind us, and a sizzling energy swept over my body, setting my hair on end. Veranna blinked repeatedly, while Hridayesh glanced around the street with the creases of befuddlement deepening across his brow.

"What exactly are we doing out here again?" he asked. "I feel like I've been asleep."

Aulus nodded to Cnaeus.

My own thoughts swam a bit, although the clarion urgency of pursuing the chalice rang through the fog.

"The time has been well-spent," I said. "But for now, we return to the temple."

When we departed the complex, I sent everyone ahead of my slower, limping pace, everyone except the little pearl dragon. The hatchling scampered along with me, always keeping me in sight, often checking upon my location between her haphazard bouts of chasing shadows or her tail.

Veranna's dodging glance implied that she still retained some recollection of our time spent in the archives. Some temporary distance served us both. I used the time of quiet walking to contemplate what both Veranna had attempted to assign to me and that which my inmost being knew must occur. Must that confounded ringing in my ears always surge at the thought of a return to the hive?

With every corner I turned in Bilearne's streets, the ruins that corralled me pleaded in silent despair. To raze was the only desire of Queldurik's minions. I could not let my own ill humors bind me with the weight of inaction—or worse, retreat.

When the hatchling and I made it back to the temple, the scent of smoke and roasting meat drifted on the light midday breeze. Both Majestrin and Eyrnir gnawed the last morsels of meat from bones while they relaxed in the shade of the north wall.

"You will join Majestrin and Eyrnir," I told the hatchling.

She tipped her chin toward me and implored with round eyes.

"None of that. I will only be on the other side of the wall, I assure you." I pointed to north side of the temple.

The hatchling shuffled the direction I pointed with a sullen pout on her face.

I stepped into the chamber where Veranna and Hridayesh sat, and an ample leg of either mutton or chevon roasted over the fire. Amazing how even the simplest of foods could smell so delectable—compared to travel rations, fresh meat, fruit, or vegetables took on a new sheen every time I re-encountered them.

Veranna rose from her chair and set her battered copy of *The Tree* on the desk beside her. "I was beginning to wonder if you would ever make it back." She eyed my leg. Her glance once again skirted mine. "Vinyanel, you'd best sit. I'm certain you're limping worse today than yesterday."

I sighed. "Somehow, I cannot quite fit you into this mothering role you have assumed, since I would guess I must be a minimum of two centuries older than you."

"Amazing how long you've managed to remain a stubborn fool, then," Veranna replied. She pointed at the chair.

I huffed. I could pretend all was back to normal, but Veranna's tentative glance rumored she was in some way re-evaluating our interaction.

A few jingling strides carried Veranna to the fireside. She cut off a serving of the roast and brought it to me on the end of a knife. "Although I came here with you with the full intention of digging my heels in until you abandoned the chalice mission, I want you to know I'm through opposing your designs —at least on this." She held the knife and meat toward me.

A conciliatory offering? I pinched off a large bite and popped it into my mouth, then proceeded to blow air through the roast as I minimized the searing to my tongue. "Am I right, for once?" I said past the mouthful.

"Only because the circumstances have changed." The prophetess handed me the knife with the remaining chunk of roast.

I took another bite and silently accepted Veranna's conditional capitulation. Whether she was agreeing with me for the right reasons or not fell secondary to my determination to make the best of her compliance before her temperamental humor shifted again.

She drifted toward the window and gazed through it for a long moment. Her voice was lowered, as if she spoke to herself more than anyone in the room. "We have a span of just under three weeks, I deem. It will have to be time enough."

~

*R*aen pursed her lips and folded her arms. She cast a wary glance around the corner of the tumbled building, while Mythrenese slunk through the block-paved street. He snuffled about the space, then turned a furrowed glance her way.

"It's like trying to follow one set of footprints when a whole crowd has passed through the dust." Mythrenese sighed. "I catch little moments of Iriscendra's trail, but there are fresher signatures of no fewer than three . . ." He scrunched his snout. ". . .humans, I *think*. Not to mention the sense of that silver dragon hangs like a fog over everything. He must be ancient."

"I know you're doing the best you can, Mythrenese, but maybe we need to search the old fashioned way from here? The signatures seem to be doubling us back more than they lead us forward."

"I don't know, Raen," Mythrenese replied. "Who knows how big this city is? Or if they're even still here?"

"It's not like we'd miss them amongst the throngs of other people in the streets." A dry smirk pulled one side of Raen's lips crooked.

"Well, no. Maybe we could press on and just check for signs

periodically. It would be a little faster, and we could readjust if we lose the signs completely."

Raen nodded. "That sounds productive."

The ruins of what Raen assumed to be a human city loomed all around her with oppressive density. Had the place been teeming with the population it must have once supported, she was certain she would never have mustered the courage to pass the gates. Amazing how a century of isolation had made even the heralds of the urban world so unsettling. The stark facades of empty-windowed buildings crowded along the streets like ranks of disapproving soldiers watching Raen's every step through their encampment. She skulked along the edges of the avenues.

"The sooner we find Iriscendra and get this whole unpleasant business over with, the better," she muttered.

Mythrenese, on the other hand, now that he was free to advance with less rapt attention on Iriscendra's muddied signature, peeked in every dark window, under every staircase, and behind every weather-beaten sculpture.

"I'd wager the people who lived here wrought some marvelous treasures." His eyes glinted. He bounded up to the entry of a tall, narrow building whose entry portico boasted fluted columns, their chapiters adorned with scrollwork, sculpted swags, and delicate leaves. A dull gleam in the deeper crevices of the architecture rumored they might have once been gilt as well. "Can't we look inside this one? Please?"

Raen folded her arms across her midnight blue bodice. "There's nothing in there that would interest a dragon. Stop wasting time."

Mythrenese's wings drooped.

A pang of guilt pricked Raen's middle. "I'm sorry. This place makes me edgy."

Mythrenese bit his lip, but he pressed onward, giving the pavers a sniff as they went.

The shadows in the streets stretched longer. Half a day of searching, and not an elf in sight, much less a hatchling pearl dragon. Raen's heart sank. Maybe they had moved on. Was it sheer foolishness that she had left the other dragons and the eggs on a shred of hope that she and Mythrenese would find a creature who could have fled to any far corner of the world?

The clamor of her brooding almost caused her to miss the sound that played at the edge of her notice. Raen froze in place. Listened.

The murmur of voices—too far to be interpreted, but voices for certain, drifted to her ears.

"Mythrenese!" she called in the loudest whisper she dared.

The indigo dragon pulled his head from the depths of an urn. He swiveled his ears. His eyes narrowed.

"Get over here."

A quick scuttle returned Mythrenese to Raen's side. "I heard it. It wasn't Elvish, though."

Raen lowered her voice. "Humans?" She shrank into the shadow of an arch between two homes.

"I think so. Both with signatures." Mythrenese closed his eyes and breathed deep. "Yes, two of the signs I have been sensing are stronger now, but receding."

Despite her roiling insides, Raen pulled the hood of her light cape farther over her head. "We'd better have a look. Stay behind me, and for Patrons' sakes, out of sight."

They crept toward Raen's best guess at the voices' location. With all the echoing walls, the distance and heading of any sound was conjecture. *Creo, show me. Please, please lead my steps.*

Raen rounded the corner of a low structure, perhaps at one time a shop, judging by its wide window and stone shelves in front. Two figures, just under two blocks ahead, caught her eye. She shrank back. Her hand shot out behind her and pressed against Mythrenese's snout. He skidded to a stop. She put her finger to her lips and glared his way.

"I'm sorry," he whispered. "There's so much gravel."

She wrapped her fingers around his snout and held it shut. A slight lean offered her a renewed view of the street beyond the corner of the shop.

The two walkers had progressed farther from her, their backs to her. They strolled across a wide plaza toward a breathtaking structure bathed in the golden remnant of sunset. Much in the city had decayed, crumpled, or sagged, but not this place. Stained glass still gleamed in the windows. And right beside it, the evening light glinted from a mound of mirrors.

Or rather, a reclining dragon.

Raen's breath caught. The massive, metallic-scaled wonder. Whether she understood the companions he kept or not, the silverlord was astonishing to behold. Raen shrank back around the concealing corner of the shop and held her breath. Ecleriast had once said the mature silver wyrm was not safe, but that he trusted him. But that likely meant the creature still saw the use of his abomination as acceptable. The wyrm seemed so much larger here when compared to architecture, rather than the majesty of the falls. She would have to tread carefully, depending on how bonded this creature was to his rider.

Despite the obvious risk of the dragon, and the less-certain issue of the men, Raen steeled herself. "We have to get closer to that temple."

Mythrenese nodded. "If we backtrack to the last alley, it might cut that way, without forcing us right into the plaza."

"I trust your sense of direction better than my own," Raen said. "Let's try it."

They ducked into the cool dark of the alley, which ran sufficiently parallel to the southeastern edge of the plaza to ease them nearer to where the dragon lay. When they had sidled within what Raen guessed to be forty or fifty paces, still a building's depth away from the square, Raen paused and listened.

"Forty-seven, forty-eight . . ." a voice grunted from somewhere up ahead. It paused. "Forty-nine . . ."

"You don't have anything to prove to me, Vinyanel," another speaker rumbled. The depth of his timbre vibrated the stone beneath Raen's feet.

"Fifty!" someone blurted, more growl than voice. "And just for good measure. Fifty-one." Another groan. "Fifty . . . two!"

"Must you?" a gentler male voice asked. He spoke Elvish, but his accent was unfamiliar to Raen. "Can you not give your wounds time to mend?"

"I am not using the wounded leg."

"Impossible," a third, hard-edged voice replied. "If you need us, you know where to find us."

Raen edged between two buildings, the easement between them hardly wide enough to allow the scant breadth of her shoulders. When she neared the end of the narrow way, she crouched and peered into the square again. She first caught sight of the length of the silver dragon's spiked tail. Her glance progressed in a hesitant crawl across the dragon's serpentine body, studded with dorsal plates. Just beyond the creature's winged shoulder, she spied an elf who stretched in a plank position on the overgrown greensward that ran alongside the temple. A swath of the plant life had been tamped down, and a trio of horses browsed through the high weeds beyond the dragon and the elf.

A sack of something bulky weighed on his shirtless back. He had his platinum hair lashed into a tail.

A lump wedged in Raen's throat. There was no mistaking him. Fury burned in her chest, and the soldier's physical near-perfection only intensified her sense of injustice.

Ecleriast, eyes closed, perspiration dripping from his nose, sucked a breath. "Five more. Do you know how much more . . . strength it takes to fly than it does to ride land-based? It has caused me to find muscles I never knew I had—muscles that are getting soft as we mill around this place."

He slowly bent his elbows and lowered his body a hair's breadth from the ground. He raised himself again, the musculature of his shoulders, chest, arms, even his hands banding with the effort. Raen stared for a moment, but a sudden surge of—what, embarrassment?—tightened her neck and shoulders. She cast her glance to the ground.

The silver dragon swung his neck around, his eyes narrowed. Raen shrank back in the easement. Quiet stretched on, with only the slow intake and exhale of Ecleriast's breath to underscore it.

"Those were your five," the dragon said. "Take a break, Vinyanel. You make me tired just watching. And two days hardly amounts to milling."

Raen dared half her face beyond her hiding place again, just in time for Ecleriast to rotate his body until the sack on his back slipped to the ground with a heavy *whump*. He plunked on his rear, then swept a forearm across his sweaty brow.

"At least we shall be on our way in the morning. What of the hatchling, though? Do you think I could convince her to stay behind? We could always come back for her. In the meantime, she has proven herself adept enough at fishing, and the river . . ."

Raen's sudden gasp pulled her away from the end of the elf's statement. So she *was* here. But where?

"I doubt it," the dragon replied. He extended a rumpled tunic on a curved claw. "You really fail to grasp the full scope of the situation."

Ecleriast snagged the garment from Majestrin. He dried his face with it, then pulled it over his head. "If you would cease speaking in half-statements and implications, I might know better. My knowledge of dragons begins and ends with you, you realize . . ."

Bristling annoyance crackled through Raen's flesh. To think Iriscendra had risked her own safety jaunting after this complete stranger. She saw no point in confronting him in his ignorance with accusations that would likely shatter on his steely front with no real impact. No, better to handle this like every other dragon liberation upon which she had embarked.

"There are some topics I would rather not discuss if there isn't pressing need." Majestrin angled his face away from the conversation.

Furrows creased Ecleriast's forehead. "This situation does not qualify as pressing?"

"No."

The elf scratched his head. "The more I get to know you, the more I realize how long it might take me to understand. Ah well. We have time." He bent down, picked up a scabbard and belted it, and cupped his hands around his mouth. "Little one! It's time to go. Uncle Majestrin's had enough of us for one evening."

A heavy scrabbling erupted somewhere overhead. The roof of the building to Raen's left, perhaps? Ecleriast turned toward the sound, and Raen held her breath. She backpedaled from his potential line of sight as his attention angled her way, even if it aimed more for the roof than her location.

"There you are!" he continued. "Sunning up high again? I would leave you to it, but it is getting dark. Who knows what other dangers might be lurking in the corners of this forsaken place, just waiting for cover of darkness to emerge."

Noisy galumphing and Elceriast's laugh—a strong, assured laugh—receded.

When Raen dared peer toward the temple again, only the dragon remained. Let the Delsin have their silver behemoth. Waiting for darkness, indeed. If Ecleriast only knew.

By daybreak, she and the hatchling would be long gone.

~

a sickle moon fought its intermittent way through rushing clouds, and Raen minced her way across the square on soft-soled shoes. She pulled her hood low and skulked from corner to pile of rubble, from tree trunk to archway. Around the rear of the temple, a secondary entrance led into the hall where she had determined the elf and his companions had taken up residence. Surely he must be asleep by now. Raen stifled a yawn. Shivers seized her limbs, beyond the effect of the cool autumn wind.

She stared at the bank of windows for half an age, her heart gaining speed with every beat. *Stop being such a coward!* How many dragons' eggs had she managed to liberate from corrupt parents by now? Surely coaxing one little dragon who already knew her back to the placid life she offered in the vale would prove no challenge.

A quick dash covered the distance between the archway and the window of the elf's quarters. Raen clapped her body against the wall, then scanned the surrounding churchyard for watching eyes one more time. All stood still under the moon. Raen edged her nose over the windowsill.

Curled near the hearth, before a mound of glowing embers, Iriscendra slept. Raen's eyes stretched wide. How she had grown. The hatchling was easily twice the size she had been during her final days in the vale. What had she learned while here in the ruins amidst this inexplicable troupe of travelers?

Raen clenched her fists. Surely nothing that could not be untaught after so few weeks. After a long exhale, she crept for the door.

The simple scrolled handle had no keyhole, bolt, or lock she could see. With a clammy palm, she reached for the handle. She grasped it. Her heart thundered as though it would batter its way straight through her temples.

A firm push turned the ancient ironwork without so much as a snick—a miracle in and of itself. Raen eased the door open, stole inside, and slipped through the interior door, left ajar. Iriscendra drowsed in what looked like a small sitting room. The door at the back of this snug chamber sat closed— the door to the sleeping quarters. Raen never took her gaze from it until she reached the sleeping hatchling's side. She placed a hand on Iriscendra's neck.

"Wake up, little Iriscendra." Raen whispered in the hatchling's ear. "We've come to take you home."

The grind of a blade leaving its scabbard grated from behind the bedchamber door.

13

INTRUDER

I stirred upon my straw mattress, mired in the murky depths that separated sleep from wakefulness. A voice—maybe Veranna's—whispered, but the words came to my ears garbled. Too low to hear, let alone understand. And something was wrong with her voice.

My stomach performed queasy gyrations. A pox on sleep— true repose would not have left me in this groggy mire. My jaw and neck hurt. Clearly the strange dreams of my short sleep had set me clenching my teeth again. My limbs dragged like lead. My eyelids fought to stay sealed shut, but slowly, I resurfaced from the world of dreams to the night-hues of my chamber.

I managed to pry one of my eyes partway open. It was not time to wake, that much I could tell from the starlit sky beyond my window. The unintelligible whisper droned again, but this time, it was no dream.

The voice swept all the weight of slumber from my flesh,

and the fire of battle instinct flooded into the void it left. It seemed whatever murmuring I heard came from beyond my chamber door. A film of sweat slicked my brow in a fraction of a moment, and my heart thundered into a full gallop. Could the hatchling be speaking? Or perhaps just trying, either awake or asleep? It was difficult to tell, with the dull ring that rose in my ears.

I reached to the floor and grasped the hilt of my sword. My legs slid free of the coverlet, and my bare feet met the smooth planks of the floor.

I shot a quick glance to my armor, piled in the corner. No time for even the under layer of chain mail, unfortunately. I gritted my teeth against the stiffness in my leg. Hridayesh, curled in the bunk against the opposite wall, did not stir at my rising.

"Don't do this!" the voice whispered. "Please. Come on."

I burst through the chamber door, sword high. A cloaked intruder crouched on the floor beside the hatchling, but as fast as I had sprung, just as quickly, the stranger flashed a thin blade overhead and deflected my downward stroke. A dark scarf covered the lower half of my opponent's face, and while I read surprise in his rounded eyes, the expression fell short of fear.

The intruder rose and spun at once, whistling a cut with a basket-hilted blade toward my shoulder. I threw my sword in its path. The hatchling cringed at the clatter.

With a circling repositioning of my weapon, I made another lunge. My opponent jumped back and out of range of the cut.

The swordsman advanced with a series of swift attacks, each of which I parried, but all of which gained my full attention. Here stood a talented warrior, with greater speed in his favor than I possessed. I could admit that. My impaired stance was no help.

I reached back with my free hand, grasped one of the stools

at the little table in the center of the chamber, and flung it at my opponent's legs. The intruder jumped out of the way, and the tactic gained me a moment to put the table between us.

"What are you doing here?" I demanded.

The swordsman just glared at me from beneath the shadow of his dark hood. He leapt to the table's edge, grabbed it, and flipped it at me. The wood top bashed against my knuckles when I blocked the table with my weapon hand, and I clamped my jaw shut. If that was how he wanted to conduct business, so be it.

My sword swept in low. My enemy jumped. The intruder's slimmer blade sliced down from overhead. I parried. The swords grated against one another until they locked at the hilts, until I lifted a foot and kicked the persistent attacker in the gut. He must have been a skinny whelp under the dark cloak, breeches, and tunic, for it required only minimal force from my kick to thrust him back.

For every advance I made with a series of hews and redoubling, my opponent answered with viper-quick flicks of his own blade. We both breathed heavy. Clearly, if I was going to master this warrior, I would have to simply overpower him—after all, the thought of causing a bloody mess in Creo's temple was distasteful, even though my enemy's strokes led with the edge and suggested he had no such compunctions.

Our swords met in dozens more cuts and parries. No matter how I sought to corner my opponent with the press of my attacks, he always found a way to maneuver to another section of open floor. My throbbing leg protested a fight that dragged on, but at least I begin to see signs my combatant was flagging. His parries rattled in his hands with less surety, and his speed lessened to the point of matching my own. My blade whistled in, and as I perceived its path, I turned the blade flat. It struck my opponent's wrist, just above the area the weapon's basket hilt protected.

The intruder yelped a high-pitched cry when my blade struck flesh. Was it possible the warrior was only a youth? The timbre of the outburst hardly had a manly ring. The weapon clattered free. I stepped on the blade and dragged it toward me with my foot.

The warrior staggered back and threw a protective arm across his face. His feet tangled and nearly cast him to the floor, but he recovered better footing. I lifted the second blade, spun it in my hand, and pointed them both at my enemy.

The hatchling whined.

My head ticked the creature's way, to find her crouched in a trembling ball in the corner, eyes brimming with tears and lips quivering. My brow puckered. I studied the sword again—something about the curving strands of its hilt struck me as familiar.

The intruder's wide-eyed glance flitted to the door.

I think not.

When my opponent darted for the exit, I was well prepared. I dropped his weapon and caught his wrist. His slight wrist.

Youth or no, he had no business setting foot in my encampment. I spared little force in jamming his hand back until it popped. He crumpled to his knees. I barreled into him and smashed him to the floor with all my weight. His cheek met the boards and I twisted his arm behind him.

"Shall we try again?" I said in a low growl. "What are you doing here?"

The hatchling bounded over to us and thrust her face before mine. Jewel-blue eyes implored. The victim beneath me groaned.

I bored into the hatchling. "Do you know something I do not?"

Still, just the stare of tortured blue eyes.

"Confound you! When do dragons learn to talk?"

"Stop!" the person I had pinned said, though muffled by scarf and floor. "You win."

That voice—neither a man's nor a boy's. Was it possible? I spied the intruder's sword from the corner of my eye. A schiavona. Yes, I had seen its like not so long ago. I released my victim's wrist and grabbed the scarf across the unfortunate opponent's face.

I tugged it free, and when I did, a shock of straight carmine hair tumbled from beneath the victim's hood. A pale, delicate-featured face, though less pale with exertion and discomfort now, glared back at me with amethyst eyes.

I eased my weight back from my prisoner. "Well. Of all the people I doubted I would ever encounter again, you were at the top of that list." I stood and brushed the rumpled folds from my tunic and pants. My tight chest and ringing ears ceased their warnings.

The red-haired elf maid thrust herself further from me. "Of all the people . . . I hoped I never would, you were chief." She cradled her wrist against her belly, sucking hissing gasps through her teeth.

A twist of guilt sank home in my gut. If I had known...but then, she *had* skulked in while I slept, for what reason I could only guess. Not the sort of ladylike behavior I would have thought to address with more chivalry. I covered my discomfort with a smile.

"Oh, come now, I am not so hard to look at—"

"Why did Iriscendra come here?"

I blinked. "What?"

"The hatchling," the maiden said. Her face had cooled, and now took on a slightly ashen tone. "Do you know what drew her to you? And I'd prefer if you answered in plain words, since I know you have a way of twisting them."

My jaw dropped. "Did you just call me a liar?"

"You said you didn't touch the egg!"

"I said no such thing. I said I did not 'handle' it." I sunk my weight back on my good leg. "Touching and handling are very different, no?" I mentally slapped away a roguish inkling to suggest ways I might demonstrate the difference. Part of me stood amazed at my own level of distraction.

"When you came barging into my home looking for your precious talismans, Iriscendra was just a day from hatching. You touched her egg and wove your signature to hers. Didn't you?" Her eyes welled, but she blinked the tears away.

Signature weaving? While I had no notion what that meant, I would not hint at my ignorance. But I did know someone who could tell me for certain. It would be enlightening to know something about why the hatchling had sought me out.

"Barging into your home? Well, on that count, we now seem somewhat even." I bored into her with a glare. "However, on counts of theft or attempted theft—"

"You have a lot of nerve!" she blurted. Her glance flitted to her cradled arm, but she clamped her teeth shut, as though to restrain further words.

The twist of guilt clutched again. "Listen. Whatever brought you here from the far border of Da-Shir, whatever possessed you to sneak in here— I swear I would not have engaged the tactics I did, had I but known . . ." I huffed. "Let me see your arm."

She shrank back from me and her eyes hardened.

"I can help. Or rather, Creo can."

"I'm sure. Thanks anyway. I think I'd rather you didn't touch me." She shifted from sitting on the floor to her knee. With the effort, her face turned sickly green, and she choked down a grimacing swallow.

"Mistress," I said, "There are members of my party who can help you, if not me." I reached a hand out to her.

She used her good arm to push up from the ground and

regained her feet. "I'll just wrap it, I think. It's probably not so bad, once I stabilize it."

"Let me see it."

She lifted her chin. "It's not necessary. I've taken care of myself for a long time. I'm prepared to continue doing so."

"When you are living in the remote wilderness, I can see the necessity. But now, you have excellent treatment at your disposal. Why must you refuse? Had you intended to spend the night in an alley or a tree somewhere?" The question I asked myself, however, was why did I care? This maid had tried to abduct the hatchling, engaged me in a melee, and argued me on every point I had made since I met her. It would be less of a headache to leave her to her own devices. And yet, I could not.

After a partial attempt to extend her elbow, which resulted in a pain-etched grimace and a grunt, the maiden gingerly cradled her injury again.

I lowered my chin and raised a brow. "Let me see it. Really. It will be easier to sort the situation if you are not spending the whole time on the brink of vomiting from pain."

She sighed. But she also extended her arm toward me.

Though my fingertips only brushed her forearm, that whisper of contact made me starkly aware of how warm my hands seemed compared to the smooth chill of her skin. I eased her sleeve up to her elbow, and the truth became quite evident. The maiden's wrist had already swollen to twice its expected size, and mottled bruising discolored the once milk-white flesh all around the joint. I had been regrettably thorough, and the strange offset of her hand convinced me that perhaps I had succeeded in causing a complete separation somewhere in the lower arm or wrist joint.

"Simply splint this? I am convinced you will lose proper use of this hand if you do not either let the surgeon or me address this." I cleared my throat and met her gaze. "I am loath to impair such talent with the blade."

The hint of a smile tugged at the corner of the maid's lip, but she tightened her features against it. The maiden stared at her disfigured joint and swallowed. "Very well. Please show me to this healer, then."

"That is the smarter choice." A few strides carried me to the door.

Iriscendra glanced between the elf maiden and me. She whimpered at the glaring maid, but then trundled to my side.

I reached out and patted her nubby head. "I'm afraid you will need to get used to a lot of swordplay if you intend to keep my company."

The hatchling shrunk her neck back into her shoulders, her eyes bulging.

I winked. "You shall have a role befitting your talents, once you have grown."

The elf maiden blew a huff. She muttered something about her dead body, but I did not ask her to clarify.

Instead, I opened the door. "This way, if you will."

I led the red-haired maiden down the hall toward the main worship chamber of the temple, destined for the wing of the building on the opposite side where Aulus had chosen chambers for himself, Praesidio, and Cnaeus. The rooms on that side clearly once housed the more significant members of Creo's clergy, as they were larger and still retained furnishings far less spartan than the simple scribe's desk and cot in my room. Our footfalls, as well as the rat-a-tat of the hatchling's claws on the stone floor reverberated through the middle-of-the-night stillness.

When I neared the worship chamber, another rumor mixed with our footfalls—tiny bells. I hesitated in the doorway and listened.

The bells jingled on—rhythmic and accented. I placed a hand on the corner of the hall and peered into the vast room beyond.

On the wide space of floor that stretched between the front row of seating and the stairs that ascended the platform, I caught sight of Veranna, her back to me, her arms stretched toward the coffered ceiling. She rose onto bare toes, kicked a leg high, then glided her foot back to earth with a graceful bend of her knees. She spun. I sucked a gasp and ducked behind the cover of the doorway. The inexplicable private-ness of Veranna's dance pricked me with a twinge of guilt for looking on. And yet, I still inched a stealthy eye past the doorframe again.

She reached and swayed, leapt, turned, and arched, all of it performed with closed-eyed abandon. It was as though a great symphonic accompaniment swelled within her soul, and through her movements, somehow I could nearly hear it too. The worshipful artistry gripped my heart.

I glanced back at the maiden I had led this far. Her rapt focus followed Veranna's every step.

Veranna's feet touched the floor once again, and she whirled toward the rear of the worship chamber. Her glance met mine. Perfect. The last person to whom I wanted to try to explain what had happened . . .

Stretching straight and tall, Veranna smoothed a tendril of raven hair away from a forehead lightly dewed with exertion. "Can't sleep, Lieutenant Commander?"

"Uh, well, I have a . . ."

The maiden rushed from behind me. "Your dancing is tremendous! I've never seen anyone incorporate bells like you did."

Veranna blinked a few times, but then a flush crept into her cheeks and she ducked her head with a demure smile. "Thank you. That's very kind of you to say—I make most of it up as I go. But forgive me—who are you?" She rolled her eyes at me. "Vinyanel has many talents, but etiquette is not one of them."

I sniffed. "I should be excused in this case. I did not have time to ask for a formal introduction between this maiden's thieving entry and the swordplay. If you will pardon us, I was taking her to see Aulus." I took a step forward, but Veranna sidestepped in front of me.

"It's the middle of the night, Vinyanel. What could you possibly need that would justify that kind of rudeness?"

"This maiden is, well . . . injured."

"And I even have a name," the intruder interjected. She curtsied. "I am Raen. The lieutenant commander and I have met once before, though perhaps he chose not to mention me." Raen's eyes swept over Veranna from floor to crown. She cocked a caramel-brown eyebrow at me.

Awkward silence hung over us all as Veranna cast Raen an appraising look in return, then smirked at me.

"What?" I blustered. "I *did* mention her. The elf maiden Hridayesh and I ran into when we were after the talismans."

Veranna sighed. "And here I thought the story between the two of you might be interesting."

"Hardly," Raen replied. "No worries—you have him all to yourself." All the while she spoke, she splinted her damaged arm against her abdomen.

"Lucky me." Veranna rolled her eyes. "What of this injury, then?"

Raen scowled. "Master over-reactor here pounced on me for my trying to speak to my baby dragon. I've been searching for her for weeks."

As if summoned by her mere mention, the hatchling scampered up to the group and shoved her snout into my hand. I patted her nose. "*Your* baby dragon? If I believed a dragon could truly belong to anyone, I still might say the current evidence contests your assertion." The short moment of fluster that had risen in my gut over Raen's obvious talent and comely face ebbed. I would not be made out to be both a liar and villain. "And I disagree that my actions were anything but justified. What else was I supposed to think when a shrouded figure snuck into my quarters and seemed to be arguing with the hatchling?"

"It's not like I was attacking her. So you break strangers' arms on a regular basis?" Raen held out her functioning palm to me in a gesture of incredulity, but winced.

Veranna approached Raen. "So that's why you're cradling your arm like that? You poor thing."

Clearly my argument of self-preservation had little foothold in the emotional tide that crashed through the maidens' sense of logic. "I am attempting to right the issue, if you would let me."

"It is needless that you should wake Aulus," Veranna said. "I will implore of Creo . . ." Her gaze became distant. She tilted her chin higher, and her eyes drifted shut. Her brow knit. After a moment more, her eyes snapped back open, and Veranna shook her head.

"Or perhaps . . . I won't. I'm sorry Raen. I cannot say why, but it seems Creo deems today's hurts mendable by earthly measures."

It would be deceitful to say a certain sense of smugness did not stretch my posture a little taller. "As charming as all this 'Vinyanel is a brute' has been, shall we call it to a close? I have a long journey to begin tomorrow, so the sooner I can see Raen's arm set right and the matter of the hatchling settled, the better."

"And here I thought interpersonal conflict was the very air you breathe," Veranna said. "Go. See to the care of this wound you've inflicted. There will be time in the morning to settle the rest."

I nodded curtly and limped for the opposite hall.

"Do you inspire this same level of civility in every maiden you meet?" Raen asked.

"I simply seem to have a magnetism for females of a particularly difficult sort of late," I stared ahead and gritted my teeth.

When we reached Aulus's door, I rapped lightly on the wood panels. Though once stained a deep mahogany, the wood's raised grain dulled its sheen. Cracks ran from the base of the door to nearly the middle.

No response.

I knocked again, though the sound of my knuckles echoing against the stone of the hallway made me wince. I was rewarded with some shuffling on the other side of the door this time.

The door creaked partway open. Aulus rubbed his brow and squinted at me. "Anything amiss?" His voice came out froggy.

"I fear so," I replied. "I regret waking you, Master Aulus, but I have a matter of a visitor who needs a bone set at worst, a joint realigned at best."

Aulus leaned to look behind me. He tilted his head, and deep furrows rumpled his brow.

Raen extended her wounded arm and groaned.

Aulus clucked his tongue. "You had best come in and sit. This is in no way tidy work ahead."

14

ABOMINATION

*A*ulus muttered a few quiet words, and his lantern sitting on his bedside table swelled to life. He pressed the heel of his hand to his forehead, closed his eyes, and blew out a deep sigh.

"We shall see if I can stretch what provisions I have packed." He opened a bulky satchel that sat beside his bed and pulled out a series of leather pouches, cinched tight, some strips of linen, and a shallow bowl. The bowl, he extended to me. "Vinyanel, if you would please fill this with water."

I took the vessel. After a quick nod, I left Aulus's room, the hatchling close on my heels.

"Iriscendra," Raen called.

For a moment, the hatchling hesitated in the doorway. Her head pivoted to me, then back to Raen. A pinched look of apology creased the creature's brow, but in the end, she trailed after me.

I slipped into my quarters, and Hridayesh stirred at my

entry. He rolled over, then met my glance. "What has you so cheery?"

"Are you joking?"

"No, I'm not." He rotated to sitting. "You had a self-satisfied grin on your face when you walked in."

I lifted a brow. "I cannot imagine why."

The hatchling, Iriscendra, so it seemed, plunked down beside my bunk but rested her head on the mattress.

At the foot of the bed, I found my waterskins amidst my gear. I lifted them and tested their volume by squeezing them. Both were mostly full. Their contents would provide just about enough to fill Aulus's request, but that would leave me no drinking water until I endeavored to refill them, and we had not yet encountered a usable well. The river was at least a mile walk from where we camped.

"Adramalech's nails, elf, it's the middle of the night. Why are you even up?"

"Not by choice," I grumbled. "We had a visitor, whose intrusion you conveniently slept through."

"Really?" Hridayesh yawned. "Of the creepy crawly sort?"

I chuckled. "No. Of the red-haired sort. A certain young elf maid who resides in a dragon's nest when she is not goading me into a swordfight."

"There's that grin again."

I squared my shoulders. "I have been provoked more than enough for one night, Hridayesh. Leave off before I start a brawl just to get it out of my system."

Hridayesh shook his head. "Well, if she stays nearby for long, it should be interesting to watch." He lay back down and shifted his blanket back over him.

I scowled, but Hridayesh simply snorted and rolled over.

Rather than keep Aulus waiting a half hour for the water, I opted to fill the bowl from my skins, leaving just a mouthful in one of them to drink in the morning. After all, how much time did I really want to give Raen to spin her side of the tale of what happened?

I forced the stopper back into the neck of the second skin. I turned to the hatchling, whose eyelids drooped. "Well, Iriscendra, shall I call you that?"

She shrugged her wings.

The name fit well enough, I would give Raen that much credit. "If you are not adverse to the name, I can call you by it. It will fit much longer than 'little one,' do you not think?"

Iriscendra smiled. She reached for the empty waterskins on the bed. She rocked back on her haunches and lifted them in her foretalons. Only one barely sloshed when she shook it.

"Yes, I shall have to fill them in the river in the morning, I suppose."

A thoughtful look crossed Iriscendra's features. She dashed out the door with the skins.

"Wait," I called after her. I jogged into the hall, but once I reached the main sanctuary, I was only in time to see her tail vanishing out the front door of the temple.

A squeeze of worry for her tightened around my stomach. I shook my head. "She is a dragon, Vinyanel. Likely safer as a baby than I am as an adult."

After retrieving Aulus's bowl from my room, I walked it as steadily as I could manage back across the building. I arrived at his quarters wet only on my right hip where the water had sloshed once.

He and Raen sat at a table, her arm resting on the surface, much straighter than it had looked before, but still red and swollen. Some thin strips of a material that looked something like bone, a pile of cloths, and the pouches Aulus unpacked waited. Raen seemed so ghostly in the lamplight, especially against the slick cascade of her deep red hair. Her lashes clustered together, recently wet. As soon as I darkened the doorway, she blinked and sat up a little straighter.

"The water you requested, Master Aulus." I set the water bowl on an empty spot on the table.

"Where's Iriscendra?" Raen asked.

"She ran off with my waterskins," I replied. "For someone who says nothing, she seems the thoughtful and competent type."

"I never met a dragon who wasn't." Raen sucked a breath. She closed her eyes and blew it out through her lips.

"The worst is over, maiden," Aulus said. He dumped differing measures of his powders into the water. "I will apply as ginger a touch as I can from here, but I do fear the splinting and wrapping may jostle things a bit more."

"I understand. I'll try to distract myself." She shifted her focus to me. "Lieutenant Commander, I should have had decency enough reunite with Iriscendra openly. But I must assert: I'm taking her home in the morning."

"Home?" I said. "Clearly what you label home was a place Iriscendra was not inclined to stay."

"I'll chalk up her choice to run off to youth and instinct."

"Or perhaps it was unbiased clarity," I said.

"What do you think you would do?" She paused to growl as Aulus passed a roll of puffy fabric under her forearm. "Drag her with you wherever you're headed in the morning? To Delsinon, of all places? You can't believe she'd want to live in a city full of dragon hunters."

The way she spat the capitol's name sent a wave of prickling protest up my spine. "Full of dragon hunters? A guild of a dozen zealots hardly makes for a city full."

Raen huffed. "At least it sounds like some sense has whittled their numbers."

"The crown has already had words with them because of Majestrin. She would not be in danger in Delsinon." I folded my arms. "Which is also irrelevant, as tomorrow's path leads me elsewhere."

"All the more reason to send her home to the vale with me," Raen said.

While we fenced verbally, Aulus mixed his binding paste with methodical steadiness and dredged the first strip into the compound. He eased it under Raen's wrist, wrapped it, and smoothed it.

"I am not entirely convinced either your will or mine will bind this hatchling's intentions," I said, my voice lower. "But I assure you, I want her to be safe."

Her gaze lingered upon my eyes for a long moment before she swallowed and glanced away. "I can understand your attachment to her, Lieutenant Commander. She's perilously winsome."

Some of the steel that had stiffened my jaw and shoulders softened. I found my attention tarrying upon the slight rise of pink in Raen's cheeks and the soft slope of her jaw. I cannot say for sure how long I let silence stretch after she had spoken, but it must have been long enough for her to notice my stare. She tilted her head as if to beg a response.

"Winsome, yes." I cleared my throat. "The hatchling . . . indeed she is."

Aulus added another paste-laden strip to the growing cast on Raen's arm.

"You're certain the setting is absolutely straight?" I asked. "It is her sword arm, after all."

The corners of the surgeon's eyes tightened. He smoothed the last wrinkle out of the fresh strip.

"But Iriscendra is still vulnerable," Raen said. "I'm sure you can see that. She would be much safer within the haven of the little sanctuary the falls offer. Not everyone appreciates the complexity of dragonkind, as you must well know."

If her intention had been to pry past my defenses by slyly including me in an elite minority of individuals who understood the marvels of the dragon, she played the hand well. So well that only part of my mind noted the tactic, while the rest of me puffed up and allowed a smug smile to twist the corner of my mouth. "So you would propose she takes some time to grow up a bit in the cover of the vale. But what of her destiny once she has gotten big enough to assert her own opinions with none to gainsay her—save perhaps a larger dragon?"

Raen's eyes widened with an innocent stricken-ness. "I would never try to hold a creature outside of its will. But so far, I find those who call the vale home love it above any other part of the available world."

Probably because they simply had not yet seen the vast wonders well beyond their borders. But the concept mattered little. I could be patient—and if Iriscendra went with Raen for the time being, I knew where to find them.

A scuffle outside Aulus's door interrupted my thought.

"Iriscendra!" the voice that called the name echoed in a shrill treble from the stone of the hallway. "Where are you going? We need to find Raen."

A pearly snout thrust through the narrow gap between the slightly-ajar door and the frame, and Iriscendra tumbled breathlessly into the room. My waterskins dangled on straps that she clenched between her teeth. She set them beside me and smiled. Her sapphire eyes sparkled.

Not a moment behind Iriscendra came the indigo dragon youth I recalled from my talisman hunt not many weeks prior. The rogue had better have stayed clear of my quarters.

He skidded to a stop halfway into the room. His eyes bulged.

"Mythrenese!" Raen scolded.

Aulus hissed through his teeth. "Please, mistress, stay still." He furrowed his brow at his work, but then released a long breath that carried his diffused concern with it.

Mythrenese shrank back into his shoulders. "I couldn't stay

hidden—not when Iriscendra came flapping right by my hiding place. And when I didn't see you, I—"

"Just how many dragons do you people keep on hand?" Aulus burst out. "In only a couple of sunrises I have gone from having seen none of such creatures in my lifetime to encountering three up close."

"It is highly unusual, Aulus," I replied.

Mythrenese sidled closer to Iriscendra, but seemed hesitant to draw as near to me as that demanded. His glance continually flicked between the two of us. "Maker's mercy you've been found! Hopefully we're in time enough that Raen won't have too much to un-teach you."

A strangled cry escaped Raen. She glared daggers at her dragon companion. At first, I had thought some part of Aulus's treatment had caused her outburst, but I considered Mythrenese's words for a moment, and suspicion heated my blood back to a low simmer.

"Un-teach? Mythrenese, is it?" I said. I adopted my iciest tone that I typically saved for headstrong recruits in need of an adjustment of perspective. "Just what might she have learned while she was outside the fair mistress's glance?"

Raen shook her head. "He speaks out of turn—"

"That is the main trouble with words," I said. "They can never be unsaid." I leaned closer to Mythrenese. "You will find, even with dragons, I can be quite persuasive. Continue."

Mythrenese did not meet my gaze. He took a pair of backing steps to Raen. "No, sir, I'd rather not, if it's all the same to you."

"It is not."

"I will not sit idly while you bully my friends," Raen snapped.

"Bully?" I gaped. "Have I so much as raised my voice? With the way you step on his words, one might question which of us bullies Mythrenese . . ."

"How dare you." Raen clenched her free fist. "Just you wait until this cast dries. I have a mind to knock you flat with it."

I snorted. "Is that a—"

"No breath."

My attention snapped to my left. "Who . . .little one? Was that you?"

Iriscendra nodded. "Raen say no breath."

The fact that her pronunciation of the letter r came out more of a w forced me to take a moment to translate. Still, I was not entirely certain what the hatchling meant. "You *can* talk."

"Congratulations, Lieutenant Commander." Raen spoke through her teeth. "Looks to me like you've gotten to hear her first words. They'll likely start coming in an avalanche from here."

"But what do they mean, is what I would like to know," I said. "You told Iriscendra 'no breath'?"

The flinty look in Raen's eyes told me I might as well ask the basin on the table what Iriscendra's statement meant, as it would likely be forthcoming with an answer before the maiden would be. "But this 'no breath' edict certainly does not apply to you, correct, Mythrenese?"

Mythrenese tipped his snout higher and lightly lowered his eyelids. "Of course it does. I wouldn't be so barbaric as to use my abomination on anything for any reason."

Raen covered her face with her available hand.

I smirked, grateful that my play against Mythrenese's youthful sense of righteousness had brought the reaction I had sought to the surface. But my expression floated just atop a roiling storm of hot words. His abomination?

"You mean your breath gifting? Is that what Raen insists you must not use?"

"Gifting?" The word exploded from Raen in a near-shriek. "Is not the dragon's abominable breath the very thing that earns this magnificent creature loathing in every kingdom?

Even the Delsin, with all their knowledge, still kill them over it."

I took a step closer to Raen, but Mythrenese dashed between us and arched his back. At least he had avoided becoming a complete craven. Advance aborted, I raised my hands and stepped back. I was in no mood for a fight with a dragon, even a young one who would not breathe on me. He still had teeth and claws, that is, unless he had been convinced these too were a source of shame.

"I am uncertain where you get your information, but the dragon hunter's guild only reacts to reports of marauders. With the perceived value of just about every last scale, tear, and tooth a dragon has, you would ask the rest to deny themselves their best defense?"

Aulus sighed. "Would you mind forgoing this debate until I have finished here, and until the cast is set? I have been more than patient, Master Vinyanel, but if you are going to keep prodding at my patient's clear aggravations, I will next insist you leave."

I made a slight bow. "My apologies, Master Aulus. I will leave the two of you in peace. Frankly, I am too tired to conduct as lengthy a discussion as this looks to be anyway. I thank you for the help with the bone setting." A few long strides carried me to the door, and Iriscendra fell in at my side. Just before I slipped from the room, I cast Raen a grin and a shrug. The hatchling and I departed together.

15

THE WEAVING'S IMPLICATIONS

*U*nfortunately, this all still left me with the question: what would become of the hatchling as I embarked to rescue Aulus's daughters and recover the chalice for what I hoped would be the last time? The journey would be dangerous. It would be foolhardy of me to jeopardize the task at hand if Iriscendra's impulsivity trumped her toughness. I dangled my arm over the edge of my bunk and rested my hand on her smooth-scaled neck.

Protection. Just how much did the hatchling need, after all? That all came down to whether or not Raen had yet convinced Iriscendra her breath gifting—whatever sort it was—was an 'abomination.' Were the porcupine's quills a horror? The skunk's spray something it should restrain? The dragon's breath gifting was no more an abomination than a Maker-given talent for swordsmanship or targeting or stealth.

And the fact remained that I knew perilously little about the needs of a very young dragon, and Majestrin grew uncharacteristically icy any time the subject came up. Even so, I needed to consult him about the matter if I planned to hold to my itinerary.

The first hints of the sun's return had eased the horizon from black to deep slate when I rose and peered through the narrow window of my quarters. I guessed I had only slept a couple of hours at best due to Raen's arrival in the wee hours. Although I made no effort at quiet in packing my gear and donning my armor, Hridayesh still snored on in his cot. How he managed an assassin's life when he slept like the dead made no sense to me.

Iriscendra's curled and slumbering form monopolized most of the chamber's floor, but I could more easily forgive her continued repose, given the time she had spent up with me, and her tender age. Did young dragons need a lot of sleep like elf babies did? Or perhaps she was underfed and conserving energy in the typical draconic manner. I wondered if Majestrin and Eyrnir had finished the meat they brought back to our camp.

Once the sun flirted with the horizon in a plum flush, I left my bunkmates to what slumber they could still collect and sought Majestrin. I found him on the grassy side of the temple once again. Thankfully, he was awake, busily gnawing meat from a joint of unrecognizable game. The pile of bones beside him stacked high.

"Good morning, Vinyanel," Majestrin said. "Is today the day we move on?"

"That is my intention," I replied.

"Excellent. To be honest, I would rather not idle here. Too many crawling things in the night to keep at bay. It's hard to properly enjoy a bona fide ruin under those circumstances."

I chuckled and patted him on the neck. "I trust those of us who slept in the temple are in your debt."

Majestrin puffed a little frost cloud from his nostrils, but smiled. "So where are we off to?"

"I fear not far from where we first met, if my guess is right." Back to the mountains where my good steed Solaris had served his last. Where I had parted ways with Curunith, the final surviving member of the squadron I had taken into the dragon-kin hive. My stomach tightened. I thrust down the quickening pulse and drew a journal from my pack. My clammy fingers fumbled to find the page upon which I had begun transcribing notes about the chalice.

A feminine voice cut into my thought. "There you are!"

I glanced over my shoulder. Raen rounded the corner of the temple and cut a straight path for me, though this morning, she no longer wore the dark tunic and breeches of her nighttime exploits, but the floor-length, midnight blue gown I had seen her in the first time we met. A silver chain belt that held her scabbard and schiavona hung at her trim waist. Flattering garb for someone who lived in the wilderness. A bright white cast peeped from inside her flared sleeve.

Majestrin lifted his brows. "So now the new signature in town makes sense."

"What do you mean, 'new signature?'" I glared at him, but lowered my voice. "She is a magic user?"

Majestrin chuckled. "No, the wisps of signature I started noticing yesterday were draconic. She must have brought along one of her brood?"

"The indigo wyrmling."

Raen closed the gap between us, but still maintained a ten-pace distance. "Has your silver companion explained to you yet what a mess you've made?"

"Good morning to you, too." I reached my hand, palm up, toward Raen.

She folded her arms.

Majestrin tilted his head and blinked slowly. "This sounds fun. What, mess, Vinyanel?"

"Her ladyship seems to have taken exception to the fact that the hatchling has made the trip here. She accused me of weaving my signature to the hatchling's," I said. "But given she snuck into my quarters and got into a tug-o-war with the little one in the middle of the night, I am not entirely inclined to take her at her word."

Majestrin pursed his lips. "That would explain quite a bit. It's no wonder the hatchling fawns over you like she does."

Raen's lips curled to a smirk.I let my hand drop. "I still fail to understand how such circumstances constitute a mess. If you would, good dragon, educate me on this so-called 'weaving.'"

The door to the cathedral swung open again.

"Ah, well someone must have realized we're talking about her," Majestrin said.

Iriscendra bolted into the churchyard and skidded to a stop beside me. I reached down and rubbed her head.

Just before I tossed a smug look to Raen, I caught a glimpse of her expression. The tight lips and creased brow of restrained pain splashed across her features, and a twinge of sympathy wiped my expression neutral.

I cleared my throat. "And be honest, Majestrin. Should this weaving have been established between the hatchling and myself, what is your opinion of the gravity of such a situation?"

Majestrin eyed Iriscendra sidelong as he spoke. "Usually the matriarch of the nest will lay her talon upon an egg just before hatching to interconnect her signature with her offspring's. That keeps the hatchling close to her and hopefully out of danger."

Raen huffed. "During that time you didn't 'handle' the egg."

I kept my attention fixed on Majestrin.

The dragon shrugged a wing. "The patriarch can do so as well, though it's less common." He barked a single laugh. "I don't know about any mess, but I don't think you're ready to be a father, Vinyanel."

Raen massaged her temple with her fingertip. "I just hope I'm not too late to keep her from ending up the type barbarians will target."

I drew a slow breath through my nose. How could one individual inspire such warring feelings? Depending on what she had said last, I seemed to have equal inclination toward teasing or tirades. For now, tirades reigned. "Who made you the elven authority on what should be done with apparently orphan dragons?"

"As if you, a *soldier*, would have a better sense?"

The way she spat my profession arced through me like a lightning strike. "Mind your tongue, mistress," I said through my teeth. "There is a great deal of sense taught to a soldier one does not gain by hiding alone in a cave playing nanny to creatures who have no need."

"Vinyanel," Majestrin said, his voice smooth, almost crooning. "I'm no scholar of etiquette, but I don't believe insults are any way to curry favor here."

Iriscendra shuffled beside Majestrin and wriggled under his wing. His eyes widened, and best I could judge, he stiffened, holding his wing above her in a less-than-warm embrace.

"You see," Raen snapped. "Neither of you has the slightest notion how to nurture this tender little soul. Iriscendra, come to me."

The hatching dropped her head to the ground and covered her eyes with the joints of her wings.

"You know she had no choice." Majestrin spoke low to Raen, but somehow, the rumble of his voice increased, taut with sobriety. "It isn't fair of you to ask her to act as though she does."

"No, I suppose she couldn't help herself." The maid leveled a glare at me. "But sometimes we have instincts that are better restrained. She could have been killed finding her way here."

"Once again," I said, "you underestimate the strength in those you claim to know so well."

"And you seem to pretend strength can solve every problem." Raen pushed her hair away from her face. "I hope you haven't gotten too attached, Ecleriast. Iriscendra, Mythrenese, and I are going."

I opened my mouth, but before I could form my first word of rebuttal, Majestrin raised a foretalon.

"I will handle this, Vinyanel." He spoke through his teeth. Majestrin's eyes narrowed, and he swung this unsettling demeanor to Raen. He took a heavy step toward her. "Remove the hatchling?" Another step. "That is your aim?"

Raen swallowed hard. She blanched. "It seemed the wisest course of action, considering . . ." She licked her lips and gulped again, and I could imagine the chalky dryness that must have overtaken her mouth.

"The council of elves here is irrelevant." Majestrin snaked his head forward, the hook of his snout just a foot from Raen's face. He fired a glare down that reptilian visage, straight into her eyes. Cold mist trickled from his nostrils. "*I* won't allow it."

Raen stroked the length of hair that hung over her shoulder with both hands. She flicked a sidelong glance to Majestrin. "I understand Ecleriast intends to embark on a mission, and Veranna has informed me just how perilous it will be." After a deep breath, she pushed her shoulders back and dropped her hands to her sides. "Were you planning on taking the equivalent of a toddler on a military excursion? She must return to the vale with me and forget all about this little visit. Anything else is insanity."

Veranna. My shoulders tightened. Why must she muddy the water? We would have words later.

Majestrin reared his head back. His nostrils flared and eyes flashed. "And you claim to know so much!" he thundered. "You come here, insisting the hatchling and Vinyanel are woven, and in the same breath, say it is best for her to leave him? You say Vinyanel fails to understand the implications of the bond, but beyond its existence, I venture you know precious little more, mistress! You speak of insanity. I say, do not speak upon matters about which you are dangerously ignorant." The silver dragon's voice rose in volume with each word he spoke, until his concluding word came in a roar. The air throbbed with the reverberation of his demand.

Even with a half century of battle training, I came very close to needing a change of underclothes. As it was, my knees quaked. The hatchling scrambled behind me, but I felt less than a shield to her in the face of Majestrin's wrath. Suddenly my similar tactic that I had employed against Veranna the previous day seemed a pale and laughable squeak by comparison.

Raen fell prostrate and covered her head with her good arm.

"Wh-what do you mean?" I managed.

The fury dimmed in Majestrin's eyes, only for a haunted look to replace it. "To sunder the signature weaving is to destine a dragon for a psychotic future. Part a hatchling from her woven caregiver too soon and you break her immature, but indeed powerful mind."

I wet my parched mouth with a swallow. "You are sure of this?"

"Beyond a doubt. And I will speak no more of how I know."

I opted against pressing the matter.

Majestrin backed off and settled to the ground. His expression, however, remained tight. Guarded. "Inconvenient or not, it will be imperative that Iriscendra remain with you, Vinyanel, for a good while yet."

My stomach flipped. While the Majestrin's assertions

brought me the victory of keeping Raen from taking Iriscendra, the implication she needed to stay, perhaps more than she wanted to, gnawed at my heart. "For how long?" My words wavered.

"Each hatchling is different, but she will require you for a shorter time than would a child of your species." Majestrin sighed. "And here is where my practical knowledge ends. Although I understand you will both know when she can spread her wings, so to speak, when the time comes."

So, somewhere between a day-and-a-half and seventy-five years. Great.

I regarded Raen, who peered only tentatively from beneath her arm. She continued to tremble, despite Majestrin's normalized voice. I breathed out my roiling questions. Instead, I forced a relaxed stance, which frankly also rested my wounded leg, which was beginning to burn.

"Care to debate the forty-foot authority on this, Raen?"

"My apologies, Silverlord," Raen replied in a quaking whisper.

Majestrin cocked his head. "Silverlord? My, it's been a long while since I've heard such formality—and never from the mouth of an elf or man. Where did you learn the title?"

"My lifelong study of dragon culture taught me some of the etiquette and customs of your kind." She straightened. "What texts I've studied did not offer any depth on the weaving's implications. Even its existence seems to be debated among scholars." She bowed her head. "Silverlord, forgive my oversight."

A half-grin curled one side of Majestrin's mouth.

"Hold on," I blurted. "A use of a title and some craven pandering is enough to sway you from fury to amusement?"

"You might just as well work on your disposal toward the maid as well, Vinyanel," Majestrin mused. "Otherwise, the trip to retrieve the chalice will be awfully long for both of you."

"Exactly, the trip for the chalice. I have lost more than enough time—" I bit off the thought. "Wait. Both of us? What are you saying?"

"You cannot send the hatchling from your side, nor leave her anywhere. You have other matters that require your full attention, now that you've committed to them. Therefore, you will need someone to mind the hatchling on your travels. Who better than the maiden so staunchly insisting she knows best?"

Raen regained her feet. "What? I never meant I intended to follow the lieutenant commander anywhere."

"So you concede you will go home instead?" Majestrin tilted his head. "And leave Vinyanel to teach Iriscendra what he will?"

Raen threw her good hand out to the side and gaped.

I scowled. "You are a scoundrel, Majestrin. Why play us off one another like this?"

Majestrin stretched his bright wings, and the eastern sun behind him illuminated them like frosted glass. "Because like you, young Windrider, I am eager to be on our way, and there really is no other simple solution."

"She has a broken arm!" I protested. It came out far closer to a whine than I was pleased to admit.

Raen folded her arms and shook her head. "You aren't exactly at peak, from what I can tell, oh Limpy Lieutenant."

"I will be back to normal in another day, I am certain."

The scoff Raen blew through her nose communicated her skepticism, but she allowed the subject to drop.

Limpy? My molars creaked against each other. Never had proving someone wrong burned so hot in my soul. Despite what measures it took, she would see.

"You can bicker about it someplace else," Majestrin said. "Maybe while you pack your supplies—which you all have in abundance, right?"

I sighed. Majestrin had touched on an important point. My

own supplies were low, which meant Veranna's and Hridayesh's were as well. I had no idea what sort of provisions Raen had at her disposal, but I was not about to lead a troupe of civilians into the wilderness and starve them. The outset of the journey would need to account for a stop in whatever civilization we could find, in search of bread and fruit—things we would have to acquire if we did not all want to end up with perpetually empty bellies and bleeding gums. It was late enough in the autumn for the forage to be failing.

"I will order the plans, Majestrin. I expect we should be ready to go airborne by mid-morning." A few more hours of preparations, and then I would finally be on my way to pulling the thorn from my heel that the loss of the chalice had driven there.

As for the inevitable new thorns Veranna—and now Raen —would jab my way, I guessed it would not be long before I started to feel their sting.

16

INTERCEPTED

A pale sun climbed toward its zenith as our group assembled in the plaza outside the temple of Creo. Most of us, anyway, since the young dragons, under the guise of fishing, had headed to the riverbank to chase one another and splash.

I extended a rolled parchment to Aulus, who sat astride his horse. "Present this to the first centaur guard you encounter within the Delsin's borders. If you follow the eastern bank of the Arin, there is no risk of you passing the city without being intercepted. Always stay within sight of the river, or you may become disoriented and lost."

Aulus nodded. "I thank you for doing what you can on our behalf."

"You're certain you cannot escort us?" Cnaeus frowned.

"My word is as good as my presence," I said.

Hridayesh laughed. "Probably better. He likely hasn't

mouthed off in the writ. If he's with you, the chances of him irritating someone important are pretty significant."

Veranna and Raen, seated on the low wall surrounding an empty fountain, met each other's gazes and joined Hridayesh in his mirth.

I shrugged it off. The opportunity to fly again had tempered the irritation that had been plaguing me ever since we set foot in Bilearne.

"Creo's protection go before you," I said. "I sincerely hope the Chancellor will see the wisdom in aiding you, but I can make no promises."

"We understand." Aulus clasped his fist over his chest and made as much of a bow as one could while mounted. "And if any of us receives Creo's protection, I wish it for you before myself. May the trail be clear." He lowered his eyelids and drew a breath through his nose.

Though I could not truly understand what he was feeling, I knew what he desired. "I will keep both eyes open for your daughters." I faced the young man who sat on his own horse, a length behind Aulus. "Your sisters."

Praesidio's lips tightened and a flush overtook his cheeks. He blinked glassy eyes. "Thank you," he rasped.

Aulus opened his eyes but did not meet my gaze directly again. "Praesidio, Cnaeus, let us be off."

They wheeled their mounts and departed at a brisk, clattering walk. Once they were out of sight, I lifted my pack and heaved it up behind Majestrin's saddle.

"Hridayesh, you ride Eyrnir," I said. "I have given him permission to make rations of you if you try to escape."

The griffon ruffled his feathers in a way that seemed something like a shudder, though the unchanging expression on his face made it hard for me to interpret his body language. Given how thoroughly our mounts had stripped two goats, a sheep, and a mule deer of meat over the past day,

I was glad their appetites did not really extend to humans or elves.

"Veranna, you are with me."

The prophetess and Raen whispered to one another like conspiring courtiers.

"Veranna?" I tried again.

Veranna rose from her seat on the fountain's edge. "I guess we shall have to finish that story another time," she said to Raen. She sighed. "Very well, young Windrider. On our way to market, then?"

"Yes," I replied. "And you are the one with the silver, right?" I interlaced my fingers in front of me and bent at the waist.

"A leg up? To what do I owe this courtesy?" Veranna cocked her head. She hesitated to take advantage of my offer. "Unless you are serious I pay the price of provisions."

"Of course I am not," I huffed. "Poor Majestrin simply does not deserve for you to clamber on him like pups fumble over their mother."

Veranna put her sandaled foot in my hand, grasped one of Majestrin's dorsal plates, and swung herself into place with ease that took me by surprise. She was so light.

Raen rose as well, cupped her hands around her mouth, and called, "Mythrenese, Iriscendra! It's time to go."

The two smaller dragons careened over the partially-collapsed roof of a nearby structure that may have once been a bathhouse whose caldarium had long gone dry. They skidded to a stop a few paces outside our group. Raen approached Mythrenese. She hitched her pack tighter on her back.

The indigo dragon's back was noticeably bare. "No barding?" I said.

Raen inclined her chin. "Mythrenese takes care of me."

I cocked my head and shrugged. "If you say so." I suspected her flights with the dragonling had been less taxing than my typical excursions.

I wedged my toe into the crease of Majestrin's foreleg, grasped the horn of my saddle, and swung my opposite leg over his back. Pain ripped through my wound. I settled in the saddle and slowly unclenched my fists as the ache ebbed.

Veranna leaned around my shoulder. "It's feeling that bad today, eh?"

"I have just lost a little suppleness in the muscle from a few days without riding," I replied. "Once I loosen up, it will be fine. Majestrin, we go. Northeast, back to the main course of the Nuruhain."

The rush of flight smoothed away the fire in my leg, or at least filled me with enough soul-gripping joy that I forgot it for a time. My glance roved about the flying creatures in whose midst I flew, and I could imagine such a group ridden by the best soldiers I would one day train. I breathed deep of the cool wind, and in little time, the remains of Bilearne receded into the golden mist of the distance.

I leaned back a bit to speak to Veranna, still needing to yell over the wind. "If I am not mistaken, there should be a human settlement—a mining operation, I believe—as we get into the southeastern foothills of the Triasteads, and if we—"

"Vinyanel! Below you!" Hridayesh bellowed.

Before I had a chance to search out his concern, something crashed into Majestrin's neck. A figure. A winged figure whose hood covered all but the tip of his scaly snout and whose moss-green cloak hung between sinewy, thrusting wings. The beast grappled the crest of Majestrin's neck, just behind his head.

Majestrin thrashed. Veranna shrieked.

"Eyrnir, come get Veranna!" I reached for a knife on my belt. With the great length of Majestrin's neck, I doubted I could reach the dragon-kin attacker, but I had to try something.

The griffon closed on us, approaching from the rear in order to dodge the span of Majestrin's beating wings.

"Prophetess, jump to Hridayesh," I commanded.

"Are you insane?" She gestured to the hundreds of feet of open sky that separated us from solid ground.

"I cannot fight with you back there. I need you—gah. Never mind." I twisted in my saddle, grabbed a hold of the back of Veranna's ruffled blouse, and caught Hridayesh's glance. Majestrin's flight path grew increasingly erratic. "You ready?"

Hridayesh's eyes widened.

"I said, are you ready?"

He nodded.

"Here she comes." At once, I lifted and shoved Veranna from the saddle.

The griffon, Creo bless him, did exactly what I required. He dropped a few feet and maneuvered beneath me. Veranna fell only a fathom before Hridayesh grabbed her. I turned back to my own plight without taking the time to focus upon whether she got seated.

The dragon-kin grasped Majestrin's neck with straining muscles in one arm. With the other hand, he brandished a black-bladed knife.

A moment before I wound up a throw of my own weapon, the dragon-kin plunged his.

Straight into Majestrin's head.

17

CRASH

*T*he beauty of flight erupted into madness so fast that Raen could scarcely comprehend what was going on. What was that thing grappled to Majestrin's neck?

"Iriscendra!" she cried. "Stay behind Mythrenese." Raen slid her schiavona from its slim scabbard, but honestly, what could she do? Even the best of strokes stood little chance of hurting that . . .thing. . . without striking Majestrin as well. Raen stared long enough to realize a hooded humanoid of some sort, though one with leathery wings and a reptilian snout, clutched the silver dragon's neck in some sort of twisted airborne rodeo.

Iriscendra complied with Raen's command with eyes wide. Her brow puckered. Lips quivered.

"Don't worry little one, we'll get him out of—"

Majestrin's roar tore through the air.

Ecleriast had raised a dagger, poised to throw, but not soon enough. Majestrin's attacker wrenched his free hand back from

150

the dragon's head, right behind his ear. The dark blade dripped with purplish blood.

The silver dragon lost two fathoms of altitude. He thrashed his serpentine neck, though whether from pain or a simple desire to throw off his attacker, it was hard to tell. More spatters of steaming, purple blood flung from his wound.

Ecleriast jammed his knife back into a sheath on his belt, and instead of waging an attack, gripped the handles on his barding. His teeth were bared, his eyes aflame. Terrifying in his fear and rage. His mount's flight path tipped and jagged left. Majestrin flapped in an erratic, spastic flail, but accomplished nothing more than becoming even more unstable. His wings and tail thrashed in disharmony.

He was going down.

The ring of steel from Raen's right tore her horrified attention from the disaster unfolding with Ecleriast. Another attacker had emerged from who-knows-where, and Hridayesh held the newcomer's bastard sword in a parry with his wide-bladed khanda. Raen searched the canopy. *Perfect.* Yet another beast beat leathery wings to close on their position. The hand he thrust ahead of him glowed with a sickly green light.

"Why didn't I bring my short bow?" Raen muttered.

"By Creo's might, I bind your curse!" Veranna intoned, now astride the griffon behind Hridayesh. She pointed a long finger at the ascending attacker.

The creature hissed and veered to the side. His glow erupted and blew away like trailers of oily smoke. He grabbed the wrist of the curse wielding hand with his opposite claws.

"All right, Mythrenese," Raen said. "I never meant to subject you to anything like this, but we need—"

Iriscendra streaked toward the attacker Veranna had delayed in a pearlescent flash. The hatchling's foolhardiness strangled Raen's words. Whatever directive she might have conveyed to Mythrenese transformed in to a shrill exclamation.

"Little one! No!"

Iriscendra's sweet face twisted into a fearsome mask of fury and determination. The glint of the curse-wielding beast's widening eyes shone from the recesses of his hood. The hatchling reared her head back, then shot it forward.

A sick churning twisted Raen's gut. She *wouldn't*.

A cloud of pearlescent gas streamed from Iriscendra's maw. The cloud, while not huge, was enough to envelop her opponent. His every muscle halted in mid-wing-thrust.

He dropped from the sky like a stone.

Surely whatever this creature was, it could not have the fortitude to withstand a three-hundred-foot drop. That left Hridayesh's opponent. Majestrin, Ecleriast, and their knifeman were nowhere in sight.

Raen and Mythrenese wheeled toward Hridayesh and Eyrnir just as the North Deklian slashed a blow across his attacker's head. He cleaved the hood it wore, which blew back in tatters to reveal a long snout with a scaly hide, seeming hundreds of uneven teeth, and beady eyes. Curving ram's horns and dorsal plates jutted from its skull. Its scales were sandy in color, but smeared now with the crimson blood that ran from a gash stretching from the corner of its mouth to its horn. These must be the dragon-kin Veranna spoke of. The beasts Ecleriast had a grudge against. It seemed the grudge was mutual.

"Get me behind that awful thing," Raen said. She squeezed Mythrenese with her knees.

"I'll try," he replied. His voice trembled.

You're a dragon, for heaven's sake! Raen bit her lip. Not only Mythrenese's voice trembled, but his body as well. Did he not have instinct? She stroked his neck. "You can do it."

Mythrenese banked toward the tangle of combat between Hridayesh, the dragon-kin warrior, and Eyrnir. Swords slashed. Talons raked. Beaks and teeth snapped.

"Let's get a little higher and to their south. We'll make a diving pass and I'll slash while we're on the move."

"You think you can do that?"

"I have to try. I'm certainly not making you hover right where a stray—or intentional—blade might catch you."

Iriscendra whipped her head back and forth, searching the canopy.

"Iriscendra, don't you dare run after them alone. And no more abominations!" Raen shot a stern glare to the hatchling.

The tortured mix of fear and fury roiling in the hatchling's eyes gripped at Raen's chest, but for now, she dismissed Iriscendra's distress. Pursuit must wait. *Please let her find some sense!*

The crashing and roars of Ecleriast's plight had receded. A hunt for clues where Majestrin's crash took them would have to wait.

A few hard thrusts of Mythrenese's wings carried them higher and outside the fray. Raen leaned close to his neck. "Ready?"

"No," Mythrenese croaked.

"Neither am I. Go!"

They shot like a javelin for the confrontation. The dragon-kin slashed Hridayesh's forearm, and he juggled his sword, grip compromised.

Raen thrust her schiavona in her off hand, and the momentum of Mythrenese's dive plunged the blade through their target's back until the basket hilt met his lumpy cloak. The creature hissed and gurgled, and his wings went limp. He began to fall.

Only a painful wrench of her arm freed the weapon from her opponent before he dropped away. Raen's shoulder throbbed. Creo permit there should be no more lurking in the canopy.

After the initial crashing of the defeated dragon-kin

smashing through the trees below, all went quiet, aside from the flap of dragon and griffon wings. They hovered in position. Raen warily scanned their surroundings. No more dragon-kin —but then, no Ecleriast or Majestrin either.

18

*T*he cold slosh of water over my face forced my eyes open. I tried to draw a breath, but a terrifying crushing sensation in my chest prevented the proper intake of air. My body spasmed. I somehow shoved myself from my back to my side, and a cough that could not quite produce wrenched at my ribs. No decent breath, no cough to clear the way. Panic swarmed through my muscles.

Another involuntary contortion of my abdomen forced a sudden gush of water and breakfast from my mouth and nose. I vomited again, then the coughing finally began. I thrust up on my arms, coughing and retching at intervals. But at least air seemed to be getting into my lungs now, if in fitful snatches only.

I collapsed back to the pebble-strewn ground beneath me. The lapping current of a swift river numbed my legs from the knees down. Now that I had stopped heaving, I noticed a stream of cloudy red ran from me and streaked downstream in macabre curls.

I struggled to sit, which renewed my hacking, and I spat more mucous-laden water. With stiff fingers, I pried at the buckles on my cuisse. The saturation made the leather stiff and unyielding. I wrenched my gauntlets from my hands and threw them down, then went back to work with wrinkled fingertips on the buckle on the side of my thigh. Once I had pried the damaged cuisse free, I found a deep burgundy stain covered my entire pant leg beneath the plate. I bunched the sodden pant leg up to my hip. As I feared, Aulus's careful stitches stuck out in all directions in frayed tatters. The gash in my leg gaped like a toothless, bloody sneer. I pressed my cloak to the wound to stanch the steady flow of blood.

I needed new bindings. Those Aulus had applied hung in a loose mass around my knee, bloodied to saturation. But where was my pack?

With Majestrin. Where was Majestrin?

I staggered to my feet, but dizziness and the dark haze of threatening unconsciousness prevented me from taking any steps. The deep quiet of wilderness surrounded me. A swift river, whose far bank I could hardly see for the great span of the water, rushed by. Behind me, tall granite cliffs loomed, and a forest of conifers reached for the sky from the level places atop the rock face. I was utterly alone.

With one hand, I kept my cloak pressed to my wound, and with the other, I reached for my hilt.

My heart plummeted into my gut. My scabbard was empty.

I plopped back on the ground. Part of me yelled it was just a hunk of steel. The rest of me cringed at a horrifying sense of nakedness. Vulnerability.

I needed to think. Sort out how I had gotten here. Ah, yes, this morning, we had set out from Bilearne, and hardly put the city behind us before the attack.

A curse burst from my lips. We should have been more wary. Of course the dragon-kin scout Majestrin intercepted would not have been alone. The scout must have been the only villain to press on, though sun sick, long enough to allow Majestrin to discover and collect him. Had we taken the time to scout the area ourselves, we likely would have seen others of his kind, encamped and waiting for cover of darkness to close in on us.

As bitter as the thought was to swallow, having Galdurith along would have made much difference, I guessed, in the way we prepared to set out. Every award I had won for tactics mocked me from their little case in my quarters back in Delsinon. My haste, my determination, my frustration had all driven me forward with complete disregard for what I knew.

And now, what had happened to Majestrin? How lethal was the wound the dragon-kin had dealt him? It certainly destroyed his ability to fly. Our plummet from the sky that finally smashed through the canopy and then into the cliff face had been doubtless the most terrifying experience of my two-hundred-forty-three years. We could have easily flown several miles before we finally crashed. Whatever happened after that hid in the gaping hole in my memory that spanned the time between the lash of the canopy and my awakening on the beach.

First things first, however. I needed to get the leg wound bound again if I intended to accomplish anything else. The pressure had slowed the bleeding from a flow to more of an ooze. I untied Aulus's bandages and frowned. With no equipment, the only option I had was to reuse them.

My leg screamed its protest as I lowered myself to the river's edge again. The water ran clear over a rocky floor. I plunged the bundle of bindings into the river and scrubbed them against one another. Their burgundy and brown softened to a lighter pinkish-beige, and what blood I rinsed from them drifted away, downriver. Once the water I squeezed from them flowed clear, I wrung them out and flattened them.

Field medicine had always been one of those disciplines to which I had only committed the barest study. My academic neglect of the finer points of the art now seemed perilously foolish. I did not know exactly why, but wrapping my wound in wet bandages seemed less-than-ideal, so I shuffled away from the shore to a cluster of boulders that the sun bathed in morning light.

I spread the bindings on the warm surface of the rocks. Hopefully a few hours of air and sun would dry them enough to apply to the cut. With no means to stitch the gash, I could only hope that sitting still during that time would complete the clotting process and further seal the wound. Once the bandages all had a place to dry, I sat again and leaned my back against the rocks. Weariness dragged at my eyelids and my limbs.

"Creo," I said. My voice sounded small and raspy. "This is quite the mess, is it not?" A bitter smirk tugged at my cheek. "But I think of the others. Majestrin especially." What kind of knife had the dragon-kin used that had bit so thoroughly through his scales? And a knife wound to the head? My eyes stung. "Please, please rest your mighty hand on him. Keep him from . . ." My chin dropped to my chest. Before I was even aware, my shoulder shook with silent sobs. The dragon-kin would not take Majestrin from me. The very idea ripped my heart open and shredded it like a pack of jackals would a carcass. I wanted to pray further, but cohesive thoughts eluded me. I curled in a ball and let the mercy of an exhausted sleep quiet my agony for a time.

When I awoke, the ground was cold, and no sun reached into the river valley, for it had dipped to the west behind cliff and bough. I was stiff, sore, and freezing. What idiot falls asleep in plate mail and wet clothes? My teeth chattered, and my movements came with sluggish pain.

At least the bindings were mostly dry. With shaking hands, I re-wrapped my leg wound and then strapped on what pieces of my armor I had removed.

My stomach rumbled. The only weapons I had were a pair of knives on my belt. My aim was typically good, but hunting with thrown knives? I groaned. My best hope lay in finding the others.

~

*I*riscendra sped back and forth across the sky. "Yennel! V'yennel?" she cried in a voice that grew weaker and more pitiful with each repetition.

Raen slid from Mythrenese's back and landed on the crest of a rocky pinnacle that overlooked the forest of firs and spruces. She beckoned the hatchling. "Iriscendra, come here. Please."

The hatchling drifted to Raen's side and settled on the rock. "He hurt, Myf'rnese?"

Mythrenese drooped his neck. "With the way Majestrin was—"

Raen lay her hand on Mythrenese's withers as though to lean on him, but used the gesture to conceal the fact that she pinched him. Hard.

"Ow!" the dragonling yelped. "What?"

"I hear Ecleriast is very resourceful," Raen said. "Don't worry, Iriscendra."

Eyrnir set down beside Mythrenese, and Veranna dismounted and dashed to Raen in one motion. She grasped Raen's hands.

"Thank you for your help in the battle." The prophetess

pushed a waving tendril of hair from her eyes. "I had no idea you had sword skills."

"I would have done better with my actual sword arm." Raen's beleaguered gaze lingered on her cast. "Hopefully we won't run into too much more of this kind of thing."

"We need to prepare for the chance, though. First things first—we need to find Majestrin and Vinyanel."

Raen glanced at the hatchling. Iriscendra curled at Mythrenese's feet and stared into the distance. "The trouble is, won't he also be looking for us? If we're all moving about hunting for one another, we're bound never to find each other."

"You have to send a search party while the rest stay in one place," Hridayesh said.

The bite in his voice jabbed Raen's patience like a thistle. She straightened her posture and withdrew her hands from Veranna's grasp. "That's wise advice, Hridayesh. I believe the job is best accomplished by Mythrenese, with his gift for sensing."

Hridayesh snorted. "He's little more than a child."

"So you propose one of us travels with you instead?" Veranna lowered her chin and fixed her gaze on him.

Raen stopped breathing. Was she mad? She knew little about the North Deklian, but intended to assume the worst until he proved otherwise.

He groaned. "Let's at least send Eyrnir as part of the search party then. I'm not willing to risk waiting somewhere for days because the dragon baby decided to chase rainbows instead of doing what he ought."

The heat of a flush warmed Raen's cheeks. She clenched her fist.

Veranna placed a light hand on her shoulder and spoke in Elvish. *"Na uvennet e lir."*

Don't rise to it. Raen drew a breath. "Very well. If Eyrnir is amenable to going."

The griffon lowered his head, as though in a bow.

"Before you lift off, however," Raen said, "the rest of us should find a more sheltered spot where we can make camp for perhaps a day or two."

Iriscendra's head shot up. "I going. Not waiting."

"It's too dangerous." Raen shook her head. "There could be more of those dragon-kin about."

The hatchling's eyes narrowed to smoldering slits. "You try stop me, I run away."

A quickening heartbeat thudded against Raen's ribs. "Now just one minute, little one. Is that any kind of tone—?"

Air hissed between Iriscendra's teeth. Air drawn in.

Mythrenese dashed between Iriscendra and Raen. "Don't! I can understand why you . . ." He swallowed. ". . .did that during the fight. But you really mustn't. It's so heinous."

"Why?" Iriscendra and Hridayesh said as one.

Raen bit her tongue. The last thing she wanted to do was forge some kind of alliance between the assassin and the hatchling by giving them a mutual grievance. "All right, Iriscendra. I know you're worried about Ecleriast, so I will let you go with Mythrenese and Eyrnir. But you must all come back to us by nightfall. Is that clear?"

Something between a scowl and a pout and a worried furrow wrinkled Iriscendra's snout and brow. She nodded. "Found him 'fore. Find him this time too."

19

———————

THE MASKING CURSE

"*L*ord Hanash, a report." Warrior Khagrosh poked his snout through the tent flap. "Your permission to step in?"

Naghax set down the text clutched in his hands. *This had better be important.* Hanash did so little to protect his time from well-wishers, prodders, snoopers, and general interruptions. And it always seemed like Naghax's audience times, rife with complicated details, were the appointments to suffer the most frequent distraction.

Hanash leaned back on his cushion and waved the burly Khagrosh forward. "The information I have been waiting on, I hope?"

"Indeed, Your Most-revered Excellency." Khagrosh bowed.

What a bootlicker. Hanash had not been lord long enough for anyone to have yet made a serious attempt on his life, and here Khagrosh was pandering to him like he was a high priest.

"The Elgadrim and the elves have parted company, my lord.

The Elgadrim went south, and the elves northwest. The scouting squadron attacked Ecleriast and his band of fools. Completely took them by surprise."

Hanash grinned. "And?"

Khagrosh hesitated. He regarded Hanash with a sidelong glance. "Two of ours perished. Their half-elf witch hexed Shannak, and then either a dragonette or else a surprisingly bold hatchling with them paralyzed him. He fell to his death. Radneth perished by more conventional means."

Naghax snorted. "But what of Oglech? This is sounding less and less like a successful ambush."

A low growl rumbled in Khagrosh's throat. "You stick to the fairy-tales, pen pusher."

A swell of smoldering anger rose in Naghax's chest, but he blew it out with a huff. The thug wasn't worth the energy and loss of focus.

"I will have civility in my quarters," Hanash hissed. "And I do echo, what of Oglech?"

The simmer in the messenger's eyes cooled. He puffed his chest beneath his suit of plates and straps. "He downed the silver dragon and perpetrated the masking curse on Ecleriast before the blasted elf went over the falls. *If* he lived, no one will be finding his signature for at least three moonrises."

"The she-elves are still abroad, then?" Hanash asked.

"Lordship, I fear that is the case, but the remainder of the squad has narrowed down the area where they believe the females and the North Deklian have made camp."

"Excellent." Hanash rose and stepped to the tent sidewall. He pulled a flask from his pack, raised it to Khagrosh, and smirked. "I say the investment was worth the payoff, then. Thank you for the update. You are dismissed."

Another deep bow from Khagrosh set Naghax's eyes rolling. The warrior backed from the tent.

"That's it?" Naghax burst out. "Assume Ecleriast dead and no concern for the rest of the group?"

"Much to the contrary, Naghax." Hanash took a swig from his flask. "Let the softbellies regroup. Getting what remains of them back together in one place makes my next order for Khagrosh's ilk that much simpler."

"So you intend to strike them again?" Naghax asked.

"Of course. With Ecleriast out of the way, that leaves us with some interesting options with regard to the females." A wicked smirk stretched across Hanash's maw.

His smirk had a contagious quality that spread to Naghax's face as well. "That sounds like a fate worthy of the pains they've caused us. Good thinking."

"It's this kind of thinking that makes me the natural choice as Scitherias's successor." Hanash scanned Naghax's pile of carefully-penned notes and calculations. "Between this strike on the elves and our inevitable success with the chalice, there could be a noteworthy future ahead of you, my friend."

~

I huddled by a meager fire while the crickets chirped their raspy songs from the underbrush. Goose-bumps washed over my flesh in waves. Just what I needed—some kind of cold or other illness to take hold of me now. I could not recall the last time I had suffered so much as a sniffle. I inched closer to the flames and threw another bundle of sticks on top of them. The misfortune of having no tools prevented me from collecting any wood thicker than what I could break with my bare hands, and that dictated I feed the fire often.

My stomach rumbled. There were only so many black walnuts a person could eat, and the forest gave up nothing more within the radius I could travel on my reopened injury. As much as my conscience said I should stay put and ease the search—if indeed Veranna and the others were actually searching for me—the lack of food in my vicinity would determine how long I could remain. I fingered the weave of my cloak. Could I pull a thread of yarn from it and make a fishing line? Even if I could get the string, how would I fashion a hook? Cannibalizing my armor was the last of last resorts.

I shivered and barked a curse at the shadows. A pox on the dragon-kin! My every grievance I could trace back to them, and if I caught up to them, I would savor each morsel of vengeance I could get.

Vengeance. Is that what I wanted? Did I have any hope of seizing it, if the time came? Or would my body and mind betray me, as they often threatened of late? What kind of warrior was I if I suddenly could no longer breathe at the start of a fight? Or if my vision darkened? Or if senseless panic locked up my battle skills? I swallowed the lump that formed in my throat at the thought.

I rose from my position by the fire, since it seemed to have little power to warm me anyway. The bank of the river boasted a field of stones, most rounded and worn from days when the river must have run higher. I lifted the lightest one by my feet, a stone that was almost white. After hefting it for a moment, I placed it beside another stone of similar paleness.

While working my way along the shore, I gathered every white stone I saw and placed it with the others until I had a pile about a foot high and four wide. By then, my leg wound raged with excruciating fire, drowsiness made my head feel three times its weight, and yawn after yawn made my eyes water. I gave up my little project and curled on the uneven ground by the fire. If I slept at all, it would be a miracle.

Apparently I drowsed at least a short while—enough to jolt awake at the gray hour of dawn. My glance darted every direction, and beads of sweat ran down my brow. I tried to sit up. An explosion of misery in my leg flooded to my stomach and forced a retch, and the burn of digestive fluids seared my throat.

I half-crawled to the river's edge and cupped some of the water in my hands. My first tentative sip went down without causing further heaving, so I took a deeper drink. Once I had cleared the bile from my mouth, I plunked back on my rear.

Why was this confounded leg wound becoming *more* bothersome rather than less?

The bindings on the wound displayed a disgusting palette of rust, brown, yellow and green. I loosened them carefully.

The wound was puffy and purplish, and the width of the gash only narrower due to the immensity of the swelling. A musty funk met my nose, one that reminded me of a week-old battlefield. The chills. The clammy sweat. The look of the wound. They all mocked the professed strength of Aulus's anti-infection agent.

I needed to clean the gash again, and I doubted the bandages would improve much with another scrubbing. Without hot water, who knew what filth might linger in their weave and perpetuate my troubles? If I could just submerge my whole leg for a while and let the river's current sweep away what grime it could.

I glanced about. My clothes were finally dry—I was not about to soak them again after enduring their damp cold for most of the previous day. The weather was not in the least bit warm—rather, it was solidly autumnal. Hardly the ideal for bathing in a river. But there was no alternative.

I stripped off my clothes and laid them on the bank, then hobbled to the river's edge. *Gah*, the water was colder to bare feet than it was to hands. I gulped a breath and slogged into the river as fast as my lame gait would carry me. I stopped once the water's depth reached the upper extreme of the gash, high on my thigh. I would be cursed before freezing any part of me higher than that. The occasional lap of river water mocked my sense of self-preservation, as the icy water occasionally lapped my—well, areas above my wound—and wrenched yelps from my that drove a flock of starlings from an overhanging tree.

Strangely, the pain in my leg lessened as I lingered in the water, though whether from the decreased weight on it or the numbing temperature of the water, I could not pinpoint. I remained in the water as long as I could bear it, shivering, and I am certain, blue-lipped. With my luck, this would be just the moment some member of the group found me. Though if the searcher to find me turned out to be Raen . . .

Blast it, I was becoming addled. I turned for the bank.

The swelling looked a mite better once I patted myself dry with my cloak and wrapped it around my shoulders again to steady my convulsive shivering. But the skin was mottled and ugly. And I would have to do without bindings for now, at least until Majestrin brought me my gear. He would. Soon. I clung to that.

20

LITTLE LOVE LOST

*R*aen sat on the ground, her legs crossed, elbows on her knees, chin in her hand. The small portion of dried apple she chewed was bland and leathery, but it could have been the most succulent slice of fruit on the continent and she would have possessed no palette for it.

"It would be nice if the flyers returned prior to sunset," Raen said, "but I'm not hanging any hope on that outcome."

"Nor am I." Veranna stared into the distant sky, her face drawn. "I'll pray to that end anyway, though."

"Can you pray and gather wood at the same time? We should build a large, smoky fire, in case Majestrin and Vinyanel are looking for us."

Hridayesh scowled. "Let's just lead the rest of the dragon-kin in the area to us. That sounds like wonderful fun. Maybe they'll stay for finger sandwiches and games!"

A few swift strides carried Veranna straight to the North Deklian. "Getting our group back together is likely going to involve some risk. There's a reasonable chance any dragon-kin in the vicinity are pitching camp and getting out of the sun by now. We need to use our daylight hours as best we can to lead *Vinyanel* to us."

A disdainful curl pulled at one side of Hridayesh's upper lip. He stepped back from Veranna. "Did you not see the disaster on wings Majestrin became? They're probably dashed against a rock face somewhere like hurled eggs."

"It won't be long," Raen said. She stood and took a place beside Veranna. "If the weaving led Iriscendra halfway across the continent to find Vinyanel, the matter of a few miles will be short work."

"Does a dead elf, or dragon for that matter, still emit a— what did you call it? That magical trail you could just be making up . . ."

"Signature." The blood drained from Veranna's cheeks.

Raen narrowed her eyes and took careful stock of Veranna's demeanor. In addition to the paling cheeks, she clutched her skirt with one hand. The prophetess blinked a few too many times in a short span. The answer to Hridayesh's question must have been no.

"There's a lot we don't know about signatures and weaving," Raen said. "Give the dragons time. I am sure they'll return with news tonight. Or sooner." She marched to the edge of the clearing, bent down, and lifted a stick about the circumference of her bicep. "The fire will still be useful."

Hridayesh turned and ducked into his tent.

Raen sighed. "I guess that makes it up to us."

Raen's broken arm made gathering wood laborious, but by the time two hours had passed, they had a strong, tall blaze crackling. Raen fed armloads of leaves and pine needles onto the flames. A thick, white smoke rose straight into the windless sky.

"You lit that fire faster than I ever could have." Veranna

stood with her arms wrapped around her middle. Dark circles shadowed her amber eyes.

"A century of living in the wilderness makes you good at certain things." Raen shrugged. She lowered her voice and slipped closer to Veranna. "You're very worried."

The prophetess closed her eyes. "Majestrin's plummet must have carried them quite far. I noticed Vinyanel's signature growing fainter after he disappeared through the canopy, and then I lost track of it as we dealt with our own problems. But since then, I haven't been able to pick it back up."

Raen's glance flicked to Hridayesh's tent. "What do we do if . . . well . . .nobody picks it back up?"

"I'm not sure." Veranna stretched her hands to the flames. "I can't simply close my eyes to the fact that three little girls are on their way to be horrifically sacrificed, and the results of that sacrifice could spell chaos for so many."

Did she mean to forge on even if the worst had befallen the Windrider and his mount? Was it complete insanity? Alone, yes. Together—perhaps a little less doomed to failure. Did it really matter to Raen and her dragons, though? Iriscendra was found. Mythrenese was still unscathed, so far. If Ecleriast and his driving perspective were really no longer a factor . . .Raen chewed her cheek. "You really think we have a hope of catching up to the girls on our own?"

A small smile blossomed on Veranna's lips. "We're never really on our own unless we choose to be. Remember that."

Raen nodded. She leaned very close to Veranna and offered the lowest possible whisper. "But what about him?" She cocked her head toward Hridayesh's tent. "Is he always this surly, or is he reacting to the stress of the situation? I don't get the sense he has warm feelings toward you. What exactly is his connection to this group? I'm a bit unclear on that."

"It's rather complicated—but he and Vinyanel have gone back and forth between trying to kill each other and saving each other's lives enough to somehow share some kind of warped bond. Vinyanel has promised to bear witness for Hridayesh to the Delsin Court in a pending trial."

"Trial? Dare I ask what for?"

Veranna chuckled. "An assassination attempt. On Vinyanel."

A churning sickness rolled around in Raen's middle. "I don't like this. If Mythrenese and the rest don't get back tonight, I think we had both better watch the night together. We can catch up on sleep once Ecleriast is back."

"Honestly," Veranna said, "I think Hridayesh is going to try to slip away."

Raen pursed her lips. "If we're lucky."

The suffering look in Veranna's eyes caught Raen by surprise. "If only it were that simple." Veranna rubbed her temple. "Vinyanel has already stretched the bounds of his authority by embarking on this chalice mission. It's possible, no matter the outcome of this excursion, that he'll face some unpleasant discipline when he gets back home. If he also loses a prisoner in the process . . ." Veranna's glance fell. "I feel an obligation to prevent as much damage to Vinyanel's career as possible."

"You seem pretty wrapped up in him on quite a few levels," Raen said. "You're sure the antagonism between you isn't just a forced attempt at preventing . . . other . . . entanglements?"

The sudden laugh that burst from Veranna came out in a near-snort. "Yes, I'm entirely certain. I'm more an admirer of the lute-plucking, verse-scribbling types."

The image of Ecleriast with a lute was enough to bubble laughter up and cover some of Raen's anxieties, for the moment. "All right, so we have to wait things out until the fliers can give us a report, and in the meantime, make certain our trio here in camp stays intact. That should be sufficiently agonizing to keep my attention."

~

*B*irds sang in a jabbering choir and the crickets provided metronomic accompaniment under the purple light of a failing dusk when Eyrnir, Mythrenese, and Iriscendra circled the camp and made a gentle descent. But Raen's sense of relief lasted only until she caught a glimpse of Iriscendra's face.

The hatchling's babyish features crinkled with the pressure of worry. Her efforts to fold her wings were tremulous and clumsy.

Raen pressed her lips together. Iriscendra's exhaustion emanated from her slumped posture. A whole day of flying was too much to ask of one so young.

Drying sweaty palms on her skirt, Raen eased to Iriscendra's side. "You'll be able to look again tomorrow."

"Why I no-know where V'yennel is, Raen?" Iriscendra spoke in a thin voice. "Always know where, even from far 'way."

"Well." Raen toyed with a lock of her hair. "You're getting older. The weaving doesn't last forever."

Iriscendra narrowed her eyes and bored into Raen with her gaze. "You don' think that w-w-rrreal rrreason."

Confounded dragons. Even fresh from the shell, they were more perceptive than seemed fair. "I wish I knew what was going on. I promise we'll do everything we can to find Ecleri-ast." Raen ran her fingers along Iriscendra's small horns.

The hatchling closed her eyes and sighed. "Go fish now. I hungry."

Raen smiled. "*I'll* go *fishing* for now. "*I'm* hungry." She glanced across the camp. "Mythrenese, please go with her. None of us should be alone right now." *Especially one of us who might run off on her own and keep searching if the rest of us aren't careful.*

The two dragons departed, assumedly for the river, which

was farther from sight or hearing than Raen liked. But as fast as hatchlings grew, she conceded Iriscendra's need to eat. Eyrnir, as was his wont, withdrew about thirty paces from camp, circled, and lay down on the needled forest floor.

"Did you really just correct Iriscendra's grammar?" Veranna laughed. She closed the cover of her copy of *The Tree* that sat in her cross-legged lap.

"You teach your students one thing," Raen said, "I teach mine another."

"I find it interesting that she's chosen to speak Elvish. How much do you think she understands of what we're saying?"

"Every word."

Veranna blinked. "What? How?"

"I'm not exactly sure." Raen moved to Veranna's side, crossed her feet, and sat. "But Fiernoth—he's the oldest dragon in our pod—says that dragons just somehow innately understand languages. He always knew what I was saying to him from the time he was a hatchling, and when he's been near human settlements, he understood them too. None of the pod has ever run into a speaker whose language they couldn't translate."

"Fortunate dragons," Veranna said. "All the years and headaches I've endured in studying Vareinorean and Unsundered Elvish in an effort to translate Utterances..."

Hridayesh emerged from his tent and stretched. "You hens want to keep it down a bit? Your shrill voices carry."

Raen narrowed her eyes. "All caught up on your lazing, then?"

"You two would have done well to 'laze' a bit. The watches get long when you start them tired."

"I don't know what you're used to," Raen said, "But I'm no pampered pet that can't take care of herself. I don't need your advice."

"Your self-sufficiency doesn't improve my opinion of you."

Hridayesh's lip curled. "How are we dividing the watches tonight?"

Raen's glance flicked to Veranna. "Well, Veranna and I were planning on splitting it. If you want to pick a half and watch, that's up to you. I wouldn't presume to give you any instructions."

Hridayesh's sneer turned to a smirk. "At least you're figuring out the way of things a little. Now if you'll excuse me—do you trust a prisoner enough to go relieve himself, or do you need to come watch?"

Veranna grimaced. "We'll send Eyrnir with you." She craned her neck toward the griffon. "Good Eyrnir, would you mind performing a soldier's duty in the stead of our missing two-legged soldier?"

Eyrnir rose, reached his front talons out before him, and stretched his beak in a wide yawn that curled his tongue. He nodded. Just a few paces behind Hridayesh, the mount followed the assassin into the shadows.

Until Hridayesh emerged once again from the cover of the trees, Raen tapped a tense foot on the ground. But return he did, and Eyrnir seemed in no way ruffled or challenged. Perhaps Veranna was right—that there was some sort of bond between Ecleriast and the North Deklian that checked his behavior and the typical prisoner's inclination to make a dash for freedom.

Veranna slipped into her tent once it was fully dark, though the ladies had agreed she would not sleep. The fire from the day glowed at its core, where a few smoldering coals pulsed with a fading orange light. Raen hugged her knees to her chest and waited.

Hridayesh reclined against a tree trunk beside his tent and cleaned his khanda. At one point, he pulled a whetstone from his pack, placed the edge of his sword against it, then shook his head. He tucked the stone back amidst his gear.

In an effort to watch Hridayesh without being hawkish, Raen kept him in her peripheral vision. The hours crawled by, but the tightening grip of nervousness prevented Raen from falling victim to drowsiness. What was taking the dragons so long to fish? The dusk hours should have been ideal. The waxing moon rode high enough in the sky to peer between the summits of the trees, and it shone down on the campsite with cold impassivity.

A rustle to the west caught Raen's ear. She sat up straight.

"Mythrenese?" she said, though in a hushed tone. "Is that you?"

The reedy sound of a puff of air supplied her only answer, which preceded, only by seconds, the griffon's shrill yelp. Eyrnir stumbled to his feet. He took a few staggering steps, then crashed, beak-first, into the pine needles.

Raen leapt up. She sprang behind the nearest tree. "Who goes there?"

Another puff. A whistle through the air. Raen ducked. A *thock* rang out against the bark of her cover. Though she hardly dared look, she spied the fletched end of a dart protruding from the tree trunk mere inches from her shoulder. It still vibrated with the force of the impact.

She jammed her hand into the protective basket of her hilt and swept her schiavona from the scabbard. "Veran—"

Dragon-kin, at least a half-dozen, crashed into the camp from all sides. At least two brandished swords, while others circled some kind of cable above their heads. Raen did not wait, but charged for the beast closest to her. He was a dull, rust-colored creature with one horn half-shorn from his head and gleaming yellow eyes. His slit pupils were wide, and a psychotic grin stretched across his crooked-toothed snout.

He caught her sword stroke between the teeth of his serrated sword, and he wrenched his weapon with a twist of his wrist. The tug jolted Raen's arm, but her fingers fused tight around her grip, and she yanked her blade free before the brute either disarmed her or sundered her weapon. She came around for another stroke. It connected with the dragon-kin's chest, but chattered across his scales like a mallet down the bars of a xylophone. The mark she scored wept no blood.

Across camp, Veranna burst from her tent, but a red-and-black-robed dragon-kin and two warriors closed on her immediately. Some arcane-sounding words echoed from Veranna's lips, but the thundering response of the robed villain drowned them out. Crackling tore through the air and a strange, nose-tingling smell filled stung Raen's nose. Veranna braced herself and barked the final word of her chant. Raen could not interpret what had just transpired, but she was satisfied that Veranna seemed unscathed.

Opponents surrounded Raen. She lunged and spun. Her blade found a path between scales and sunk deep into the chest of one of her enemies. He dropped back, but not before something struck Raen's legs and wrapped around her with bruising force.

She swung again, but her grappled legs prevented a proper stroke. Her balance faltered.

Another impact battered her ribs and pinned her cast arm to her side. Bolas. Raen gritted her teeth and dug with her toes, but to no avail. She crashed to the ground. Her crowd of opponents roared.

Face pressed to the loose footing, Raen writhed to search past the tramping talons of the dragon-kin, and on the edge of camp, caught sight of Hridayesh. He met her glare with a dark-eyed gleam. He shrugged one shoulder, performed a two-fingered salute, and backed into the shadows and out of sight.

21

OF SYMBOLS AND SHELTER AND SICKNESS

As awful as I felt, as much as I shivered, and as many times as my stomach pain bunched me into a ball, I could not sleep. I hobbled around the shore I had declared my base of operations and arranged my collection of white stones in a large ring. It was a remarkably round rendering for an elf who was dizzy and miserable. I even managed to stave off passing out on a couple of occasions where my pain surged and filled my body with sickening heat.

After the ring was complete, I began arranging more stones in the shape of an outstretched wing within the circle. At least I hoped that was what it looked like. It was hard to tell with the twelve-foot span of the thing. I ran out of rocks half-way through the project and had to venture further downriver to gather more. It was tedious and painful, but better than laying on the ground wishing sleep would overtake me.

After what I guessed must have been about two hours of this limping occupation, my leg declared it had endured enough, and I lay back down in my nest of dry leaves and needles at the cliff's edge, where the wind had gathered enough of such chaff in a rocky cleft to make a decent bed. Well, at least a more decent bed than a rock-strewn shore. As hard as it was, I would need to endure at least another full day of lingering in one place before I began conducting my own search of the area for Majestrin and the others. Hopefully they had not gotten themselves into some kind of impossible bind without me.

Eventually, sleep transformed a few of my overnight hours from waking pain to dreaming delirium, where I relived the terror of the crash. Snatches of a struggle with a charcoal-scaled dragon-kin flashed between snippets of conversations and conflicts with officers and subordinates back in Delsinon. My attacker's stab into Majestrin's head interpolated through lessons Veranna taught from *The Tree*—her expression ever patient, and sometimes even bright when I finally grasped a nuanced concept. The guttural words of a curse rumbled from the dragon-kin's maw.

I did not remember any effect from the words. Had his curse failed? Had that happened at all, or was it just a product of fevered imaginings?

When I awoke to a cloudy, dismal morning, where a fine, drenching mist hung in the air and shrouded everything more than a few yards distant into gray silhouettes, I struggled to sit. I eased my pant leg up to my hip once again. My mottled flesh, which I had thought yesterday could not possibly look any worse, defied my most gruesome imaginings. The edges of the wound had developed blisters full of dark fluid, and the smell that clouded from the wound made me cough. I swore. If I lost my leg over a chance encounter with a statue . . .

My initial anger gave way before a wash of despair that gripped my chest with crushing force. What if I did lose my leg? Could I learn to ride again with only one? I had no useful skills other than the sword and the rein. I re-covered the festering wreckage with my pant leg.

"Where are you?" I thundered at the sky.

My voice fell dead in the dank air. A single, scoffing laugh shook my shoulders. *Where are you.* On the surface, I had meant Majestrin. But the more I thought about it, the more I knew the question was meant for Creo. Why had he splintered my group into who knows how many fragments? *The Almighty is the keeper of the innocent and the helpless.* Were the Elgadrim girls not just that? How did stranding me in the wilderness with a necrotizing gash use me as a vessel of his mercy? If things progressed as I feared, I would become a laughable bearer of his might.

My mouth tasted like I had fallen face-first into a rubbish pile. I licked my lips, and peeling skin snagged against my tongue. First things first—a drink, then perhaps a little foraging. I did not feel in the least bit hungry, but the intermittent sweat and chills, along with the constant throbbing that now blighted the region from my toes to my ribcage probably masked the fact that I had not eaten a decent meal in . . . how long had it been?

I hauled myself to my feet, and the earth tilted. My elbow, hip, knee, and cheekbone collided with river rock. Only when the twirling ceased did I open my eyes again. The foul coating already in my mouth mixed with the metallic taste of blood. I did eventually make it to the river's edge, but in more of a shambling crawl than a walk.

After a few sloppy sips of water, I rolled onto my back and stared at the sky. My strength was non-existent. Today I would rest and give my body a chance to beat back the fever—then I would be able to search for my companions.

The weather that day deteriorated from a hanging mist to a cold, pelting rain. I dragged myself to the forest's edge in search of some branches I might prop into a triangular shelter, but only gathered a half-dozen before I collapsed, utterly spent. I was freezing, but I was sweating. My stomach was empty, but it heaved as though I had gorged myself for days on end. Incapacitated as I was, I fumbled upright and leaned the boughs against one another. They fell over. Continually.

Creo, steady my hand to build this. I was not too proud to beg. Not now.

From one knee, I finally managed to brace three of the stoutest boughs against one another. I imagined a Patron holding each in place as I hauled my few smaller sticks up to prop between them. With a hand that shook so violently I could hardly close it around the clasp of my cloak, I unfastened the garment.

I swept it toward my shelter frame, and the whole thing toppled. I would have cried, but only the tremors of sobs took me. No tears spilled from my hot, sticky eyes. Dropping the cloak, I started again.

Prop some sticks. Rest, out of breath. Add another. Lay still until the careening earth steadied. I dug my fingers into the sodden weave of my cloak. My lank hair hung in dripping bundles over my eyes—its platinum color more akin to ash with all the grime. It took me another unreasonably long span of minutes to drag my garment over the wobbly, shabby shelter frame I had erected. But at least this time, it stayed upright. In a final expulsion of effort before my vision failed altogether, I flopped beneath the partial protection of my construct.

~

"*I*s it him?"
        "Is it *he*—but never mind, nobody says it like that. Anyway, I can't tell. Whoever it is has no signature at all. Do you sense one?"

"No, but s'more like plugging your nose than sumpin' has no smell."

"I know what you mean. We'd better go closer. What do you think these white rocks mean?"

"It looks like a ring—and what's that inside it? A wing maybe? Eyrnir, like your barding!"

I tried to stir, but my leaden body would not move. Whose voices did I hear? The padding of many footfalls ground rocks against one another. I opened one of my eyes just a slit—that seemed to require all the strength I had. Through the gaps between my shelter boughs, I beheld scaled talons and a set of large, tawny paws.

Someone gasped. "Creo's mercy—we can't find anything but problems today!"

A childish voice cried, "V'yennel! V'yennel, you awake?"

But after that, the voices drifted away, and a sea of oblivion absorbed me.

~

*R*aen rolled her head on a neck raw from the scraggly rope tied around it like a leash. The opposite end of the rope wound around the trunk of a stout maple, bare of leaves. She wriggled the fingers of her un-cast hand, but nothing she did seemed to ward off the tingling. The dragon-kin tied tight bonds, no doubt of that.

Rain dripped from the hem of her hood. Cold seeped into her shoulders through the wool that had hours ago ceased to repel the rain. Mud splattered her skirt.

She glanced to Veranna, who sat with her feet together, knees bent, and forearms propped upon her knees. Her hands, too, were bound, and she chafed under the same noose. The rain soaked the prophetess's hair, but only coiled its raven waves into tighter curls that framed her lovely, copper face with greater drama.

Some girls had all the luck.

Raen chuckled at the absurdity of the thought at such a desperate time. Luck was something they both seemed to lack.

The rusty-colored dragon-kin who had descended upon Raen in the wee hours of the morning approached from between the tents of the dragon-kin camp and nodded to the bronze-scaled creature that stood guard over the maidens. Had it really been less than a day since the attack? How could just hours feel like an eternity spent as captives?

"Did they let you know if you get to keep what you caught, Khagrosh?" the bronze guard asked.

Rusty-scales—Khagrosh apparently—rasped a repulsive hissing noise that scarcely passed for a laugh. "Lord Hanash makes that call." He stepped up to Raen, grabbed her chin and forced her face upward. "I can hope to Queldurik his lordship sees it my way, though. It's been too long since we've had anything quite so luscious in the spawning camps."

Raen fixed a glare over her horror. She hoped their words were somehow figurative, but regardless, she had no intention of finding out.

Khagrosh slapped Veranna's foot with his tail. "You interested in this one? I can put a word in for you."

The bronze guard guffawed. "A noble offer, but your word won't surpass the bidding, no matter how deep you're in with Hanash. The chances the witch will spawn a curse-bearer are too great for them to waste her on a grunt like me. Now if you don't mind, I need to go get some tonic, if we have any more. I'm starting to feel run through."

Khagrosh released Raen's face. "By all means. A pox on the blasted sun. You'd think all this rain would help, but it really doesn't."

The guard turned to depart. "Blame the elves, like the

saying goes. Some of them will pay a little back. Soon." He sneered at Veranna and Raen, then turned his back on them and tramped from sight.

Khagrosh took up bronze-scales's post and blew a long sigh. He planted the butt of his halberd on the ground and yawned.

"Veranna," Raen whispered. "*Tre mesnesir vocet—*"

Khagrosh wheeled on her. "None of your gibberish. You keep it up, I'll move you to opposite sides of the camp and you'll each get your own guard."

A thousand questions raced through Raen's mind. How long a journey did the dragon-kin intend to drag Veranna and her upon? How long did they dare wait before attempting escape? If what the bronze guard said about how poor he felt by the end of his watch was consistent, they stood the best chance of escape near the end of the guard change, during the daylight hours, the next day. Where would they be by then? How could she coordinate such a risky endeavor with the prophetess if speaking to one another risked having them separated?

Raen shifted her attention to Veranna. The half-elf held her head high, face skyward and eyes closed. The prophetess mouthed words, but her expression lacked the creases of worry Raen could feel deepening between her own brows and around her pursed lips. Veranna's countenance not only lacked fretfulness, but exuded peace.

Whatever words Veranna prayed, it could not hurt if Raen echoed a few of them from her own heart. She breathed deep and bowed her head. *Almighty Maker, I'm out of ideas, but I'm listening.*

J was vaguely aware of some lifting, shoving, and shuffling. Some degree of bickering and frustration volleyed among those who had joined me. They rolled me to my back, and rain spattered my face. I grimaced and turned my head to the side. More tugging jostled my ribcage, and I groaned.

"Here, Iriscendra—your talons are smaller. Can you try these fasteners?"

Iriscendra. The hatchling. And the other voice must have been Raen's indigo dragonling. What had she called him? Myth-something.

More prodding at my side ensued. "Too tight. V'yennel? You need take off, um, elf-shell?"

Myth-what's-his-name laughed. "Elf-shell?"

My thoughts exactly. What was she talking about?

"Ohhhh," the dragonling continued. "You mean armor. It's called armor."

Take off my armor? "Why?" I rasped.

"Eyrnir can't get a very good grip on you because of it."

I inched a weary hand over to the breastplate's side buckles. "Is he still wearing his barding?" My eyelids were too thick and heavy to open them and find out myself.

"Yes," Iriscendra said.

"Lash the plate to it," I said. I gasped for breath for many moments. Even those few words had sapped me like a long run. "I will not lose the suit."

My sluggish fingers pried at the fasteners until they slipped looser, and then scaled claws took over the task. As much as I wanted to help, I simply flopped about like a sack of meal as they worked me out of the armor. Even so, they cradled me in gentle grasps, slipped the breastplate over my head, and rolled me to my side. Bad leg up, thankfully, since the motion still hurt like the bites of a hundred fiends.

184

A few moments later, a powerful grip bunched the padding across my back. Strong limbs gathered me against a warm body, and for once, my chills abated. The scent of a warm-but-clean fur wrapped around me.

"It appears, young dragons, we have found the Lieutenant Commander just scarcely in time." The speaker's voice was creaky but resonant. I had heard the voice so infrequently that it took a long stretch for me to recall its owner. Eyrnir, the griffon member of my Windrider Battalion. Or what was left of it. The thought galled me.

"Let us hope Majestrin knows better than we what to do for our liege's affliction." The feathery whoosh of wide wings filled my ears, and we thrust upward.

Majestrin. Eyrnir's words implied he still lived. For the first time in what seemed like forever, I let go of consciousness in relative peace.

22

_____

RESCUE

_R_aen lay on her side in the back of the rough wagon, scarcely able to care about how the planks rubbed her cheek raw. Her gnawing hunger eclipsed those scrapes and the rope burns. The gray of dawn lightened the eastern sky, dimming the stars that had finally emerged from the previous days' rain. Dawn meant the dragon-kin caravan would soon come to a halt, and that meant Raen had just a few hours to finish the final planning for how she would enact escape for her and Veranna.

She fixed her gaze on the eastern sky. Sunlight—the only advantage they had in this whole mess. When the time came, would they even be able to flee? A couple days of no food and very little water had left her limbs shaky. Veranna did not seem the type to endure lean hardship with much fortitude, but then again, how could she know? It was not as if the dragon-kin had made it possible for Raen to learn much from the prophetess.

Would Veranna be plotting an escape of her own? All it seemed she was doing was praying, hour after hour. They praying probably didn't hurt, but they needed to *act*.

A growing rumble of conversation from up ahead caught Raen's ear. At least she guessed it must be conversation—the dragon-kin's language was so guttural and alien, it was hard to imagine the syllables acting as words. She writhed into a sitting position.

The wagon had reached the apex of a hill, and ahead, perhaps to the northwest, an encampment sprawled. Scores of tents stood in rows, and armored dragon-kin paced the perimeter. A crackling fire towered at the camp's center, around which stood a half-dozen robe-clad figures. On the far side of the fire, Raen found a rough, thick-beamed table, and on its surface sprawled . . . her eyes bulged. Who was that? Could it be someone else from Ecleriast's party? Or even Ecleriast himself? Her throat caught at the notion.

But no, the flickering firelight revealed the man lying on the table was dark-haired. Stocky. And very dead. Raen averted her gaze from the gruesome, gaping cavity the dragon-kin had opened in his chest. So much blood.

Veranna was also upright in the wagon. When she had moved from seeming sleep to observing had gotten past Raen's notice. Their dragon-kin entourage seemed to have their attention aimed at the encampment, so Raen dared lean over to Veranna.

"Do you think that's what they have planned for us?" Raen's whisper came only with great effort, her throat was so dry.

"I doubt it," Veranna whispered back. "Their talk of bidding and claiming insinuated something much more horrifying."

A surge of panic rose in Raen's chest.

A sharp whack of wood on wood cut the conversation off. Their guard shook his spear at them. "Don't get chatty."

Raen clamped her lips shut. The wagon rolled down the hill, closer to the encampment. The fifteen dragon-kin in their caravan had been problem enough for her to turn over in her mind. Now they had to outwit a hundred. She beat back the shard of despair that threatened to pierce her.

When the wagon lurched to a halt about fifty yards within the encampment layout, Khagrosh grabbed the arm of a passerby. He grunted something in his impossible tongue.

Raen frowned. "I wish their disgusting language wasn't so un-learnable," she muttered.

"Hush," Veranna replied. "Creo has granted me the inter- pretation of tongues today. I'll keep an ear out for anything important."

Not that they would be able to discuss anything under such close watch. Raen drew little comfort from someone else knowing what the beasts were saying.

"He's looking for someone named Hanash, but Hanash hasn't arrived here yet. They're waiting for him. He has somethi —" Veranna clamped her lips shut and looked at the bed of the wagon when the guard came marching behind her.

"Not uncomfortable enough yet, I see," the guard snarled. He whipped a filthy rag in the air beside him with a snap, then jammed it in Veranna's mouth. He tied the ends of the strip behind her head.

The prophetess turned amber eyes fathomless with long-suffering toward the captor, and he blinked. The overly-quick way he turned away betrayed the conflict he must have felt when confronted with Veranna's expression—she had a power in her eyes that Raen could not deny. The guard stepped away. He re-established his glare and aimed it at Raen.

"You keep your trap shut or I'll find a gag for you too."

Raen nodded.

The dragon-kin continued an exchange of words, which

included some pointing and gesturing to the west—deeper into camp. Khagrosh nodded and waved the wagon onward.

"You're in luck, my lovelies," he said. "Seems they see fit to put prisoners in tents around these parts."

Raen mulled the comment over for a moment. "That won't keep our friends from finding us!" she blurted. "They'll rescue us yet, you'll see."

Veranna furrowed her brow at first, but then nodded emphatically. "Mmm-hmmm," she managed from behind the gag.

Khagrosh laughed. "I don't think so. But if that thought keeps you going, believe what you like. I have it on good authority that your pals are either dead or deserting. Look around and get used to this," he said with a wave of his arm. "We're all you've got now."

The longer he keeps thinking we're looking for a rescue, the better. Sadly, I fear he's at least partially right. Veranna and I are on our own. Raen faked a crestfallen expression.

The wagon slowed to a stop, and Khagrosh unhooked and lowered the tail gate. "Out. Straight to the tent or I'll throw you in."

By the look of his banded arms, Raen did not doubt he might deliver on his threat. She could not help but eye her schiavona strapped to his back as she passed by, however. A few more hours of waiting, and she would need to have a plan to eliminate him quietly, get her sword back, and see Veranna out of the impending nightmare.

All things considered, the tent was not a bad place to linger. Khagrosh tethered both maiden's neck ropes to the center pole, which re-awoke the burning pain at Raen's throat, but she gritted her teeth through it. He checked both their wrist bonds, then left. His shadow outside the flap assured Raen he had gone no farther than to assume a guard post just outside. Talking to Veranna would still be impossible, especially as the camp quieted with the rise of the sun and all concealing environmental noise came to an end.

Not that it mattered. The moment Khagrosh left, Veranna lay down and closed her eyes. By the tempo of her breathing, it seemed plausible she had gone straight to sleep. How? Escape plans would not churn in her mind as they did in Raen's?

Raen attempted to follow Veranna's example and reclined as well. After all, if she might have to fight for her life and then flee as fast as feet would carry her later that day, a little rest would be a great help. As she suspected, though, plotting, planning, and worrying made the morning hours drag. Eventually, fatigue did grant her occasional snippets of sleep, but every rustle, sigh, or animal snort woke her and sent her heart hammering.

As did the high-pitched scream that woke even Veranna somewhere around midday.

Raen strained to listen through the rising scuffle beyond the tent wall. A group of dragon-kin yammered in their abrasive voices to one another, but amidst it also came whimpers. Crying children? The tramping of feet and sniffling sobs drew nearer. Would fortune have it that she and Veranna would be held in the same camp as the Elgadrim girls?

Stretching her leg as far out as she could, Raen poked her toe under the bottom seam of the tent. She lay on her side as far from the center post as her noose would allow, raised her leg, and peered through the space she had opened.

Her skewed vantage point only afforded her a glimpse of the group that passed perhaps twenty paces away, and that glimpse only displayed figures from about the knees down. Four shuffling dragon-kin—two in armor and two in black robes, surrounded three pairs of grubby, bare, human feet. Ragged tatters of what must have been shifts or nightdresses hung in filthy rags about those legs.

A gust of chill air blew through the gap Raen had opened

by lifting the tent. A flame of fury sprang up in her gut, fanned by the cold. Children, barefoot at this time of year—and terrified? Could the dragon-kin exhibit any viler behavior? The concrete reality of the girls' presence demanded swift action.

The group passed from sight, and Raen released the tent canvas. Holding it up was beginning to make her thigh muscles knot up anyway. Her anger threatened to boil over and steal any degree of calculated planning she might undertake, so she took a long breath and closed her eyes. What horrors awaited her fell secondary now—those girls must see liberty, at any cost.

∼

I know Eyrnir did his absolute best to keep from jarring or jostling me as we flew, but when I regained consciousness, every beat of his feathered wings drove through me and racked me with pain. I shivered convulsively, although I could tell my skin radiated dry heat. We followed the course of the river for what might have been hours or days...it was probably hours, but the agony of each semi-lucid moment distorted their duration.

At a time when the late-day sun glared and lanced my eyes with pain, we left the river's course and headed west, into the mountains. Our descent took us toward the wide mouth of a cave, though the crevice's ceiling was low. I cringed as we glided beneath the cave's eaves, sure Eyrnir would bump his head or wings upon it. He navigated it with ease. I reminded myself that griffons were cliff-dwellers—of course he would know how to make the approach without bashing either of us into the rock face.

I lowered my heavy eyelids again once the cave's dark swallowed us. It would take a moment for my vision to adjust anyway, and I did not even possess the energy to focus my eyes long enough in the dark to force the issue. Eyrnir lowered me gently to the ground.

"Silverlord," echoed Mythrenese's voice. "We've found him, praise the Maker!"

"Praise the Maker, indeed!"

The response sent the first sensation of true elation I had felt in ages. Unmistakably, it was Majestrin's deep rumble. I felt it through the stone of the floor as well as heard it. If I could have moved, I would have run to him and hugged him. If no one was looking.

Mythrenese continued, "But he's in terrible shape. We're not sure what's wrong with him."

Majestrin sniffed. From the scraping over stone that neared, I assumed he drew nearer to me. "Something's rotting, can you not tell?" In a quieter voice, he urged me, "Vinyanel, can you hear me? Can you speak?"

I pried my eyelids open. Silver scales filled my field of vision, as Majestrin looked down at me with leaf-green eyes, fraught with concern.

"What's going on? Why can't I sense your signature?"

"I cou'n't either, 'Jestrin," Iriscendra piped up. She scampered to Majestrin's side and added her own furrowed regard to his. Majestrin shrank away from her a half step.

"None of us can." Mythrenese shook his head. "Very strange."

I thought back to the guttural words of the dragon-kin's curse—the one that seemed to have no effect. "Could it be..." A retch claimed my sentence for a moment. I swallowed; not that I had any saliva to work down. I might have even been out of bile by now. "Is there . . . a curse that . . . remove your signature?"

Majestrin reached up with a scaled talon and scratched his cheek. That's when I noticed the traces of purple blood that crusted the scales on the back of his head and cheeks. "It's possible. I don't know of anything firsthand, but then, I've never made it my business to know much about curses at all. You know what they say about getting too deep in the counsel of the enemy."

Iriscendra cocked her head. "No. Who's 'they,' and what they say?"

I could not restrain a chuckle, even though laughing ripped at every muscle I had. I whispered, "*Seek ye the light and know it as a beloved companion. Tarry not on the paths of Darkness, for what wisdom might linger there is bought with grief and suffering.*" I panted for breath after reciting the passage. "Sage words from the scribes . . . who penned *The Tree*."

"Ohhhhh," Iriscendra replied. Her narrow eyes took on a faraway look as she seemed to churn through what I had said.

I turned as best I could to Majestrin. "Someone help me sit up."

Eyrnir positioned himself behind me and nudged my shoulder with his gold-plumed head, but the moment I lifted my upper body from the ground, the world tilted and spun again. "Gah...no, no...never mind. Set me back down." I clapped a palm to my forehead and waited for everything around me to stop twirling.

"You look as though you feel much like I did," Majestrin said.

"That is what I want to know," I said, though weakly, owing to my vertigo. "How did you survive being stabbed in the *head*?"

"We dragons are thick-skulled," Majestrin said. "In many ways. But I'm certain this dragon-kin wasn't fool enough to think he could kill me. His attack pierced the area right behind my ear that controls my flight stability. Without the ability to coordinate my wings and tail, down I went. I do apologize I did not care for you, my rider, better."

I guffawed. "Are you joking? Majestrin, I thought you were as good as dead. You have nothing to apologize for." I choked up. It took me a moment to regain any ability to wrangle words. "I am glad to see you again."

"Any guesses when you might be able to fly again?" Mythrenese asked, his voice timid.

Majestrin paused. The muscles around his eyes tightened, and he blinked away a flicker of doubt. "My walking balance is much better today than it was, but flying is still out of the question. I've never had this kind of injury before, so I don't know how long I'll be constrained."

The initial elation seeing Majestrin alive only lasted a short while in eclipsing my symptoms, however, and my violent shivering re-emerged. At Majestrin's command, the small dragons covered me with the blankets I had in my gear—Maker's mercy, I had my gear again—but even the heavy wool did little to comfort me.

Huddled under the blankets, I muttered. "I am going to have to sit up. And Mythrenese, I need you to find the field surgeon's kit in my saddlebags. I have a wound that desperately needs re-dressing."

"Something new, or the leg still?" Majestrin asked. The note of reproach in his voice rankled me, but I shoved down my pride.

"The leg."

The young dragons propped me up against the cave wall. It took a full minute at minimum for my vertigo to slow from a wild, stomach-twisting careen to a mere rocking sensation. I worked my pant leg up with sluggish, clumsy fingers.

A collective gasp broke out when I revealed the gash in my thigh. Iriscendra whimpered.

"Forgive my saying so, Vinyanel," Majestrin choked, "but that's disgusting."

He was right. It was awful. Enough to make even a seasoned warrior's stomach turn, though the stench the wound emitted compounded its nauseating impact. I fumbled through the medical bag for a long strip of linen bandage, which I rolled sloppily around the wound. I might have had some salve in the pack, but it seemed to me the equivalent of whitewashing rubble at this point. At least with it covered, the tension in the cavern eased a bit.

"I'll be much better after a little rest, now that I have shelter."

"I'm sure you're right," Majestrin said. His tone sounded far less assured than his words implied.

But what to do next? Something was missing in all this... right! Incessant nagging. Where was Veranna? And what about the red-headed baby dragon thief? That fact that Veranna was not hovering over me, pestering, was somehow discomforting. "Why aren't Veranna and . . .what was it? Raen...? And Hridayesh. Where are they?"

Eyrnir sighed. "We don't really know. When the dragonlings and I went searching for you, they vanished."

"Vanished?" I turned my head enough to frown at the griffon, though I doubted I seemed very intimidating.

"We fear for them, sir," Mythrenese said. "Their camp did not appear intentionally broken. As a matter of fact, all their gear remained, but we haven't seen them."

Under the circumstances, even Veranna would not have simply wandered off. I steadied the hundred imaginings of what might have drawn the rest of my companions off. "Have you sought them? Are there any clues to follow?"

"It was a hard choice, but I insisted we keep looking for you, first." The griffon padded toward me and sat beside me. The warmth radiating from his fur was soothing, even if it failed to halt my shivers.

"We found 'Jestrin first," Iriscendra said. "He still had...sig... sing-a-chur?"

My chuckle hurt like a pike in the gut. "Signature." Icy

fingers of concern plucked away the shred of levity. "Thank the Maker you found us both."

Majestrin added, "I agree, but enough talk for now. You need to rest. And once you're strong enough to ride, we'll begin our search for the maidens. And Hridayesh, if you insist."

23

A CHILD'S PRAYER

*J*ust how deeply did dragon-kin sleep, and if they did not, how debilitating was the daylight to the foul creatures? Raen prayed the sun's effects would make the villains' feet less fleet than her own and their ears dull to her plans.

The dragon-kin camp had been quiet for several hours, and Raen might have mistaken the stillness for the deep of night, were it not for the sun illuminating the canvas of Raen and Veranna's tent. So far into the wilderness, the silence rang ominous. No birdsong lilted outside, no cricket chirped, as if every living creature had fled the dragon-kin's vile presence.

Khagrosh must have been feeling the uncomfortable effects of his waning "tonic" by now. Raen inched her way toward Veranna, who sat with her back against the tent's center post. Would she be able to convey any semblance of a plan to the prophetess without speaking to hash her idea out? The moment she chose to open her mouth would be the one Khagrosh tramped in to silence her.

Raen eyed Veranna's gag and her hands bound behind her. Would it be possible to remove the gag by tugging at the back of it with her teeth? Only one way to find out.

She nudged the prophetess's shoulder with her own. Veranna turned her head only partly to Raen and raised an eyebrow. Raen nudged her again, this time leaning into Veranna's shoulder to encourage her to sit forward. Veranna obliged, and when she did...

The tail ends of her gag fell slack, and the rag hung from between her clenched teeth.

Raen stifled a gasp.

A quick nod shook the rag from Veranna's mouth, and she reached up, hands free of chafing ropes, to rub the reddened corners of her mouth.

I'll have to hear this story later, I guess. Raen shrugged.

In a swift and silent moment, Veranna worked Raen's bonds loose, both wrists and neck, and without a word, Raen undid the knot at the prophetess's nape. The exhilaration of freedom flooded into her head and drove away her nagging hunger and thirst. They might just have a chance. But the trickiest part lay ahead...hopefully the prophetess would catch on.

"It's the only way," Raen whispered, but louder than she really needed to for Veranna to hear.

The prophetess snapped her attention to Raen, her face quizzical.

Trust me. Just listen. "Put these in your mouth," Raen said. She gave the prophetess nothing. "The moment we swallow them, we'll be dead, just like that." Her eyes flicked toward the tent opening.

A rustle outside the tent. "How many times do I have to tell you . . .?"

The spark of understanding ignited in Veranna's face. "Will

it hurt?" she asked. Her eyes pleaded in a convincing show of trepidation.

"Only for a moment, but then all this will be over. On the count of three, then. One—"

Khagrosh burst into the tent. "Oh, no you don't!" Raen's schiavona glinted on his back.

She prepared a foot sweep for his stout legs.

"Creo's judgment befall you!" Veranna intoned, although in a husky whisper. She leapt to her feet and thrust her hands toward the approaching dragon-kin

Simultaneously, Khagrosh said, "Now you spit out whatever you put in your—what?" He stopped, mid stride. His hands flew to his throat. A hissing and popping sound arose in the tent, a sound that seemed to come from Khagrosh himself.

In an instant, his eyeballs sunk, shriveled, and disappeared into their sockets. His flesh shrunk around his bones, reduced to a third of its volume. His atrophied hide split in dusty fissures like hard clay in years of drought. He opened his maw, but not a scream, a hiss, or a curse was forthcoming. The warrior collapsed under the weight of his plate armor, and when he hit the tent floor, his shrunken corpse broke into pieces.

Raen froze in place, stunned. What in creation just happened? She shook off her surprise. "Let's get out of here."

Revulsion and morbid curiosity warred within Raen's will, and she could not decide whether to look away from the ruinous pile of what used to be Khagrosh or to stare. Despite her conflicted emotions, she reached down and plucked a knife in a sheath from the rubble. And then her schiavona.

Raen poked her head from the tent and surveyed the camp. As she suspected, no one moved amidst the tents. Doubtless, there would be perimeter guards, but they would deal with those only when they must.

"Ready?" she whispered. "Let's—"

Veranna stood in the middle of the tent, her hands splayed before her, and her horrified gaze locked upon them.

"Veranna?" Raen buckled her sword belt around her waist. "We need to hurry. Are you all right."

The prophetess's only reply was a silent shake of her head.

"I don't pretend to understand what just happened, but it appears you don't either." Raen took a few steps back to her fellow prisoner. She pressed Khagrosh's knife into Veranna's hand. "I think Aulus's girls are here. They're little. Barefoot. Maybe freezing to death."

Finally, Veranna made eye contact with Raen. She tightened her fingers around the sheath. "In this encampment? I thought I heard crying but wasn't sure if I had dreamt it."

"You didn't. We need to find them before sundown and get them out of here."

A deep breath brought Veranna back to her usual composed expression. "You're right. Where do you think we should start?"

Raen scanned the ground to the right, where the girls must have passed when she watched them. The previous day's rain left the ground soft, and the activity of the camp had killed much of the grass in the spaces between tents. With tension tying her middle into knots, she scanned the surroundings, but the narrow causeways between tents could have hidden doom just around the next corner. She strained to listen.

Certainty was a luxury beyond Raen's means. And time was doubly precious. Before phantom footfalls and worry crumbled her resolve, she stole over to the place where she thought the girls had walked.

A multitude of tracks churned the ground, but most of them proved to be of the three-toed variety. Occasional boot prints intermixed with the clawed prints.

"I'm not really much of a tracker," Raen sighed. "This might be—"

"There!" Veranna pointed to the earth to Raen's left. Sure enough, a petite print of a bare foot compressed the mud.

Raen bent low, and with a glance as scattered and wary as a hunted hare, searched for further prints.

She and Veranna skirted close to tents, but the child-prints did not lead them far. The tracks veered into grassier territory along one of the rows of tents. But at least they had a small lead before the tracks failed. Raen pushed her tangled hair from her eyes. A better woodsman would have been able to track the girls, even in the grass. If she survived this insane ordeal, it would be something to practice.

The encampment, Raen discovered, consisted of five spokes of about ten tents each, all arrayed around the central altar. They had followed the tracks a third of the way around the wheel before the trail headed down one of the spokes.

The clank of armor, or perhaps a scabbard against strides, rang in Raen's ears. She pulled Veranna between two tents. A perimeter guard, perhaps? Hopefully the girls were not housed in one of the outer-edge tents. Raen took comfort from the fact that would be a stupid choice, inviting escape—and the dragon-kin weren't stupid. Once they found the girls somewhere in the interior, though, they would still have to navigate the perimeter. It was crazy to even try to rescue them. And hopeless. And non-negotiable.

Once the metal clanking receded to Raen's liking, she crept from between the tents again. "One tent at a time," she whispered to Veranna.

"I think it's best if we peer under the side if we can." Veranna licked her lips. "Less prone to revealing too much of us to the occupants."

The first tent was empty. The second revealed the winged back of a sleeping dragon-kin just inches from where Raen inched the canvas up. Her breath snagged in her throat.

Veranna tapped Raen's shoulder. The prophetess jerked her head toward the next tent. She cupped a hand around her ear.

In the stillness, Raen bent her attention on nothing but sound. She wanted to close her eyes to focus further, but did not dare, lest she miss the approach of some danger.

Sniffling.

Raen sprang for the next tent. She placed her ear right against the canvas.

"I'm here with you, Cassia. Creo will hear our prayers," a girl within the tent whispered.

When Raen turned for the front of the tent, Veranna had already slipped through the opening. A quick glance indicated no observers, so Raen ducked in as well.

Three young girls, ranging from barely old enough to begin learning her letters to one closing in on adolescence, huddled together in one of the rear corners of the tent. Their long hair hung in ratted clumps, the color of the strands hard to determine with how dirty it was. Grime smeared their faces. Their lips peeled. Ropes bound them hand and foot. All three stared with round, gray eyes.

Veranna held a forefinger to her lips.

The littlest had her knees drawn up to her chest, and new tears had cut pale tracks down her cheeks. She leaned toward the eldest. "Are they Patrons?" she whispered.

The middle child scoffed. "Think a moment. *The Tree* says the Patrons are all men."

"Male," the eldest said, her voice scarcely audible. "But who cares." She shot an accusatory glare at Raen and Veranna, but the faintest spark of hope flickered under her suspicion. "Why are you here?"

"What have you been praying for?" Veranna asked. Her voice flowed with such warmth, it smoothed even Raen's tight-wound nerves.

"That Creo would send someone to save us," the littlest peeped. A genuine smile broke over her face.

"Well, then. "Veranna smiled in return. She cut the eldest girl's bonds. "What are we waiting for?"

Raen stepped forward to help with the ropes, but a flap of canvas behind her crackled. The girls shrieked. Raen spun. Two dragon-kin stood in the gap, swords bare.

Without a thought, Raen lunged. The point of her schiavona found a swift path between the lead dragon-kin's bands of armor and into his chest. His partner grabbed his slumping body and tossed it aside, nearly wrenching Raen's sword grip from her hand. She tugged the blade free, but not before her victim's toppling weight yanked her off-balance.

The remaining dragon-kin swung at Raen, and only in the last possible moment did she manage to put the center tent post between herself and the whistling blade. The weapon met the post with a splintering crack.

Raen wheeled and swept her sword in an upper cut, which cleft a gash in the rear of the tent. "Out!" she cried.

Veranna had managed to free the eldest girl entirely and the feet of the middle child, but the youngest still struggled against both sets of bonds. The eldest bent and scooped her up before she fled through the exit Raen had made.

Her parry caught the dragon-kin's next attack with a loud ring. Confound it! Between the girls' shrieking—who could blame them—and the sword clatter, the whole camp would be up in a matter of moments. Veranna and the girls were clear. Time to go on the offensive.

Raen ducked her opponent's next swing and repositioned her stance. Like a viper, she struck. Her sword-point turned on an armor plate, however, and only scored along the beast's ribcage. Dark blood wept from the wound, but not enough. *Deal death or receive it.*

She caught the next attack in low guard, then leaned to the

side and thrust the fullest-force kick she could muster at the dragon-kin's knee. Her foot landed with a sickening *crack*, and the creature's joint collapsed the wrong direction. He staggered.

Good enough for me! Raen darted out the back of the tent, after Veranna and the captives.

24

A WOUND'S DEPTH

"*Why do you coddle him?" Father snapped.*

"*Coddle?" Mother replied. "I simply offer him the tenderness a child deserves. If I seem to give more than I should, perhaps it is because I must do enough giving for both of us." A tear slid down her pale-as-cream cheek.*

I shrank back from the crack I had opened between my bedroom door and its frame. Rarely did my mother fling such sharp words. Were they arguing about me? My chest tightened. How would he respond? The ensuing silence goaded me back to my limited view of the discussion.

Father gripped his forehead in his hand. "I do not mean for this to come between us, Lirallyn. It is so . . . very . . . hard."

"*Then let it go," Mother whispered.*

Father snapped his head up. "Let it go? I cannot simply blithely convince myself it doesn't matter that our son is dead. Gone. Never to become . . . all because of Vinyanel's recklessness."

The words raked across my soul like claws. I recoiled, and tears sprang to my eyes, but I blinked them back. I was weary of crying. The sea of tears I had already shed had done nothing to wash away death. They certainly would not cleanse my father of his hatred for me—in fact, if he caught me sniveling, it would probably only under-gird it.

"Vaedhreth, you know that's not true." Mother paused. She took a tremulous breath. "Vinyanel never intended for that afternoon to go so wrong."

"I did not say it was intentional," Father replied. "I said he was reckless. He is the eldest, and it is high time he developed some judgment. But even should he become the most temperate, wisest elf in all creation, I still call Findellis's life too high a price for that."

I crawled over to my bed, climbed in, and pulled the covers over my head.

"So in losing your youngest son, you would discard the one who remains?" Mother said.

Father replied, but I did not hear it, because I dragged the pillow over my head and mashed it against my ears.

"Lieutenant Commander..." A muffled voice worked through the down.

I shook my head. Lieutenant Commander? I was just a youth. Who was the voice calling?

"Lieutenant Commander, can you hear me? Vinyanel?"

The dark of my little bedroom, the crinkle of my pillow faded away. There was only rough wool over me and a bed of rock below. My eyes fluttered open, and Majestrin's gleaming snout filled my vision.

"Take a drink," the dragon said. He pushed my waterskin toward me. "You're muttering and thrashing again."

My tongue felt thick, like it filled most of my mouth. I had no strength—and no will—to lift my arm for the skin. I closed my eyes again.

"Mythrenese, come here," Majestrin said. "Pour a sip of this into the Lieutenant Commander's mouth. The skin's so tiny, I'll just end up dousing him."

The vague sensation of something cool trickling over my lips and tongue encouraged me to swallow.

"No more," Majestrin said. "He'll simply vomit again."

"Has he eaten anything since we found him?"

"Nothing that's stayed down."

Someone gripped my shoulder and shook it. "V'yennel! Be awake."

The hatchling. Could I muster the will to live for Iriscendra's sake? I forced one eye open just a slit. A beaming smile lit up her pearlescent face.

"You see, getting better!"

Majestrin sighed. "Maybe, little hatchling. Why don't you and Mythrenese go fishing? We'll need something for him to eat when he's up and about soon."

"K, 'Jestrin!" Iriscendra scrambled toward the cave mouth.

Mythrenese huffed. "Fishing? But we need to look for Raen before the prophetess's trail fades too much and we can't track her."

"After the fishing. Now go, before you lose track of the hatchling."

"Iriscendra, slow down!" Mythrenese's voice trailed after her, and after a leathery flurry of wings, all fell silent, except for an occasional distant drip somewhere deeper in the cavern.

"How long do you give him?" Eyrnir asked in a low voice.

"I'm no medic," Majestrin replied. "He's a fighter, but unless something changes, and soon, this is going to kill him. In days at best."

The small part of me that still had a shred of fight left bristled at the fact that Majestrin was calling me as good as dead. Another part of me thought of the hatchling—essentially orphaned and looking to me for parentage, as absurd as that seemed.

"Majestrin," I rasped. I opened my eyes so I could look at him. "If I die, you need to take care of Iriscendra."

"What?" Majestrin snaked his neck back to recoil from me.

"Is that so horrible a request? Who does she have? Raen? She could be dead."

"Well..." Majestrin rubbed his chin. "There's Mythrenese."

I rolled my eyes. "He scarcely has enough sense to take care of himself. And with the way Raen has somehow convinced him his breath gifting is evil, how long will he last on his own? You need to teach her to be a real dragon." I heaved for breath. Just a few sentences robbed me of air worse than a sprint in full gear.

"I can't, Vinyanel." Majestrin's head drooped.

"You cannot, or you will not?"

"I will not because I cannot." Majestrin's eyes flashed. "I am no parent."

"Many people find themselves in the position to have to parent unexpectedly," I said. "They figure it out."

"I tried figuring it out . . . once." He clapped a talon over his face. Tension rippled beneath his scales. "The world has an insane marauder to contend with, thanks to my parenting skills."

I turned the statement over in my mind. Had Majestrin not said something before about the breaking of the signature weaving the perfect way to corrupt a dragon? I opened my mouth to speak again, but coughing gripped me instead. A splash of burning yellow fluid churned up from my stomach and onto the cave floor.

"Lay still," Majestrin said. "I know you're just going to kill yourself asking me questions, so here it is: I had a mate once... millennia ago now. She was the loveliest of silver dragons, graceful, quick, and with the brightest laugh." He paused. He blinked slowly. "She bore our first egg, and just before it hatched, went through the ritual of entwining her signature with our daughter's. I still remember how magical the day she hatched was. My mate and my daughter were an extension of one another—beautiful, full of joy. Creo's masterwork.

But the hunters came, like they always do. A hundred of them en masse. We went to battle, defending our lair and our hatchling." Majestrin no longer looked at me, but into the distance, and I knew the day flashed across his mind's eye, as vivid as when it occurred. How often had I not done the same with the day I took Findellis riding?

"They swamped her, took her down like an animal—when we had never so much as eaten one of their chickens. Her dying request was that I flee with our daughter, so after a final blast of cold to the hunters, that's what I did.

But the signature weaving kept us from being as close as we needed to be. She mourned her mother, wasted, and I forced her to eat enough to stay alive. She fought me on every bite. Over time, she went from sad, to rebellious, to irrational. The insanity took her, and eventually, she tried to kill me. She needed the one to whom she had been woven." His whole body sagged. He sniffed and blinked away tears.

"And that is why, Lieutenant Commander, I forbid you to die."

If only the will of a dragon could sway such things.

~

"*W*hat do we do?" the eldest of the liberated girls cried. She clutched the little one to her chest.

"Run!" Raen replied. She jabbed a finger toward the woods. "That way."

The girls staggered forward with Veranna close behind, and Raen retreated backward, her glance sweeping the camp for signs of further pursuit. Dragon-kin stumbled from more tents than she cared to count. Raen spun and broke into a full-out dash after Veranna.

The girls' short legs, bare feet, and probable lack of nourishment slowed their escape. The sharp hiss of an arrow flew past Raen's ear, and she flinched. It stuck in the ground just inches from Veranna's foot.

"Veranna!" Raen cried. "Has Creo got any more judgment to deal out? We've drawn more company than I'm interested in entertaining."

The look Veranna shot back to Raen was far from amused.

Point taken. No time to be cute. Two more arrows whistled in. The cries of dragon-kin closed upon them. When Raen looked back, a quick survey revealed a score of the villains on their trail. Most wore the banded mail of warriors, but toward the back of the group, a black-robed creature wearing a gargoyle talisman around his neck roared the bulk of the commotion to the group. The sickly green light that pulsated from the talisman gave Raen the shivers.

The black-robed dragon-kin swept his hand in a circular gesture before him, and the talisman flared to bright white. The roar of flame broke out ahead. Raen whipped her head around.

A wall of green flame towered in front of Veranna, who recoiled and shielded her face from it. The girls wailed.

Raen skidded to a halt. *The girls couldn't be in the flames, could they?* No, the screams and whimpers were those of fear, not pain. *Still, what a disaster.*

"It completely rings the girls!" Veranna hollered back to her. "There's no way—"

The prophetess abandoned her explanation in favor of diving off to one side as more arrows sought to bring her flight to a close. Only two of the pursuers had bows, thankfully, and it seemed they were incapable of a shot on the run, as they halted to loose their arrows. Their sloppy form also implied their struggle with the effects of daylight.

A horn bugled somewhere in the middle of the encampment.

The pursuers could only be fifty strides behind, at best. Their lumbering gaits prevented them from being very fast, but with the curse-bearer in their midst, a fight grew increasingly unbalanced, especially if Veranna had no counter. The harsh truth crushed Raen's chest.

"We have to leave them." Veranna's assertion only under-scored Raen's own realization. If they tried to contend with the fire, the warriors, and the curses, they would all face only death as their reward.

Raen broke into a run for the cover of the trees. Veranna matched her speed, stride for stride. Another arrow sped past. Fiery pain erupted in Raen's shoulder, and she stumbled. A quick grab from Veranna prevented Raen from sprawling head-long into the dirt. They staggered onward.

"We have to come . . . back for them." Raen panted between words. She reached back and plucked a flopping arrow from her flesh. Blood smeared her hand, but thankfully, the wound did not seem too deep.

"We will. With the right help," Veranna replied.

Despite the haze of pain that clouded Raen's eyes, she barreled onward. The green glow of the eerie flames receded, but the girls' screams followed Raen for much longer, far past the eaves of the wood.

Much of the dragon-kin rumble also died down once Raen and Veranna had pressed far enough into the woods to no longer have the encampment within view. But the snap of branches and the churning of leaf litter told Raen they were not so fortunate as to have shaken all their pursuers. She took the lead and chose a game trail that allowed for decent running.

A flapping sound like canvas whipping in the wind closed in on Raen and Veranna from behind, passed overhead, and with a crashing thump, one of their pursuers landed before them. He folded his wings and leered.

The maidens dug their heels in for a clumsy halt. *Why do they have to fly?* Raen curled a lip. *They don't deserve the pleasure of it.*

A trio of villains closed from behind. The effort of raising her unbroken arm sent arcs of pain through Raen's entire upper body. The trio fanned out.

"Surrounded," Veranna whispered.

More flapping sent Raen's last scraps of hope into the shadows.

An eagle's scream, only ten times louder than any hawk Raen had ever heard, ripped through the air. The reptilian captors' glances flashed upward.

A golden-plumed creature plummeted through the canopy. It screeched again.

"Eyrnir!" Veranna practically sang.

The griffon raked at the dragon-kin with his claws, and his victim toppled to the side, a spurting gash opened across his neck.

An indigo blur joined the descending fray. He opened his maw, drew his head back...

He wouldn't. Raen stared, transfixed. Horrified.

Mythrenese shot his head forward, and caught one of the dragon-kin's arms in his teeth. He snapped his head to the side, and the arm in his grasp made a sickening crack. Eyrnir dove in again with slashing talons. The victim he mauled collapsed.

The remaining dragon-kin backpedaled, holding his sword at mid-guard and his eyes bulging. Eyrnir grabbed the back of Raen's cloak and dress in one claw and caught hold of Veranna in the other. He beat his wings with furious strain but managed to lift them from the ground.

A wash of pain from Raen's shoulder and relief from the depth of her soul swept over her. Her limbs grew heavy. A sudden flash of heat sickened her, and the world faded from sight.

The next thing Raen knew, treetops passed beneath her, and bright sun warmed her cheeks. Her shoulder burned. Eyrnir clutched her to his underbelly, and she had to admit, it was a perfectly lovely way to see the world. The terrain between the trees boasted a great deal of rock, and it was clear they worked their way through the mountains, flying into the sun, so likely southwest.

"Are we nearly there?" Veranna's voice came from above, but it was muffled. She must have been mounted on Eyrnir's back.

"Nearly, prophetess," Eyrnir replied.

"Do you really hate flying so much?" Mythrenese asked. "I don't know if you've lifted your face from Eyrnir's back once."

"I hate it with a passion eclipsed only by my sense of duty to Creo," Veranna replied.

"I think you could learn to like it," Raen called. Her voice squeaked, hoarse.

"Raen's 'wake!"

Whose was that childish voice? Raen craned her neck to find the owner. Ah yes, Iriscendra. The whole reason she left home in the first place. What a quagmire Iriscendra's escape from the vale had created.

"Where are you taking us?" Raen asked.

"Back to Majestrin," Eyrnir replied. "And Vinyanel."

"Thank the Maker." Raen's whole body relaxed, although regret at their retreat nagged at her heart. "At least getting the group reassembled will give us a position of strength from which to tackle the next phase of this mission."

Eyrnir and Mythrenese exchanged a pained look.

"What?" Raen's heart picked up speed. "What's going on?"

"Things are complicated at present. It's better that you see it than we try to explain." Eyrnir pulled his wings in and dropped into a dive. Veranna shrieked.

When the griffon leveled out, Veranna's wail petered to a whimper. Their course drove them toward the mouth of a cave.

Raen smirked. "Has she been doing that the whole time?"

"Only most of it." Mythrenese chuckled.

They glided into the cave, and right away, a fetid odor caught in Raen's throat. Before her eyes could adjust to the dark, she groaned. "Ugh. Do you dragons have a kill in here you haven't finished? I think it's time for it to go, or someone's going to get sick."

"Welcome back." Majestrin's deep timbre vibrated in Raen's chest, like the lowest notes of a pipe organ. "And no, we're not keeping anything around to poison ourselves. No one but Vinyanel, I think."

Eyrnir set Raen on her feet, and her legs wobbled a threat to drop her to the chalky floor. Mythrenese flashed to her side and caught her arm. Bright spots flashed before Raen's eyes, but slowly, they dimmed.

"I beg pardon, Silverlord." Raen lowered her eyes. "I don't know what you mean."

Iriscendra bounded to Raen's other side and caught her hand in a pearly talon. "V'yennel very sick." She implored of Raen with round eyes. "Hardly ever wakes up--days and days."

"It's the leg wound he sustained in Bilearne," Majestrin said.

Was *that* what was causing the awful, spoiled meat stench in the cave? Raen grimaced. "Well, I better have a look."

Ecleriast lay in the rear of the cavern, covered in two blankets. His pallor had a greenish cast. A water skin sat on the floor beside him, and a wet rag draped across his forehead. Raen reached for the rag, and when her fingers met it, she gasped at how hot it was.

Iriscendra's anguished gaze locked on Ecleriast's sweaty

face. "Cool rags won't stay cool more'n a few moments," Iriscendra whispered.

Raen reached with hesitant fingers to draw the blankets away from Ecleriast's leg. Veranna stepped up behind her.

"Do you have a strong stomach, Prophetess?" Raen asked. "This may be gruesome."

"It's best I know what to pray for," Veranna replied.

Raen left the blankets over the rest of Ecleriast's fevered body but worked the pant leg up. Dried fluids stiffened and stained his clothing. The bandage underneath was a saturated ruin of green, yellow and brown. The rotting smell intensified, and Raen's stomach churned.

"Is there a knife anywhere?" Raen asked. *More likely, I need a bone saw.*

Mythrenese handed her a knife. It was her own horn-hilted knife with a narrow, curved blade. One she had honed herself from an antler she stumbled across in the vale she called home. The valley seemed so distant, and the thought weighed heavily on Raen's heart.

She smiled. "You gathered my equipment?"

Mythrenese mirrored Raen's expression and nodded.

Gingerly, Raen slipped the blade under Ecleriast's bandage. She sawed lightly, and the fibers parted. A gag twisted her stomach and clutched at her throat. It was worse than she imagined. Worse than any infection she had ever seen.

"How in Creo's dominion is he still alive?" She placed a fold of her cloak over her nose and mouth.

"Frankly," Majestrin said, "I'm surprised he is. Do you think there's anything we can do?" He clamped his maw shut, and his eyes misted.

Raen rubbed her forehead and pushed a lock of hair from her eyes. "It's a scant chance at best. Do you have any meat . . . uncured?"

Majestrin shook his head. "No one has been hunting since

Eyrnir, Mythrenese, and Iriscendra went looking for you. Dragons who can't fly can't hunt, you know. We're not exactly stealthy on the ground."

"I could get something," Eyrnir said. "How big a piece do you need?"

"Not much," Raen said. "Even a rabbit would suffice. I just hope we can keep Ecleriast on this side of the Grand Entry long enough for me to try my plan."

Eyrnir nodded, then turned and loped from the cave.

Veranna rifled her own gear for her skirt and belt of bells. She pulled the skirt on over the trousers she was wearing, and then worked the pants off. A few slow, deliberate strides took her to the center of the cave; the tinkling of her bells echoed back to her from the stone walls. She reached for the ceiling, cocked a knee, then brought her arms down in a slow arc. She twirled.

Her every motion was fluid grace. Raen sat transfixed by the rawness and the beauty of the dance Veranna performed. The bells on her garb created a self-contained, rhythmic accompaniment, and the prophetess danced with no regard for any that watched. It was a dance for her lord and Creator alone.

Raen turned her attention back to Ecleriast. Until Eyrnir returned with some meat, and until she could apply her last-ditch plan, only Veranna had a way of helping the dying warrior. Raen pulled off her boots, rose, and slipped to the prophetess's side.

At first, she mirrored Veranna's leaps, lunges, spins, and stomps. Starting in a slow trickle, the hundred years of Raen's dance training returned to her limbs. But with each step she performed, the trickle grew to a steady stream of recollection until it swelled to a flood. Her tutored style was much more controlled and refined than Veranna's visceral performance, but she could use it as an offering. Had that not been her desire so long ago?

The two maidens danced on, for how long, Raen lost track. But it was good to abandon herself to the bliss of movement, even with the pain of her mounting wounds. When she danced, she forgot pain. Hunger and thirst were meaningless.

Eventually, as if by mutual agreement, both Veranna and Raen's dances waned to a close. A heavy sweat dampened Raen's back and brow.

"We had best take some food and water if we mean to keep this up," Veranna said.

Raen nodded. She drew a waterskin from the pile of supplies near the wall and took a deep draught. She handed it to Veranna, who also drank.

"Water never tasted so good," the prophetess said. "By the way, you are very talented."

Raen laughed. "No, you're talented. I'm just trained."

Veranna crossed her feet, lowered herself to the floor, and swiped at a glistening brow. "I cannot go on without some decent food, though. I'm terribly dizzy now—but the compulsion at seeing Vinyanel's state was too strong to do anything but implore of Creo on his behalf."

Raen took a few shaky strides to the packs again, but Mythrenese beat her to them.

"I believe you still have some dried fruit and black walnuts, mistress...and a bit of waybread, though I fear it has gotten beaten into quite a few pieces with all the lugging around." Mythrenese reached in the pack and produced the smaller oilskin pouches Raen used for food. They were lighter than she would have preferred.

"That will do." She sat cross-legged next to Veranna and drew out a modest portion of the nuts and fruit Mythrenese had brought her. The wine-like quality of the walnuts and the cherries' tartness offered a pleasant distraction from the otherwise foul atmosphere of the cave.

Raen offered the pouch to the prophetess. Veranna poured herself a scant handful of the food as well. They ate in silence.

After a period of quiet, Raen leaned forward and propped her elbows on her knees. She sought Iriscendra and found her sniffing the air at the cave's mouth, at least twenty yards away. "We're going to need to devise a strategy that assumes Ecleriast's absence," Raen whispered.

"May I ask your plan for preventing that?" Veranna replied.

"The dead flesh needs to be removed from the wound, and he needs medicine I don't have." She glanced down at her cast. "I wish we had Aulus with us. Are there any cities near here?"

Veranna popped another bite of bread into her mouth and shrugged with a sheepish curl of her lip.

Mythrenese shuffled closer. "I saw a human settlement of some kind to the west. It will be harder to get there with Majestrin unable to fly and his rider so ill."

"But we have to try," Veranna said. Her mouth tightened with emotion and her cheeks flushed.

"I know nobody wants to see somebody else die," Raen said. "But I'm actually a little surprised how . . . important Ecleriast's recovery is to you."

Veranna released a sad laugh. "The amount of time I've spent in his head has had a profound effect on me. There is anger and brusqueness and bravado on the surface, but beneath all that, there is deep wounding. Deeper than even those wounds he bears from the loss of his squadron over this cursed chalice. While at times I want to strangle him, I am continually awed by how much he does while in so much pain. Heal his wounds, and he will be unstoppable."

Raen studied Veranna's face while she spoke. Her admiration, even perhaps love, for Ecleriast was undeniable. She herself even had to admit, in the short time she had spent with him, he had a powerful impact on anyone with whom he came in contact.

The way he lay there, just breaths from becoming a corpse rather than a patient, gripped Raen's middle. He needed saving. And so did the girls he intended to pursue. *I must save him to save them. I can't hope to do it alone, not even with Veranna's help.*

At the end of their meal, Raen leaned her back against the cave wall. Drowsiness plagued her, but her churning mind stole any hope of repose. No matter what angle she viewed the Elgadrim girls' plight, she could find no likely solution.

Veranna crouched beside Vinyanel, her eyes narrow. Her lips were tight and brow furrowed.

"The ritual the girls were to be involved in was to take place at the new moon, right?" Raen asked. Her words came slowly as her weariness fought with her diction.

Veranna nodded. She stood and stepped toward Raen. "That gives us just over a fortnight, I believe."

Iriscendra shuffled across the cave, her tail dragging, to Vinyanel's place. She sat back on her haunches and picked up the waterskin beside him, then drizzled water on the cloth she had been using to cool his brow. When she draped it across his forehead, he made no response—not even the flutter of an eyelid. With a ginger touch, Iriscendra combed the elf warrior's hair away from his chiseled features. She lightly raked through the strands with her claws, which made some improvement in his bedraggled appearance.

The hatchling heaved a sigh, set her head down on Elceriast's chest, and whispered, "Wake up V'yennel. Please? No more sleeping."

Raen forced her attention out the mouth of the cave. Poor Iriscendra.

After a very long, very quiet couple of hours, Eyrnir returned. He swooped through the cave mouth with a feathery whoosh. In one talon, he carried a limp bighorn goat.

In the other—a very sour-faced Hridayesh.

25

RAEN'S HOPE

The North Deklian tumbled to the floor when Eyrnir opened his claws. He righted himself and rubbed at his underarms.

"Come now Eyrnir," Majestrin said. "No one in his right mind would eat that." He blew a puff of frosty air from his nostrils and narrowed his eyes at Hridayesh.

"Enjoy your few days of freedom?" Veranna marched toward him. Her barbed tone widened Raen's eyes. "I hope shackles are a favorite accessory for you, since you're probably going to be wearing them for the rest of your life."

Hridayesh lowered his brows in a deep frown. "Freedom? I spent it looking for Vinyanel. I found this." He reached behind his back and pulled a bare-bladed sword.

Raen squinted at the weapon. The blade had a clean edge, and the crossguard's design was a simple, brushed steel, but the leather wrapping of the grip was much-worn, the strips of hide fused together with use.

"Vinyanel's sword," Veranna said. "I'm glad, for his sake, that you came across it." Her expression remained stony. "But you're still a treacherous viper."

"We were hopelessly outnumbered." Hridayesh gaped.

"You abandoned us!" Veranna said. "I wouldn't be surprised if you set up the whole attack."

"Delusional tart," Hridayesh countered. "I couldn't do any good in that mess."

Raen scoffed and joined Veranna. "The two of us managed to escape quite a few more dragon-kin without you. If you had shown some . . .well . . . you might have spared Veranna and me a lot of suffering."

"It's too much to hope that he would care." Veranna folded her arms and looked away.

"I don't owe you heathen harlots anything!"

Mythrenese charged to Raen's side. "You might not make a good meal, but you'd still better watch what kinds of names you're calling people." He drew a deep breath.

"Don't you dare," Raen said under her breath.

Mythrenese sunk his neck back into his shoulders and dropped his glance to the floor.

Hridayesh sneered. "So where is the Lieutenant Commander anyway?"

Raen cocked a brow. *Oh, right. He's human. He probably can't see much in here at all.* "He's deeper in the cavern." She nodded in Ecleriast's direction. With the only individual for whom Hridayesh had any respect on his deathbed, did the North Deklian pose a danger? Or rather, was he more dangerous close at hand than he was out of sight? Someone had said he was an assassin, right?

No one else in the cavern gave any more specific details about Ecleriast's exact whereabouts. It seemed no mystery anyone who knew him at all harbored misgivings about him.

"Why are you all holed up here?" Hridayesh's glance

scanned the chamber. He sniffed. "Couldn't you have picked a campsite that doesn't stink?"

"We're reassessing our strategy," Majestrin replied. "But as the most senior servant in the Windrider battalion available at the moment, I deem you back under constant watch, for your questionable conduct with regard to the maidens' plight."

"Adramalech roast you all!" Hridayesh roared. "Some thanks I get for trying to arrange for aid. No, I should have just let the scaly monstrosities capture me and spill my vitals on one of their putrid altars."

"You're a liar," Raen said. "I saw your smug face when you skulked off."

"Simpleton. Enemies don't pursue someone who looks like a deserter. The moment I seemed I might be going for help, they would have piled on me. Since I'm not as useful to them as you could be, my chances of survival were next to none." Hridayesh stomped in an aimless circle. "I need to speak with Vinyanel."

Raen looked to Majestrin, whose glance volleyed to Veranna.

Hridayesh halted. "He's dead."

"'Nuf!" Iriscendra yelled from the depths where Ecleriast lay. "V'yennel NOT dead. Not *going* to be dead." She tramped up to Hridayesh and snatched the longsword from his hand. She carried it back to the lieutenant commander. A quick rifle later, and she produced his pale hand from beneath the blankets. "Look, V'yennel. Scowly-man brought you something."

Ecleriast, though slowly, closed his fingers around the sword's grip. Iriscendra shot a look that combined smugness and fury back at the rest of the group.

"She knows how to give him strength," Raen breathed.

"Of course she does." Majestrin's voice caught. "She's woven to him."

. . .

*R*aen took the goat carcass to the cave entrance to dress it, though the task proved just short of impossible with a cast on one arm. Work she could have completed in three-quarters of an hour took three times that. But in the end, they had meat to roast and a pile of scrap gathered on a sunny, flat rock. The meat would be a luxury compared to rations, but the scraps mattered more. A warm afternoon breeze ruffled her hair, but Raen thought only of the night. How cold had it been of late? Had there been consistent frost?

Veranna stepped out to the cave threshold. "Can I help you clean up? These guts are going to get stinky here in the sun."

"That's what I'm hoping." Raen cleaned the blade of her knife.

Veranna frowned. "You're not one of those mystic types who looks for fortunes in entrails—?"

Raen laughed. "Heaven and earth, no. Don't worry, you'll see."

Veranna propped a fist on her hip. "Why all the secrecy?"

"My plan is a little. . . distasteful to some, but it's all I have right now. Something I saw work—a long time ago." Raen wiped her uninjured hand on a rag, then took Veranna's slender fingers in her own. "Please, trust me. And pray I'm right about what we should do."

～

*W*aiting. It was the most interminable process. Well before dawn, Raen awoke, even though she had concluded her watch just a few short hours before. The desire to dash outside and check on the trimmings she had left pulled at her, but it was too soon. Nightfall would be the soonest she could hope for results.

Even so, when dawn lit the sky, she stepped out onto the

rock shelf that formed the threshold of the cave. Her breath steamed from her nose and lips. Had there been frost? The surrounding rocks and trees wore a layer of dew, but no ice crystals. Raen took some comfort from this.

Just outside the cave mouth, Mythrenese sat in the spot appointed to the night's watchers.

"Anything to report?" Raen stretched stiff limbs. The arrow wound was thoroughly scabbed and little more than a nuisance. The weight of her cast made her right shoulder tight. She rolled the tense muscles. Still weeks to go within the confines of the heavy plaster. Weeks of fighting with her off hand.

"I had to shoo some ugly birds away from the pile of guts." Mythrenese yawned. "But not much else."

"Well, thank you. It was not a wasted effort." Raen glanced at the scrap heap. Once-pink organs and tissues had taken on a grayish hue in the open air and the remainder of last after-noon's sun. Their souring smell advanced Raen's cause. She nodded. "Well, the sun's up, as most of us will also be soon, so your watch is complete. Why don't you take Iriscendra fishing again?"

"All right. I can fill the water skins while I'm at it." Mythrenese jogged into the cave with Raen a few strides behind.

Iriscendra slept, her head still on Ecleriast's chest. The warrior had one hand resting on her shoulder. When Mythrenese came within five paces, the hatchling's eyes snapped open. She sprang to her feet and arched her back. An angry hiss poured from her wide maw.

Mythrenese recoiled. "Whoa...what? It's just me!"

Iriscendra blinked and her eyes softened. "Sorry, Myth-nese. Bad dreams."

"Want to come fishing with me?"

Iriscendra looked back at Ecleriast. His facial bones showed plainly through his skin—the rims of his eyes especially. She shook her head. "Not really wanna." A slow wriggle worked her back under Elceriast's limp hand.

Raen tread softly toward the young dragons. "We'll watch over him, Iriscendra. He'll be safe. You don't have to worry."

"I don't want to miss when he wakes up," the hatchling whispered.

A smile tugged at Raen's lips. "If he does wake up, I won't let him tramp off anywhere. You need to eat. That goat won't stretch to feed us all."

"You bring me fish?" Iriscendra asked Mythrenese. "I won't come. No more asking."

Mythrenese sighed. "If I get any. You're better at fishing than me."

"I'll help you," Eyrnir said. He rose from his corner, stretched his front talons out before him and lifted his hindquarters in a long, feline stretch. "Even though he won't admit it, Majestrin has got to be hungry, having been stuck here all this time."

The silver dragon continued to snore softly in the rear-center of the cave, behind a row of short stalagmites. Raen chewed her cheek. He would sleep more and more, the longer he went without food—the typical draconic defense mechanism against the need to consume unthinkable amounts of game.

The griffon and indigo dragonling loped away, thrust their wings, and disappeared over the lip of the cave.

The day progressed with little change, other than the shifting light from morning, to noon, to afternoon. Veranna prayed and read her copy of *The Tree* at intervals. Hridayesh nibbled rations, cleaned his weapons, oiled his armor, and generally kept as great a distance as possible between himself and the maidens as the confines of the cave permitted. Vinyanel occasionally muttered and writhed, which actually gave Raen a faint hope he was not as close to dead as he appeared. Every time he struggled, Iriscendra combed through his hair and hummed a little tune.

"Where did you learn that song?" Raen asked her in a low voice, after Vinyanel had settled from his latest fit.

"Made it up," Iriscendra replied.

Raen raised her brow. The tune was fairly catchy for someone who may have never heard any kind of organized music. Could Ecleriast hear her? Did her constant presence soothe him at all? She made yet another trip to the cave entrance. A pleasantly warm afternoon sun beamed down, and the mountainside that spread below her wore a golden haze over the mixed palette of prickly, bare branches, green conifers, rust, and gold. A few stubborn trees that clung to autumn leaves offered the flashes of color.

A fly buzzed past Raen's ear. She smiled. The insect's drone was a song of hope.

As the sun sank and dusk brought with it a descending chill. In the canopy the northeast, a flutter of activity caught her eye. She squinted toward it. A bit of gold, and some indigo—yes, it must be Eyrnir and Mythrenese returning. The dragon and griffon shapes grew in clarity and size, and within just a few moments, they glided in for a landing on the shelf.

Before Raen could even greet them, Eyrnir marched straight toward her.

"We need to move. Soon," he said.

Raen blinked. "We can't yet. I need another day. Why the urgency?"

Mythrenese's jaw trembled. "There's an encampment of dragon-kin just about an hour's flight from here. We can't be sure, but they may be hunting for us."

Raen's heart thundered. Her face heated. No doubt, Ecleriast was too weak to consider moving. And if Majestrin could not fly, they'd make such a tramping through the woods that the dragon-kin, if they were tracking the group, would find them with no trouble.

"I must respectfully assert you're wrong, Eyrnir." Majestrin approached the mouth of the cave. "This is the one defensible place we might make a decent stand if the little monstrosities do want to attack. How many were in the encampment you saw?"

Eyrnir bowed to Majestrin. "It was difficult to tell, since they were asleep with only a couple of posted guards. There were about a dozen tents."

"Did the guards see you?"

Mythrenese cringed. "I'm pretty sure they did. I heard loud voices as we left."

Majestrin growled. "How were the guards positioned? Spread out, or together?"

"Standing together," Eyrnir replied. "On the north side of camp."

"And it didn't occur to you, Mythrenese, that you had the capability to fly in, eliminate those scouts, and *then* come back?" Fury sparked in Majestrin's eyes, and Raen locked her knees against the desire to flee.

She clenched sweating hands and stepped between Mythrenese and Majestrin. "If you're implying he should have used his abomination on those guards, I would appreciate it if you would stop suggesting it."

"Abomination? Where does this idea come from?" Majestrin stretched as tall as the cave ceiling would allow. "Among dragons, we refer to this as our gifting, which none of your protégés would know, of course, the way you've isolated them."

Raen's whole body quaked, but she planted her feet shoulder-width and forced her gaze to meet Majestrin's. "Is it not, Silverlord, the dragon's breath that makes humans and elves so fearful of you? That drives them to hunt dragons and wipe them out?"

"And so you suggest that we simply roll over and tell them where to stick the spear?" The dragon's eyes stretched wide, and his mouth twisted in a sardonic sneer while he spoke. But then he paused. Drew in a long breath. Blinked slowly. "Many of them hunt for sport, or for scales, or in search of whatever elusive interior body part makes our particular breath possible."

"But don't you see?" Raen clenched her hands together. "If we could change the world's perception of dragons...help them see how magnificent you are, and that you're really not a danger—."

"Is that what you're trying to do? Create some kind of new, toothless, spineless generation of dragons?" Majestrin huffed. He directed his attention to Mythrenese. "When the dragon-kin squadron comes, you have to ask yourself what you are. Did Creo make you with the ability to protect yourself and others from many enemies? Or would you rather pray your young scales will hold out against tempered steel?"

The indigo dragon shrank back. "I—I . . . don't know."

"Well, now is a good time for some deep reflection." Majestrin turned back for the cave's interior. "As for me, well, I advise you all stand clear of the cave's mouth when the assault begins, because there are likely to be some sudden storm conditions. And I shall never apologize for that when it comes to defending the defenseless."

~

*E*ven though it was daylight, the group posted a guard at the cave mouth all day. About mid-afternoon, Hridayesh took a turn, though under Eyrnir's scrutiny. He emerged on the shelf, sniffed, and grimaced.

"All right. It's really time to get rid of this stinking pile of entrails," he said. "It's crawling with maggots now."

The nap that had closing a slow grip upon Raen vanished. She scrambled to the cavern threshold. "Maggots? Did I hear you right?"

Hridayesh curled his lip at her. "You *would* be pleased about something so vile? They make me gag just to look at them."

"Well, if you want Ecleriast to live, get over it." She knelt beside the trimmings, and indeed, white grubs wormed their way about the rotting flesh. With careful fingers, she gathered the insects into a rag. Admittedly, the process made her gag, too, but she masked her reaction.

Raen bustled back to Ecleriast. "Iriscendra, I need you to get out of the way."

The hatchling lifted her head and regarded Raen with haunted eyes. "Why?"

"Please, just listen to me," Raen said. "I have ... medicine."

Iriscendra's frown conveyed plain skepticism, but she shuffled back. Veranna joined the group just as Raen set the rag down on the floor and opened it.

Veranna squealed. "Ugh! What?"

With flying hands, Raen uncovered Elceriast's black-blistered wound again. His whole thigh was shiny red and inflamed, taut like an over-full wineskin. Raen gulped back the lump in her throat, breathed through her mouth, and picked up a pinch of maggots. She dropped them into the gash.

Veranna covered her face. "Are you sure this is a real practice? I've heard of this sort of approach, but I wasn't convinced anyone had really tried it."

"The skin and muscle that's dead is poisoning Ecleriast's whole body. We need to get rid of it for medicine to be of any use. I'm hoping that once we get the worst of it cleared out, we can at least move him without the risk of pushing him off the lip of the cliff he's on."

Raen deposited the last of her little rot-eaters in their new home and re-bound the wound loosely to keep them corralled.

"Now what do we do?" Iriscendra hunkered down at Ecleriast's shoulder and lay her head on his chest..

Raen brushed her hands together. She shook off the shiver that skittered across her arms. "We wait some more."

26

HELLO AND GOODBYE

*I*t was quiet. Not a quiet where low sounds drifted in the furtive distance, nor where speakers near at hand forced quiescence. The air itself seemed unstirred by my passing. My bare footfalls landed without even a patter. Neither cloth nor surface gave up a rustle or thud as I drifted down a white, windowed hall, a place where the brightness should have inspired a squint, but I remained nonetheless wide-eyed.

I wandered to a padded bench against the tall arches of the windows, sat, and gazed through the glass. My mind felt muddled, and I could not make sense of the blurry shapes beyond. I brushed at the loose folds in the crème linen pants and airy tunic I wore. While comfortable, I did not recognize the clothes. Where had my companions taken me? Who had re-dressed me?

Motion in the distance drew my focus. A door of polished glass opened at the far end of the hall, and a tall, narrow-featured elf stepped out.

My breath caught in my throat. *Beriadhan.* Wait, what? Beriadhan? Oh, no. No, I was dreaming. I had to be.

He breezed toward me on lanky strides, his sandy hair loose and hanging about shoulders armored in tan leather. The spreading tree of Creo embossed his breastplate, and a sabre in a silver scabbard hung at his hip. He stopped at my side and folded his arms.

I stood. Any grogginess I had felt swept from my mind like driftwood on crashing waves.

Beriadhan extended his hand, which I clasped. I yanked him to me and clapped him on the back with my free hand. When I stepped back, he did not return my broad smile. The grin fell from my features in broken shards.

"I am not yet pleased to see you, my friend," Beriadhan said.

I blinked. "I'm dead, I suppose."

A little chuckle puffed through his nose. "Not quite. But very nearly. And unnecessarily."

Stepping around me to the bench, Beriadhan sat on its smooth seat. "So much has happened, and yet you remain so much the same, Vinyanel."

My shoulders tightened. "And why should I not? Must I be completely unmade before Creo can use me or his people accept me?"

"Why will you never listen to counsel?"

"I . . ." The words lodged in my throat. The cane of Beriadhan's accusation stung. I took a moment to allow the heat to ebb from my cheeks. "How am I to lead if every decision must endure debate? Those who have not seen a battlefield in centuries forget that sometimes the quickest strike is best."

"And sometimes quick is hard to discern from hasty. You even eschew the admonition of those beside you in the fray." Beriadhan leaned forward and propped his elbows on his knees, his fingers intertwined in a loose clasp. "A true leader weighs all options and makes sure his followers feel heard.

Would you follow Creo if you felt he did not care for you as an individual? You can only bind so many to yourself for so long by your strength of will."

"You fought beside me!" I said. "You followed with willing steps—there was no coercion between us."

He placed a hand on my shoulder. "There was no need. You trusted us."

"I knew you."

"And you do not know those in your company now because you will not allow yourself to!" Beriadhan stood. "You cannot confide in those you do not trust, and you cannot trust those you do not know."

I turned burning eyes on my friend. "You are in the easier place. You can lose nothing here."

"You envy me for dying?"

I faced the window. "Sometimes."

"Vinyanel." Beriadhan sighed. "Your shoulders have always been more apt to the task than mine. You are fit to lead, and there is much Creo can do with you, if you would just stop trying to do it all alone."

"I must be strong—and those that follow me must be positive I am. Otherwise, what am I worth?"

"That's your father talking," Beriadhan said.

A sudden fire flared up in my gut. Few times in my life had I been tempted to connect my knuckles with Beriadhan's impeccable nose, but the urge now tensed my every muscle.

"Stop letting his pain define who you are, Vinyanel." My friend clasped my shoulder again. "You are capable. Extremely. If you do what you know how to do, people will see that and believe it."

"But every time. . ." I stopped in order to rein in the rampaging doubt that threatened to pull me to pieces. "Every time I lead, I kill people. My brother. You."

"Those examples hardly amount to 'every time.'"

I pressed the heels of my hands to my brow. As infuriating as it was, he was right. I had only suffered a few bad turns, but those failings had been complete enough to rob me of the two people I had loved most in life.

Beriadhan leaned closer. "You don't have to shoulder this load alone. You don't have to figure out how to live with your pain and your fear without help. It will never entirely go away... but if you are willing, you can learn to manage the thudding heart, the shortness of breath—"

"The confusion?" I chimed in. "The sense of disorientation is the worst part of it all."

A bright laugh lit Beriadhan's face. "I can see that being particularly hard for you—the one who always had everything planned, down to the amount of weapon oil we'd need on an excursion."

His contagious laugh coaxed a smile from me. "This 'willingness to feel dependent' lesson is clearly not my best subject."

"Creo knows it is easier to share a load with those you can see and touch. He gives you people—and in your case, dragons, you lucky fool—as his representatives."

My thoughts drifted to Majestrin, to Iriscendra, even to Mythrenese, with his annoying quirks, and the corner of my mouth curled. "I have been given much." If I was being honest, even Hridayesh served his part in keeping me honest and seeing me for what I was.

"You will need them all, comrades with wings and without, if you can get where you are going. But you still may not, if you continue to let your stubbornness and pride poison you."

"And here I thought it was my leg."

Beriadhan laughed. "Consider it a metaphor."

I rose and met my ex-comrade's eye. "You left quite a hole in the ranks, my friend. We all miss you."

"You would leave a bigger one. Humble yourself, Vinyanel.

Be who you are, but like a good mount, keep a soft mouth to the bit, won't you? It is possible to both lead and follow."

The hallway around me blurred. The walls, the windows, the ceiling blended with the subtle textures of rough stone, as if the ghosts of such shapes emerged slowly through a thick mist.

Beriadhan glanced left and right. "It seems our meeting comes to a close, Captain." He cleared his throat. "Lieutenant Commander, that is. Some things do change." He took three steps backward, clenched his fist over his heart, and bowed. His figure grew transparent, while boulders and stalagmites grew more distinct. "On to greatness."

And with that, he vanished.

"On to greatness," I whispered. The hall darkened to gray and brown, and chaos crashed around my ears.

$\sim$

Swords clanged, and their ring ran up my spine. Where was I? This recurrence of waking up in unfamiliar places was growing extremely wearing. My clothes, my ordinary, grungy tunic and pants, clung to me as though I had been doused with a stable bucket's worth of water. But for once, I did not tremble with unchecked chills. My leg felt stiff, but was not throbbing, for once.

My surroundings appeared to be the same cavern that faded into the environment while I talked to Beriadhan. Talked with Beriadhan? The notion seemed absurd. But it had been no fevered dream. In some way or another, that had happened.

Hridayesh's voice met my ears. I turned my head...though it took the effort of wrangling the steerage of a warship in a tempest. The slight motion darkened the edges of my field of vision and turned my stomach.

The North Deklian stood on what appeared to be a ledge just outside a cave in which I was laying, and he held a dragon-kin warrior's thick, ugly sword in a bind. He thrust his leg out behind him to catch another attacker square in the gut.

Raen, too, slashed at a reptilian warrior. She spun and clobbered another with the plaster cast on her sword arm. The beast staggered back, clutching his head with one hand, his eyes bleary.

My instinct screamed to join them, but when I tried to lift even a hand, I found I lacked the strength. Dragon-kin outnumbered Raen and Hridayesh three-to-one. Their combat warped and shimmered, as though I watched it through a thin sheet of water.

"Ramenna ceardeth sinithwe!" echoed from behind me and to my left.

Veranna—it had to be. I forced my limp neck to crane my head toward the voice, and I caught sight of the prophetess. She stood with her feet apart, and she wove her hands before her in fluid patterns. Her eyes were closed.

"Arrows!" Hridayesh yelled.

I forced my glance his way just in time to see a handful of flying shafts hit the undulating curtain near the front of the cave and bounce off. A dozen other red-fletched arrows lay scattered on the floor, also on the opposite side of the barrier.

"V'yennel!" The shrill voice made my head pound. "V'yennel's eyes open!"

Iriscendra eclipsed my field of vision. Her blue eyes sparkled.

A cry burst forth from within the battle. The sword *shhhhick* that followed was all too familiar—the sound of a weapon slipping from flesh. The cry was of a masculine timbre.

"Move!" the bellow clearly belonged to Majestrin.

"Too few have come up yet," Hridayesh yelled back in a strangled voice.

"Move!"

I turned my sluggish head in time to see Raen and

Hridayesh dive to opposite sides of the cave mouth and vanish outside. A roar like storm wind tore through the cavern from somewhere deeper in than I lay. A turbulent, cold wind ripped past me. The rippling barrier dissolved.

The column of deadly frost crashed into the dragon-kin at the cave entrance. They split at the middle of their formation, and the maneuver saved the outer two attackers. The center four, however, froze solid and crashed onto the cave's outer shelf. Their limbs and wings shattered when they hit the rock. The snout of one snapped from his head upon impact. It was something like watching the destruction of an ice sculpture— works of exquisite detail artisans crafted in Delsinon during the Winter High Feast—broken to bits. Except the elven sculptors always chiseled things of beauty, not grotesque monsters like these.

Iriscendra cringed close to me. "We'll fight them away, V'yennel. Don't worry." She arched her back. Her scales stood on edge, and her face twisted in a fierce snarl for one so little.

"What are they up to?" Veranna whispered. "Well, if they didn't know Majestrin was with us, they do now."

A renewed clash of weapons drowned out Veranna's conjecture. Hridayesh and one of the remaining dragon kin swung swords, though the condition of the threshold, slick with ice, threatened to sweep their feet from beneath them. The ice seemed only part of the reason Hridayesh's coordination faltered, as he clutched his hand over a growing dark blotch on his lower left side.

A leather flapping grew in volume, and another cluster of dragon-kin appeared at the lip of the shelf, swords drawn. Raen leapt back into the fray and sunk her slender blade into the chest of the first besieger with deadly grace.

They will never outlast reinforcements. I threw every ounce of will I had into sitting up, but I scarcely succeeded in arching my back. My leg sent shooting pains up into my abdomen and down to the sole of my foot. I panted for breath.

"Stay still," Iriscendra pleaded. "Too sick."

A hawk's scream echoed down from the night sky outside the cave. In a golden blur, Eyrnir plummeted into the group of dragon-kin. With claws and beak, he opened gashes on two victims, and the force of his body drove another two to slip, then plummet from the edge of the cave shelf. Their cries and the crack of rock receded. It must have been a long way down.

Hridayesh's right foot lost traction on the icy ground, and it shot out in front of him. One of his opponents lunged, and while Hridayesh ducked that thrust, another dragon-kin caught his sword-arm in a vicious, two-handed upswing. I wanted to avert my eyes, but my horror bound it to the disaster.

The wide blade of the attacker's bastard sword swept straight through Hridayesh's upper arm. The limb dropped away in a spray of blood. Hridayesh crashed to the ground.

The dragon-kin bellowed a coarse laugh and kicked Hridayesh's severed limb, still gripping his khanda, over the stony edge.

My heart hammered. It ran me through to lay there, unable to so much as utter oaths at the attackers. The faster my blood coursed, however, the weaker I felt. My eyelids began to drag too heavily to keep open. My grip on consciousness loosened.

What good was I? Nothing but a liability.

"Stop letting his pain define who you are, Vinyanel."

Was I even worth protecting? My father might have said no.

Majestrin lumbered into motion, and the cave shook with his footfalls. Or was that my own renewed trembling as my soaked clothes cooled in the night air? His massive silver form blocked my view of the proceedings outside.

"Vinyanel," Hridayesh croaked. When had he arrived beside me? "I'm sorry." The North Deklian flopped to his side, and his normally-deep skin had faded to a mousey taupe. Iriscendra slunk backward away from us.

I stretched my eyes as wide as I could manage, which still only amounted to slits. "For what?" I slurred. I counted the fact that any words came out at all a minor miracle.

"This is my fault. I left the girls. It *did* look like a losing situation—" He shivered violently. "But I left because I decided not to care. Watched my own back. Looks like I got what I deserve for that." He glanced at the stump of his arm. Blood ran in a pulsing torrent. It spread on the floor of the cave in an ever-widening pool.

"That is not Creo's nature," I said.

He half-smiled. "I know . . . many things, I know better now. Thanks to you." He grabbed my arm with his remaining hand. "You'll apologize to them for me?"

"You shall do so yourself," I said. "Majestrin will end this battle, and then—"

"You believe the part about Majestrin, but not about me. You're . . ." His breaths grew labored. "Lousy liar. Stay that way."

He had paled further. His eyelids fluttered. But he dug into my arm with tightening fingers. "Make sure you take the flask."

"The what?" I could hardly understand his words for the way he drawled.

"The . . .adamantine . . .flask. Just a hunch. You'll . . .need . . ." His eyes rolled back. He shuddered. Then went still.

At the back of my awareness, the cries of battle still rang in the night air. I stared. Was he truly gone? Just like that?

A giant pool of blood under the stump of his severed arm hammered home my supposition. No man lost a limb and lasted more than a minute or two. I crawled my fingers along until I had dragged the weight of my own arm to touch Hridayesh's face and press his eyelids closed.

Find peace, wanderer. Creo gather you in.

27

GROUNDED

"*H*e did wake up!" Iriscendra cried. Her voice warbled, or perhaps whispered.

Either way, it felt as though my hearing was not entirely functional.

"Did you catch any words?" That one was definitely Veranna. Had it not been for her voice, the growing volume of bells gave her away.

"Talked a bit with Hri...Hri...one who died."

"Well," a more matronly voice chimed in. Probably Raen, "if he's coming to even in the slightest, we should try to get some water into him. The way his skin is crinkling. . ." She pinched the back of my hand. "See how it doesn't spring back? It's not good."

"Ow," I growled. The word raked my throat as though I had just coughed up a thistle.

Someone gasped. "He *is* back." Raen again. "At least a little. Bring me the waterskin."

A cool hand slid under my neck and shoulders and pulled. I wanted to help whoever tried to lift me and sit up, but I felt as though my mind had no connection to my body, and I could not so much as tense my abdomen or brace my arms against the ground. My torso moved from horizontal to reclined, and the change in position threw everything off-kilter. I flailed, albeit involuntarily.

"Whoa there, it's all right. Vinyanel, can you hear me?" Raen whispered. "I have a drink for you. Please, you must try to swallow some."

Something pressed against my lower lip, and icy water spilled over my mouth. My thickened tongue fought to respond, and the drink went astray in my mouth. I lurched and coughed.

"Maker's mercy, I'm sorry," Raen said. When my coughing stilled, she pressed the lip of the waterskin to my mouth again. "I'll give you a smaller sip. If you can hear me, please . . . try again."

The near-tearful earnestness in her voice drove me to give it my best effort, even though my body felt shackled to weights. A little water trickled into my mouth, and by tensing every muscle in my neck and shoulders, I forced a swallow.

"He took it!" Veranna squealed. "I saw his larynx lift and settle back down."

The following swallows came more easily than the first, and the fire in my throat calmed to an ache. My tongue also loosened a little.

"Where are we?" I asked. Or at least, that was what I meant to say. It came out more of an indistinct moan of several pitches.

Both Raen and Veranna shrilled again. "Majestrin!" Raen cried. "Vinyanel is awake. Sort of. The maggots must be working!"

Someone sniffed. "It does seem to smell less bad over here."

If I was guessing right, that was the indigo dragonling. When I regained my faculties—

Raen lowered me back to the ground and tugged at my pant leg. She hitched it well up my thigh. "See, look! There doesn't appear to be any new pus on the bandage." Some more tugging, and cool air drifted over the wound. She clapped her hands. "Many of them are gone, and it looks to me like they've cleaned out all the rot."

My prolonged unconsciousness must have addled my sense, because it took me a few moments to piece together what she was talking about. Rot? Bandages? Pus? And what was gone? I worked it over in my mind for a moment.

Maggots?

My eyes shot open. "Wha--wha's going on?"

"Welcome back, Lieutenant Commander," Majestrin said. He shuffled in close. "What a scare you gave us all."

Raen placed her wrist on my forehead—her touch was ice cold. "Hmf." She then leaned down and pressed her cheek to my brow instead.

Some intoxicating combination of scents--lavender, maybe a hint of rosemary, wafted faintly from her hair.

"He's not exactly tip-top yet." She sat back up, "He's still feverish. We need to get him to a real healer to make sure he doesn't take a turn back down the slope."

I swallowed again. "What's this talk of maggots?"

An uneasy laugh escaped Raen. She tucked a carmine lock behind a delicate ear point. "Well, it was the only thing I could think of. Your leg, you see—it's deeply infected."

I strained to crunch my abdominal muscles together and peer at it.

"I don't know if you want to . . ." Veranna said.

An angry, inflamed, open gash cut a canyon across my thigh. The wound was clearly still wide open, but the black blisters and the multi-hued ooze had disappeared. Something wriggled in the deepest part of the crevice.

"Agh!" I shuddered. My whole body crawled with the sensation of insect feet swarming me. I turned my face as far from the sight as my stiff neck would allow.

Raen cleared her throat. "I think we can safely clean the whole thing out now, but we'll need to boil the water we use. Mythrenese, please stoke the coals and add more wood."

"I'll help him get the water ready," Veranna said. She padded off, and somehow, the sound of those bells brought some comfort to my soul.

A few silent moments passed, moments I had no energy to fill. It was Raen who broke the quiet. "You should know . . . Hridayesh . . ."

"Yes, I know. He bled out," I said. "He wanted you to know he was sorry."

Raen pursed her lips. Her glance dropped, and she sighed. In a quieter voice, she added, "We burned his body, in accordance with North Deklian practices."

Whatever had transpired between them must have been painful, for a multitude of emotions swirled in her fleeting glance.

"He bringed this," Iriscendra drew closer and held something long and slender out to me.

I blinked my blurry eyes. When they finally came into focus, I blinked again. "My sword? But how?" Shaky as my hand was, I took the grip from Iriscendra. But in the back of my mind, I did remember the feel of it in my hand, even while all else was pain and darkness.

"He claims to have found it after he," Majestrin took a breath, "got separated from the group."

I pressed the crosspiece to my chest and closed my eyes. Whatever Hridayesh's failings, this gift covered many of them.

That, and whatever sense of loyalty drove him to deliver the weapon rather than pass it by.

Raen gently cleared away the remainder of my bindings and took a long look at the wound. "Well, I think you're finally improving, and I won't pretend I'm not surprised."

A hint of a smile emerged on my face. "You have seemed to shed some of your surly disposition toward me for all the inconvenience I have caused you."

Raen smirked. "I get invested in my projects."

The idea pricked like a splinter. *Projects?* Like her dragons? A handful of barbed responses rushed to mind, but only in the last moment did I bite them back. I was still weak, feverish, and relatively helpless. No use antagonizing the helper. Not to mention, Raen inspired a maddening mix of emotions, between her misguided philosophies, her undeniable sword skills, and subtler qualities that challenged my vow to abstain from emotional entanglements.

"Dare I ask the phase of the moon?"

Veranna returned, brushing her hands on her skirt. "A day after full."

A surge of panic struck through me like a flash-fire. "Then we cannot waste the time it will take to go for med—"

Raen placed her fingers over my lips. A lump formed in my throat.

"The town where we can get what you need isn't far. It isn't even particularly out of the way, according to Majestrin and Veranna."

"We'll get to the girls," Veranna said. "I pray the Maker gives them fortitude against their suffering in the meantime." She stared toward the mouth of the cave with a stern cast to her lips.

The resolve in her voice took me by surprise. A few days lingering on the outskirts of death, and I had missed a change in Veranna. It appeared to be a change I could work with.

~

*A*s it turned out, once Majestrin waded into the dragon-kin battle, that ended it. Eyrnir, who had been serving as scout, was confident that they had left none of the detachment that came after us to report back to the larger host. Although I wanted to depart right away, Raen in particular insisted that we remain sheltered for one more night against the frosty cold that had settled in.

The next morning, I spent a few moments inventorying Hridayesh's gear—something I always hated doing in the field, but was common, necessary practice. He carried surprisingly little, and true to assassin's form, nothing that would identify him. At the bottom of his satchel, I found the flask. Why had he wanted me to take it? I shook it, and it seemed quite full.

When I removed the cap, the odor that drifted up from the contents was familiar, but I could not say why. It certainly did not seem like something anyone would drink, with the way the scent of it burned the lining of my nose. I tipped a little of the contents onto the cavern floor. When the clear liquid hit the stone, the floor hissed and bubbled, and the liquid left the stone beneath it pock-marked and partially dissolved.

I replaced the cap. Why in the Maker's creation Hridayesh chose to carry this flask of caustic stuff, I could not fathom. But puzzling it out could wait for another time. I shoved the container into the bottom of my own satchel.

With Eyrnir's help, I hauled myself onto Majestrin's back, utilizing only my upper body and my good leg for the task. I settled into the saddle. The motion pulled a roar of pain from my throat as flexing my thighs to grip Majestrin's sides awoke blinding pain worse than anything I had ever felt. . . except perhaps the time Lord Scitherias had tried to crush me with dark magic. I blew out breaths and sucked them back in through my teeth.

Majestrin craned his head around to meet my glance. "You're going to have to ride with a lot less leg contact than I think you're used to, if you're going to ride at all, Vinyanel."

I narrowed my eyes. Bad riding technique in others rankled me enough, but to slacken to it myself?

"Don't worry." Majestrin chuckled. "I'm no strong-willed horse that will take advantage of you."

I sighed. "If only we could fly—that would take my mind off the pain. Any idea when you'll fly again?"

Majestrin looked away. "You mean 'if.'"

The notion crashed into the pit of my stomach like catapult shot. Might we both end up crippled from this endeavor? The possibility was too horrifying to ponder.

We set out, picking our way up the cave mountain first, and then weaving down the more gradual opposite side. The view from the peak displayed evidence that a glacier or other cataclysmic terrain-altering phenomenon had shorn the cave side of the mountain to a wall of stone. No creature could have ever assailed the place on foot. Eyrnir and Veranna took to the sky and scouted ahead. Iriscendra frisked along beside Majestrin, and Raen rode Mythrenese, still bare of any tack, and perched side-saddle, owing to her gown. Astounding she could do it, really.

"How far is this town?" I asked.

"On foot?" Raen replied. "We've estimated about a day and a half. It's in the western foothills of this arm of the mountains, where two large highways intersect."

"It is a settlement of significant size, is it not?"

Raen nodded. "I haven't seen it myself, but that's how Eyrnir has described it. How did you know?"

"My knowledge of this region, from previous excursions, leads me to believe this city we are approaching is Barrington. It is a mining settlement just over the border of Velon." I rolled my eyes. "Though I admit, my bearings could be off.

From Barrington, we should be able to use the eastward highway to cover a lot of ground in getting back toward the dragon-kin hive. But even the highway becomes treacherous within the mountains." I clenched my fists. *Too late* was not an option.

We lumbered along, and the pain in my leg, even though I tried to simply let it hang and did not tighten the muscles as all, gripped my entire lower body. We had to stop far more often than I would have allowed otherwise, when the continued pummeling on my body had sapped my strength to the point where I feared I would fall from the saddle.

On one such stop, Raen focused long scrutiny on her cast. She probed it with her other hand.

"I think I must have cracked this when I used it to club that dragon-kin," she said. "If we find a surgeon for Ecleriast, I would have this looked at too, but. . ."

I shoved away my own haze of agony for a moment, "But what?"

"Surgeons are expensive in the human world."

"Pssh." I waved a hand. "I am certain I can manage any mortal fee for care. The important thing is that your sword arm has proper support until it heals."

Raen's eyes rounded. "I—you—that's not necessary."

"Of course it is," I pressed. "If you can fight like you did back at the cavern with your off-hand, well, let us just say I should mind my manners around you once you can fight with your sword-arm."

Raen flushed. "Stop trying to wheedle your way onto my good side, Ecleriast."

I smiled. "You can call me Vinyanel."

Raen straightened her back and looked down her nose at me with a little half-smirk pulling at the corner of her lips. "I'll think about it."

I half-expected a snide remark to come my way about the

bit of thaw between Raen and me, but the lingering silence after her words reminded me: there would be no more ribbing from Hridayesh. That reality stung with surprising acidity. I blinked against the prickle of tears in my eyes.

I beat back the notion that I had led yet another comrade to his death. In both Beriadhan's and Hridayesh's honor, I fought to frame my thoughts in truth. It was a persistent loss, however, and it mocked me from the darkest recesses of my mind whenever the journey grew too quiet.

Our route led us by nightfall to the Trans-Velonese highway, which ran north-south and enjoyed blessedly welcome maintenance. For all their scrabbling disorganization in other areas, the Velonese humans did keep good, gravel-surfaced roads that they graded well to prevent ruts and pooling. They even saw fit to mark the leagues. We made significant progress until well after dark, until I, even in my urgency, conceded we must make camp and rest.

The next day, we put many leagues behind us, but I lost much of the journey to drowsing. The weather was cold and damp, but I shivered more than I should in such conditions. My fever was rising again, and my joints ached. I wearied of illness. If the surgeon insisted he would need to take my leg in order for me to be well again, could I accept that? Who would I be without swordsmanship and riding to define me?

The longer I spent feverish and racked with pain, the more inevitable life-altering prospects began to seem.

Even worse, not even Majestrin had words of assurance for me. The farther we tromped, the lower his head drooped. In times of rest, he sank to the ground with deep sighs.

By late afternoon, I grew vaguely aware of conversation drifting around me.

"They can't, of course, come close to the city. The people here might have an all-out riot. I heard at the gate: there are already reports coming into the city of dragons abroad on the highway." Veranna's tone was grave.

"But look at him," Raen said. "Do you think he's going to walk on his own strength the last half-league?"

"No," Veranna replied. "But I think they'll tolerate Eyrnir with better fortitude than the dragons."

Majestrin blew out a long breath beneath me. "The memories of Scalgroth the Black are likely kept alive in fireside tales, particularly here. Veranna is right. Mythrenese, Iriscendra, and I should hunker down in the woods."

Iriscendra squawked. "Not when V'yennel still looking so . . . tired. Go with him."

"You can't begin to understand how bad an idea that is, little one," Majestrin replied. "Out of fear or greed, the humans would not think before they attacked you."

I opened my eyes and sought Iriscendra. She crouched low like a hunted creature. Her glance flitted from face to face, and I could practically hear her heart thundering. "But when he gets far . . . I start feel so . . . confused. Angry. Afraid."

My stomach knotted.

I hauled my wounded leg over Majestrin's back and slid to the ground. Instantly, the leg buckled. Raen and Veranna jumped to my side. They slipped a shoulder under each of my arms and prevented me from toppling.

"Take me closer to Iriscendra," I said through a clamped jaw.

We jostled our way to the hatchling. I reached a hand out and placed it on her head. "You must be brave. I will not put you at risk. Mythrenese and Majestrin," I shot the silver dragon a plaintive look, "will watch over you until I come back. It will be very short, and I will be much better then."

Iriscendra's lip quivered. "But—"

I glared her into silence. "Majestrin, you will take the two younger dragons to a high point, where you can watch this spot on the road." I gestured to the rectangular standing stone that marked the league. A deep *one-half* was graven into its surface on all four sides, near the top of its story of height. "We will return to this marker when it is time for us to reconvene."

Raen pulled a small, flat charm from the neckline of her dress. "I'll use the signal, Mythrenese."

The indigo dragon nodded.

"Before you go, however," I said, "I will have my armor. And I will need my sword and scabbard, and my belt pouch." Even if I was a sorry mess, I did not have to appear one. My chances of looking far worse *after* we found a surgeon loomed over my soul like a hammer, ready to strike.

28

THE BASIN OF SEEING

*B*arrington sprawled across a bowl-shaped valley, and the humans who lived there constructed its thousands of thick-walled buildings from the mottled gneiss readily available anywhere in the hills. Outside the city wall, ranches dotted the tumbled countryside, where young boys tended flocks of goats and sheep. We passed a large creamery, seemingly managed by several households that ringed their pastures and barns. By the roadside, a wooden stand displayed an array of hard and soft cheeses, jugs of cream, and crocks of curd. How long had it been since I had eaten a meal, let alone a fresh one?

A girl whose unlined features implied she had only just embarked upon her adult years sprinkled something into a wide bowl of curd. She began to toss the bits in a practiced motion, where she thrust the bowl out in front of her, then drew it back in a way that flipped its contents.

She glanced up from her work and her eye met mine. Her

eyebrows shot up. Although I had drawn my hood, my cloak did not conceal my armor, and even if it had, I was riding a griffon. Her surprise was warranted.

"Uh . . .try a squeaky curd, master?" she said. "I just turned them out now." She propped the bowl on her hip and tugged at the triangular scarf holding her hair back. The laced corset around her waist imparted a feminine shape upon her billowy, shirred blouse.

The Western tongue. How out of practice had I gotten? Little in the life of an elf required the clunky language's regular use. I formulated a few words in my mind before trying them aloud. "A small taste." Truth be told, I was leery of testing my stomach, with my recent propensity for vomiting. That would likely distract this girl from offering me information.

The milk-maid grabbed a pair of tongs and plucked one of the little cheese lumps free of the batch. She extended it to me. It was less than a bite, but I still only nibbled half. A salty, creamy, divine nibble at that . . . the best thing to have passed my lips since perhaps officiating Delsinon's tournament months ago. And it even stayed down.

I smiled. "Thank you. Could you tell me if there is a good surgeon in the city?"

The girl turned her head slightly, scrunched her brows together, and bit her lip. "My apologies. A what?"

I reviewed the words I had used. Had I chosen the wrong word for surgeon? Could I make it simpler? "A person who mends . . .hurts? Broken bones. Cuts."

The milk-maid leaned forward, her expression intent. "Oh! A *surgeon*. Now I understand. It's just your accent." She flushed. "I mostly only sell to locals."

Veranna snickered. "It *is* pretty awful, Lieutenant Commander."

I turned half a scowl to Veranna.

"But to answer your question," the milk-maid continued.

"I'm pretty sure there is. I'd have to ask Papa to come up with a name. Can you wait?"

"We can."

She spun, and her long woolen skirt flared with the motion.

"But before you go, perhaps a small satchel of—what did you call it? Squeaky curd?"

Her simple face blossomed into a bright smile. "My pleasure." She used a metal scoop to dole out a portion of her fresh cheese onto a cloth, then tied it up with twine. "Five pennies, please."

I fished in my pouch for a coin. I had nothing but gold with me. I handed her one of the coins.

Her eyes bulged. She held the coin between her fingers and stared at it a long moment. "This is like art. I don't even know how much it's worth."

"I don't need change," I said. "But hopefully the remainder of the coin after it pays for the curd will compensate you for your trouble in getting that name for me."

She nodded. "The surgeon. Right. One moment." A quick dash later, and she had vanished around the house behind the cheese stand.

"Well, I must say," Veranna said. "You handled that far more civilly than I would have guessed you capable."

I shrugged. "I feel too awful to act myself. And the cheese is good." I extended the pouch to Veranna and Raen.

*E*ven without the dragons, we still drew plenty of notice as we made our way into Barrington. The maidens had drawn their cloaks close around their garb and hoods low over much of their faces, but this seemed only to arouse more curiosity than it dispelled. Armed with the surgeon's name, Ackley Adelharde, we passed the simple, swinging gate in Barrington's low wall amidst whispers and stares.

My brief spurt of civility weakened as I rode. For the first time in my life, the desire to dismount and lay down somewhere—anywhere—overwhelmed my usual infatuation with riding.

Barrington's streets were a tangled, illogical mess, clogged with vendors, beggars, and well-dressed loiterers offering commentary on it all for one another's amusement or consternation. The city was apparently set up in several districts, each with its own central hub. The surgeon kept a shop somewhere in the Guardsman Hill section of the city on the western side. Having entered through the south gate, I assumed if we worked our way left and uphill, we would find it. If only any street would continue straight for more than a half-dozen blocks.

Raen hugged her arms around her middle and seemed to shrink the farther into the city we progressed.

"Are you feeling all right?" I asked.

She eyed the graceless-but-functional architecture on either side of the narrow street with wary suspicion. "It's been a while since I've been anyplace so . . . confining."

"We were in Bilearne not so very long ago."

"It's different when the buildings are empty, but it was still bad enough." Raen shuddered.

True, Barrington's streets sometimes grew a little tight, but in terms of size and population, Delsinon dwarfed the place. I shrugged and pressed onward. Turn after turn carried us through the meandering streets. The dead ends and unexpected forks in the road steered us along the skirts of the hill, but never up, and no sign we passed indicated a surgeon's presence. The foot traffic in the byways thinned as we passed from a market district into a residential area. The few residents in our path cast us nervous glances before bustling inside or out of sight.

Thanks to the snatches of conflicting directions we were able to gather from the few locals willing to speak with us, the sun was well on its journey to the horizon when we found Ackley Adelharde's shop. Over the front door, a wooden sign with burnt letters read *Adelharde's: Bones Mended, Ailments Cured, Wounds Tended.*

I slid from Eyrnir's back, and this time, Veranna and Raen were already in place to keep me from collapsing.

"Ugh, do you really have to wear all this armor?" Raen said.

"No," I replied. "But unless you would prefer to carry my casket back to Delsinon, it has proven useful on multiple occasions. I guarantee the coffin would be heavier."

"Now that's the Vinyanel I know," Veranna said. "Mean for no reason." She pulled open the door. "Come now, in we go."

"One moment," I said. "Eyrnir. No use waiting here with so many fearful eyes upon you wherever we go. Watch for us at the south gate."

Eyrnir glanced around the street, his gaze lingering on the goggle-eyed boys and the mothers who gripped their children's shoulders with protective strength. The griffin rolled his eyes and shrugged his wings, but eventually bobbed his head in a hawkish nod. "As you wish, sir." He turned. After a few strides, thrust his wings and launched skyward.

Only two of us could squeeze through the surgeon's shop door at the same time, so Raen remained my crutch, and Veranna trailed in after us. The entry of the shop was a tight room of tile with a counter along one side and three doors on the back wall. A stick-figure of a man stood up from a stool behind the counter.

He scratched his head, further mussing his strawberry-blonde curls. He lowered bushy, straw-gold eyebrows at us. "What's this, dare I ask?"

"Are you Ackley Adelharde?" I asked.

He straightened his back. "By your talk, you've come a long way looking for leech craft, I'd warrant. But yes, I am. And who are you?"

I reached up with my free arm and pulled my hood back. "My name is Lieutenant Commander Vinyanel Ecleriast, Windrider Battalion of the Delsin."

"Delsin? You've come farther than I even guessed. But why come to me? I'm sure I know little, compared with the elves."

"You were closer," I said. "As to what you know, we shall see."

"Please forgive the lieutenant commander's disposition," Veranna said. "He can't help himself." She turned her head over her shoulder. "Wounded or not," she added in an Elvish whisper.

He eyed my armor, particularly the rent in my cuisse. "I'd venture the issue you're looking for me to mend whatever is behind that tear in your . . .um . . ."

"Cuisse," I said. "Yes. Can you stitch a large gash that involves muscle and skin?"

Adelharde rubbed his chin. "A deep one, eh? Well, if it's complex, it does cost more. Of course, you understand . . ." He looked at me sidelong, cracked his knuckles, and rubbed his hands.

I huffed. "Of course. I would rather not banter. As you can probably tell, standing is not exactly convenient."

The surgeon gulped. "Very well, I meant no trouble. If you'd come this way." He jabbed a nervous point toward the left-most doorway

We tromped our way toward the room he indicated. Beside the doorway hung a polished oval mirror. As we passed it, Raen gasped.

"Why didn't anyone tell me I'm such a sight?" she cried. She stopped outside the doorway. "I look like some kind of madwoman whose principal fear is water, with a side phobia of soap!"

"Traveling in the wilderness for weeks on end will do that."

I pulled my arm from around her shoulder. "If you need more time to gape, I can limp from here."

Raen clutched my arm before I could work it completely free. "And undo all my handiwork? I think not." She craned her neck back toward the surgeon. "Where would you like him?"

Adelharde shooed us through the doorway. "There's a cot inside. He can sit on that. And if you want, there is a washroom with a full tub of hot water in the third room . . . not a free bath mind you, but—"

"Perfect!" Raen beamed. She hustled me to the cot and turned so I could sit.

The surgeon's skeptical glance at Raen's cast snuffed her smile. "Maybe Veranna could at least help me wash my hair?"

"If there's a smaller basin in the room to work with," Veranna said.

Adelharde nodded, and the two maidens headed out.

The act of lowering my weight to the cot squeezed a growl from my lungs, despite my best efforts to keep it contained. I clenched the sheet that covered the stuffed mattress with whitening knuckles.

"Whenever you're ready," Adelharde said. "No rush. But shall we have a look?"

I worked the buckles loose on the rent cuisse, but it took both of us to work it off my leg, owing to my reluctance to lift my thigh. I scrunched up my pant leg.

Adelharde cut the bandage free with a pair of shears, and I had to admire the fact that his expression remained flat upon his first glance at the wound he revealed. He leaned closer.

"Laceration of significant depth . . . moderate infection in the surrounding tissue." He tapped his chin. "My guess is that there's been tissue loss. Is that what the girl was talking about when she said 'handiwork?' Has she already surgically removed tissue from this injury?"

I shuddered. "Not exactly surgically. She did treat it, though."

Adelharde waited with a cocked brow.

"It was surrounded by blisters filled with a dark, noisome fluid. My understanding is that she packed larvae into it while I was unconscious."

"Did she?" The surgeon clapped his hands together. "Well, tidy work, that! You owe that girl your life, if it was as bad as you say."

Part of me already knew that, but I still shivered at the thought. "You can patch it up the rest of the way, correct? I am hard-pressed to complete a mission I've begun."

"Complete a mission?" Adelharde scratched at his head. "I can stitch it, but you'd do better to rest the leg for a couple of weeks, at least."

"Two weeks? Can I ride during that time?"

Adelharde grimaced. "Let me put it this way—if it hurts, it probably isn't rest. And if I may be so bold, a man who's been in as bad a shape as you were is usually talking bone saws or headstones with me, not rest. I'd do my best to recognize a miracle, if I were you."

So, no bone saw in my near future—thank the Maker for that.

I rubbed my forehead. "Not that I lack gratitude. I simply have some unyielding circumstances I have to align."

"One moment, if you will." Adelharde meandered from the examination room, and the clinks and rustles of rummaging ensued. A moment later, he returned with a brown glass bottle, only about an eighth full. He pulled the stopper with a pop. "You need to drink this. I fear it's short dose for someone of your, um, rather . . . bulk. But it's a start. You'll need more, though."

I took the bottle and sniffed it. The alcohol of the medicine seared the inside of my nose, but I tipped it back anyway. As the scent rumored, the dose burned from the moment it touched my lips until it reached my stomach. I coughed. "What is this?"

"White willow tincture, primarily." Adelharde beamed. "That should start in on the fever. But you'll need poke root and echinacea salve too. I can probably have both in the morning."

"Probably?" I looked at him from under my brows. "I do not have time to dawdle about this . . ." I restrained the colorful descriptor on my tongue. "City."

Adelharde took a step back and wrung his hands. "You don't have to follow my advice. But then, you don't have to get well if you don't want, either."

~

*R*aen opened the door to the bathing chamber, and a cloud of steam warmed her cheeks. A little taste of home, in some ways. How she had come to take for granted constant access to hot water like she had in the springs back in the Vale—where bathing daily was as simple as stepping from the cavern she called home. Had she even brought enough soap to remedy the mess she had become?

Square tiles of pale marble lined the floor of the room and covered the lower three feet of the walls. Narrow windows of frosted glass allowed the afternoon sunlight in. In the room's center stood an enormous marble bathing tub, propped on iron feet, and beneath it, coals glowed in a shallow pit. Wisps of steam curled from the water's surface.

Veranna immediately swept over to a long side table in the chamber and picked up a turned wooden bowl. She dipped it into the main tub and filled the basin about half way, then set the vessel on the floor.

"So, maybe if I pull a stool up to the edge of the tub, I could lean over it, and you could help me wet my hair, since I can only use one hand?" Raen said.

Veranna pulled a ring from her left hand, then held it up before her at arm's length. Keeping her eyes focused on the jade circle, she replied, "In a bit. There's something I must try first."

With a tiny splash, the ring dropped into Veranna's basin of water. The prophetess sat cross legged by the bowl and raised her face to the heavens for a silent moment. She cast her gaze to the basin and there it remained.

Raen waited. Veranna uttered not a word. After a long stretch of uneventful waiting, a faint light began to illuminate Veranna's features from below. Raen edged closer.

The ring at the bottom of the basin glowed bright and golden. The water in the basin shimmered and shifted, until the waves of gold on its surface coalesced into a form—the faint contours of a face? Raen stared. Transfixed. What could Veranna be doing? The face in the water moved in such a way that mimicked the facial expressions of speech, but all Raen could hear was the discussion between Ecleriast and the surgeon in the next room.

A thousand questions rampaged through Raen's mind, but would interrupting Veranna somehow break the enchantment? Painful as it was, she bit her tongue.

Nearly a quarter of an hour passed with Veranna still staring into the vessel, so Raen eventually stepped away and contemplated if there was a way she could go ahead and bathe without the prophetess's help. Just as she had resolved to go ahead and dunk her head in the tub, a rustle from across the room caught her ear.

Veranna stood, rubbing her temples. She had returned the ring to her hand, and the basin contained nothing more than ordinary water.

"I've never seen an enchantment of that sort," Raen said.

Veranna lowered her voice to a whisper. "One of the little ways those in charge of Vinyanel, whether he chooses to remember them or not, keep track of his exploits. The conversation went better than I could have hoped."

"So Ecleriast's superiors aren't overly peeved at him?" Raen asked.

"Oh, I didn't say that." Veranna picked the bowl up from the floor. "Let's get you cleaned up, since it looks like you might end up meeting some of them."

29

WEAK SPOTS

*T*hough the trip to the surgeon lightened my pouch by a half-dozen gold pieces, his meticulous stitching proved well worth the price. Although even expertly-administered stitches still hurt like fire and salt. He sent me on my way with crutches and his promise to get further tinctures and salves from the apothecary as soon as the chemist opened his doors in the morning.

He reinforced Raen's cast where her use of it as a club had cracked it, and we all left clean. While I had not given half a thought to how filthy I had gotten, the ashen color I left the wash water told the extent of the tale. It was good to feel civilized again, for now.

Once Adelharde had shut his shop door behind us, I adjusted my crutches under my arms and said, "Back to Majestrin, then."

Veranna cocked her head. "Wouldn't you rather remain here for the night? It seems silly to travel hours back and forth."

"Back and forth?" I squinted at her. "Why?"

"For the medicine you need," Raen said. "That's probably more important than the stitches, you realize."

Veranna gestured to the wattle-and-daub buildings on either side of the cobbled road. "Surely there's a respectable inn somewhere nearby. Hot food, actual beds... but if we camp with Majestrin for the night, we end up having to make the long trek back in the morning."

"We are not returning in the morning." I crutched my way forward, through the deepening shadows of the buildings around us. "I see little reason to lose nearly a day of travel better used to close in on the chalice ..."

Raen frowned.

" . . . *and* Aulus's daughters. Surely neither of you would contest the necessity we avoid leaving ourselves too little time on that." I pressed onward, and my companions flanked me.

"It's only a matter of hours, Vinyanel." Raen stepped in front of me, blocking my path. "Hours your leg could use to finally scab a bit. Surely you didn't intend to march toward the hive under the dark of night. Even you need to sleep sometimes."

"I suppose I could concede a few hours' rest once we get back to the dragons. But a trip back here once civilians have begun business?" I scoffed. "Too great an expenditure for questionable benefit."

The pleading in Raen's eyes caught me off-guard. "We've come all this way, and you have a chance to get everything you need to become entirely well. Please don't throw that away."

An awkward heat crept up my neck. Raen's pinched brow suggested a level of emotion I preferred not to contemplate. I played it off with a quip. "Oh come now. Surely you have enough projects to keep your attention that you do not need to add me to that list."

Raen's expression of concern gave way to indignation. She

swung a backhanded punch right at my new stitches. When her knuckles connected with my wound, stars exploded across my vision. My leg gave way. I lost my balance. My hip connected with the cobblestones.

"Blast, Raen," I clutched my leg and sucked deep breaths against the inferno of agony pulsing through it. "What was that for?"

Veranna gaped. "He just got put back together."

Raen gestured to me. "If I can knock Ecleriast down with a single punch right now, how will he stand against dragon-kin who will do far worse? Do you send wounded soldiers to the front lines? Even wounded horses?"

"This is a time-sensitive operation that lacks the luxury of reinforcements." I rocked and groaned.

"How far are we from the hive?" Raen asked.

I took a moment to make a mental calculation, when a sudden reality struck me. With Hridayesh's death, we again had enough airworthy mounts to fly. The fact brought with it both freedom and the sting of loss. "If Veranna and I ride double on Eyrnir, it occurs to me our timing depends solely on what sort of pace Majestrin can keep."

Raen faced Veranna. "And how many days until the new moon?"

"Twelve," the prophetess said.

"But did the surgeon not say you needed to avoid activities that cause you pain in the wound if you want it to actually heal?" Raen said. "Riding hurts, there's no hiding that."

"I thought you were taking a bath, not eavesdropping," I grumbled.

"I wasn't eavesdropping." Raen huffed. "You two were going to no pains to keep quiet. Let's discuss a worst-case and assume we have to go on foot still. How long?"

"About ten days," I said.

"And so that leaves time to both wait for the medicine and

time to get there," Raen said. "If Ecleriast will agree to rest on the way, then maybe he won't go prone at the first dragon-kin that clubs him with its tail."

I sat in silent pain until my vision cleared. Raen was right. I would get them all killed if I could not withstand even a simple blow.

"Very well, you two win this time." I heaved my way back to my feet. "But once we acquire the medication in the morning, we put this city behind us."

The next challenge in a list of impossibilities: to cross a mountain range and rest at the same time.

~

*N*aghax frowned at the small, weaving script of the texts spread on the table before him. He blinked burning eyes. Diagrams, scribbled notes, and scraps of vellum containing clues he dared not misplace hung on every spare inch on his study's earthen walls. His heavy chair creaked as he leaned closer to the manuscript on top of his central pile.

Pounding on the door jolted him from his concentration.

"Who's there?" he said.

"Hanash," came the answer.

"Enter." Naghax sat back and stretched his stiff muscles. So many hours of hunching over scrolls and crumbling books had bound his travel-weary muscles into knotted cords.

The door *swooshed* outward, fluttering Naghax's research documents.

"Inquisitor Ezio requires a written report on the status of your preparations for the sacrifice." Hanash delivered the edict in a flat tone.

"Does he?" Naghax replied. "Since when did that softbelly, no matter how important he is within his own herd of uncivilized cretins, become privy to my gleanings?"

"Since he made the summoning's success a condition of the treaty." Hanash stomped into the little room. "We've lost a degree of favor with the escape of the half-elf witch and her lethal little friend."

Naghax pointed to the half-dozen sets of writings that littered his desk. "How does that deflect onto me and become my problem? Does he think weeding through five languages, one of them nearly extinct, is something one does in just a handful of days? Even if I had all my notes transcribed in the order I will need them, we have yet to harvest and dry enough of the nightshade fungus. Slaying the girls is only a single facet of a ritual of web-like intricacy."

"Then your documents had best convey both the intricacy and your competence. It is important we re-establish his confidence."

Naghax snapped. "To summarize what I'm doing is a waste of time that I don't expect his inferior human mind to comprehend. And frankly, I trust Ezio and his sword slingers little."

"Are you truly so thick-skulled? With the number of fiends we can summon through the Chalice's power, we need more curse-bearers to bind and command. The Tebalese offer us that, as well as foot soldiers who suffer no ill effects in a daylight battle."

"I don't like it," Naghax said. "Power is a notoriously difficult commodity to share. And Ezio continually stinks of horse and cheap liquor."

Hanash turned to depart. "Then I advise you breathe through your mouth and fake some cordiality. The Inquisitor will be here to gather the document he's requested tonight. And he mentioned he'll bring a marking knife in case you're less prepared than you say."

"So now you're threatening me in his place?" Naghax snorted. "How quickly you've become the pet lizard of that scale-less imbecile. We're lucky we didn't end up killing the

Elgadrim girls with the pace he demanded we set just to get back here. Now get out of my study, if you want me to get any closer to adhering to your leash-holder's pointless demands."

"Pray you can do so. My understanding is the fates of those the Tebalese mark are particularly deplorable," Hanash said. "And while you're working, you might want to meditate upon whom you keep as allies." The door clicked shut behind him.

Naghax turned his attention back to the writings. Allies, indeed. His scowl deepened. While he had entered this plot as the scholar needed to execute Hanash's plan, it looked more and more as though working with Hanash meant answering to Ezio. Naghax clamped his maw tight.

Somewhere beyond the walls and twisting corridors of the dragon-kin's mountain hive, he could sense the sun had already risen. He thrust away his weariness and focused on the study of the incantations to be pronounced over his sacrifice knife. Did Hanash fear he lacked enough true authority to rule the dragon-kin without Ezio as a prop? Was there any concrete edict that said their ruler needed to wield curses? An inkling brought a conspiratorial grin to Naghax's face.

Sleep could wait.

30

LOCATE, ASSESS, ENGAGE

I stashed the jar of balm in my pack, as well as the bottle of tincture, my belt pouch even lighter of gold than I dared imagine such remedies could make it. The medicine had drained me of more than my stitches and Raen's cast repairs combined.

"One last purchase, and that should do it," Veranna said.

I threw my hands up. "Are we on a holiday by the sea? We have restocked our provisions, been gouged for herbs, ate multiple meals in actual inns for a change . . . I could court both of you with less pampering."

Veranna scoffed. "Your idea of courtship is lean indeed. What we need is perfectly unromantic, so that should suit you. We need a cart."

"What in the blazes for?" I asked.

"For you to ride in," Raen replied. "Eyrnir has already agreed to pull it."

Of all the ridiculous notions. "And when people see us

coming, they will call for acrobatics and sword swallowers. What a ridiculous troupe we will—"

"Could you, just for one moment, try to forget how you'll look?" Veranna said. "Do the girls who the dragon-kin have dragged off to a dungeon you yourself have said is a place of horror care if you show up on a charger or in a cargo bed? They simply want someone to show up at all."

I ground my teeth. "Very well. Let us hope a cartwright is easier to find in this town than a surgeon."

～

*G*rumbling under my breath, I shortened the backstrap of the harness to accommodate the way wings and a leonine body mismatched the fit of horse tack. I rechecked the collar, the shaft pockets, and the girth. "You are certain you are comfortable?"

Eyrnir nodded. "I will be fine, Lieutenant Commander."

No beast had suffered so much as a saddle sore under my care. I smoothed the portion of Eyrnir's mane that ran under the collar.

The cartwright pulled a light, two-wheeled rig up behind the griffon, set the shafts down and cast the griffon a wide-eyed glance. "You seem to know your way around this sort of thing, master," he said. "You want to finish the hitch?"

"Ow!" Veranna cried.

I wheeled toward her. She held the sides of her head and had her eyes squeezed shut.

"What?" My pulse quickened. The last thing we needed was another delaying issue.

"It appears whatever phenomenon was masking your signature has now worn off," Veranna said. "I don't know why I expected I would begin sensing your signature again in some gradual way, but you're definitely back. I feel as though I've been clubbed with a cactus."

I shuffled. Would I ever grow accustomed to Veranna's ability to feel my presence? "One more mystery out of the way, then." I faced the merchant. "Yes, I can take things from here."

I pulled the shafts of the cart up on either side of Eyrnir, threaded them through the pockets, and unrolled the leather traces attached to his collar back to hook them to the cart's singletree. After I clipped the shafts to Eyrnir's breeching, Veranna and I boarded the cart while Raen opted to walk beside it. We made our way for Barrington's south gate.

After about a quarter hour of bumping along streets that never seemed so uneven until we rolled hard wheels over them, a light blur diving toward us from the sky caught my eye. I snapped my head toward it, just in time for Iriscendra to open her wings wide and slow her descent.

"V'yennel!" she cried. "There you are! Your sing-a-chur's back."

"What are you doing here?" I said. "You were to wait for me with Majestrin and—"

Mythrenese arced over a rooftop to the left and joined us as well. "Raen! Veranna, Vinyanel. Come quickly!" He panted for breath.

My blood sped through my veins. "What has happened?"

Iriscendra grasped my shoulders implored with sapphire eyes. "It's 'Jestrin, V'yennel. Men got him."

The news pummeled me like a battering ram. "What do you mean 'got him?' Be more specific. And what kind of men?"

"Men with a long bunch of colored . . . um . . ." Iriscendra pursed her lips in thought.

"Wagons!" Mythrenese cried. "More wagons than we could ever count. The women dressed a lot like Veranna, but they were darker of face."

"Caravanners, then," Veranna said. "What did they do to Majestrin?"

I braced myself, unsure if I wanted to know the answer.

"Caught him!" Iriscendra blurted. "He told us fly 'way. Didn't fight at all. Just let them tie him up."

If I had been standing, I would have collapsed with relief. "Where are they now?"

"Headed this way, but very slow with all those . . ,wagons . . . and people walking too." Iriscendra tugged on my cloak with her teeth. "Gotta help him."

"You are right, little one," I said. "Show us the way."

We proved maddeningly slow, even with Eyrnir towing the cart at a gallop. The road from Barrington provided the primary route for commerce and to the mines upon which they based their economy, and was thus choked with morning traffic. The terrain off the road proved too rough for driving.

Due to Barrington's location in the foothills, the road snaked among rocky hillsides dotted with twisted trees, The journey progressed at gallop-crawl-maneuver-gallop intervals that threatened to part me from my sanity every time we hit a snarl of carts, pedestrians, or riders.

Veranna tapped me on the shoulder, jarring me from introspection. "Given the situation, I don't think it will be wise to simply barrel up to the caravan. Unless you want to run the risk of losing Eyrnir too."

"I do not understand." I swiveled to her. "What about these folk should I know?"

"My best guess is that they've captured Majestrin as a centerpiece to an ultimate sideshow," she said. "Why he allowed it, I can't begin to imagine. But it's likely they number a thousand road-hardened individuals or more. Even a carvanner child is a person not to be trifled with."

I rubbed my tightening neck. "Then we shall need to keep the young dragons and griffon clear of them as we proceed. We will locate them, make a tactical assessment of the situation, and then engage the target. Standard procedure enough."

Raen narrowed her eyes at me. "I think that depends on what you mean by 'engage the target.' Surely you don't mean to blaze in with your blade whistling. Even if you were in your best form, the sheer numbers Veranna is talking about would spell calamity."

"I shall fight on one leg if I have to . . . if that is what it will take to see Majestrin free."

Veranna sighed. "While we're still on our way, I think you'd best spend some time praying for persuasiveness."

I opened my copy of *The Tree*. Lifting my face to the heavens, I prayed, *Creo, guide me to wisdom. May what I read here arm me with convincing words, should I require them.*

Though why the mightiest creature I had ever beheld might need my help to recover his freedom was a mystery I could not even begin to unravel.

31

CAGE OF TIMBER, CAGE OF ICE

*G*audy banners flew high over a broad tent city atop a plateau on the west side of the road, about an hour outside of Barrington. The caravanners had parked their wagons in a wide circle to create a contained fairgrounds of sorts, and they pitched their tents within. We drove at an unhurried walk on the highway, amidst the traffic passing by, but our beast of burden was now a very ordinary-looking dun horse we had purchased at one of Barrington's outlying ranches, rather than a griffon. Iriscendra lay curled under a pile of tent canvas in the small cargo bed of the cart. Mythrenese and Eyrnir flew somewhere to our northeast, seeking cover until we could make some decisions about Majestrin. Raen sat beside me on the cart's driver's seat.

Once we drew within about a quarter mile of the gypsy caravan's encampment, the cry of accented voices reached my ears. Men bearing parchments paced along the length of the road, handing the bills to any passersby that would take them.

Veranna walked beside the cart, on the far side from the gypsy caravan. She wrapped her cloak tighter over her garb. "I have no idea who the caravan master might be of this group, but for safety's sake, I think one of you had better do the talking if one of those hawkers approaches us."

"Better one of us than someone who shares their heritage?" I said.

"You make enemies when you run away from the circus," Veranna replied.

Raen started. "Wasn't that a long time ago?"

The prophetess sighed. "Not long enough."

A man in a wide hat rimmed in bells, a ratty doublet, two-toned pantaloons, and a shirred tunic stepped up to our vehicle, waving one of his parchments. "Come tonight! The show begins. Beautiful damsels, feats of daring, and a glimpse of the silver terror! A sight never seen by mortal eyes, 'least none that ever lived to tell the tale—'til now."

I pulled my hood low and reached for the bill. A lunging, serpentine silhouette sprawled across the center of the paper. "A beast like this?" I said.

"More terrifying than you can imagine," the hawker said, his face alight with a mischievous grin.

"Alas, we will not be back this way tonight. Could we come now?"

The hawker laughed. "Oh, no, no! Tonight. Change your plans. You don't want to miss this. Pledge me coin now, and I'll be sure you get a spot right up front."

I warred with the notion for a moment. Was it worth gold to buy access to Majestrin's location? He would be easy enough to find. "No, I cannot," I said. "Pressing business. My loss."

"Indeed. The tales you hear will make you regret declining." The man laughed, snapped the parchment from my hand, and moved to the next traveler.

Once we had continued past the reach of the caravan's

criers, Raen took a long look back at the tent city. "Do you see what sorts of ridiculous behavior stem from people's misconceptions about dragons?"

From a limited angle, yes, I could see why Raen chose the path she had with the dragons in her keeping. But the plan seemed so short-sighted. "It is completely impractical, Raen," I said. "Your few trained creatures, as charming as I am sure they are, cannot undo centuries of fear and superstition. And what of the crazed dragons that are worthy of dread?"

"We just need to intercede," Raen said. "If the marauders have eggs, claim them, as I have. I'm certain I have prevented the corruption of at least four dragons so far. With enough careful attention, evil dragons would eventually become extinct."

Of course, her plan rode solely on the supposition that evil was a learned behavior, or at least one that could be trained out of a creature. That was a larger debate for another time.

"Wait . . .you have stolen eggs from four separate, maniac dragons?"

Raen stretched taller and regarded me with heavy lidded eyes. "Six, if you count the two whose mates were present."

I blew a whistle. "But going forward, you propose to find every one? The world wide?"

A cunning grin curled her lip. "I'd have a better chance with help."

I batted away the whisper of intrigue attached to that statement. Deeper moral questions rumbled under the surface. "There are people who will never understand dragonkind. How many can say they have known the caress of the skies, as we have? The joy and the power—and at the same time, the sense of complete insignificance that comes in riding the wind? No Raen, they cannot truly know, and in fact, few sane people want to."

She listened to me, wide eyed and silent. A furrow deepened between her eyebrows. Her attention shifted inward.

"Consider the dragons who are not psychotic, though. We cannot ask them to cease being dragons in order to eliminate the sense of threat to those who will forever consider them alien." I said. "Out of my respect for Majestrin, I could never demand he be something other than what Creo made him to be. I think you would be amazed to see what your brood could do, if you would give them the rein to explore their gifts."

"Do you truly mean all this—I mean, I know you do about the abomin...the breath, but about the flying?" Raen asked.

"I always say what I mean," I replied. "Even when it would have been better had I kept my mouth shut."

Raen's eyes brightened. "I've just never heard anyone talk about flying the way you did." She tugged her cloak tighter. "I figured you simply viewed it as a means to an end. A military tool."

"An excellent tool, I will admit," I said. "But even riding horseback has been a passion for me from the first day I put my foot in a stirrup. And I admire the symbiosis between rider and mount."

She nodded and fell silent again.

Had she finally heard me? Her smile, laced with warmth I almost feared to believe, kindled satisfaction in my heart. It was good to know someone understood, at least in part, the thrill that owned my joy.

*A*fter an agonizing afternoon of waiting with the dragons and Eyrnir in the shelter of a copse of fir trees about a league from the encampment, Raen, Veranna, and I traveled back toward Barrington and the spectacle that awaited there. Only because Iriscendra could once again sense my signature did she concede staying behind.

"This very un-magic place," Iriscendra told me. "Can find

you and 'Ranna quick with no other sing-a-churs to confuse me."

I laughed. "Remind me to work on your grammar when we get back."

Torches lit the perimeter of the place the caravanners had set up, burning in a spectrum of hues. Some of the flames guttered in green, others blue, some lavender, while others danced in every warm color from pale yellow to blood-red. Jugglers, acrobats, singers, soothsayers, and dancing women whose neck- and hemlines wedged a lump in my throat all warred for patrons' attention. There was food, song, and far too much drink.

People celebrated in a frenzy as though only a few short hours would contain all the abandon they might enjoy for the rest of their lives. For a while, the spectacle drew my fascinated focus, but it took little time for my interest to sicken at the futility and desperation behind the dark-lined eyes, powdered faces, and fortune-telling cards. It was no wonder Veranna had fled this life, though the full tale of that, she had not yet divulged. At least not to me.

We pressed through the throng, slowly due to my crutches, and often forced on a circuitous route by the press of the crowds. But finally, we reached the northwest edge of the fair, and there we beheld it—a towering dome of bent poles, hewn hastily from stripped young trees and lashed together with scraggly hemp. Inside, Majestrin lay. He did not stir, but from the way the scales around his closed eyes crinkled, it was apparent he held his eyes shut rather than slumbered.

A length of rope bound his snout closed, wrapped around countless times. Heavy chains ran between both his front and hind legs, though I doubted even they would withstand his strength if he chose to strive against them. More rope wound around his tail, which ended at a series of a dozen knots around a pole driven into the ground.

Rage mounted in me with each coil of rope, with each link of chain I observed. Why had he not simply swept away every one of his captors when they tried to wrap his tail? He could have crushed anyone who dared come within ten paces of his talons. Did many caravanners lose their lives to a frosty end before they managed to bind his maw? He bore no visible wounds, as aside from the gash to his head the humans did not deal him.

"Who dares step into the cage with this spawn of death itself?" a man cried over the thick crowd around the cage.

I moved to raise my hand, but Raen grabbed my arm. "What are you doing? I thought this was the tactical assessment, not 'Ecleriast makes up the plan by himself.'"

The barker chose a drunk Barrington youth. "You're sure, now? I assure you, this is a real dragon, able to bite you in half if something goes wrong."

The drunkard laughed. "I'll stab him through the eye if he tries." He patted the hunting knife on his belt.

Enough of the crowd scoffed for me to satisfy my indignation for the moment.

The barker cocked his head. "If you say so. Five silver." He put out his hand.

Veranna pulled Raen and me close. "We should come back when this all winds down," she whispered. "It will be in the wee hours, but don't you think we could sneak in and find a way to get him out of here less likely to bring the whole sideshow crew down on us?"

"C'mon, ya big lizard. Too much of a coward to even look at me?" The man who elected to brave the cage kicked Majestrin in the snout. The crowd around us gasped as one.

I lunged forward. Both Raen and Veranna dove at me and grappled my arms. If not for my blasted crutches, I would have broken free.

"I know this is awful, Vinyanel, but try to think for a moment," Raen said.

I wheeled on her, but I swallowed my outburst when I beheld the tears welling in her eyes. After choking the lump down, I said, "Why does he do nothing?"

"Who knows?" Veranna said. "But what we do know is that Majestrin is ancient and possesses the wisdom that comes with that. We need to get into a position to talk to him, then we can decide what to do. We see the battlefield, young Windrider. Have the patience to run the campaign only when the time is right."

We meandered the carnival grounds to pass the time, while I also committed as much of the layout of the place, and its potential obstacles, to memory. Veranna insisted we purchase food, drink, and the occasional trinket to mask our lingering.

The drinking, shows, and pagan revelry lasted later than even Veranna imagined, but eventually, sideshow guards armed with clubs and spears began to suggest the last die-hard revelers depart the rows of tents and booths. Merchants and performers wearily lowered tent flaps and closed the side panels to caravan wagons.

"Come again tomorrow night," they bade the lingering patrons. "There's always more to see."

I, for one, had seen more than enough.

We huddled behind the wagon nearest Majestrin's sorry excuse for a cage, and I placed a hand on both Veranna and Raen's shoulders.

"Ready?" I said.

"You're sure how this works?" Raen's voice quavered.

I was not. "Absolutely," I said anyway.

"Almighty Maker," I intoned, "grant us Delquessa's Zephyr, shadows amidst shadows will we drift. Swift, silent, and to your glory."

A buzzing energy swirled in my chest and spread through both my arms in a tingle that might have inspired me to laugh if my brow was not bathed in the sweat of fear. The maidens faded before my eyes, as did my hands, my arms, my legs, and finally all of my body that I could observe. Veranna and Raen held feminine forms, but had grown almost completely transparent, in smoky tones.

I stepped forward, but drifted rather than walked. My wounded leg meant nothing, as my feet had no need to touch the ground. My sheer will moved me any direction I desired with gentle swiftness. The glance I cast back to Veranna and Raen confirmed they too had discovered the means of movement, and the faint contours of Raen's features bloomed into a smile.

When a trio of armed gypsies marched past, I instinctively shrank back against the side of the wagon, but none of the men glanced our way. I led Veranna and Raen to the cage bars.

"Where is that door they used?" I whispered. When I caught sight of it, I restrained an oath. "Locked."

Veranna chuckled. "Vinyanel, you're a vapor. Drift through the bars."

I could do that? I would not break up and drift away? "Right." I willed myself forward.

A disorienting sensation of stretching and pulling overtook me, and while not painful, it was definitely alien, and I was grateful when my form took what I assumed to be its normal shape again on the inside of the barrier. I eased up to Majestrin's head. Now he did appear to be asleep. Did I dare wake a sleeping dragon, even one I had come to rescue?

"Majestrin, can you hear me?"

He breathed on in the deep rhythm of slumber.

"Wake up!" I said in a louder voice. My swift survey of the area confirmed no caravanners passed within earshot. "We have come to free you from all this."

Majestrin snorted, and the force of his breath buffeted my

wispy form. My heart fluttered in an irregular gallop. What would a stiff wind do to me?

The dragon opened his bright green eyes, and for a moment, stared, uncomprehending. His line of sight focused on me, and a crestfallen agony swept through his expression.

I reached for the bonds on his snout, but could not grasp them. My hand simply lost shape and spread around the contour of his scaly face.

"I release the Utterance, for me alone," I said.

The groundward pull of my weight settled me back to earth, and the weakness in my leg became all too apparent again. I pulled one of my crutches from my back and leaned on it. In a swift stroke, I slid one of my daggers under Majestrin's bonds and cut them. I ripped them away.

The dragon closed his eyes. "I did not want you to see me like this. Did the young dragons not tell you to continue on the mission without me?"

I guffawed. "Go without you? Nonsense, we can have you out of here in moments."

Majestrin kept his head on the ground. "Why bother?"

I stammered a few words that failed to form any cohesive thought. Finally, I spat out, "I do not understand."

"What good is a flightless dragon to the eventual High Lord of the Windriders? I'm nothing but a bungling liability. What am I but a pet in a cage, fit for nothing but mockery and scraps to grow fat upon?"

I shook my head in bafflement. "Did something happen? You are not making sense."

"Vinyanel." Majestrin met my gaze. "Go, leave me here. It won't be many years before Iriscendra will be large enough to serve as your mount. I am unfit for service."

Anger began to bubble up under my confusion. "How can you ask I do such a thing? You yourself even said you do not know how long it will take for your head to heal—"

"Ecleriast, pipe down!" Raen whispered from behind me. "Someone is going to hear you."

I leaned closer to Majestrin and whispered. "You cannot say with any certainty whether you will fly again. And even if you cannot be my mount . . ." My voice caught. "I need you. As a friend. As somebody with bushels more sense than me."

"We haven't even known each other for long enough for you to believe that." Majestrin's point came across faint-hearted.

"Long enough!" I reached down and lifted his face. At least I put pressure under his chin, and he agreed to lift his head and look me in the eye. "Do you know how it rent my soul when I contemplated the possibility the dragon-kin had killed you when we crashed? I could not leave you here even if it were the right thing to do."

"It's the most sensible one, given the urgency." Majestrin glanced to the sky overhead, where wisps of glowing cloud skirted across the moon.

"And yet, the choice I will not make. If we have to walk the whole way to the hive, fine. I need you with me to the last possible moment before I must face that place again."

Majestrin huffed. "It's not as though I can help you once you're inside. Or after."

"I know that, and I have all along. Listen to me," I said. "I cannot say how I know this, but deep in my soul, I know you will fly again."

"Are you sure you're not grasping at vain hope?" Majestrin said.

I shook my head. "It is as though Creo has promised it to me, not in words, but in a deep sense of assurance that no other mount will carry me through my role as commander of the Windrider Battalion. Perhaps you do not trust me, but trust Creo."

"The Maker can be enigmatic at times . . ."

"When we met, you were certain of his calling on your life.

Or else why would you have taken up with such an impossible, unteachable, troublesome idiot like me?"

Majestrin chuckled, halfhearted. "I suppose *that* took some faith."

"You must believe that Creo can work miracles if you have ever trusted he can make me into something he can use."

"What if I accept that he can bring you to your ordained destiny with or without me?" Majestrin settled his head back down.

"Now you are just feeling sorry for yourself." I propped a fist on my hip. "And when you find out that I am an utter disaster without you, then you will have guilt on top of your self-loathing."

A slow smirk spread across the dragon's lips. He blinked. On the second blink, his green eyes cleared, and a measure of their spark returned. "When you put it that way, how can I insist upon staying?" Majestrin lifted his snout from the ground. "You make it sound inevitable that you'll single-handedly undo everything we've worked for so far."

"You doubt that for a second?" I clapped him on the neck. "Now come. I am certain if you exert even a little effort, the rest of these sad bonds will fall away."

Majestrin thrashed his tail, and the post to which his captors had lashed it ripped right out of the ground. I did have to take a blade to the rope to loosen the overabundance of length they had wrapped around him, however. He lifted his body on sinuous legs. The chains snapped, and links flew.

One of the club-wielding guards rounded the corner of the nearest wagon, and when he turned his attention to Majestrin's cage, his eyes went wide.

Veranna's misty form coalesced, the Utterance dispelled, and appeared behind the guard.

He blurted, "The drag—mmph! Hrmph."

Veranna's hand clapped over his mouth. She wrenched his other arm behind him before he thought to resist.

"Vinyanel, release the Utterance for Raen," Veranna said.

A thought later, Raen appeared before the gypsy and pressed the edge of her schiavona against his throat. "The dragon is going, and only fools would try to stop him."

"The Maker seal your lips," Veranna intoned.

Veranna's prisoner broke away from her, and he opened his mouth in what looked to be a furiously colorful string of words, but no sound emerged from his flapping lips.

"Shall we?" I said to Majestrin.

He reared and slammed his horns into the dome of boughs above him, and the structure exploded into kindling. I shielded my head with my forearm. Another swipe of his tail thrust rear third of the timbers out of our way. Raen's opponent fled, and she made no effort to hinder him.

Commotion stirred in the caravan wagons closest by.

"Now what? Here they come," Raen said.

Majestrin grabbed Raen and me in his claws and tossed us onto his back, and Veranna he plucked from the ground with his teeth. Craning his neck around, he plunked her behind Raen.

A half-dozen caravanners came running, and Majestrin sucked a gigantic breath.

The approaching responders skidded to a halt. "It's loose! Run!" they screamed.

Majestrin backpedaled a few steps and released a torrential gush of cold, but he swung his head back and forth in such a way as not to swamp the fleeing men, but to plaster the six caravan wagons nearest to us with ice. A fortress of crystals covered their sides and webbed the narrow gaps between them.

"Hold on!" he said. Majestrin bounded left.

I did not have the heart to complain about how painful holding on was, especially since he did not have his barding.

When he reached the next section of caravan wagons, another breath gushed from his maw, once again walling the wagons in glittering spikes of ice at least a foot deep. "We'll see how they like trying to find a way out of a cage."

As Majestrin rounded the circled caravan wagons that made up the perimeter of the encampment, their owners fled him amidst the tents. In a matter of three more breaths, he had encased the entire encampment in ice, curls of cold snaking from its surface. The few caravanners who thought to flee the circle, Majestrin allowed to pass, but he then walled up the caravan behind them. Chaotic cries of panic echoed from inside the crystalline trap. The dragon stepped back to survey his work, and he blew one, final puff of frosty mist.

"That was a lot of breaths, my friend," I said. "Very close together. How?"

"Really, it was only two, divided to manage the job. Covering something in ice isn't nearly as demanding as trying to swamp enemies in open terrain."

Raen leaned around me. "It's staggeringly beautiful. Like you've created an arena of glassy spires and crystals. If it lasts until tomorrow, you've probably given these rogues another way to draw crowds. That is, if they're willing to brave climbing the carts to get out and take the gawkers' money."

"Did you see how thick it was?" Veranna said. "It will be there a while in this autumn weather. I'm almost sorry we won't get to see it in the sunlight."

"Amazing work, my friend," I said. "Even from the ground. Now let us put all this far behind us."

Majestrin turned and loped into the night. Every time I glanced back at Raen, I found her staring over her shoulder, and she continued until the ice fortress disappeared from sight. "Amazing indeed," she murmured.

32

A Dragon's Determination

*E*ven Ecleriast did not insist they be ready to depart at the first hint of dawn the next morning, since it would have meant only an hour's rest after the encampment escape. They rejoined the young dragons and Eyrnir within the cover of the copse of firs. Raen unclasped Ecleriast's waist and slid from the giant wyrm's silver back with a hint of reluctance tugging at her to dally.

"'Jestrin! Jestrin!" Iriscendra frisked all around him. "I knew you'd come back!"

Majestrin snorted, but there was a smile beneath it. The haunted expression still lingered in the depths of his eyes, however. Their victory lacked the potency to rid him of his deepest-rooted melancholy, or so it seemed.

Raen pulled Mythrenese aside as the others discussed departure plans and where they needed to stop to recover Majestrin's barding.

"I want you to tell me just what happened with Majestrin's capture." Raen said, her voice low.

Mythrenese pressed his belly to the ground.

"No one's in trouble." Raen knelt beside him and stroked his cheek.

"Not even the dragon whose fault it was?" Mythrenese whimpered.

"It's over now. But I need a better picture of why a Silverlord would let men bind him and lead him off."

Mythrenese glanced over his shoulder, then leaned in toward Raen to speak in a hushed voice. "Iriscendra went too close to the road—she kept going down there waiting for Ecleriast, and she wouldn't listen to anybody. Heaven and earth—she gets mean when he's not around."

"It's not her fault." Raen's chest squeezed. "Anyway, what happened?"

"The caravan of men saw her, even though she thought she was hidden, and she came blazing back to us with fifty of them on her tail and gaining. They had nets."

Raen heaved a sigh. "She's not very fast yet."

"And so, when Majestrin saw her coming, he got this tortured look on his face . . . well, even more tortured than he's been since the, um, you know." Mythrenese shrunk in a sheepish posture. "Anyway, he leapt out there, and he demanded the men let her go. They pulled out bows and started to panic. He said not to shoot, he'd go with them. And that was it. He yelled at Iriscendra—told her to stay with me and wait for Ecleriast, and that we needed to stick to the mission. Made her cry. The rest, you know." He stifled a yawn.

Raen rubbed her temple. Her eyes felt hot and sticky with fatigue, but this all demanded more contemplation. Did she dare broach the subject with Majestrin himself? One look at his astounding length and ancient eyes squashed that notion, at least for the time being. But with the way he resisted using his abomination to swipe a quick path right through the men who had captured and mocked him suggested a level of restraint Raen never expected. The vision of his frozen master-piece lingered in her mind's eye.

"Do you have any idea why he insisted?"

Mythrenese shrugged. "I didn't quite catch what he was saying. The men lassoed his mouth in the middle of it, but he scolded Iriscendra, something about having the risk of how far the men might have taken her before Ecleriast got back."

Raen pursed her lips in contemplation. True, Majestrin had no way of knowing the caravan would stop outside Barrington. What if the men had taken Iriscendra and kept traveling? What if circumstances prevented Ecleriast from going after her? They could have been headed back to Thelenalon, for all anyone knew. Ecleriast might have had to choose between the mission and Iriscendra's rescue. If he chose the mission, how long would it have taken for the madness Majestrin spoke of to over-take her?

And there Raen had her answer. In order to avoid any chance of Iriscendra's madness, Majestrin offered himself as a substitution, rather than risk Ecleriast never finding her again. He put the needs of a hatchling he did not even like ahead of his own.

Raen unbundled her bedroll for a brief repose, her heart and mind brimming with the events that had challenged so much of her dragon-rearing philosophy.

~

Snow swirled like baffling eddies around us, and while it did not fall heavily, the fat, drifting flakes still made following the mountain road treacherous. The way often narrowed to a width scarcely greater than the wheelbase of the cart Eyrnir pulled behind him. Mythrenese and Iriscendra traveled ahead and back to us in a constant cycle, spying out the road and warning us of obstacles along the way, most of which consisted of debris in the road from rockslides. The elevation in the middle of this section of the range ground a biting edge onto the wind, and we all suffered continual running noses and stiff fingers. My wounded leg was stiff and sore, but feverless. But the lands remained empty around us, and for that, I was thankful.

Raen woke me for my watch on the sixth day of the journey, and when I sat up and stretched, something immediately struck me as out of place. My pulse quickened until it pounded in my temples. My breath caught in shallow gasps. What was wrong? I whipped my head left and right.

Where was Majestrin?

Raen placed a hand on my shoulder. "Are you feeling all right? You look awful all of the sudden."

"Why is Majestrin out of sight?" I cleared the rasp of sleep from my throat.

Raen smiled. "Stretching his wings, I believe."

"What? You had better not jest."

"Why would I do that? He said he needed to keep them from weakening."

"How long ago did he leave?" I scanned the skies for flashes of silver.

Raen stepped closer to her tent. "About a third of my watch, as best I can guess."

I heaved myself from the cart. My wounded leg, though the gash had improved to a patchwork of scab and newly-formed, bright pink tissue, threatened to give out under my sudden weight. It was always so unstable when I awoke. I mumbled an oath.

"Not so fast," Raen said. Her voice softened. "How is it you constantly forget? It wasn't that long ago that you were nearly dead."

"I have been nearly dead more often than most elves you will meet," I replied. "I wish you would desist in telling me to be careful, to slow down, to favor this leg. I do not have time for it to linger in weakness."

"It's like you think you can choose how long even your own healing will take." Raen shook her head. "Will I ever understand you?"

"You would be the first, if you did." A flutter rose in my chest and my mouth went dry. I scratched the back of my head.

The way Raen's gaze lingered on me in a mix of inquisitiveness, consternation, and concern troubled my spirit. I limped a few paces away. "Well, anyway, get some rest. We need to make better progress tomorrow than we have been."

Raen said nothing more, but ducked into her tent. I scolded myself for the niggling sense of disappointment that she gave up so easily. Sometimes, it might have been useful to be less convincing.

About halfway through my watch, the crunch and clatter of falling stone erupted behind me, somewhere up the mountainside. I spun to find Majestrin clinging with spread claws to the steep face of the shale slope. He steadied his stance with wide wings. A wave of relief spread through my body and loosened my tight shoulders.

The dragon worked his way down the slope, noisily enough that the rest of the winged members of the encampment stirred. Iriscendra frowned and tucked her head under her wing. Mythrenese shot his head up.

Eyrnir stood and stretched his foretalons out in front of him, then yawned. "How did it go?"

Majestrin padded his way to us. "It could have been worse. The landings were pretty sloppy." The look of utter disgust that narrowed his eyes and pulled his mouth into a frown convinced me to pack my questions away.

Eyrnir cocked his head. "Sloppy landings, or crashes?"

I grimaced. Perhaps the griffon had developed a deathwish?

Majestrin puffed a swirl of frosty air from his nostrils. "All right—if you must press the point, more crashes than landings."

"Just so we're clear," Eyrnir said. "There are certain elves who might get ahead of themselves if it was construed you were back to normal."

"Still, you did get airborne?" I worked my way over to Majestrin in my uneven gait.

Majestrin huffed. He plopped down and curled his tail around him. "Flight means nothing if the flier cannot return to the ground safely. Not even you, with all your riding talent, could have stayed seated through all that banking and weaving."

"It still sounds promising, for a first attempt," I said.

"I hope you've been working on those other plans for your battalion, Windrider." He swung his head away from the group and plunked his snout on the ground.

Majestrin's surly dismissal punched me in the gut.

The breeze pushed thin clouds away from a moon, near its third quarter. I drew a long breath. A future of commanding the Windrider Battalion without Majestrin? I kicked a rock into the distance. Creo's unspoken promise seemed a frail hope. A hundred questions, that all began with "Why . . ." shouted at me long after the encampment fell into silent repose again.

33

REINFORCEMENTS

*W*ith a scrape and a lurch, the wagon wedged in yet another run-off groove in the road. I caught my thrown weight with my right hand, and my copy of *The Tree* tumbled face-down to the floor of the vehicle. Had I not just had my nose deep in a passage about bearing trials with wisdom and temperance, more than a few unsavory words might have spilled off my lips.

Eyrnir leaned into the collar of the harness he wore, but the cart would not budge. I rose and climbed over the side of the vehicle. "We have made half the progress we would have on foot, even with me limping." I thrust my shoulder into the rear face of the cart. It rocked forward, then rolled back and thumped into my ribs. Despite my armor, pain shot across my side.

I bellowed a wordless cry and slammed my shoulder back into the cart. It hopped forward, and finally, the wheel rolled free of the gully. A crack on the opposite side of the cart rent the air with a sharp, wooden note. The cart sagged to the left. Eyrnir's head drooped.

"Now what?" the griffon moaned.

Veranna rounded the cart. She propped her fists on her hips. "Now that's done it. I think the axle's cracked."

I inspected the situation. A large rock had blocked the left wheel just beyond the gully, and indeed, the axel had splintered. The wheel hung by a last few fibers of wood that had not yet given up their hold on the rest of the apparatus.

"You had your way for a few days," I said. "But now, we must make it to the hive in five days or less. We are not halfway there." I turned to the rear of the group, where Majestrin picked his way along the narrow causeway. "I do not ask out of selfishness, friend, but we must try to fly."

Majestrin implored with his eyes. "I could kill someone with the way I bank and weave."

"And the dragon-kin *will* kill the girls, given the way I walk. They will only be the first victims."

"Your wound is finally starting to look like skin and not raw meat," Veranna said. "You can't force your leg astride a mount."

I wheeled on her. "The next individual who opens his or her mouth to tell me what cannot be done—"

"I could try'n carry you, V'yennel." Iriscendra sidled close to me.

Frustrated as I was, a smile fought back my scowl. Iriscendra had grown visibly, even in just the past week. She stretched a good eight feet in length, but her wings were still small in proportion to her body, at least compared to Majestrin's wing-to-body ratio. "I do not doubt you would give the effort much heart. But no, I likely still outweigh you."

"So, what cannot be done is fine to come from your mouth, then," Raen said. She folded her arms.

Majestrin stomped his foot. "Enough bickering. We have troubles enough without everyone indulging raw nerves and short tempers. Iriscendra is correct that it would be best for someone to carry Vinyanel. I will, so that he need not stress his healing leg, and we will simply need to glide in short spurts, keeping very low. It won't be as fast as real flight, but it will pick the pace up considerably, so long as I don't bash us into a mountainside too often."

"I shall wear my helm," I said. "Thank you for offering a solution, Majestrin. And as for you, Veranna, Raen—from this point forward, I need soldiers on this endeavor, not wet nurses. If you want to help save these girls, you need to think less about who might get hurt and worry more about who might die."

Veranna cast her gaze to her feet. "Sometimes one of those is the result of the other."

"Creo will fortify where mortals can leave only breaches." I settled my helm upon my head and buckled the chin strap.

Veranna nodded. "Well said, Lieutenant Commander."

The maidens mounted Eyrnir and Mythrenese, and Majestrin reached around my chest with one of his front talons. I clenched my fists and released them.

"Ready?" I said.

"No," Majestrin replied. "But here we go anyway."

He took a few running steps on three legs, then thrust his wings and we were airborne. He immediately tilted right—the side I was on. His muscles strained against my back, and he over-corrected to the left. He clipped his wing on the steep, rocky slope on that side. Down we went. With a grating rattle, his hindquarters skidded on the ground, and Majestrin scarcely salvaged the landing.

"You see?" he blurted. "I knew—"

"Try again," I said.

"But I can't compensate for your weight on one side. I—"

"Try again." This time, it came out like an order.

Raen, Veranna, and their mounts waited about fifty yards

ahead. Iriscendra sat beside me, her brow puckered and lips tight.

"I don't appreciate the scrutiny," Majestrin said.

"Iriscendra," I said in a soft voice. "Join the others. No worries. We will catch up in just a moment."

Iriscendra nodded. "Yes, V'yennel." She fluttered in her haphazard way ahead to the group.

Majestrin drew me in tighter, closer to the center of his body.

I clutched the dragon's barding in gauntleted hands. Majestrin heaved a breath, ran a few strides, and flapped his wings again.

The liftoff was more stable this time. Majestrin's flight, while wobblier than when he was in good health, took us to the rest of the travelers in a few wing beats. They thrust skyward, and we all journeyed together for about another quarter-mile.

Then the mountain to our left opened into a valley, and a stiff crosswind caught us in its rush through the low place. It buffeted Majestrin. He banked and plummeted. His bank transformed into a half-roll, and we hit the ground three-quarters of the way onto Majestrin's back.

"I'm all right," he said through clenched teeth. "Just caught a little off guard." He rocked back to his feet, careful not to so much as brush me against the dry grasses of the valley floor.

We spent the balance of the day repeating this type of semi-flight performance. But even with the crashes and corrections, we traveled at more than twice the speed of walking. I was a little bruised when we stopped to eat and make camp, and of course my leg throbbed its complaints, but I mentioned it to no one.

"*Y*ou are keeping a very sharp eye, correct?" I asked, fixing a skeptical glance on Veranna and Eyrnir. "I find it suspicious that we have encountered not a single dragon-kin scout on this side of the mountains."

Veranna nodded. "The way ahead is quite clear of enemies."

"Which is inconsistent with my previous experience in this area." The last time I had ridden north through these foothills, my squadron and I had to eliminate or avoid patrols twice, if not thrice, daily. The clear passage might have seemed a blessing to some, but to me, it felt like an ill omen or a trap. Trusting a prophetess to scout could prove poor judgment, I feared.

Over the days it had taken us to cross the mountains and reach the flatter terrain south of the hive, Majestrin's flying had improved, but only slightly. He still dared no height or distance. The height was just as well, though, as the further into dragon-kin territory we forged, the less wise it would be to forsake the cover of the hillsides.

We rounded the south side of a grassy foothill and turned north, all walking for now. Clustered in the valley between the hills ahead, stood dozens of rows of tents, about a half-mile in the distance as best I could determine.

I shrank back behind the trunk of a thick cypress a few steps downhill. "Quite clear?" I pointed to the encampment. "Are you blind?"

"No need to be insulting, Vinyanel," Veranna said. "I said it was clear of enemies."

I squinted back toward the tent rows. The group flew no banner, and no one moved between the pale canvas structures.

The dense branches above me shuddered, and my hand flew to my hilt. A figure in dark clothes dropped from the concealment of the tree, flipped on the way down, and landed in a crouch.

My sword flashed from the scabbard, and I leveled it at the newcomer. My heart thundered, and my nerves screamed, battle ready.

The dark-clad individual rose, tossed a thick shock of sandy hair from his eyes, and shot me a bemused grin.

"Well, if it isn't everyone's favorite, nervous officer," Major Galdurith Emynon said. "Oh, wait, my mistake. You're nobody's favorite."

I thrust my sword back into the scabbard. "Ha, ha. What in the Great Patron's name are you doing out here?" My heartbeat relented, thumping now instead of pounding.

Galdurith tugged his black, tooled leather breastplate straight. "Just following orders. You should try it. I think you'd find yourself with a lot fewer headaches." His glance flicked down to my leg. "Or should I say, festering wounds?"

"I must be in trouble," I grumbled. "What other reason could you have for being in such a chipper mood?"

Veranna took a few demure steps toward the major. He grasped her hand, bowed, and pressed the back of it to his lips. "You cannot imagine how happy I am you're safe."

"Did you know we were coming?" Veranna said.

"Only in the vaguest way. Simply a charming coincidence that I ended up being on this perimeter watch to intercept you."

I turned back toward Majestrin. Raen hung back by his shoulder, and the smaller dragons were out of sight. She regarded Galdurith with a hint of skepticism from the corner of her eye.

"Galdurith," I said. "This is Raen. We—uh—encountered her in Bilearne. Raen, Major Galdurith Emynon, Blackwatch."

"A friend of yours?" Raen asked.

"More of a colleague," I said.

Galdurith chuckled. "You must not know the Lieutenant Commander very well."

Veranna took Galdurith's arm. "You're not being very nice," she chided.

"We are distracting the major from his duty anyway," I said. "Do we have leave to enter the camp, civilians and all?"

"You could leave one of the civilians here." He focused on Veranna.

I folded my arms across my chest. "Save your fraternizing for when you're off duty, Major. Who is the senior officer with this detachment?"

"Chancellor Lerendir."

My jaw slackened. The Delsin military must have been brewing a bigger engagement than I first assumed. "It seems I have much to hear from the Chancellor. Dragons, I leave it to you as to whether you choose to come down or make yourselves comfortable somewhere nearby."

"Dragons? Plural?" Galdurith cocked his head.

Raen stood on tiptoe to look over Majestrin's back. "Don't be afraid, Mythrenese."

Iriscendra rounded Majestrin's posterior and scrambled toward me in a sloppy run. The indigo dragonling eased his way from his concealment with warier strides. A few long leaps brought Iriscendra to my side.

"Myth-nese kept me back." She glared over her shoulder.

"I do not fault him for doing so," I said. "Caution is a useful lesson to learn early."

"So when are you going to make a study of it?" Galdurith said.

Iriscendra sharpened her glare and aimed it at him. "I not like smug Major."

After a step back, Galdurith cast a glance about the group. "All right, I'm done. Lieutenant Commander, you and your . . .party . . . may report to the chancellor."

I reached over and turned Iriscendra's snout toward me. "You dragons may come to the perimeter of camp only. I will always be close by, but you, Iriscendra, cannot be frisking along behind me all afternoon. I have business to attend."

Majestrin shot me a pained look.

"Let Mythrenese serve as hatchling-sitter. I have little fear trouble will prod at this large an assembly of the Delsin army." The truth was, I anticipated a fair number more hard words flinging my way as I entered camp, words Iriscendra might not deal with in as mature a fashion as I needed. My own behavior was difficult enough to manage without a headstrong hatchling to restrain.

Mythrenese pouted. "Seems you have orders for everybody."

"It is my job to give orders," I said. "Just be a help. I will find you something shiny to compensate you, if need be."

Mythrenese brightened. Raen cupped a hand on her forehead.

"Looks to me like we all agree enough." I took a few strides toward camp. "Let us leave the major to *his* current orders."

Veranna sighed and drew away from Galdurith. "When does your rotation end?"

The major smiled. "Dusk. I'm sure I'll be able to find you."

Galdurith clenched his fist over his heart and saluted me with the requisite bow. I tapped my fist on my chest in perfunctory return. Try as I might to mask it, I still limped down the hillside toward the tent rows.

~

I blew a long sigh as the camp physician pulled my cuisse away from my thigh and set it aside. He bunched my pant leg. His study of my gash caused him remarkably less alarm than I thought it might, and at his stoicism, I released a pent-up breath.

"You're going to have quite a bit of scar tissue once this is done healing," he said. "The muscle fiber will never be the same. I won't lie to you."

Never the same. I met his eye. "You mean I will forever limp?"

"I'm afraid so, Lieutenant Commander."

"But will I be able to ride again?" I braced myself for the worst.

"I cannot imagine why not," he replied.

I collapsed back in the bolster at the head of the cot. In the end, whether I could still employ a mount was all that truly mattered. My pulse drummed against my ribs. "Do I need to stay off the leg still?"

The physician tapped his chin. "No, the wound is closed enough that moderate activity will help the tissue grow as normally for use as possible. The trouble is, I understand you're not slated for *moderate* activity over the next couple of weeks."

The flap of the physician's high-roofed tent drew back, and Chancellor Lerendir stepped through, followed by another, dark-haired elf carrying a wrapped bundle in his arms. I recognized Lerendir's companion as King Saransaeloth's personal armorer.

I stood, though I caught the edge of the cot with a hand as my weaker leg threatened to go out from beneath me upon its sudden use. I steadied my stance, straightened my back, and saluted the chancellor.

"There you are," Lerendir said. He smoothed graying hair back from his forehead. "If we didn't need your expertise right now, I'd probably have you court martialed."

I swallowed but still maintained eye contact. "I understand, and I will accept whatever disciplinary measures I have garnered when you deem it the right time."

"And if you think you can just . . .wait. What?" Lerendir pressed the heel of his hand to his temple. "No excuses?"

"Just because I was the highest ranking officer in the field, sir," I said, "that did not necessarily give me leave to invent my own next set of orders. The repercussions of my rashness will linger with me."

Lerendir's gaze swept me from head to foot. "It must have been quite a journey, Lieutenant Commander. But it's not over yet. The Elgadrim emissaries informed us what the dragon-kin have planned. What do you propose next?"

"To accept whatever orders I assume you have brought in lieu of the court martial."

The chancellor laughed. "You don't get off that easily. I have plans for this battalion, but we're here more to bluster and distract than invade. Since you're the only one who's been in this cave network, we need you to plan the specifics of the reconnaissance."

"Very well," I said. "After all, I did not come this far without some ideas."

"I beg pardon, sir," the armorer said from behind Lerendir.

"Oh, right. First things first." Lerendir took the bundle from the armorer and set it down on the cot. "I believe you have a cuisse in awful shape?"

A hot flush swept over my cheeks. As I looked at the piece of armor on the side table, it really was a disgrace. The twisted rent. The grime in the grooves between plates. "The past weeks have not treated it with gentleness."

"Well, open the bundle."

I reached for the heavy hide wrappings around the package the armorer had brought, then threw the edge of the fabric aside.

Inside the wrappings lay a brand-new, ebony replacement for my destroyed piece, but this one bore some unusual embellishments. Running along the outside of the thigh plate, there was a long rod that connected to the plate by short posts, riveted and soldered in place. The rod ended in some sort of fastener, attached by a series of mechanical joints.

"I will need to make some modifications to your tasset and knee plate in order to integrate the support rods with the rest of your suit," the armorer said. "But this series of rods and housings should take a lot of the demand off your thigh muscle and transfer it to your hip and knee."

"Will I still limp when I wear this?" I asked. I ran a finger along the slim rod that ran the length of the apparatus.

"Less," the armorer said. "The challenge will be to avoid taking too many blows against the mechanism. It's sturdy, but not indestructible."

"What I fail to understand is how you knew to bring this. What compelled you to develop the extra support for my leg?"

Lerendir clapped me on the shoulder. "You owe the prophetess some thanks for apprising us to the deterioration of your situation."

Embarrassment surged through my muscles and drew them tight. "She somehow tattled on me?"

"No need to view it in that light," the chancellor replied. "She saw a need for extra resources. Would you, as a commander, allow your pride to keep you from calling for reinforcements in a battle stacked against you? You needn't worry. I will still save the most insane part of the mission for you."

34

*T*he next morning, I stood outside the armorer's quarters, on both feet equally, with only a barely perceptible discomfort in my leg. The armorer tightened the last fastener at my knee for the new, enhanced cuisse, which fit my thigh as perfectly as my destroyed piece had before the gargoyle had torn it open.

"Remarkable," I said.

"A little testing is in order, however, before you forge into the field," the armorer said. "I understand we have little time to linger over adjustments."

I glanced at the pale crescent of the setting moon, white against a rose and lavender morning. "True. Very little." In a swift arc of my arm, I drew my longsword. I held it in a long guard for a moment, then broke into the paces of hews and parries I practiced every morning when not campaigning. The familiar rhythm soothed my otherwise crackling nerves. I could feel the mechanical joints in my armor enhancement shifting and bracing to redistribute the force every time I put weight on my bad leg, but the workings compensated with fascinating efficiency. I spun and slashed. Crouched and positioned a block. Pivoted and swung a high cut.

My sword clashed against another blade. I jolted from my reverie.

Raen held her schiavona aloft, its slender, bright steel delicate and frosty in color in comparison to the darker, broader breadth of my longsword, my trusted companion through many trials.

She quirked a mischievous smile. "It seems the handicraft of the Delsin will make quite a difference for you."

She still gripped her sword in her off hand, but the casing around her other wrist was much trimmer and now almond in color, rather than heavy and mired with weeks-worth of grime.

"The old cast was failing?" I lowered my weapon.

"Threatening, at least," Raen replied. "The unit surgeon supplied me with a much lighter support, which he thinks I should be able to have off entirely in a couple weeks at most. Enough small talk, though. When are we heading out?"

"We?" I returned my sword to the scabbard. "My reconnaissance squadron will be on the move in less than two hours. You should be safe wherever Lerendir chooses to post camp for the rest of the battalion."

Raen shook her head. "I'm not interested in being safe. I need to make sure those Elgadrim girls are."

"You are wounded. The very—"

"So are you."

"You are a civilian."

"So is Veranna, and she's been with you on missions. And you're skirting awfully close to being a civilian again yourself, as I understand the trouble you could be in with your superior officers."

"Raen," I said. "Things could go tragically wrong. The

mortality rate on my last endeavor to this location was astronomical."

"So you plan to go in alone?"

I rolled my eyes. "No, but only because I have been deprived of that option. Lerendir has assigned a group. Which I need to meet in moments."

Raen stretched to her full height and lifted her chin above parallel with the ground. "What if I told you Lerendir granted me permission to join you?"

"Then I would say the old elf pays too much heed to the batting of eyelashes," I said.

Raen eased closer to me. "Can we put aside the constant toe-to-toe for a moment? I told those girls I had come to save them, and then had to run and leave them behind. If they're still alive, I have to help them. I won't be a liar."

The words pricked my conscience. Had I not made Hridayesh the same promise, once? I rebuked the shame—it would not fetter me in my current purpose. Not with so much at stake.

"You are helping the girls," I said, my voice lower. The scents of lavender and rosemary drifted to my nose again. "You saw to it I stayed alive so I could complete the mission to deliver them." A lump rose in my throat. "I never . . .well . . .never properly thanked you for that."

Raen blushed and brushed at the skirt of her midnight blue gown, apparently cleansed of the stains of travel. "I'm not very good at receiving thanks."

"The people who deserve it most never are." I clasped her shoulder and rotated her toward me. "You are excellent at caring for people. And dragons. I need you to stay back and make sure someone does everything possible for Iriscendra if I—"

Raen averted her gaze, even though I prevented her from turning her body. "Don't say it."

"Tell me you will stay. And in the worst-case scenario, that you'll pour everything you have into keeping Iriscendra from going wayward."

Raen swallowed. "You're annoyingly convincing, Lieutenant Commander." She sighed and met my eye again. "I'll stay in the battalion camp with Iriscendra until you get back."

"Thank you." This time, my glance fled hers. "It means, well . . . much to me."

Raen's wide, caramel-lashed eyes searched my face. I reached up and carefully smoothed her satiny tresses back from her forehead, tucking them over her ear point with my gauntleted fingers. Her light blush deepened. She dipped her chin only to have the same lock of hair slip forward over her face again. "Get going before I change my mind about staying behind."

I released her shoulder and took one step back, then another. The tightness around the corners of her mouth betrayed the emotions she fought to corral. My breath caught in my throat, and the flutter in my chest threatened to undo what mental preparation I had made for the trial ahead. I took a long draught of air, turned, and undertook a swift march to find my squadron.

~

"I thought you said Ecleriast was working alone!" Inquisitor Ezio burst through the entry to Naghax's study with such force that the iron latch on the door smashed into the wall and sent chips of limestone flying.

Naghax juggled the vial of wyvern bile, barely replacing the stopper before the caustic substance sloshed from the mouth of the container. "All the reports indicated it was just him, the females, and the North Deklian."

"Then why am I now hearing that half the cursed elven

army is two days from here?" Ezio slammed his palms down on Naghax's work table. The single iron gauntlet on his left hand gouged the wood.

"Mind your flailing," Naghax hissed. "There are many weeks of irreproducible work on this table your temper could destroy, and then where would we be?"

"And I say you make it all look more complicated than it is. Get your fiend army in place, you bat-winged vagrant. If you can't deliver on your portion of the strategy, I'm sure Hanash would be happy to take over."

Hanash. Naghax clenched his jaw. How he would love to take credit for every aspect of the summoning. Earn himself a spot in a higher circle. Already he had assured so many fools he would prove a more powerful fiend binder than Lord Scitherias ever was. But the truth was, Hanash was nothing without Naghax's meticulous research and attention to minute detail. Details so important that should even one go astray . . .

The machinations of Naghax's mind began to churn. "I assure you, Inquisitor, I have every aspect of this summoning well in hand. No one will be disappointed. Have the scouts keep a close eye on the elves—I have a feeling the pointy-eared softbellies will regret provoking our anger when they see what we have arrayed against them."

∼

I reported to the center of camp, where my squadron had assembled for departure. Veranna, Galdurith, and once again, Sergeant Althoron joined me on orders. At least they were a familiar lot. Two more soldiers completed our numbers, brothers, both privates.

"Private Thederonde, Private Asmenius," I said, pacing before the small line of soldiers, my hands clasped behind my back, "welcome to the detachment. I understand the two of you are in the process of determining which eventual division you will pursue?"

"Sir, that's correct," the taller of the two young elves replied. Thederonde.

"As it is the Delsin custom to send a mix of disciplines on specialty missions such as today's, this squadron will familiarize you with the roles played by the Blackwatch ..." I nodded to Galdurith. "By Windrider." I placed my hand on my chest. When I settled my attention on Althoron, my brow lifted. "And as I understand it, Wardancer?"

Althoron blew a breath through his mouth. "Sir, so you've been informed? Let me assure you, you were an excellent commander and—"

I raised a palm. "Say no more. I have seen you fight on foot, and talent like yours belongs on your own two legs. While I hate to lose you, I cannot deny the Wardancer Division is where you belong."

"Sir, I thank you for both the compliment and the understanding," Althoron said.

"You are welcome. Now, with that out of the way, we have work to do. Major Emynon, Private Thederonde and Private Asmenius, when we liberate the Elgadrim subjects, you three are assigned primary responsibility for seeing them back behind our lines. Althoron, you are with me in the acquisition and retention of the Chalice of Gherag-Tal."

"And I assume you will give me no specifics, as usual," Veranna said.

"Whatever hedge or advantage you can give us of the divine sort, I would thank you for."

Veranna stepped forward and patted my shoulder. "You seem to forget, I'm not the only one with the gift here, young Windrider. I have a few Utterances I believe you would do well to focus on over the next couple days it will take us to reach the hive."

I swallowed. Somehow, my Thaumaturgical role in the coming gambit troubled me more than any other. I could learn every utterance in *The Tree*, but knowledge alone would never be enough.

"We break camp and move north in an hour." I turned from the group. "Check your provisions—we travel light."

～

"You cannot imagine how much I wish there was a way I could have you with me." I leaned back against Majestrin's side, stretching my legs in front of me on the cold ground. "Lerendir's attached two privates to my squadron. He knows what happened the last time I had inexperienced soldiers in this environment." I squeezed my eyes shut, as if to forbid the images that threatened to break loose of their containment in my mind.

Majestrin craned his neck around to bring his long face close to me. "And so now you know how to better ensure your squadron's survival. You can count on one thing only, Vinyanel. This trip into the hive will be different from the last."

"Potentially worse," I said. Already, days out from the actual maneuvers, beads of sweat rose on my brow. "More difficult, with young girls to usher out. And we have no room for error. According to Lerendir's estimate, we will arrive at the hive on the morning of the new moon."

"This was your idea, if you recall," the dragon said.

"Perhaps foolhardy to embroil myself in, but on the other hand, how could I not? I could not turn a blind eye to the potential horror." I leaned forward and dropped my head into my hands. "What started as blind vengeance has transformed into an honor-bound compulsion. But tell me, Majestrin, what is valor's worth if its continual companion is death?"

The dragon fixed his gaze into the distance. "Death comes

in many weights. To die for others? For what is right? There can be no nobler spending of one's days. To die inside because you have ignored the compulsions of conscience in pursuit of your own comfort, only to await a physical death to relieve you of your emptiness? Nothing is more tragic. To die at the hands of evil? It is valor's calling to interpose between the innocent and such designs."

Nothing Majestrin said was new to my mind, but could I allow such truth to break through the stony shell around my heart? The briefest thought about the dragon-kin hive made me nauseated. But not as nauseated as the idea of three young girls losing their lives so the dragon kin could mete out their blood and bones as ingredients in a diabolical recipe. And not as sickened as I became at the thought of the dragon-kin wielding an army of summoned fiends.

"This is too large a job for me," I said. "No elf has ever achieved my rank at my age. I am beginning to think it is for good reason. I am too frail to bear its enormity."

"You're right." Majestrin's green eyes exuded sympathy. "Look beyond yourself. Just like your new armor gives you strength you do not otherwise have—seek sources of strength you know are there. You have already done the hard part— admitting the need for them."

How could I argue with a message I had now heard twice, from both the dead and the living? I sat back up. "I will try. If you will excuse me then, I have some armor to test a bit further. And some inner strength to seek in *The Tree*."

If only the waves of terrified reluctance that churned my insides to foam would still long enough for me to accomplish either task.

35

ESCAPEE

I stared down the narrow ravine in the mountains, along whose floor ran a swirling rill of silty pale green. The twisted vegetation on the bank offered my squadron and me some concealment, but a constant electrified sense of vigilance still set my nerves on edge. My neck and shoulders coiled into rigid knots and cords. Beyond that canyon wall lay the twisting halls of the dragon-kin hive, and my heart knew it all too well.

"We have given ourselves far too small a berth of hours," I whispered. "This place is, as best I can recall, on the far side of the hive from the dungeon access."

"You needn't guess," Althoron said. He reached into his pack and produced a folded stack of parchments. The papers were soiled, battered, and their edges bore the coffee-brown scars of scorching. By extending his other arm, he created a shelter for the documents beneath his cloak, since the freezing rain strafed us from the pre-dawn sky. "Your sketches and notes from the previous hive excursion."

My pulse accelerated at their sight. "Everything I noted?"

"I believe so." Althoron looked at me sidelong. "Sir, are you all right? You've paled."

The thought of confronting the same locations where I watched the dragon-kin whittle my last reconnaissance squadron down to nothing had me edgy enough, but to have, in hand, the documents where I had to chronicle the tragedies chilled my blood far worse than the foul weather.

"I will be fine." I took the parchments from Althoron. "Leave it to you to have visited the library before heading into the field."

Mimicking Althoron's care of the documents, I extended my cloak and gently shook the folds in the parchment open under the shelter of the garment. The first page contained my best guess as to the layout of the main entry of the hive, the area Lerendir's force prepared to bombard at the sun's first glimmer.

Well, what would have been the first glimmer, were it not for the rain. I switched to the next page, which detailed my group's ascent from the dungeons where the dragon-kin had kept us as prisoners, unaware that we had sanctioned our own capture as a means of access to the complex. A shop-worn strategy, always risky, but initially effective during my previous visit.

"In cross referencing your notes," Galdurith said, "and making our own assessments of the site exterior, we were able to locate this potential point of entry." He pointed through the branches of the close thicket where we huddled. "There. Do you see the flat portion of the rock face straight ahead? The brush is crushed and thin in front of it."

I squinted in the direction he pointed.

Veranna tapped my shoulder. "There's a curse on that place."

"Of course there is." My crossness sharpened my tone. "It is full to the peak with dragon-kin."

Veranna huffed and cupped her forehead. "I don't mean figuratively. I mean on the flat spot, specifically. It's cursed as a means of keeping it shut, as best I can tell. I have more learning to do in the field of reading signatures."

"Aha." I rolled my shoulders, but the stretch made no improvement. "And you suggest?"

"The countering Utterance, followed by the Utterance of Passage."

"Very well, can you perform them from here?"

Veranna tilted her head. "Not me. You, young Windrider."

"Confound you, woman!" I clenched my fist. "Stop calling me that. And is this really the time for drills?"

"When better to utilize something than when it will be most useful?"

"The more immediately, the better," Galdurith said. "We don't want to discover this entry unusable and ruin the timing of Lerendir's attack."

After a quick glance around our surroundings, I tucked the maps and notes into the inner pocket of my cloak, then emerged from the thicket. Cautious strides carried me across the water and to the supposed entry to the hive.

I ran my hand along the wet rock, and while it was flat, artificially so, I saw no seam that would indicate the actual perimeter of the door. Veranna skulked up beside me and pulled *The Tree* from her gear. She flipped a few pages.

"Here we are." Her forefinger rested at a set-apart section of text.

I turned my attention to the words. After I had read them through—they were familiar enough—I closed my eyes.

"Flawless Maker of beauty, Crafter of righteousness, by thy holy might, sweep away the dark defilement in this place." I spread my palm on the surface of the rock. "I submit to thee my flesh as thy vessel."

A swelling heat ran from my shoulder to my arm. The stone beneath my fingers trembled. A sharp sensation, as if the surface had suddenly turned to shards of glass, each one driving its point into palm, burst across my flesh. The sensation could not be a true, physical manifestation, though, with the triple layers of fine black chain that covered my hand. I clenched my teeth and leaned all my weight on my palm.

"Creo is master, before which no darkness can stand," I said. "Begone, foul curse, in the name of the author of judgment and mercy."

Like the clash of cymbals, the war between the heat of my hand and the stabbing pressure erupted in a pain I was sure would shatter every bone on the right side of my body. Just as suddenly, it all subsided. I let my head hang loose on my neck and leaned heavily on my hand. Rivulets of rain ran from the lip of my hood.

"You can see why I prefer prophecy to Thaumaturgy," Veranna said. "I don't have your tolerance for pain."

I turned my head. To my surprise, my breath came in heavy gasps. "I haven't felt a sensation like that before in any of the other Utterances I've worked."

"This was a very strong curse, and if I'm not mistaken, the first enchantment you've endeavored to break in a direct assault. The Darkness doesn't release its hold willingly."

Galdurith joined us at the hive wall. "Looks like you've revealed our door, Lieutenant Commander."

I turned my face toward the rock face, and saw that indeed, the distinct outline of a rectangular slab now marked the area that before offered just flat, unbroken stone. But the slab showed no handle or other means of opening. All around the seam, runes cut in short strokes of straight lines framed the presumed entry. The crinkle of pages turning caught my ear.

"Now for the Utterance of Passage," Veranna said.

I stood up straight and again focused on the words she offered. "As the Maker passes through all places, so I cross this threshold. Creo opens all doors he dictates his faithful pass."

The Utterance pulsed from my chest this time with a series of distinct, low peals. The force of it knocked me a step back before I steadied my stance against the force.

Scarcely a moment after I had widened the placement of my feet enough to keep from falling, the slab before me shuddered. Every irregularity in the stone glowed with a golden light. A flash. The door's surface retreated from my fingers, until it finally collapsed into a pile of coarse sand.

One of the privates, still back in the thicket, blew a low whistle. "Is that how it always works?"

Veranna shook her head. "Creo's Utterances manifest themselves in ways as individual as the Thaumaturgists he uses to enact them. Somehow, it doesn't surprise me you would end up reducing rock to dust. Your signature is hardly bearable when you're uttering."

I waved the rest of the squadron onward. "This is only the first of many obstacles ahead, soldiers. Let us pray we succeed in eliminating the rest with such thoroughness."

I led the way into the low tunnel the slab opened to us, and we began the unavoidable descent into the dragon-kin lair.

～

Iriscendra and Mythrenese sped by the small slit left open by the flap of Raen's tent, with the indigo dragon in splashing, laughing chase of the hatchling. No matter the pelting, icy rain. Iriscendra had woken that morning with a playful attitude, a total reversal of the morose moping she had done for the prior two days. Maybe having Ecleriast out of sight for his mission would not prove as great a challenge as she worried it might. Raen peered through the slit to see Irsicendra skid around the tent at the end of the row. Her bubbling squeal of a laugh brought a smile to Raen's lips.

"Try not to crash into any of the soldiers," Raen called after the dragons.

The day had been dark and dreary since daybreak, and although no one saw the moon the night before, owing to the miserable weather, a sense of pregnant anticipation hung over the military camp. The new moon was upon them.

Somewhere, two miles distant, siege engines creaked and sprang. Two hundred elven archers, at least as many cavalry, and a compliment of foot soldiers that outnumbered archers and cavalry put together, waged the largest feint in history on the western edge of the dragon-kin hive. Would the dragon-kin take the bait and focus enough attention on the assault to give Ecleriast the slim chance of infiltrating the complex? The brief look Raen had gotten of the carven stronghold, with its towering stone gates set deep in the face of a mountain, with only a narrow, zigzagging road for an approach, had not bolstered her hope.

Maybe she and Mythrenese should get another quick flight in, despite the weather. Being cold, wet, and informed seemed better than huddling in a semi-dry corner, waiting for news. Somehow, no one placed much urgency on delivering progress reports to the dozen or so elf maidens who served as camp followers. As soon as Mythrenese and Iriscendra came by in another lap, she would intercept him. Majestrin could endure minding Iriscendra for just a short while.

Time wore on, filled with the melancholy patter of ice. Raen hugged her arms around her shoulders, but the raw chill of the day had reached a depth where no amount of rubbing or pacing drove it back. Where had those dragons gone? The most intent listening revealed nothing of their galumphing return.

It's been too long. Raen's middle clenched with unease.

Motion to the left of her tent caught Raen's ear, and she leaned through the flaps and into the rain. Through the clouds of swirling mist and smoky haze generated by the smoldering fires of the camp, something stirred. The motion coalesced into a pair of elf soldiers. Not dragons.

Raen turned to a corner of her small accommodations and grabbed an oilskin cloak the army suppliers had been kind enough to part with. She threw it over her shoulders, and forged out into the rain.

Past the cook pots and sickbeds the camp followers had set up, Raen bustled her way across turf that had grown both squishy and slick. Twenty paces behind her tent, just beyond the perimeter of the camp, stood the tall pavilion Lerendir's army had erected as shelter for the dragons. Perhaps the young wyrms had sought the pavilion for some shelter against the weather few would endure voluntarily.

But no, only Majestrin lay within, breathing the slow, deep draughts of sleep. Raen stepped under the high roof, out of the stinging ice that streamed from the heavens. Still no sight of Mythrenese and Iriscendra. Dare she wake Majestrin to ask him to help her locate them?

"Majestrin! Majestrin!" Mythrenese cried from somewhere behind Raen.

Well, at least I didn't have to be the one to do it. Raen spun to find Mythrenese scrambling in the ice-laden grass toward the pavilion, his breath steaming from his mouth, and his eyes wild.

He met Raen's gaze, skidded to a stop, then shrank his neck back into his shoulders. A quick survey behind him confirmed the fear that squeezed in Raen's chest. He was alone.

"Where is Iriscendra?" Raen asked.

"Majestrin!" Mythrenese persisted.

The larger dragon snorted. His eyelids fluttered. He sighed and shifted his head away from Mythrenese.

"Please!" the indigo dragon said. "I need your help."

Majestrin rumbled a growl. He dragged his head back around, and his eyes opened to slits. "This better be important."

Mythrenese swallowed. "It is, I promise. Iriscendra and I were playing." He glanced over his shoulder. "It was going so well. She was having fun and not moping at all. We played for at least an hour, but a few moments ago, she got ahead of me, where the tents are really close together, at the center of camp."

"You lost sight of her?" Raen wanted to shout the question in a hysterical rant, but she tempered her voice. She only had herself to blame. The weather never should have kept her from maintaining clear sight of the hatchling.

"I'm really, really sorry, Raen." Mythrenese hovered on the brink of tears. "Her signature led back this way, I thought. But with the way we've woven around the whole camp today, I can't figure out what's newer and what's from earlier. It's like trying to follow a single thread through a pile of yarn."

Majestrin blew a beleaguered breath. "How long have you been looking for her?"

"About a quarter of an hour," Mythrenese replied between gasping breaths. "Maybe a little more."

Raen pressed the heel of her hand to her temple. "She's far too clever—muddying her own trail."

Majestrin heaved to his feet. "All you need to do is circle the perimeter of the camp, although there's not really any question what direction her signature will lead once you discover at what place she left."

"There isn't?" Mythrenese said.

"Her path will follow Vinyanel's, of course." Majestrin stomped his foot. "Curse my drowsiness. I need to eat more and doze less."

Raen chewed her lip. The fire of self-recrimination burned in her gut. "My share of the blame is as great if not greater. Ecleriast tasked me with her keeping. Looks like I'm in for a trek in this weather I hid from when I should have been watching."

Mythrenese collapsed to the ground and covered his eyes with his foretalons. "One time was bad enough . . . I'm the worst dragon-minder there ever was."

"You have unusual factors working against you," Majestrin said. "But now, you two had better get moving. Even with little wings, she must be very close to the hive, if she's not there already."

"I was bluffing when I told Ecleriast that Lerendir was going to let me go on the mission," Raen said.

"You're not going on the mission," Majestrin grumbled. "You're intercepting a very foolhardy little dragon who has no idea what she's getting into."

Raen nodded. "Sounds about right. I'll get my pack."

~

"*T*here! Finally," Mythrenese said. "Though why she chose to emerge here on the southwest side—"

"Because it's the opposite of where we thought she'd head," Raen said. She leaned close to Mythrenese's neck and pulled her hood lower, but it still could not seal out the needles of ice that numbed her cheeks. "What a horrible day to have a battle."

"Is there such a thing as a good one?" Mythrenese eyed the clouds, his expression sour.

"Until now, I would have said no," Raen said. "And maybe there's no such thing as a good day that contains a battle, but necessary ones, perhaps. Is Iriscendra's signature clear?"

Mythrenese nodded. "Pretty clear. It rounds the camp."

They flew as fast as haze and cold allowed, over tumbled, chalky mountain slopes, bare of most vegetation except the few stubborn, twisted trees that gripped rock against the swirling wind. Water ran in milky rivulets down the stones, and in many places, built into frozen cascades that created row upon row of jagged fangs along the mountainsides.

In moments, they reached the place where the elven front line had entrenched, where catapults hurled massive boulders quarried from the environment around them to assault the main entry to the hive. The remnants of pillared architecture lay in crumbled heaps. Fifty yards in front of the ruins, armies clashed in the deep of the valley.

Raen squinted down at the battle, which she and Mythrenese skirted to the south. The elves, in their bright armor, high-domed helms, and colorful heraldry by division stood out clearly on the field. Their opponents, however, garnered Raen's lingering notice. None wore the deep hoods of dragon-kin in daylight. No, these leather-helmed and fur-caped opponents were men.

What that meant, Raen did not care to contemplate. A century of isolation in the vale allowed her to remain blissfully ignorant of the political goings-on of the wider world to her west. For now, the task remained. Follow the signature. Intercept Iriscendra before she got herself killed.

Thankfully, Iriscendra's signature did not pass the front lines, but instead ran parallel to the elves' blockade of the narrow pass that led to the hive. Then it wove into a tight canyon.

Mythrenese banked and wheeled, climbed and dove to make his way through the ever-tightening defile. Had the circumstances not been so dire, Raen would have loved to fly the place for leisure and scenery. The dragonling jammed to a halt.

"Ow!" he cried. He shook his head as though trying to rid himself of a clinging, clawed attacker.

Raen wrapped her arms around the dragonling's neck. "What? What's going on?"

"There's a horribly 'loud' clash of magical residue here,"

Mythrenese said. He lowered to the canyon floor and rubbed his eyes.

"A what?"

"I don't know how else to explain it. Intense powers strove against one another somewhere nearby. When you trail a signature into such a place, it's sort of the magical equivalent of inhaling those spices you grind back home."

Raen slid from Mythrenese's back. At first, all she saw was weeping, icy rock, a narrow slice of gray sky above, and the churning bubble of a swollen stream at the canyon's deepest point. But then, about fifteen paces ahead, an irregularity in the left canyon wall caught her eye. She gripped her hilt and skulked forward on furtive strides.

A rectangular opening yawned black in the rock face to her left. Deep runes covered the cracked surface of the stone around the opening, graceless characters of a geometric, straight-lines-only design. A pile of sand mounded on the threshold, and the sand held numerous boot prints. The cold, musty smell of deep places drifted from the entry.

"Let me guess." Raen pointed into the fathomless depths. "Iriscendra's signature goes that way."

Mythrenese's wings drooped. "Of course it does."

"Looks like finding her just got a lot more complicated." Raen's breath tightened in her chest. Her palms grew slick with perspiration. The runes, the unknown beyond, and the certain danger ahead all shouted that she should flee. But if she would be in peril, so would Iriscendra.

Raen squared her shoulders and prepared to face whatever lay beyond the yawning entry Iriscendra had dared to pass. If a hatchling had the nerve, should Raen not be able to muster it as well?

36

*N*aghax tramped past the roughly-hewn pits in the deep passage. The bars blocking each hole in the floor bore a red, flaky crust from the constant weeping of moisture in the cavern. The stenches of open chamber pots, rarely emptied, illness, and trench foot hit him in pockets as he made his way to the farthest cell of the row. He reached the last barred hole in the floor, about his arm span wide. The pit below widened in a conical shape.

Naghax leaned over cell entry and peered into its depths. The enclosure housed a half-dozen softbellies—the three Elgadrim girls and three older females harvested from other conquests. His iron club rang against the bars.

All the females jolted from slumber and immediately scrambled into a huddle. The tallest of them, an emaciated, dark-haired Velonese woman, glared up venomously at the bars.

"Save your energy, spitfire," Naghax said. "You and the other elders in this cell will clean the little ones. Spotless."

"With what?" the spiteful woman said. "Our own spit and what's left of our clothes?"

A distant boom echoed through the cavern. Naghax narrowed his eyes. What devilry was going on in the upper levels? This was not the day for one of Hanash's insane experiments. "For your tongue," he said, "I should make you work with just that. But no, this is a task that must be done well, and so the guards will bring tubs of water and soap. Perform well, and we might even let you hags use some of the supplies for yourselves. So much as wash your own toe before these girls are perfect to inspection, and one of you dies. Slowly. In front of the brats."

Though the proclamation did not mellow the fury Spitfire's eyes, it did keep her lips together, so that was enough. The guards tromped up, carrying a half wine-barrel by rope handles. The slosh of water slapped on the barrel's wooden sides. Two more guards stood with swords pointed at the grate that covered the pit entry while Naghax opened it. The water bearers shuffled to lower the barrel by ropes tied to the handles. It tilted and a cascade of water streamed down.

"Careful, you imbeciles. How many trips do you want to make lugging that much?" Naghax pulled a bundle of champagne-colored silk from beneath his arm, and he held it over the cell opening for the group to see.

"Array the girls in these when you have finished." He dropped the bundle.

Spitfire caught the bundle in a juggling grasp. Her black-rimmed nails and scabbed hands struck a barb of concern through Naghax's chest.

"See they are not soiled." After the water carriers dropped bundled burlap that contained the soap, he clanged the grate shut again and turned down the hall. "I will return in one hour for the inspection."

Another boom echoed from somewhere above.

"Or sooner." He waved the guards after him. "Follow me. I have a feeling I'm not going to like the answer to what that sound is."

~

e worked our way down a narrow corridor of natural construction, judging by the rough walls, full of jutting prominences and fissures, as well as the varying ceiling heights, Veins of quartz and gypsum ran through the crumbling limestone. The floor threatened treacherous footing at times, where fallen rock littered the way. I led the group, my sword drawn and shield slung over my arm, though I used the weapon primarily for clearing thick, sticky curtains of cobwebs. Veranna followed me, then came Private Asmenius and Private Thederonde, then Althoron, and last, Galdurith. The corridor rounded a bend, and I paused. I pulled out my partial map.

"I am not entirely certain where this will let out," I whispered. "I recall sleeping chambers and a kitchen and buttery on this side, if we are on the middle level. If not, we could step out by the forge and armory. Either way, places that stand a good chance of being popu—"

The floor shuddered beneath my feet, and a thunderous *boom* cut me short.

"Sounds like the catapults have delivered their invitation to the game," Galdurith said. "An aptly timed distraction."

So it began. Would Lerendir's strategy goad the dragon-kin into conflict? The more swiftly we completed our tasks and got out, the better.

We resumed our careful-footed advance down the hall, and

after another small bend, I caught a glimpse of the outlet. I placed my back against the wall and inched toward the flickering light ahead. Torches? But why? The dragon-kin had no need of light.

"It's probably the kitchen—the middle level," Althoron said. "If it were the forge, we would be hotter."

I nodded, then placed a finger over my lips. Another step. Two more, and I finished rounding the last curve.

Fifteen paces ahead, the end of the tunnel boasted a black iron portcullis. Its vertical bars stood sheathed in the stone floor, and on the opposite side, sliding latches bolted to the floor locked the gate down. Beyond the gate, I glimpsed a massive butcher block, empty of any foodstuffs. It was an orderly place, with knives all sheathed in a block, wooden bowls of varying sizes nested within one another, not even a spare rag laying about. The surroundings spoke of civility, really, until I caught sight of the row of smoked carcasses hanging at the far end of the kitchen, just inside the buttery doorway. They were humanoid in shape--beheaded and deep brown in color from the preservation process, but still recognizably stout enough to rumor they were perhaps dwarves. Whatever roots the dragon-kin had in a great culture of old, clearly the years had faded any recollection of those standards. I averted my gaze and settled it upon the undulating light that came from a wide hearth containing red coals of an old fire.

"Shouldn't someone be about breakfast now?" Thederonde asked. "They'll spot us."

"This is the end of their day," I said. Another crash from somewhere outside shivered the floor. "Likely many of them are rolling unrested from bed at Lerendir's summons."

Indeed, echoing, harsh voices grew, but they were indistinct, as voices that passed through walls. Scuffling feet accompanied the chatter. I shrank back behind the curve. I raised a cautioning finger to the squad.

Galdurith nodded, his lips set tight but expression collected. The two privates glanced to one another, but then met my gaze with the steel of determination. Veranna, eyes closed, mouthed prayers. Althoron kept a sharp eye to the front. Commotion continued in a thrum, but none of it seemed to clatter closer. I pointed to Galdurith and then jerked a thumb over my shoulder toward the portcullis.

Galdurith nodded. He slipped past me, strides silent, crossbow in hand. We waited. After an excruciating minute or two, he glided back to us.

"Nobody's cooking this morning, but the slide latches on the floor are so pitted and rusty, I'm not sure we'll ever get them open. They need a swift whack with a hammer."

"We must find a way," I said. "Or else it is back to the outside and seek another entrance. Squadron, stay here. The Major and I will go decide how to best work our way out of this slot."

As we drew nearer to the portcullis, I wished the commotion that rumbled somewhere beyond our limited field of vision were louder. Beyond the kitchen and buttery, the occupants of the hive must have been rousing to answer the crashes at the front gates. Three sharp impacts sounded.

"Could have used those to cover some hammer strokes," I muttered.

"That might work," Galdurith said. He crouched by the portcullis and picked up a stray rock on the floor of our unkempt hallway. "At least our sounds won't be alone."

Again, we waited, and I began to wonder if the elves outside were ever going to fire again. Just as the temptation to throw my hands into the air and return to the squadron risked boiling over, another boom came. Galdurith pounded on the slide lock with his rock.

The rock crumbled. Stupid limestone.

But the latch had budged a fraction. I bent down and handed another stone to the major just in time for another catapult impact to sound. He pounded again. This time, his rock held together, and he got another stroke from it before it too, disintegrated.

The third rock proved the stoutest of all, and the first slide-lock finally worked free. One more to go.

The longer we had to work at the release, the quicker my heart galloped. The sense of entrapment squeezed my chest. My head began to swim. I leaned against the wall and drew a few long breaths. Galdurith banged away.

"There! That's done it," he said.

I opened eyes that until that moment I had not realized I had closed. Galdurith reached through the bars of the portcullis and worked the slider the rest of the way free. I stepped forward and gripped the iron. The gate weighed more than I could lift, but the two of us together could likely produce enough leverage.

Galdurith rose and gripped the bars as well. We heaved. The gate squealed.

Just in time for an aproned man with ash-colored skin and hair in matted coils to step into the kitchen entry straight ahead.

I glared. So the reports of Tebalese amidst the dragon-kin bore out.

Without so much as a glance to one another, Galdurith and I heaved the portcullis the rest of the way open and charged the human. I dove at the man and tackled him. I had him pinned, face down and my knee in the middle of his back in less than an instant. Galdurith stood over us with his crossbow trained on my prisoner.

"Keep quiet," Galdurith said in a low growl, in the common tongue.

"But answer us this," I added. "What are you doing here?"

The Tebalese captive whimpered. "Coming to make breakfast."

"Are you the dragon-kin's slave? Prisoner? What?" I pressed.

"None of those."

I pushed the man's forearm further up his back toward his shoulder blades.

"A cook, a cook for Inquisitor Ezio!" he yelped.

I groaned. Just what we needed—a Tebalese Inquisitor somewhere around the hive. Likely with both sword skills and curses to bring to bear against us.

"Why are you here?" I asked. "And are there more men besides you and the Inquisitor?"

"They don't tell me these things, I'm just the cook, like I said," the man replied. The tremble in his voice reinforced my sense he probably was little more than a servant dragged into strange business.

"Take a guess then. Have you seen other Tebalese here?"

"Yes. I don't know how many, though. You can't get a look at much in this place. The Inquisitor mentioned some kind of ceremony." He wriggled beneath my weight. "Please, I can't breathe."

He was right about the poor range of vision in the hive, with its winding hallways and blind turns.

"He's no use to us," Galdurith said.

I glanced up. Veranna and the rest of the squadron had moved up behind the major.

"What say you, Veranna?" I asked. "The Utterance of Repose?"

She nodded, and her lips curled in a satisfied smile. "You recall it?"

I nodded in return, then placed my hand on the back of the cook's head. "May sleep unbroken fall upon you."

My captive's body went limp, and he ceased his feeble

struggle against me. I rose, releasing his arm, and it flopped to the floor.

"How long will that last?" Althoron asked.

"No telling," I replied. "But nothing will rouse him until the duration of Creo's choosing expires."

"Just in case that's not very long," Galdurith said, his glance darting to and fro, "let's put some safeguards in place. We'll bind and gag him and lock him in the corridor we used, Lieutenant Commander?"

Better to leave him that way than to kill him, as some warriors lacking scruples might have done. "Do so," I said.

Thederonde and Asmenius carried out the order while Galdurith and Althoron stood guard at the kitchen entry. With a trembling hand, I added details to my map with a stub of vine charcoal. I gritted my teeth. *Focus, Ecleriast.*

Once the portcullis locked into place, we skulked into the hall at the far end of the kitchen. The stone floor, covered in scree, made our footfalls crunch and grate. I winced with every noisy step. The resounding booms of the gate assault punctuated our progress.

The hallway I chose was short and ended in a jagged arch. Heavy, bronze-hued curtains hung from a rod at its end, only one of which was fixed back. We inched our way forward and peered beyond the divider.

To my relief, I had chosen the passage to the great hall of the place. The other hall I recalled in the section ran through a long wing of sleeping quarters--and terminated in a dead end. This chamber stood cold and empty with a still pool at its center. A momentary flash of memory--where curling trails of blood reddened that water, where lifeless eyes of lizard warriors stared blankly as their rent bodies crashed into the pool—gripped me. My strides locked. I grunted, blinked the recollection away, and forced myself to press on.

Today, the water simply reflected the jagged points of

dozens of drip formations that hung from the ceiling in glistening layers. A vast stone table occupied a dais that ran the width of the room to my left. These were familiar. The tables packed in every available spot along the main floor of the hall had not been present the last time I ran through this room in the hope of sparing my lost squadron's lives. I shuddered. But part of me was grateful the room looked different. Not that my heart did not still thunder enough to make my head hurt.

"That way." I pointed to the rear exit from the chamber, one mostly hidden by the dais and table upon it.

"Looks like they're prepared for a crowd," Asmenius surveyed the space.

"Well, the cook did say something about a ceremony," Thederonde whispered to him.

"Likely all connected to the moondeath sacrifice they have planned," Veranna said. "I have an urgent inclination that we need more haste."

"Only as much as we can employ without blundering into the arms of trouble," Galdurith said.

I pulled out my maps again, with sweating palms. My teeth squeaked against one another. "Althoron," I barked. "I place you in charge of updating the information." I thrust the map and charcoal into his keeping.

He regarded the stack with bewilderment. "Sir, a privilege."

I marched for the exit, determined my gait would convey confidence despite my racing pulse. Another winding hall lay ahead, one that would branch at its end to another bank of sleeping quarters or a long corridor bound for the main gates. The sounds of hive activity that had droned beneath our investigations thus far seemed to swell in volume as we headed this way.

Galdurith raised a hand. We stopped on the threshold of the hall.

"I will scout it out. Did you map this section?" he asked.

I nodded. Althoron produced the sketch.

After a brief survey of my notes, Galdurith slunk off. Somehow his steps were immune to the crunch of the flooring. We waited. No sudden cries erupted, so that encouraged me he remained unseen.

When he returned to us, he regarded us from beneath lowered brows. "A handful of Tebalese men in the hall to the right, strapping into armor and gathering weapons. I know little of their language, but their discussion of battle seemed to come in a griping tone."

The floor shook beneath our feet and limestone dust showered us. I stifled a cough. "Lerendir had better not do too thorough a job if he does not aim to bury us in here." I waved off the cloud of stone particles in the air. "Let us all move up. Those soldiers will join the fray soon enough for us to pass to the left. That is where we will access the dungeon level."

We minced our way, one by one—except Veranna, who went with Galdurith—down the hall and around a bend that took us away from the Tebalese soldiers. I caught a couple words to the tune of "not our job" and "nobody said anything about an assault," but I left them to their complaints. I shook my head. There was little in my mind more confounding than a soldier who enlists and expects he will never see battle.

The next hall had a painfully claustrophobic feel. The walls jutted into the corridor and made the way treacherously windy. Niches hardly large enough to hold a bed and a trunk opened at intervals along the way. Despite their lack of square footage, however, the inhabitants of each bunk hung from their walls and furnishings a charming array of skulls, bones, and sometimes-fresher body parts as evidence of their prowess in battle.

No one had any hope of swinging a sword in this corridor. In fact, there were times my shoulders nearly brushed the walls. The gripping sense we could not put this section behind us fast enough made my breaths shallow.

Voices straight ahead of us caught my ear. I whirled and pointed to the nearest sleeping culverts. The group split and dove into the nearest openings, just as a door at the end of the corridor creaked on hinges.

"Leave it to the elves to ruin a well-planned party," a deep, gravelly voice said, fortunately in the common tongue, though his odd accent marred the words. "The Moon Death revelry will be hard to appreciate with those softbellies pounding at the gates."

A more resonant voice with a singer's smooth quality answered. "Our combined forces will drive them off at nightfall —you needn't worry about their antics. They should have started sooner if they meant to foil the summoning."

I pressed my body against the wall of the culvert. What could we do? Perhaps Galdurith could snipe one of the subjects, but both?

The conversation continued, but an undercurrent of indistinct whispers also mingled with the discussion. Despite my growing panic, I strained to hear anything defining in the whispers, but failed. Tingling plagued my hands. My vision blurred.

"Perhaps we should pass through the lower level," the gravelly voice said.

"I thought we were going to the gate chamber?" the second protested. "You cannot expect me to commit my men and go without reports of how they are faring."

"We can come out right at the gates if we pass through the lower level and use the ramp up on the opposite side. That will take us past the infirmary, and then we'll see for ourselves if you have any casualties brought in from the field yet."

The whispering ceased.

"If you insist."

Footfalls receded. Silence bore down on me and made my limbs feel rubbery. I cupped a hand over my nose and mouth while focusing on slowing my breathing, and my spotty vision cleared. A cautious glance into the corridor revealed it was empty. The rest of the squadron inched from their hiding places like cautious prey from little dens.

"That was strange," I said.

Veranna shook her head. "Just a little Utterance of diversion. I was not interested in those two villains, whoever they were, coming down this hall. They were both curse-bearers."

"But now they're headed to the dungeon level." I raked my hand through my hair. "That is where we must go, you know. We could very well run into them again."

"Less of a chance if we avoid the infirmary, I guess," Althoron said.

I leveled a scowl at him. He made a sudden study of the map.

Veranna folded her arms. "I don't choose the distraction, I just ask for the intervention. You know that much."

I pressed my lips together. There was no remedy for their destination. "We will give them some time to get well ahead of us, then."

We progressed slowly into the sloping passageway that led down to the lower level. It wound and wove, likely taking advantage of a natural fissure in the mountain's structure, but unlike the corridor we had used to gain entrance, this one offered no assurance of disuse. The silt-laden floor boasted tracks old and new, and the middle was quite clear of any debris. Occasional rusty smears marked the outcroppings along the walls.

Thederonde stopped and scrutinized one such mark. "Dried blood."

"The blood of the oppressed cries out from every stone of my enemies' stronghold." Veranna recited the passage from the "Justice Annals" of *The Tree*. "But you, Almighty Maker, see and hear."

I breathed in her words, and for a coveted moment, my pulse slowed.

The temperature rose steadily the farther down we progressed, and an undulating roar grew in volume with the climbing temperature. Trails of sweat snaked their way down the small of my back. At least the corridor was wide enough for me to draw my sword.

That proved no small benefit when we reached the bottom of the passage.

THE FORGE

had scarcely set foot upon the threshold of the next cavern before the whistle of a blade through the air alerted me to dive to one side. Never mind the stifling heat or the ear-battering throb of flame, bellows, and grinding machinery—two burly dragon-kin swung ugly, fat-bladed swords with the clear intent of depriving me of my head. I brought my shield around to deflect a blow. My low chop caught one of my attackers in the shins, though I credited that to sheer providence more than my own skill.

A mechanical *twang* sliced the air, and the dragon-kin whose shins I had already gashed grabbed for his throat. Fletching stuck from it.

Althoron spun from the corridor and into the fray, but the dragon-kin still in play caught the sergeant's parallel strokes with his blade. Cries of anger or alarm broke out from somewhere to my right.

Also in that direction, the industry of a giant forge churned.

A giant side-oriented wooden wheel rotated slowly, powered by at least two—maybe three—colossal centipedes harnessed to it. A black-scaled dragon-kin froze beside one of the segmented beasts, mid-whip stroke, to gape at our arrival. No fewer than a half-dozen more forge workers ceased in banging on anvils or cooling steel.

I righted my posture and lunged at the nearest opponent. My guess was that he and his now-prone friend must have served as door guards, but the leading edge of my sword parted him from both his head and that obligation before he could bring another stroke to bear upon me.

The group of smiths abandoned their projects to grab finished swords, morningstars or axes. They charged toward us.

The forge cavern lacked anything I would have called an advantageous tactical position. It was a clutter of barrels and tools, flanked on the left with the wheel the centipedes turned and the glowing forge their apparatus fanned. But for now, it seemed none of the occupants of the forge would join the fight with anything more daunting than mundane weapons.

"Althoron, Asmenius—back to back!" I yelled.

They positioned themselves, and to my relief, Galdurith interpreted the order to apply to him and Thederonde as well. Veranna hung back in the corridor.

I barreled toward the closest centipede. A straining leap landed me on the creature's back, and a sword slice cut its harness free of the wheel. I reached forward and grabbed the creature's left antennae with my shield hand. When I yanked on the antennae, the beast wheeled that direction. I smiled.

It scrabbled away from what I guessed had been its only place to tread ever since the dragon-kin had gotten their claws into it. An occasional tug on its appendage corrected the creature's course into the battle.

I hewed right and left when the centipede clattered

between two of its prior captors. Their weapon strokes glanced from my armor. Mine cleft deep.

We overturned cooling basins. Crashed over crates of pig iron. Scattered half-wrought weaponry. Eliminated the taskmaster who sought to recapture the centipede. The ruckus was intolerable—we would bring the whole hive to us at this rate.

My squadron members fought with admirable efficiency, laying their opponents low in few strokes, though Asmenius took a fierce morningstar blow to the chest. I was sure the strike must have cracked no fewer than three ribs. Just as the final smith fell to Galdurith's crossbow, a shout outside the smithy chamber echoed. The language must have been that of the dragon-kin, judging by unintelligible words.

Two black-robed dragon-kin as well as a red-cloaked and armored Tebalese man appeared in the smithy's entry. The taller reptile lowered its snout and narrowed gold eyes at me.

"Ecleriast. Of course," he said. "You did not get your fill watching your friends die last time?"

My heart skipped. Scitherias? No, he was dead.

The Tebalese man wore a jeweled clasp at the throat of his long cape, a gargoyle and triangle talisman. The spiked gauntlet on his right hand marked him as a member of the order of Inquisitors. He blustered to the shorter dragon-kin in Tebalese, something about being told the hive could not be breached.

"We will not stand by as you ally yourselves with dark powers over which you cannot hope to maintain control," I said. I tightened my calves against the shell of my insectoid mount.

"The trouble is," the taller dragon-kin said as he took a few slow steps into the chamber, "this conflict does not really involve you Delsin at all. You just keep stepping into the middle of a grievance that would have no effect on your people if you would simply mind your own business."

"I mind Creo's business," I said.

He rolled his eyes. "Ah, piety. The great eliminator of reason. Listen, Ecleriast, I am Scitherias's successor, and if you found him troubling, you will find me unbearable. I give you and your squadron this one chance: we escort you through the front gates. You call off your band of jackals outside, and you all walk away from this with your hides. Well, at least those who Ezio's men have not yet hewn out on the field. No need to add more blood to your stained hands."

I clenched my free hand, the one that did not bind the centipede to my will. "You think I believe you would honor such a surrender agreement? And that I don't know how much blood will spill if I do as you suggest?"

The Tebalese man—Ezio, I supposed—heaved a sigh. He thrust his hands out before him, and a greenish-white pulse of light lanced forward from his palms. His shorter reptilian companion clutched a half-dozen scrolls to his chest and dropped back a few steps behind Ezio.

In the same instant, Veranna leapt forward with a cry. "Creo is my shield!" The same, nebulous barrier I saw in the cave outside Barrington spread before me, and Ezio's bolt shattered into wisps upon it.

Scitherias's successor laughed. "Came slightly better prepared this time, I see. But not well-equipped enough." His face twisted in a snarl, and he jabbed a finger toward us. The air between us warped, and his curse collided with Veranna's shield with a concussive burst. She flew backward and crashed on the ground, sliding on her side for several yards before coming to rest. Galdurith ran to her.

"You have not seen the half of what we bring to bear upon you." I drove my heels into the centipede's body. The creature lurched forward on its countless legs.

The Inquisitor's eyes widened. "Hanash, this is madness," Ezio said. Finally, an entire sentence I understood.

"Softbelly," Hanash shot back. "You coward." He wove his hands before him again.

The way the creature beneath me charged, it either had a grudge against its captors or else was not a simple beast meant to tow weight. It screeched and clacked giant mandibles.

In one motion, I flung a knife from my belt at Hanash. It glanced off his clawed hands, but the gash it scored caused him to wheel to the side with a hiss. Whatever curse he had been preparing evaporated with his broken concentration.

Every breath I took only filled my lungs a fraction of the amount it should have. *Keep your soldiers alive. That's the first duty of an officer.* Was Veranna right to have wanted to skirt these two, the curse-bearers I could only assume she sensed upstairs? Breathless or not, I closed on Hanash.

The centipede reared, then dove at the Hanash, and he backpedaled with a scathing glare. "Naghax, get a sword in there, you craven!" he yelled at the other dragon-kin.

I squeezed my mount's side with my left leg. It rotated away from the pressure. So it was a trained riding beast. I released the antennae in favor of steering with my seat and legs.

My sword whistled around, but Hanash ducked the cut. From the corner of my field of vision, I was aware of Althoron, Thederonde, and Asmenius charging Ezio and Naghax, who had shrunk further from the battle.

My own opponent reached down and snatched an axe from the floor. He swung it up in time to catch my next attack against its haft. I circled my blade away.

The centipede dove again at Hanash, and its mandibles clamped on his free arm. The dragon-kin roared. He hacked at my mount with the ax, but the close range robbed his strokes of power, and the blade skittered over the creature's carapace.

I plunged my sword, and the point sunk between Hanash's

ribs. His eyes bulged in pain and hatred, but he still managed to drop the ax and clap his hand onto the centipede's head. Smoke rose from his hand. A flash of heat spread through my legs.

The quickest, messiest dismount of my life pulled me clear of the creature just before the centipede's entire length burst into flames. It released Hanash in a hissing squeal, thrashing and writhing. The cavern filled with the choking stench of burning tissue.

I righted myself from the semi-sprawl I had suffered in my retreat from the now-engulfed centipede. In clouds of smoke, I lost sight of Hanash. No wheeling scan of the chamber revealed his whereabouts. Sword clashes and shouts rang somewhere beyond the smithy.

The centipede crashed into a ruined, flaming pile. My cloak pressed over my nose and mouth, I ran for the passage that led from the smithy, opposite where we had come in—the direction from which the clashes came. Still, the thick, oily smoke made my eyes water and my head spin.

A twist and a turn down another semi-natural corridor led me to a narrow, low ceilinged chamber with a bridge arching over a subterranean river. The dark water churned by. My three squad members had chased Inquisitor Ezio and Naghax to this the bridge.

Ezio fought with a curved knife. Naghax parried with a serrated scimitar. The moment I emerged into the chamber, Althoron slashed two cuts across Ezio's body from opposite sides with fluidity and grace almost too lofty for mere war. Ezio recoiled, and in a motion the complete opposite of Althoron's in terms of quality, Thederonde rammed his shoulder into the Inquisitor's chest.

The Tebalese man staggered back and hit the low bridge railing. To my eye, it seemed he would recover his stance—that is, until Naghax spun in a clumsy parry, and his thick crocodilian tail caught Ezio behind the knees. The Inquisitor tipped over the railing at his back. His heavy upper body carried him headfirst toward the water. Thederonde nearly pitched over the side as well, but Althoron grappled his comrade around the waist. They staggered away from the edge.

In the moment my squad members staggered back, Naghax flung his serrated sword upward in a cut that caught hold of Asmenius's blade. Asmenius's weapon flew from his hand.

Ezio sank. He resurfaced momentarily in the turbulent water before the rushing current whisked him downstream. The rapids thrust him through the mouth of a natural tunnel and out of sight.

Though Naghax had disarmed Asmenius, he spun away from the fray instead of attacking my squad member again. Asmenius backpedaled defensively toward his weapon. Naghax seized the opportunity to flee the bridge and vanish through a dark doorway on the opposite side. And unless my eyes misled me, it seemed to me he shot a small smirk at the river's surface before he left.

I dashed with lopsided strides for the group—there was only so much my armor enhancements could account for, after all, and running seemed to tax their limitations. "Did Hanash come this way?"

Althoron swept a sleeve across his sweat-drenched fore-head. "Who?"

"Hanash—the dragon-kin priest . . ." I gasped to catch my breath.

Galdurith entered the cavern with Veranna hanging limp in his arms.

I gawked, a shot of panic sizzling through my chest. "Galdu-rith, Veranna's status."

He puffed for air. "Unwounded. But unconscious. And as for the dragon-kin priest, he slipped away. Back the way we came."

I pounded the railing with my fist. "We have little choice than to keep moving. He will have the whole place on alarm looking for us in moments. If not him, then his companion. This way."

We ran over the bridge, rounded a tight bend to the right, and I skidded to a stop. To my left, a hammered iron door hung partially ajar.

Galdurith raised a brow.

I jerked a thumb toward the door. "Guard house," I mouthed.

A long listen revealed nothing—not a cough, a sigh, a clink of sword belt. The closest examination I dared on the space between the door and jamb revealed no activity. Only a partial view of an empty stool.

Galdurith eased Veranna into Althoron's care, then advanced on the door. He pressed his back to the wall beside the opening. One quick glance. Then another longer look.

"It's empty," he whispered.

Empty? Odd. But fortuitous. "Into the hall then. Spread out. Each of you check the pits on the right for three young girls."

I took the less palatable job of investigating the left hand side of the hall—the cluster of three torture chambers. While I doubted the dragon-kin would house the girls in such places, I preferred not to risk one of the newer recruits confronting the reality if they did.

The group leaned over the barred trap doors to search the pits' interiors, and I threw the first chamber door wide. Only the funk of blood left unmopped met my senses, though it was gut-twisting enough. The second chamber, however, stabbed me with a shock I never expected. But shock is understandable when a soldier finds someone he knows hanging from shackles.

38

A Familiar Face

I blinked at the back wall of the torture chamber, where a gaunt figure stretched, arms held wide against the walls in iron cuffs clamped just above his elbows. His weight hung against the restraints, which had gouged deep into what little flesh lingered on his bones. A second set of cuffs held his wrists, although the left wrist ended in a gnarled stump. His head dragged heavy on a thin neck, and matted clumps of dark hair obscured his face. Tatters of what may have once been pants covered his bony hips and stringy thighs—his knee joints larger in circumference than any other part of his legs. Only the balls of his grimy bare feet reached the floor.

I closed my eyes and turned my head.

"You're wasting your time. I won't beg your mercy."

That voice! I knew it. It belonged to—

I returned my glance to the victim. He had lifted his head, and although shriveled eyelids fluttered over sockets deprived of the orbs that once occupied them, there was still no denying the truth.

"Curunith!" I choked. Curunith, the soldier who had lasted to the end of the previous campaign in this place, who had broken off from Solaris and me to create a false trail for the dragon-kin who pursued us so many months ago. "You survived." From the looks of matters, it might have been a mercy had he not.

"Now I know I've finally lost the last of my mind," Curunith said. "If you don't sound like an impossible captain I once served with."

"No, you have not gone mad," I said. "It is Vinyanel, if that is who you mean."

"Took your time getting to me."

I grabbed my head. Never had it occurred to me that the dragon-kin would have captured him and not killed him in the field. "I—I . . . it was not possible—"

Curunith's sudden burst of laughter challenged my earlier assertion that he had not succumbed to madness. "Of course it wasn't. I never expected anyone."

I shook off my horror and shame. "Can we get you free? Do they lock the cuffs?" In a few swift strides, I reached his side, though the stench of his unwashed flesh lodged in my throat. Simple pins held the cuffs shut. I reached for one.

"It's no use, Captain," Curunith said. "I can't stand anymore."

"But you still live." I slipped the first pin free. "I know healers who will build you back up."

"It's been months since I last hoped that."

"Lieutenant Commander," Althoron called from behind me. He sucked a sharp breath. "Creo's mercy. . ."

"Somebody outranks you here?" Curunith chuckled, but it broke into a fit of wet coughing before he stilled again.

"Uh, no." Why did admitting my elevated rank to him

somehow fill me with waves of self-consciousness? "Lieutenant Commander means me now." I switched sides and slid the next wrist pin free. "What is it, Sergeant?"

Althoron stepped closer. "The girls aren't in any of the pits. Only two contain prisoners, and none of them will tell us anything. But we did see some tattered, child sized nightdresses in a pit with three grown women."

I turned these facts over in my mind. The revelation that the girls were not in the dungeon dragged on my soul. At what hour would they perform the sacrifice? Moonrise, I thought.

I recalled our calculations as placing moonrise close to dusk. Surely it was still early, but who could tell in this dreadful labyrinth?

And the only member of our party I was confident would know the time for the ritual for sure was unconscious.

"Girls?" Curunith said. "Are they who you're after?"

"Althoron, help me get Captain Curunith down." I reached for his second elbow cuff, but choked down a lump in my throat at the crusty seepage of wounds that mired the iron. "Yes. Three Elgadrim girls. But we shall take a moment to help you first."

With Althoron's help, we managed to release Curunith's ruinous skeletal form from the wall.

"The priests came and took the girls in quite a hurry—that's why they left me hanging, I think. More pressing matters, so I hear. Speaking of what I hear—what are the thuds up above?"

"Chancellor Lerendir is leading a force to bombard the gates," I said. "That is why we need to get you out. The medics at the base camp can help you."

"I'm not sure I want them to." Curunith's face twisted. He swallowed. "I had gotten fairly acquainted with the idea of dying soon."

"Enough," I said, though it came out with a crosser edge than I had set out to offer. "Althoron, go tell Asmenius we will escort him back to the kitchen passage, and he will take Curunith to the base camp."

Whether Curunith thought he wanted to live or not, this much of my previous campaign I would salvage, now that circumstances had offered me the chance. As for what the healers could do for him once he reached the camp, I would have to leave that in Creo's hands, for surely Curunith needed miracles. The other prisoners' release would have to wait until the next phase of maneuvers.

Curunith proved a distressingly small burden as I bore him over my shoulder back toward the kitchen. Dragon-kin and Tebalese soldiers jogged the hallways on the upper levels now, which forced us to hunker down for a quarter hour, at least, in the privies we found at the edge of the barracks. Every set of footfalls that approached wormed their way under my skin until I was nigh upon writhing. Thank the maker for door locks, as at least two passers-by rattled the latch to our places of concealment.

The interminable wait and close quarters made me want to scream. To have come this far and end up missing the time of sacrifice—no, I could not allow my fretful mind to dwell on the possibility.

After an agonizing eternity, the hallways outside the privies stilled. On furtive strides, I eased from my hiding place. I summoned the rest of the squadron into the empty hall and led them at a brisk clip back to the kitchen.

The portcullis we had lowered to contain the Tebalese cook stood open when we arrived. Galdurith swept by me and passed into the darkness of the tunnel. Again, we waited.

"Althoron, please give me the sketches of the sacrifice chamber," I said.

He shuffled through the parchments in his stack. Once he produced the requested page, he extended it to me.

I reached for the sketch, and as my glance fell upon the

reproductions of the runes I had chronicled upon it, a sudden sweat beaded on my lip. My stomach turned. The hot spatter of elf blood on my cheek made me flinch. My knees weakened.

Althoron caught my arm. "Lieutenant Commander, are you all right? Should I take the Captain from your shoulder?"

I reached up to touch my cheek. Looked at my fingers. No blood. For a moment, I scanned the room, confused about my own whereabouts.

The kitchen. We are in the kitchen.

All right—the parchment had simply spawned a momentary recollection of my last endeavor in the sacrifice chamber. I blew a breath.

"No, that will not be necessary." I took the parchment.

Galdurith emerged from the tunnel beyond the portcullis.

"The way is clear. You're certain you want to divide the group?" He fidgeted with his quiver strap, and his glance darted from doorway to doorway.

"While I would rather not lose an excellent help, I cannot in good conscience leave Captain Curunith a second time." I nodded to Asmenius. "Creo shield you from unfriendly eyes."

"Thank you, sir," Private Asmenius said, his voice tight. I transferred Curunith's frail weight onto Asmenius's shoulders, and he grimaced—likely his battered ribs provided a sharp reminder of the blow he had taken on the forge level.

"No matter how this goes, it will be good to feel sun on my skin again. Or is it night?" Curunith said.

I smiled, though sadly. "Daylight it shall be. Rainy, but daylight."

"Make that snow," Galdurith said.

I threw my cloak over Curunith. "Haste, Private Asmenius."

"Sir, absolutely." He clenched a fist over his heart, turned, and ducked beneath the portcullis.

I watched them until they vanished into the darkness

before I turned to Althoron and Thederonde. "What of Veranna?"

Althoron shook his head. "Still no sign of waking, sir. No signs of trauma or shock, but no response to any consciousness measures either."

"Which leaves me in another dilemma. The soldier who carries her will not be combat-ready as we press on. I put both the prophetess and her bearer at risk by continuing to take her ith us. Perhaps I should send—"

Pattering footfalls from the side hall leading from the kitchen caught my notice. I wheeled, blade bared.

The door burst open, and through it leapt a quadrupedal, white blur—no, a pearly one.

Iriscendra.

I clapped my hand to my forehead. "What? How could you be . . .?" The initial swirl of bewilderment gave way to the heat of fury. "I am going to wring someone's neck!"

The hatchling skidded to a stop at my feet and groveled. Her brow puckered in a genuine slight. "You wish me go? " She grimaced. "You wish me *to* go?" The words came slowly, each one chosen with care and pronounced with extra precision.

"You should not be here," I said. "This is very dangerous." The last thing I needed, should the campaign take me to my dying breath, was for the hatchling's sanity to take that blow. Surely witnessing my death would be more traumatic than a simple lack of return from battle.

"I can help," Iriscendra said. "But I know you not . . . knew you would not believe me unless I sounded, um, more ready."

I growled. "I would send you away, but I think I know all the good it will do." A few swift strides took me to Veranna. Althoron had laid her on the floor of the exit passage. Iriscendra joined me at her side. I dug my fingers under my hair to my scalp.

"She needs . . . bad magic . . .peeled away," Iriscendra said.

"What? A curse?"

Iriscendra sniffed Veranna's hair. "Yes. It's like 'Ranna's trapped inside a curse."

"Sir." Galdurith knelt beside Veranna and placed a palm on her cheek. His face was drawn. "Do you know what to do?"

All my squadron's eyes locked upon me.

"A curse countered," I said. "Right." I placed a hand on Veranna's shoulder. Frankly, I had no idea how to do what Iriscendra suggested. Could it be something like overcoming the hiding curse on the door? I pushed all the air from my lungs in a slow stream, and imagined my mind clearing of every distraction. I listened only for the inclination Creo would suggest.

The uncanny sense of a will outside my own flowing into my limbs and my lips swept through me. My mouth moved. I could not really hear what I pronounced. The world around me shimmered indistinct, as though on the opposite side of a curtain of water.

When the sensation abated, Althoron, Galdurith, Thederonde, and even Veranna all stared at me wide eyed. It had worked. Well, *something* had worked. Veranna definitely appeared fully conscious.

Iriscendra sat on her haunches, her chin high and a smile on her lips.

My whole body shuddered as a short, violent chill took hold of me. Once I had steadied myself, I cleared my throat. "Why are you all gaping?"

"Your eyes started to glow white, sir," Thederonde said. "And then you spoke in this voice, but it did not sound like yours—it echoed."

"But it was not loud," Galdurith added.

"In fact," Veranna sat up and rubbed her eyes. "I'm not certain it was aloud at all. It seemed more in my mind than ears, if that makes any sense."

I shoved my unsettled, tangled emotions behind a forced grin. "Not much, but I have grown used to that from you." I stood. "Glad to have you back, prophetess. As you might guess, we need to move."

Galdurith aided Veranna to her feet. "Where now?"

My stomach flipped into my chest. "Up. The level above us is the sacrifice chamber."

39

Narrow Escapes

e skulked through the kitchen toward the great hall, but a voice beyond the archway halted our progress about halfway down the passage. One speaker, dragon-kin most likely, since I did not understand a word of his guttural noise.

Iriscendra clamped her teeth onto my wrist and dug her talons into the loose footing. "Not go—don't go that way," she said in a muffled whisper. "They're getting instructions to hunt you and take you to Han-somebody."

"We must fight our way through—this is the only way up," I said in the lowest voice I could manage and still be understood. "Wait, you know their language?"

"Dragons understand all words, remember? I show you 'nother way, if you don't mind climbing."

I glanced toward the great hall. "I am willing to give anything a try, especially if it gives us an unexpected route."

Iriscendra beamed. "You see? Told you I'd help."

She spun and bounded the opposite way. In the narrow hall from which she had emerged when she found us, she pointed at a crumbling hole in the wall about my height plus half up the wall. The hole could not have been more than two feet wide.

I rubbed my temple. Why was I following the equivalent of a toddler around this labyrinth? "Iriscendra, we are not gnomes. How are we supposed to—"

She launched into the air and rammed the wall near the hole with her head.

"What are you—stop that!"

My words had no effect. She continued to head butt the wall, but to her credit, the limestone cracked. My glance flicked behind us. How loud were Iriscendra's efforts? Were they reaching the great hall? Upon her third assault, a chunk fell inward, revealing a crevice now about four feet wide, but still only as high as the original hole. Even wriggling on our bellies, it would be a tight fit. My shoulders knotted instantly.

"It gets a little bigger inside. This crack leads into an up-and-down tunnel. Just enough room to climb straight up, like a lumpy...uh...chimney," Iriscendra said.

"Where does it let out?" Galdurith asked.

The pearl dragon squeezed into the gap and vanished.

I took a step forward and spoke through my teeth. "Iriscendra, get back here! What are you doing?" I pressed my fingertips to my temples. The better question was: why was I letting her out of my sight in this abominable place?

She popped her head back out of the crevice. "Some kind of little room with a railing on one wall and some knives and bowls. And a square fire pit."

I nodded. The description fit one of the side prayer chambers on the sacrifice level. "Do we have anything to wedge that kitchen door?"

Galdurith frowned. "I can spare a knife."

"So can I," Thederonde pulled one from his belt.

The two of them jammed the blades into the wood frame of the door and an angle that would hold the entry for a few moments, but not long against a determined assault.

Tramping and scuffling caught my ear. And the nose-burning scent of dragon-kin. I grabbed Althoron by the shoulder and shoved him toward the newly-widened passage. Iriscendra jumped down into the hall beside me.

Althoron gripped some protrusions that offered insufficient handholds, but Thederonde sped Althoron's ascent by grabbing his thighs and hoisting him. He squeezed into the crevice, turned, and put his hand out.

I sent Veranna next. The footfalls neared. Galdurith cocked his crossbow. He aimed it at the door.

Thederonde jumped and caught hold of the crevice lip. Between my shoving and the hauling of those already in the crevice, he scraped inside.

The door rattled. Words of what sounded like frustration volleyed on the opposite side.

"V'yennel! Hurry!" Iriscendra butted me with her head.

I pushed her aside. "You and Galdurith first."

He turned a look of protest to me. I pointed at the crevice and set my jaw in my staple 'that's an order' position.

Galdurith kept his crossbow trained on the door while he backed to the wall below our escape. I boosted him. A solid *whump* sounded against the door. One of the knives angled looser.

While the subordinate soldiers hauled Galdurith up, Iriscendra jumped to the escape route easily, aided by her wings.

Another boom. The loose knife clattered free.

Military training had built my vertical leap to an enviable height when I had use of both legs, but I despaired of what kind of jump I would manage now. I thrust upward with all my might. Thankfully it was enough to clap the full length of my arms over the chasm lip. My squadron's heaving finished the job. I scraped across the fissure floor, wincing for what rents the abrasive motion probably raked through the black lacquer on my breastplate. No sooner than I had tucked my feet into the tight space, wood splintered, and the following *whack* of planking against wall told me the door had given passage.

The squadron dragged themselves deeper into the "lumpy chimney" Iriscendra had opened to us, and as best I could see past broken rock, they all stood in a tight huddle about ten paces away. The tramp of leathery footfalls grew in the corridor below. I lay flat and still.

I gripped my sword hilt. Should one of the dragon-kin search this way, would I even be capable of taking a slash at the beast, prone and nigh upon pinned by rock as I was?

The tramping passed below my position but kept moving, amidst the indiscernible grumbling of the pursuers. Only when all evidence of their passing faded from hearing did I dare resume my retreat deeper into the crevice.

When I reached the place where the horizontal slit in the rock opened into a tall, rough chamber, Galdurith had already begun the ascent. The rest of the group watched from within the chute. I remained in place within the crevice, since the chute up offered no more standing room.

Every time someone shifted their feet, their movement made a muffled crunch, and it was then I noticed they stood in a litter of burnt bones and ash. A long bone, maybe a femur here, small bones there. Off to the side, a crumbling, blackened skull leered at me. I averted my gaze.

After a quick span of moments, Galdurith returned to us.

He brushed chalky limestone dust from his black leather. "There is no one in the chamber at the top of this chute, and the climb leads to a grate—but it is on hinges and has no latch.

I heard voices beyond the curtain over the doorway, so I did not want to risk trying to shift the grate without help."

"Many voices?" I asked.

"No," Galdurith replied. "Just two in conversation. Although that's no reliable estimation of the population up there."

I nodded. "Agreed. We shall move the whole group into the chamber, then address what lies beyond it."

I emerged from the escape niche and squeezed my way through the group, my expression steeled with purpose. Though in truth, my palms were slick with sweat inside my gauntlets. I knew what lay beyond the chamber curtain, and the cracking bones underfoot only foretold a fraction of what we could face there.

~

"Get down!" Raen cried. She grabbed Mythrenese's head and shoved it toward the floor.

The dragonling collapsed flat upon the dais. Echoing voices entered the great hall from the far end. A quick survey of Mythrenese's position stabbed a barb of panic through Raen's chest.

"Your tail!" she whispered. "Pull it in!"

The length of the stone dining table offered cover to all but the spiked tip of his tail. He snaked it around his body. Raen exhaled in a slow stream, then peered from behind the table to seek who had joined them in the chamber.

A mixed group of men and dragon-kin, more of the latter than the former, gathered in the space near the chamber entry, since the rest of the room suffered the crowding of tables around the still, central pool. An extremely agitated dragon-kin in a black robe tramped about and threw his arms around in gestures of utter frustration. A series of throaty syllables poured from his snapping jaws.

"Better talk in a language we understand, lizard-man," one of the Tebalese men called out in the common tongue. He folded his arms across his chest and frowned.

The dragon-kin halted. "Halfwits!" he yelled. "Find Ecleriast and his party and bring them to me. In pieces, if need be."

"We don't take orders from you, Hanash," another Tebalese man said. "Where is Ezio?"

The robed dragon-kin—Hanash, as best Raen could guess—turned a chilling glare on the Tebalese man. He pointed a clawed finger at the Tebalese dissenter and barked, "*Chargrath-da!*"

Hanash's target collapsed to the floor and writhed. He dug his fingers into his dread-locked hair, and his piercing screams rang in Raen's ears.

"Anyone else care to question whether you need to hear from your so-called Inquisitor before you heed me?" Hanash said.

The dragon-kin within the group sneered, while the Tebalese men cast each other round-eyed glances.

"I thought not."

A resounding *boom* shook the floor. Stalactites broke free from the ceiling and plummeted down. One crashed amidst the group Hanash had assembled, scattering them all directions, and a handful more splashed into the center pool. A cloud of stone dust descended upon Raen from the formations that shattered on the surface of the stone table on the dais.

Raen clapped her hand over her mouth and nose, since an inhalation at just the wrong time had drawn a load of the airborne stone dust right into her sinuses and throat. Her eyes watered as she stifled the throat-gripping cough that demanded its freedom.

A loud sneeze rang out behind her.

She snapped her head around. Her horrified glare landed on Mythrenese, who rubbed at his eyes and running nose.

"What was that?" Hanash said.

Mythrenese's watering eyes pleaded Raen's forgiveness. How could she bear him a grudge, as close as she had been to the one to make noise?

The two-dozen enemies charged for the dais.

Raen leapt to her feet, whirled, and dashed for the door behind the head table. From behind her, another gravelly exclamation broke out.

Just as she reached for the door handle, Mythrenese squawked. "Don't, Raen."

Not in time. Her hand landed on the iron pull, and shooting pain arced through her body. The agony tore up her arm and spread through her like a river of broken glass filling her veins. She could not release the door handle. Her body jerked involuntarily in a manic dance.

Finally, the gripping pain released her, and she collapsed to the floor, vaguely aware of a chorus of mirthless laughter that rang out somewhere. Her ears seemed stuffed. Her muscles only spasmed when she tried to turn toward the oncoming crowd.

Mythrenese leapt into motion. He grabbed Raen's cloak, soaked from the foul weather, and wrapped it around her face. "Don't take that off your nose and eyes. No matter what."

Not that she could if she wanted to. She lay in cold, wet darkness. Heard the leathery whoosh of Mythrenese's wings. Then rushing wind?

Cries and sudden coughing, gagging, and hacking followed the rushing sound. Strong, clawed hands lifted her from the floor. Raen reached to clear the cloak fabric from her face.

"No!" Mythrenese said. "Wrap your face tight. I've got you."

She bobbed into the air. The rush of flight rustled in her ears. The coughing and moans of pain receded.

"We'll have to try another way," Mythrenese said. "There, I think we're far enough now. You can unwrap."

The twitching in Raen's muscles had abated enough that she could grasp the wet wool of the cloak and free her face. "What happened?" Her voice came out hoarse.

"The dragon-kin put a lightning curse on the door."

"Oh. I wasn't really asking about that. What was all the gagging and moaning?"

Mythrenese turned his face away and squeezed his eyes shut. His chin quivered. "I had to, Raen. There was no other way." He set her down in a chamber full of looms and huge skeins of yarn that opened from a twisting hallway. Tears welled in his eyes.

Raen reached up and touched his cheek. "You're right, Mythrenese. There was only one choice. I'm glad you used your ... gifting."

The dragon's eyes lit with a sudden sparkle. "Really? You think it was the right thing to do?"

A smile blossomed on Raen's lips. "Yes. And I think it will be the right thing more than once in this foul place. You're going to get us to the girls and to freedom. I can tell."

40

A *Burden Shed*

*M*y back pressed to one side of the chute and my feet to the other, I paused. I strained to listen, but the voices in the next room drowned beneath the throb of my own heartbeat in my ears. I was going to fail again. How could I possibly get this entire squadron through this boiling maze of enemies, when we had not yet even sighted the Elgadrim girls or the chalice? A bead of sweat ran down my temple in a ticklish trail.

"Lieutenant Commander? The next move?"

I swiped the perspiration away with a rough gesture. Why was Galdurith always on hand the moment I felt as though panic and bewilderment were about to snuff me out? I took three long breaths without apologizing for the continued delay. My heart rate at least steadied, if still too fast.

I pushed on the grate with my sword arm, and it lifted on a smooth set of hinges. The chamber above was likely only a dozen paces across, and in its center, a stone slab bore the blackening marks of repeated flame intermingled with streaks of dull red and brown that left meandering tracks over the slab's edges. A trail of partially swept ash led from the slab to the grate from which I peered. How tired I had become over the past months of the many styles, sizes, and executions of Quel-durik's altars. My study of the cult led me to believe this one likely existed for private penitence and the quiet offerings of the ashamed.

I dragged myself from the ash-chute and waved Iriscendra up next. The voices Galdurith had heard rumbled on at an argumentative pitch. "What are they saying?"

She cocked her head. "Something about the right time." She paused. "It's too soon, says one. The other, the one that keeps coughing, says the instructions are looser than the other one thinks. The coughing one is mad about the army . . . and someone called Ezio. And you."

"Keep listening," I whispered, then nodded to the rest of the group.

One by one, the squadron emerged from the chute. My eyes fixed on the surface of the altar. A growing nausea pulsed through me, as though an unholy heartbeat throbbed inside that stone, and its reverberations scrambled my insides. The deep recesses of my mind wanted to tear my gaze from the place of sacrifice, and yet, my muscles froze and would not assent.

How many had lost their lives to Queldurik's insatiable need for slaughter? Would this mission put a stop to it?

No.

A few steps carried me to the altar's edge. I leaned on it and hung my head. My inner monologue taunted me: I would never make any kind of real difference. Perhaps harry and annoy for a time, until I finally made that fateful error that delivered the death I had earned a dozen times already, but escaped due to others' clarity in the crucial moment.

"There is whispering falsehood in this place," Veranna said.

A war raged in my skull. Falsehood? Or was it bald truth that tormented me?

I was an impulsive fool with just enough ability to foist my will on others to drag them along with my idiocy—I had started young. Gotten a lot of practice.

"Vinyanel Ecleriast, come back. You hear the assault— rebuke it," the prophetess said, her tone a smooth, near-chant.

I snapped from my self-beratement and fixed my gaze on Veranna. Her eyes held the far-off look that always overtook her when she prophesied.

No, you simply hear the metal and wheels in my head breaking down. My thought held a bitter edge. Did Veranna perceive it?

Veranna's voice drifted through my mind like a breeze among soft grass. *Stop listening to the lies, Vinyanel. The darkness plants untruth and accusation in your heart, tends them so they'll take tenacious root. I cannot discern your pain, for how deeply you've buried it, how well you shroud it from even yourself, but know this: uproot it now, or forever it will lame you. Perhaps some wounds will never entirely heal, but that doesn't mean you neglect to stop the bleeding.*

I traced a finger along the mechanisms of my new armor. The strength from without. The unwavering stares of my squadron weighed upon me.

A child's fearful whimper echoed from somewhere beyond the chamber curtain. The cry lanced me to the core.

I slapped my hand on the altar's surface, stood up straight, and drew my longsword. *Today, at least for this moment, I leave my shame here. It belongs to the darkness, and I will not let its burden open the gate for another's suffering.*

"Squadron, you have your assignments," I said. "Let the moon be the only maid to suffer death today!"

41

Dark Fire

*R*aen and Mythrenese barreled from hallway to chamber, up slopes and over debris, much of it new, loosened by the catapult assault on the gates. Had the place not been put to such ill use and so full of villains, the natural caverns interspersed with the tunneling might have wooed her heart from the waterfall vale.

She and the indigo dragonling huddled in a side chamber just off the main foyer of the complex—one of the few areas the occupiers had worked for aesthetic appeal, to dazzling effect. Relief sculptures marched in a continuous parade around the semicircular foyer, figures of beasts and of dragon-kin, rendered more regal than their real-life counterparts, with long trains on their robes and high bearing. However, the constant refrain of violent and graphic depictions of dragon-kin domination that appeared at intervals throughout the frieze marred the impeccable craft with obscenity.

Another *boom*. A series of cracks ran up the wall like bolts of lightning. Dust and pebbles rained down. Between the fresh cracks, the wall over the hall to the main gate shifted.

It's coming down. Raen's breath wedged in her throat.

"Run!" she screamed. She grabbed Mythrenese by the horn and dragged him toward the curving staircase at the opposite end of the foyer.

A deafening series of crashes roared behind her. She did not look back. She and Mythrenese bounded up the stairs. Twenty steps up, a group of five dragon-kin appeared around the bend, axes and swords drawn, eyes bulging.

"Get on," Mythrenese cried. "And cover your head again."

Raen swung onto Mythrenese's back, then pulled the wet length of cloak over her face. The dragon's ribs expanded under her legs. His neck plunged forward, nearly from Raen's grasp.

Shrieks pinched into fits of gagging and choking. Mythrenese leapt forward. They passed the incapacitated enemies on the left but as they put their agonized vocalizations behind them, Raen's eyes began to burn. And her nose. She pressed the wet folds of wool to her face with a tighter grip. The ascent continued.

"Are we clear?" Raen asked, her voice stuffy under the cloak.

"Yes, you're safe now," Mythrenese answered.

Raen pulled the fabric away from her face and took a deep gulp of air. The breath stung deep in her chest like a draught of freezing winter cold.

"Uh oh," Mythrenese said. "I guess we shouldn't have run right through the cloud. Your eyes and nose are all red."

Raen swiped at her face with her sleeve. "Nothing like what those awful beasts are experiencing, I'm sure." She forced a smile despite her discomfort. "We can't go back out that way, can we?"

A sad shake of the head preceded Mythrenese's answer. "It

looked to me like the whole bottom of the stairwell is blocked now."

Raen hugged her arms around her middle. "I guess it's up we go then. Any sign of Iriscendra's signature?"

"None through here. We'll have to hope we can pick it up again someplace else."

The distant ring of steel from farther up the staircase caught Raen's ear. "Well, I doubt the dragon-kin are fighting with themselves up there." Raen drew her schiavona. "Slowly now. Surprise will prove a better ally for you and me than haste."

～

"Iriscendra, do not go tooth and claw against any of these beasts. That is an order." I threw the chamber curtain aside and charged into the main temple of sacrifice, my sword high above my head in a posture of challenge. The arched ceiling soared above us, and black shadows danced in every culvert. The light from smoking braziers tinted the stone architecture crimson, and oily smears climbed the walls above them. A loud crash assaulted my ears, and a downpour of limestone showered us. Ahead, somewhere in the hazy center of the high-domed chamber, childish wails slashed the air.

"*Chal*, Naghax!" a black-robed dragon-kin screamed. Our friends from the dungeon level, it seemed. The sticky, stained folds of his robe that clung to his ribcage helped to confirm that fact. He and another, smaller dragon-kin stood over three human girls. The maidens clutched one another, eyes squeezed shut, all of them clad in champagne-colored silken wraps. All three huddled against the pedestal of Queldurik's profane, blood streaked altar.

The girls exuded an innocence and pure loveliness I never

expected, and upon catching sight of them, my charge faltered. How frail they looked.

Hanash swiped a smoky bladed, curved knife from the carven stone altar behind Naghax. Guttering flames from the tall candelabras glinted from the dark steel. He raised the knife high.

Naghax grabbed Hanash's weapon hand with both of his clawed mitts. "*Nach! Ci dnet ghe xathit aberranin. Ci pelech krogu zhuoller*—" His snout jerked toward me. "What? How?"

"*Hae ochleg?*" Hanash's voice pitched higher with each outburst to the point of near-hysteria. "*Chal! Ak finest.*" He coughed, and a spray of dark mist clouded from his mouth.

Just keep on arguing. My pace resumed, and in my peripheral vision, I noted Galdurith and Althoron circling wide around the edges of the chamber. Thederonde, tall and lean, outpaced them to reach the far door of the temple and block any dash the villains might make with the girls.

Hanash's crimson eyes, bloodshot and swollen, stretched wider with fury. He flipped the knife around in his hand and shot the other for the nearest girl. His claws bounced back from a glassy dome that appeared over the prisoners.

Naghax took a backpedaling step. He twisted left, then right. His mouth gaped in a pant. His posture spoke clearly of flight.

"Do not let him run," I said.

Althoron, on strides fleeter than the great harts of the southern forests, closed on Naghax, his swords singing as he spun them in a dazzling intimidation tactic. Naghax clapped his crocodilian maw shut and drove away the panicked expression that had overtaken his features at our arrival.

The serrated scimitar he wore on his belt swept free of the scrolled scabbard and met Althoron's blades with a discordant clang. A quarrel flew from Galdurith's crossbow, but it caught only the fabric of Naghax's hood.

Hanash drew his hand back, and a ball of flame sprang to life in his palm. He swung his arm forward, and the fireball hurtled toward me.

I dove to avoid a full collision with the fire. It sailed straight over me, hit the floor, and exploded. The force of the blast threw me forward, tumbling me end over end like a tomcat thrown from the creamery. I skidded to a halt. Beneath my prone form, deep cuts marked the chamber floor. A curved edge. Intersecting grooves. My heart galloped out of rhythm.

Hanash cackled. "You should have left while you still could, Ecleriast."

I shook the stars from my vision, scarcely hearing Hanash's taunt over the clanging in my ears. "As I recall, it was you who ran from our last meeting, coward." I spat the blood that pooled in my mouth.

"You should have considered it mercy." He crossed his fore-arms over his chest, pounding his shoulders with his fists, and a cloud of swirling green smoke seeped from beneath them. The smoke snaked around his body. His garments burst into sudden flame so bright I flung an arm up to shield my eyes.

The glare lessened, and when I looked again, Hanash's robes had ridden away on the air in nothing but ashes. Orange light glowed between his scales, in a cracked network across his freakish body, illuminating an unnerving blend of reptile and man. A bright slice of light lanced from the place between his ribs where I had wounded him before.

I hauled my body upright and then onto my feet. The metallic twang of Galdurith's crossbow rang out. The bolt struck square between Hanash's folded wings. The dragon-kin took a stumbling step forward, but as a bright beam erupted from the wound Galdurith dealt, Hanash leered. The wooden shaft of the bolt burst into flame.

Nausea crashed over me once again. My legs locked. My chest tightened. No breath. Though my mind screamed to warn the squadron to avoid his touch at all costs, my lips would not move.

I needed to put some distance between Hanash and the girls. For all I knew, he might kill them without the sacrifice ritual, simply out of a spiteful desire to prevent their rescue. Though Veranna's weaving gestures and quiet Utterance shielded them for now, my lack of surety how long that would last pressured me to action.

So many to protect. So few working tactics.

Again, Hanash broke into a chant of impure words that made me want to ram his putrid altar down his throat. He thrust a hand toward the ceiling.

"Vinyanel, above you!" Veranna screamed. The girls' dome of shielding winked out.

My chin shot up. The ceiling directly over me glowed much like Hanash's flesh, with white-hot light streaming through imperfections in the rock, but all concentrated into a circle of stone about an arm span wide.

A pillar of flame roared down from the spot. A wave of scorching heat preceded it. I tumbled aside only quickly enough to spare my body the assault. The flames did, however, catch my cloak. The fibers kindled. I smothered the flames by balling the fabric up and pounding it.

Enough of this dodging Hanash's devilry. Now that the threat of death had loosed my muscles from trauma's grip, I flung a knife at the dark priest. It stuck in his leg. Hanash hissed at me, but in the next moment, he smirked and looked down at the weapon.

The wound leaked bright light, and in mere moments, my knife glowed as white as a brand in the forge. The crosspiece sagged. The weapon dropped from his leg in a warped ruin. He cackled.

What would happen if I dragged my sword through his cursed flesh? Would I destroy the blade? I had no chance to attack Scitherias the last time I saw this phenomenon, so I could only guess.

Althoron and Naghax continued to exchange slashes and parries. Thederonde and Galdurith made their move. In a swift dive between the two dragon-kin, they made a grab for the girls.

"Run!" Galdurith cried in the common tongue. "You must run."

The girls staggered to their feet, but the long silks around them hobbled them to a shuffle. Thederonde reached down and grabbed the two smaller maidens, one under each arm.

"Oh, I think not!" Hanash roared. He wheeled and swung a claw at the private.

Thederonde made a masterful attempt at evading the strike, but despite the twist of his body and a nearly sideways stride, Hanash still caught him across the chest. The tabard of the Delsin and the chain mail Thederonde wore burst into flame and turned to a mingled slag. He screamed and thrust the girls back onto their own feet before he staggered and slumped. Galdurith urged the eldest ahead, her sisters following toward the chamber exit.

Bereft a direct combat option, another wild concept came to me. I slammed my sword back into the scabbard. I reached back behind me, then swept my arm around to the front in a wide arc that ended in me pointing at Hanash.

"Creo's flood of judgment!"

With an ear-splitting crack, a fissure opened in the wall nearest Hanash, and a roaring torrent of water came churning through.

"Grab those girls!" The direction went to no one in particular—I could only pray someone near the prisoners would prevent the deluge from drowning any of them.

Hanash gaped a moment too long, and the gush of water collided with him. Steam exploded from the meeting.

Maker's mercy, let this work.

The water splashed and ran in all directions, and its swift current crashed like a tidal wave over the altar. It knocked everyone in its path off their feet—the elves, Naghax, and the little ones. The clutter on the altar's surface washed along with the flood.

Veranna sprang into motion somewhere behind me. I had no attention to spare for her actions.

The cloud of steam thinned, and through it, Hanash staggered back to his feet, using only his left arm and leg. His right side, the side the torrent had struck full force, no longer glowed with underlying heat. The hide of the right side of his reptilian face had the look of black, pitted rock. So did his arm.

He lifted his left leg in a stride toward me, but could only haul his other limb, as well as most of his tail, I noted, in a lumbering shamble. I drew my sword.

"Give it up, Hanash." I met his furious countenance, unfazed. "We will take the Elgadrim girls and the chalice, and this will be the end of this ridiculous game of keep-away."

"The treaty is already signed, fool," Hanash said, though the immobilized right side of his face marred his words. "You force the Tebalese and the dragon-kin to annihilate your soft little people with your murder of Inquisitor Ezio and your assault on this temple."

"You might want to take a closer look at who really killed your ally." I shot a glance heavy with meaning at Naghax.

Uncertainty flickered in Hanash's eyes. He snapped a quick glance to Naghax, but the scribe's swordfight with Althoron dragged on and prevented any meaningful exchange.

Throughout this pause in my melee with Hanash, I kept a close eye on the glowing chinks in his hide that continued to pulse. The light seemed to eat slowly into the rocky side of Hanash the water had marred. Was it just a matter of time before he was back to his superheated self? How much time, if so? The water had run through the chamber, into some of the side prayer rooms, and down the exit hall, leaving only gleaming liquid in the intricate theurgic circle graven into the floor of the place.

A streak of motion flew over my shoulder. I ducked.

Iriscendra swooped toward Hanash, but before I could order her otherwise, opened her maw and blew a cloud of iridescent gas toward him. He swiped a claw at her, connected with her shoulder, and sent her spinning to crash to the floor ten paces behind him. She squealed on the way down.

Fury boiled up in me, fiercer than the torrent Creo had unleashed.

"Iriscendra! Oh no . . ." The voice was Raen's. Sure enough, there she stood in the archway that led to the stairs. With Mythrenese behind her.

I spat an oath. Too many variables. People outside my strategy. But at least she would see to the hatchling's hurts while I wrung payment for them from Hanash's loathsome hide. As a matter of fact . . .

I grabbed a four-foot candelabra from the floor, where Creo's flood had knocked it from standing beside the altar. "Mythrenese, come here."

The indigo dragonling hunkered down. I had no idea dragons could pale until that moment, but his face drained to a sickly, grayed saturation of his normal hue.

Hanash waved away the small mist of Iriscendra's interrupted breath attack and laughed. "This should keep you busy. *Skalrata, nengerra leqaven!*"

The floor vibrated beneath my feet, and the innermost design of the circle carven in the floor erupted with red light. From three intersecting triangles in the design, hazy forms emerged, then took solid shape. Horrible, bipedal, boar-faced and primate-bodied shapes. They all carried spiked clubs.

They snarled and barreled for me.

I swept at them with the candelabra and cursed myself for

having picked it up as a weapon against Hanash. It deflected the attacks of Hanash's new minions for the first charge, but served poorly as an offensive weapon.

Running feet caught my ear, but so did commotion by the doorway. I continued to bat away the mucous-slathered, snapping jaws, the claw-rakes, and swinging clubs aimed for me on all sides. One of the beasts screamed. The fleeting glance I spared toward the sound revealed Raen with her schiavona straight through the creature.

Something clobbered me in the side of the leg, square on the rods for my armor support. My leg shook. A monkey-boar screamed and pumped its weapon overhead.

I threw the candelabra at it. The unearthly beast staggered back. My sword shrieked from the sheath.

The first step I took onto my augmented leg nearly threw me to the floor. The rods pulled when they should not. Pushed when I did not need them to.

I still managed to aim a cut at one of my opponents, which opened a gash across its shoulder. The slash carried half the power it should have, owing to the instability of my stance.

Raen pivoted to my side. "I have your flank." She swept her sword in an upward diagonal and cleft a long rent in her opponent from hip to throat.

"The hatchling," I said.

"Veranna's with her." Raen slashed at the third monster. "She'll be all right."

She had better be. I steadied my weight, then lunged. This attack plunged with the effectiveness I had come to expect from my swordsmanship, and my opponent collapsed as soon as I withdrew my blade from his abdomen. The beast's black blood rose from the steel in dark steam.

Hanash's remaining minion swung its club at Raen, and this time, it landed a solid blow to her shoulder. Her outburst rang with pain, but she still answered with swift upward slash. The beast backed a few frantic steps. It dropped onto all fours and screamed at us with a voice like a legion shrieking in chorus.

I shivered.

A normal creature, one not summoned from the depths of the Darkness's depraved imagination, would have fled in the sight of its comrades' swift deaths. But no, we would face this abomination too, because that was what Hanash demanded of it. My stomach turned at the twisted-ness of summoning.

I caught the beast's lunge on my shield and threw the creature aside. While it lacked balance, Raen drove her schiavona into the base of the creature's neck and sent it sprawling on the floor.

She was distractingly good with that lithe blade.

"I'm finding you quite annoying," Hanash said. "*Bejtarre!*" He stamped his foot, and the floor before him buckled. A wave rushed forward through the stone, and when it reached Raen, the cresting ridge of floor threw her into the air. Only the edge of Hanash's assault rolled beneath me, and although I staggered because of my weakened leg, I stayed on my feet. Raen, however, came down with a flailing crash, flat on her back. Her head bounced off the floor. Her eyes rolled.

Draw his focus. Keep him from going for the kill. "Again, no shortage of assaults for maidens and children," I said. The step I took toward Hanash had the jelly-legged look of a drunkard's stride.

"Oh, right," Hanash said. "Better that I focus on the lame idiot instead." He clapped the heels of his hands together and thrust both palms my direction. An unseen force pummeled my chest, and instantly, my limbs lost all their strength. My good leg gave out, and I crashed to my knees. My spine lacked the strength to hold me upright. I wavered. Clapped a hand to my temple, though the effort felt as though I wore half my weight in extra encumbrance around my wrist. *Where is that craven Mythrenese?*

I would have yelled the question, but I could not muster the strength to work my jaw. It took a mammoth effort just to turn my head.

Where was everyone? No Veranna, no squadron. Just Raen's prone form, with a meandering trail of blood working its way along the stone floor from beneath her head

Veranna, can you hear me? I reached out in desperation.

Yes. Her response was tight with vexation. *Not so loud.*

Where is Mythrenese? I need a mount.

He won't do. Veranna paused. *Give me a moment.*

Raen's down.

In the silence that reigned after that report, I could sense Veranna's distress. *I'm coming. Hold him off, at least.*

Hanash stalked into my peripheral vision. "Feeling a little drained? It's just a start." He brandished the sacrifice knife again. "Which lifeline should I open and truly see you emptied to the dregs?" He bent down and pressed the knife to my throat. "This one may be too fast to properly enjoy." He re-sheathed his knife.

While Hanash gloated, I heard Veranna's voice, but only in my mind. *The Maker give you might to terrify his enemies . . .* or something of the sort. I was a bit too distracted to listen.

The priest stood up and flexed his good hand, the one the water had not hardened. The creases in his hide still glowed. "Maybe that grab at the head Scitherias was so fond of instead. That should inspire some lovely screams, even in your flaccid state. Perhaps *now* you regret your foolhardy return?"

My heart picked up speed. The sheer will to survive boiled up from my core. A surge of the instinct to destroy or be destroyed flooded my veins. I dragged my sword arm into motion. Whether I risked losing the blade to Hanash's molten interior or no, I could not just lay there and let him toy with me.

The weapon bit deep into his forearm, and a spray of luminous, orange liquid flew from the wound. My blade glowed in the center of its length as though it awaited the smith's hammer.

He hissed and recoiled.

I rolled, but not before some of his magma-blood hit my breastplate and my spaulder, owing to my sluggishness. The droplets left smoking pockmarks. "That does it," I said. "I have had enou—"

Hanash's recoil turned to a dive, and he closed his fingers around the mechanics on my cuisse. Heat seeped into my leg. Panic exploded in my chest. How fast could I get the piece of armor off? How badly maimed would my leg be in the time that passed before I could unfasten and escape the inevitable searing? The rods along the outside of the cuisse began to glow orange. Then white.

The dragon-kin's hard yank ripped the already-damaged rods from the cuisse—they stretched like taffy before they snapped. I pushed with my heels to scrabble backward, but my limbs failed to lift my weight from the floor. The use of my now-unsupported leg sent waves of pain up into my pelvis.

Hanash reared his head back and cackled. "You're too pathetic to deserve the dignity of being put out of your misery." The heat underlying his hide glowed brighter, his hand most of all. "I wonder if you'll pop like a chestnut as I roast you. Funny how that shell you call security will be just the thing to speed your death." He stepped forward.

Despite my pain and my clear disadvantage, I refused to flinch. "My true armor is Creo's will." The words slurred together. But the weight in my limbs was lessening.

"Bah. Creo's will. Too often does your butter-hearted god stand by. Lets his servants meet gruesome ends at the hands of those with the sense to strike instead of fancying themselves noble martyrs." He took another step and reached his inferno-bright palm for my chest. But his focus faltered left.

A giant, pearl-scaled tail swung over me and smashed

Hanash across the face. He staggered back and spat several teeth on the floor. Something wrenched me to my feet. I twisted against the force that hauled me by the nape of my neck.

A dragon with bright blue eyes, nubby horns and dorsal plates, and a mischievous look—but four times the size of the Iriscendra I knew—gripped my cloak in her maw.

"A mount, right?" she mumbled with a mouth full of cloak.

I did not pretend to understand, but with waxing strength, I hauled myself onto the suddenly-massive hatchling's back. On the way up, I scooped up the candelabra in my shield hand. In my peripheral vision, a dark-haired figure darted to Raen's side. Likely Veranna. At least I hoped.

Hanash steadied his stance. He wove his good hand before him again.

Before I drove my heels into Iriscendra's sides, she leapt forward. I brought the candelabra around in a lumbering upswing, graceless owing to my underperforming muscles. Despite my attack's lack of finesse, the iron shaft of the makeshift weapon caught Hanash's paralyzed stone arm, and the limb shattered. Pieces flew in all directions, leaving him with only a stump at his shoulder.

He roared and clapped his free claws to the wound. Livid hatred rounded his eyes and contorted his already-grotesque maw into a snarling grimace. We barreled past him.

"Turn around and run past him, as close as you can get without crashing into him," I said into Iriscendra's ear.

The hatchling spun. She lowered her head and charged back, dauntless.

I leveled the candelabra like a lance. A smidge short for the job, but it would do. We galloped past the altar, then closed on Hanash. He fought his stone leg and tail in an effort to flee, to dodge, anything, to no avail. The five-armed end of the candelabra drove hard into his side. The arms gouged and bent, but the haft plunged through his ribcage to lodge deep in his chest. I released my weapon as we thundered past.

At first, beams of white-hot light streamed from the many wounds the charge had dealt. Hanash sank to his knees. The light flared in fluttering pulses, and the iron of the candelabra impaling his heart glowed as well. The dragon-kin priest of Queldurik crashed prone, and the illumination within his flesh dimmed until it went dark. A curling wisp of smoke rose from the place the heated metal of the haft still touched flesh, now ordinary again. The stink of scorched skin and muscle swelled from Hanash's corpse.

Iriscendra skidded to a stop. She craned her neck back, then met my gaze with a pinched expression. "We had to, I guess." After turning slowly away, her body shuddered beneath me.

Guilt crashed over me in an avalanche. Yes, Hanash's destruction had been necessary, but in my urgency, I had not thought once about exposing the equivalent of a child to the carnage. War was the business of adults, and I stood indefensibly convicted of thrusting its gruesome reality upon the innocent.

"I am sorry Iriscendra." My voice caught. Even though she had assisted of her own volition, prudence might have dictated I eschew such help. I turned to where Veranna knelt beside Raen. The carmine-haired dragonswarder hung limp in Veranna's arms, paler than alabaster. Was she breathing? Was there something I could do—?

The clash of weapons intruded upon my inspection. I slid from Iriscendra's back, my whole body hanging heavy, though not from any curse. I limped forward a few steps toward the sound, which came from the main staircase, the one I had scarcely succeeded in blundering down last time I had fought in this place. My throat went dry.

"Help Veranna with Raen," I said. "I think I have just located the rest of the squadron."

"Nothing I can do for Veranna, V'yennel." Iriscendra tilted her head and frowned. "You still limping. You *are* still limping too much to fight." She trotted to me, ducked her head, and snaked her neck and shoulders under my legs.

Despite the urgency and remorse that warred in my heart and mind, a laugh worked its way to the top of the tangle of emotions. "Persistent little thing."

She nodded and bolted for the chamber stairs a moment before I had settled onto her back. I grappled with arms and the stronger of my two legs, and on to the next fray we charged. I could only hope that my squadron had not met with more than their match while beyond my sight.

42
___

MINGLED GIFTING

*W*e lurched down the stairs. About halfway down, we leapt over two dragon-kin who lay unwounded but also unmoving. At the bottom of the stairs, where the well should have opened into the main foyer, I found a huge pile of limestone rubble, three dragon-kin warriors, Naghax, and my squadron, embroiled in a chaotic melee. A wave of relief that Thederonde fought in their midst, even with a blackened chest, washed through me.

The Elgadrim girls huddled against the wall, where the eldest hugged the littlest. The middle girl took a defiant pose in front of them, as if in refusal to let the whistle of swords daunt her. Mythrenese guarded the girls, his fifteen feet of indigo length arced around them and the fiercest expression I am sure he had ever mustered fixed on his face. He almost resembled a dragon in that moment.

The ring of blades echoed a cacophony of conflict. Galdurith fought with a long knife, Thederonde with a broadsword, and Althoron with his two longswords, exchanging slashes and parries with the warriors. Naghax clutched an iron-bound chest close in his arms. His frenetic glance darted across the rubble.

Thederonde's opponent grabbed him by the back of the head and smashed his scaly, horned forehead into the private's face. The messy spray of red made me wince empathetically. When Thederonde staggered back, the bloody ruin in the center of his face confirmed my suspicions. He flailed a sloppy swing that glanced from his combatant's buckler.

"Thederonde needs a hand," I said.

Iriscendra nodded and charged.

Her sheer size bowled through the fighting group. She swung her body around to place me beside the dragon-kin, and after my moment of marveling at her tremendous battle instinct, I brought my longsword around. The blade connected with the dragon-kin's head. He spun and collapsed. Iriscendra swept another down with her tail, but unfortunately knocked Galdurith off his feet in the same stroke.

"You just focus on getting me into position," I said.

"Sorry." She shrank down a bit beneath me.

She actually shrank beneath me—not just in embarrassment. In size.

"Uh oh," Iriscendra said. "'Ranna's magic's running out?"

In rapid succession, Althoron swung his blades in both a high hew and a low slice, and while his enemy parried the first, the second cleft deep into the creature's knee joint. It screeched. On its way down, Althoron kicked the scimitar from its hand.

While Galdurith regained his feet, I sprang from Iriscendra's back and drove my good knee into the prone dragon-kin's chest. Bones cracked and gave way. His sword dropped from a loose grasp.

"Thanks," the major said. He swiped sweat from his brow

with his sleeve. A quick flip of his knife pointed the weapon at Naghax, who stood with his ridged back to the wall of rubble.

Thederonde blinked the daze from his eyes and pointed his broadsword at Naghax as well. Althoron and I added our points to the thicket pinning the last standing dragon-kin in place.

"I-I-I'm just a scribe," Naghax said. "I'm no threat to you." He clutched the chest closer to his body.

I kept my sword trained on him, nonetheless. "Perhaps not. But unless you want to end up like your friends here, you will be a help."

A stony *boom* sounded, and limestone showered us all so thick I had to throw my shield up over my head to avoid a pelting. A fist-sized rock bounced from its surface.

"What's in the box, scribe?" Galdurith said.

"Ah, well . . .notes." Naghax wiped debris from his eyes with his free hand. "The history of my people and their origins."

"He's a liar!"

I half turned. One of the girls behind Mythrenese stood, fists on her hips, face furrowed with a sense of injustice. "There may be some papers in there, but the main thing is a big, ugly cup with fangs all around the top. Stupidest thing I ever saw. Too big to drink out of, even if it wouldn't cut you to ribbons."

The tallest of the girls shushed the speaker. "Marilla!"

"No," I said. "Let her finish."

Marilla blinked and swallowed. "Uh, that was. . .that was all, sir."

"Perhaps you scarcely realize how much you said. My thanks." I smirked and turned back to Naghax. I pushed my sword point against his sternum with firm pressure. "Give me the box, and we will see if you deserve to continue breathing after we get a look."

Naghax's eyes bulged. "I never wanted to go through with it. But you don't say no to Hanash." His glance flicked to the

Elgadrim girls. "And if it weren't for me, those girls would already be down the ash-chute."

The thought crushed my gut. How many unfortunate souls' bones, those whom nobody came to rescue, had I waded through that day? Naghax's claim did not ring of mercy, but it did carry the whiff of repentance. A first for me, from one of his kind.

"It's sort of true, sir," one of the girls said. The eldest. "He kept them from beating us as harshly as I think they would have. He gave us what little food we got. Please, I don't really want to see any more killing."

I blew out a long breath. Why could we adults not keep our well-honed depravity and our full-fledged violence to ourselves? Why was our worst behavior always on display for those without the maturity to process it? Or at least the calluses to shrug it away? The sardonic bite of the thought stuck in my mind.

"Very well," I said. "Provided Naghax maintains good judgment, Creo deems mercy for him. For now." I turned back and put my shield hand out.

Naghax trembled in a long moment of indecision. His face twisted. He clenched his jaw and clawed fingers. He squeezed his eyes shut. At long last, he flung the chest at my feet, and he crumpled, reduced to weeping.

The chest latch bent and sprang open. There, on the gravel-laden floor, the black chalice of Gherag-Tal bounced free and rolled in a semicircle until it bumped into the toe of my sabaton. I stared at it.

Naghax sobbed, muttering in his own tongue words I could not translate but carried the agony of broken aspirations. His drama prodded at my sense of skepticism, but for now, the chalice beckoned.

I bent down and lifted the chalice. So many lives spent over the cursed thing. I raised it above my head and dashed it to the stone floor.

It ricocheted from the landing, bounced a few feet, and came to rest again. It suffered not so much as a chip. I snarled at it, wordless, and brought my foot down on it. I succeeded only in jarring my ankle and throwing myself off balance.

"Lieutenant Commander!" Veranna's voice echoed down the stairs. "More warriors."

Of course. I scooped up the chalice. Maker's mercy, Veranna and Raen, whatever her state, lay right in their path. "How many?"

"I don't know. They're coming up the chute we used." Veranna staggered into sight, Raen fumbling along at her side with a faltering gait and holding a bloody rag to her head. Despite Raen's obvious wounds, my heart still leapt to see her on her feet.

Iriscendra streaked past me, now back to her normal hatchling size. She scaled the rubble and began poking her nose around the pile. Occasionally, she knocked on specific stones with the hook on the tip of her snout. She cocked her head and listened.

Despite the uneven rhythm of my own gait and the pain it inspired, I marched to the maidens, shoving the chalice into my pack. I wrapped one arm around Raen's shoulders and scooped the other under her knees.

"What?" she said, though her voice was weak. "You're in no state . . .we'll both fall."

"No, we will not," I said. "You will not fall as long as I am still breathing. Veranna, can you block these stairs for a bit?"

She sucked in a deep breath. "May Creo be willing." She closed her eyes and whispered the beginning of an Utterance.

It required every bit of my attention to descend the stairs again, but Raen did not struggle. The unequal dilation of her pupils confirmed she had little capacity to progress on her own.

Clatter up the stairs grew. A mixture of Tebalese and dragon-kin oaths echoed down to us. A nebulous barrier filled the stairwell about ten stairs up from where Veranna stood, weaving her arms and swaying her torso in a hypnotic dance. Then the stout Tebalese arrows began to glance from Creo's shield.

My soldiers stood shoulder to shoulder, weapons drawn and faces grim. Mythrenese herded the Elgadrim girls behind them and fell in at their left flank. A swell of pride filled my chest. They would face anything that came down those stairs with bravery and skill.

A scrape of rock in the rubble blocking the foyer caught my attention.

"I'm close," Iriscendra said. "There's a way."

"Private Thederonde," I said. "If there is a way for you to help Iriscendra clear an escape, do so."

A battle cry rang off the stairwell. A half-dozen warriors, Tebalese and dragon-kin, charged around the bend and threw themselves at Veranna's barricade. She stumbled back a step and her eyes snapped open, but the divine wall held.

Something crashed into me from behind. I staggered forward, hugging Raen tight to my chest, fighting to keep my feet. I wheeled.

Naghax spread his clawed feet shoulder width and brandished a large stone in one hand. "You're steadier than I thought you'd be without your little armor-crutch." He reached for the hilt of his scimitar.

Before Galdurith or Althoron could turn their weapons on Naghax, Mythrenese pounced. He crushed Naghax to the ground. "Don't worry. *This* one won't get away from me." He leaned one of his foretalons on the scribe's throat.

The warriors on the stairs number increased to nine at least, but those I could only hear would swell their numbers further. They roared again and ran for the barricade. When their collective weight crashed against it, Veranna cried out. She heaved for breath. But her Utterance still held.

"She found a way!" Thederonde yelled. Stone scraped and rolled. He and Iriscendra pushed and shoveled as fast as they could. A gap opened in the rubble, near the top left of the pile.

"Up, all of you! Get the girls through first, then soldiers by ascending rank." I pursed my lips. The challenge remained: how to meet the fury that would face us when Veranna let the barricade down.

Iriscendra skidded down the pile and left the elves to clearing the passage. It was big enough for the girls to wiggle through, at least.

"Here, Myth'nese," Iriscendra said. "Get back." She placed her snout right on Naghax's. And sneezed.

Despite the deteriorating circumstances all around us, I still laughed. Naghax went completely stiff.

"Now you help me." Iriscendra directed her attention to the oncoming soldiers held at bay by Veranna's Utterance. "The elves can't get away if Veranna needs to keep up that wall."

"But you just breathed," Mythrenese said. "You can't go again."

Iriscendra scoffed. "That wasn't a whole breath. Now c'mon. With both of us, we can probably get 'em all."

"And if we can't?" Mythrenese swallowed.

"That's what claws, teeth, and wings are for."

The young dragons positioned themselves on the stairs right on our side of Veranna's barricade. The warriors rammed it again. Veranna clapped a hand to her temple and grimaced. The wall fluttered. The dragons reared their heads back. The warriors hesitated.

"Now!" Iriscendra yelled.

Veranna dropped the Utterance. The cluster of dragon-kin and Tebalese soldiers tripped over one another trying to backpedal. Both dragons shot their heads forward.

Mythrenese's periwinkle cloud mixed with Iriscendra's pearlescent assault. The warriors coughed, choked, recoiled, and collapsed in stiffened poses of retreat.

Good enough. I followed close on Veranna's heels as she scaled the rubble, but my legs trembled with the strain of the vertical climb. Raen's weight would have been little burden in other circumstances, but for now, each step required my full concentration.

Mythrenese swooped in beside me. "She can ride from here."

I heaved a sigh, though part of me mourned transferring Raen's slender frame to the dragon. Iriscendra plunged head-first at the opening in the rubble, bulling open a larger passage.

We emerged on the opposite side to gray daylight, the ruins of most of the foyer's outer wall, and the standard of the Delsin planted in the breach in the dragon-kin hive. A legion of tired-faced but smiling elf warriors saluted my arrival.

43

Chancellor Lerendir shouldered his way through the ranks of soldiers, his silver hair a lank curtain of strands, and his corded waistcoat and cloak hanging heavy with rainwater.

"I see the young Elgadrim subjects have made it," Lerendir said. "What of the chalice?"

"Right here." I slid my pack from my shoulder and reached for the buckle.

"I believe you—leave it covered. Let us withdraw, and then we can finalize matters." He turned toward the ranks and raised his voice. "Commanders, you have your orders. Take every prisoner who has the sense to come with his life still in his possession. The challenge to our sanctions will not meet with gentleness."

I refrained from comment, but assumed the discussion between Aulus, Cnaeus, and the Delsin leadership must have infused our position with a greater measure of steel than we had wielded of late.

Lerendir nodded to me. "The field should be clear now of opponents, but just in case, I will send a detachment to escort your party and the Elgadrim girls back behind our line."

As we made our way through the tight valley that had served as the day's arena of warfare, all the aftermath of pitched battle mixed with the slop of churned ice, snow, and earth. Carrion foul hopped in impatient circles while the survivors of the battle piled the dead. Most of those whose lives war had claimed that day were Tebalese. My heart sank at the reality that the conflict had likely succeeded in earning the Delsin an enemy we had heretofore avoided rankling.

I had been granted a tall gray destrier to make the trip back to the Delsin encampment, and the two younger Elgadrim girls rode behind me, wrapped in blankets. The littlest clung to me with quivering arms, nonetheless.

I looked back over my shoulder, but all I could see was the top of her curly-tressed head for how she pressed her cheek into my back. "Little one, what is your name?" I whispered.

"Cassia, sir." She turned round, gray eyes to me.

"You have been very brave to make it through all this, little Cassia," I said. "Not much longer now, and it will all be over."

The second girl held her blanket in clenched fists, but stared with a pinched expression over the mountainsides.

"And what about you? Could I learn your name as well?"

Her glance remained hard and distant. "Marilla."

"Well, Marilla, it is clear your strength likely saw you and your sisters through much of your ordeal."

She snapped her head toward me. "What could you possibly know? It doesn't matter how strong I am or am not. They'll keep coming for us. If not my sisters and me, others. We're the Elgadrim, you know. The forsaken ones."

The poor child. Already so angry in her hopelessness.

I sighed. "I know I cannot convince you with mere words what I have seen and understand. Creo does not forsake his chosen among Men. But hard hearts can gouge a rift between him and his beloved creation. Despair names you Elgadrim, but at your heart, you are forever Vareinor, Creo's Host of Power."

Marilla took a moment to contemplate this—I could practically hear the thoughts grinding their way through her steely mind. She met my gaze with surprising ferocity for a little girl. "Thank you for coming. I'm sorry your leg got hurt in the fighting."

"No need for apologies on that," I said. "I will not claim anything nobler than my own bullishness—my hard heart— for the state of my leg."

The girls fell to conversing quietly in their own tongue. Just behind me, I caught a glance of Raen, laying on the litter the troops had prepared for her so she would not pitch from Mythrenese's back from her dizziness. She quirked a smile at me, which I returned.

By nightfall, we reached the long lines of tents that comprised the Delsin encampment, where a bright bonfire burned, sending drifting embers on erratic paths skyward. The medics saw to all our hurts, which could have been much worse—salve and stitches soothed the cuts and burns for now, but no one in the squadron had taken wounds that tending and time would not mend. I even caught quick sight of where Curunith slept, though I did not wake him, since I imagined the repose was the first peaceful rest he had experienced in many months.

The Elgadrim girls, while understandably traumatized, suffered little more to their physical health than poor nourishment. The medics ushered them into a quiet tent and brought them steaming broth and bread to begin the amendment of their woes.

"Lieutenant Commander?"

I stood and turned. Althoron waited on the edge of the triage. "What is it, Sergeant?"

"With your leave, Cassia, Marilla, and Helena have a visitor." Althoron gestured behind him, where a man in a brush-plumed helm, a tunic and toga, and a woolen cloak stood. He clutched the fabric of his tunic in banded knuckles.

"Master Aulus." I bowed, containing an elated outburst behind an air of professionalism. "No one told me you were in camp. Please, this way."

I led Aulus to the third tent in the medics' quarter and stopped outside. "Someone to see the girls," I said loud enough for anyone within the tent to hear.

The tent flap eased aside, and Raen peered out. "Well, Ecleriast, they are sleeping at the mome—" Her attention froze behind me. "But not that weary. Please, come in!"

We stepped into the tent. Veranna rose from her seat on the floor beside the large pallet upon which the girls curled. She swept up to Aulus.

"Bless the Maker you could be here. They have been asking about you, but I did not know what to report." Veranna took Aulus's hand, the one he did not have cupped over his own forehead.

He stared at his daughters with welling eyes. One slow stride after another, he broke away from Veranna's grasp and eased his way to the pallet's edge. He knelt, and with a gentle hand, smoothed a lock of Helena's honey-brown hair from her cheek. Her eyes fluttered open.

For a moment, her brow furrowed. She blinked. Her confusion gave way to a sudden explosion of tears, and she threw herself into her father's arms. "I thought I was dreaming again. I dreamt you came for us so many times," she sobbed.

I rocked back on my heels and clasped my hands behind my back. Veranna and Raen slipped to either side of me, and there the three of us stood. If my companions' feelings at all mimicked my own, a time of unsurety as to whether to step out or to rejoice with Aulus hung over us.

The two younger girls awoke, and soon Aulus toppled under a pile of boisterous embraces and girlish kisses. Aulus laughed with the tearful joy of a man rushed back from the brink of utter despair. He and his daughters whispered words in the fluid Elgadrim tongue for many moments.

Veranna tugged my sleeve. She nodded her head toward the tent exit. I took a step that direction.

"Wait, please," Aulus called after us. "How can I express the flood of my heart? There are no words in the tongues of elves or men to convey it fully."

I turned back. "You have no need of further words, Master Aulus. What was my duty has also been my pleasure." A deep place in the secret vaults of my soul ached at the sight of those children, so enfolded in a father's arms. But I would not let the empty place in my own heart cast its dark fog over their reunion. *Perhaps some wounds will never entirely heal...*

Cassia smiled beneath shadowed eyes and cheeks still recovering from pallor. "Raen and Veranna said they would help. And they knew who they needed to save us, even if there was some trouble along the way."

Raen smoothed her hair back over her ear point. "I am sorry you had to go all the way to that dungeon."

"But we went with hope," Helena said. "Things would have turned out worse without that."

"That's a truth to hold onto." Aulus squeezed Helena to his side. "There is hope for many bound up in you, Vinyanel Ecleriast."

The hopes of others. I breathed deep. *Both an honor and an incredible burden.*

One your shoulders are amply broad to bear. Veranna's voice in my mind came through warm and as soothing as summer sun. *With Creo's help, of course.*

"I do thank you for the words of confidence, Master Aulus," I said. "It looks to me, however, your daughters are now in the most capable of hands. You are welcome to remain here with them, but if you do not mind, I will take your leave. It has been a rather long day." Truthfully, the last dregs of battle fervor had ebbed from my veins, and I was not entirely sure I could stay on my feet long enough to get back to my own tent.

"Of course," Aulus said. "Far be it from me to keep you."

We departed the girls' quarters, and it struck me that Raen's steps came slowly and along a rather crooked track. Limping though I was, I stepped to her side and pulled her arm around my shoulder.

A light flush spread across her cheeks.

"I believe I am still in your debt for tending me in the wilderness," I said. "Allow me to see you back to the edge of camp where the dragons have shelter."

Raen glanced around the bustle and close quarters of the encampment. "Vinyanel," she said as she leaned into me. "That would be perfect."

~

The next morning, I awoke to the sound of my name. I lay flat on my back. Every muscle I possessed ached with lingering weariness. "Who calls?" I said without opening my eyes.

"Private Thederonde, sir. It appears the Chancellor has a conundrum for which he seeks your opinion."

I struggled upright and pressed the heels of my hands into my eye sockets. "I see. Please report to him I will appear momentarily."

I glanced about my tent. My armor was gone, but a new tunic, trousers, and black cloak lay across the trunk in the corner. My sword, in its scabbard, stood beside the fresh attire. Someone had some sense.

After I had dressed and belted the sword, I sought the Chancellor's central pavilion. His door guards admitted me, and inside, I found Lerendir, Veranna, Galdurith, and another graying elf—I believe the King's high arcanist and chronicler—though I had never learned his name. They all stood around a circular table, upon which sat the Chalice of Gherag-Tal.

Lerendir approached me. "Ah, Lieutenant Commander. Good afternoon."

"Afternoon?" I choked. "My apologies." Never once had I slept through the dawn trumpet.

"It's understandable," Lerendir said. He placed a hand on my shoulder and walked me toward the table. "We've hit a bit of a snag in your insistence the chalice be destroyed."

"Not force, not fire, nothing makes even a scratch upon it," the arcanist said. His words were sharp with frustration. "We even tried having Majestrin breathe on it to make it brittle. No luck."

"You tried melting it down?" I said.

"We could not devise a fire hot enough here in camp to make a difference," Galdurith said. "Though I suspect even the master forge in Delsinon would still be too cool. The fires here failed to heat the cup even a little. We thought perhaps we might sail to the middle of the western sea and—"

I shook my head. "Currents and tides could undo us." What was hotter than fire, capable of melting down an object cast from demon's blood, something sturdier than the hardest stone, so it seemed?

Melting. Stone . . .

"One moment," I said. I turned on a heel and half-limped,

half-jogged my way back to my tent. Once inside, I plunged my hands into my pack and tossed its contents every direction.

"What are you doing Vinyanel?" Veranna said from behind me. "You seem determined to fracture the tenuous peace you have with Lerendir right now, storming out of his presence with no explanation."

I lifted the adamantine flask from my pack. "There you are."

"What?" Veranna huffed. "There's who? Honestly—"

I marched past Veranna again and back to the chancellor's pavilion without casting her a glance. "I have an idea. Follow me."

When I burst back into Lerendir's pavilion, the flask held high, the three elves inside jumped.

"What is the meaning of this, Ecleriast?" Lerendir said. "Galdurith is right, you are losing your mind."

"Losing?" I laughed, then un-stoppered the flask. I leaned over the table to pour the caustic contents into the chalice, but stopped just short of allowing the liquid to cascade out. "Maybe we had better try this outside."

I scooped up the chalice in one hand and tromped outside, flask in the other.

"What is that?" the arcanist called from behind me.

"Gargoyle venom," I said.

"What? Where did you get . . .?"

After setting the cup down in an open space between the commanders' pavilions and the lower ranking soldiers' rows, I once again opened the flask.

The arcanist grabbed my hand. "Wait!"

His jostle sloshed a small portion of the venom from the mouth of the flask. It just missed the chalice and hit the earth, which caused a noisome fizzing in the trampled grass and soil.

I lanced him with a glare.

He shrank back but also said, "Who knows what kind of

reaction you might get here? You're mixing both chemicals and magicks. A bit of caution would be advisable, Lieutenant Commander. Perhaps if we carefully lowered the chalice into the venom."

"You have a basin stronger than adamantine I can pour the venom into?" I held an open palm to him.

He fell silent. Lerendir, Veranna, and Galdurith added their expectant stares to the quiet.

"I shall move slowly." I turned back to the chalice. Slowly tipped the flask from about two feet above the cursed vessel. The venom trickled into the cup, clear as water.

And about as unremarkably.

Not possible. I upended the flask until every last drop of venom fell into the Chalice of Gherag-Tal.

Sighs surrounded me.

The surface of the liquid stilled. My shoulders sagged. Could no craft on the mortal plane rid me of evil's workmanship? I cast the chalice a baleful glare.

That was when I noticed bubbles, tiny at first, rising from the bottom of the cup and inching up the inside of the bowl. Then more. The venom progressed from a fizz to a hard boil to a frothing, roiling tumult. We all stepped back.

The chalice began to tremble and chatter where it stood. A high, pinched sound like a hundred ghoul shrieks swelled, and the basilisk fangs around the chalice's lip begin to fold inward, one by one, melting into the boiling froth inside. After the toxic mix consumed the last fang, the chalice itself collapsed inward like black wax.

The violence of the boiling venom spurted upward like a geyser. I grabbed Veranna and shielded her with my body, turning my back to the eruption. All fell quiet, except for a faint sizzling.

I dared look back. Where the chalice stood, all that

remained was an ugly, tarry puddle. Before our eyes, the puddle dried, shriveled, cracked, and blew away as dust.

"How did you have that?" Veranna asked, her eyes on the flask.

I intercepted her amber glance. "We have Hridayesh to thank."

And for one of the few times since I had met her, Veranna was speechless.

~

*R*aen skulked through the rows of tents until she reached the canvas quarters that belonged to Vinyanel. She paused outside and listened. No voices or other audible evidence of inhabitants presented itself. A furtive stride, then another, eased her to the slight gap between the flaps. His pallet inside was empty.

With all the stealth she had acquired thieving eggs, she slipped through the entrance, minced her way to the pallet, and pulled a folded parchment from the bodice of her gown.

A shuffling sound behind her wrenched her around and set her heart hammering.

"What are you doing, Raen?" Iriscendra blinked heavy eyelids. She stretched her maw in a toothy yawn.

Of all the times for the two of them to be in different places. "Just dropping off a little message. I didn't. . . expect you'd be here." Raen slipped her parchment under the edge of Vinyanel's blanket. Her nervous glance darted to the tent entry. "Do you know where Vinyanel is?"

"Can still feel his sing . . . sing . . .*sig*nature. He's not far. At the healers with 'Jestrin, I think."

Raen's breath tightened in her chest. *It's not ideal, but at least I only have to suffer through one of these conversations.* "I wish you could come back to the vale with me."

"You're really going." Iriscendra's head dropped. "I'll miss you."

Though the hatchling's body language, her drooping wings and downcast eyes, conveyed her melancholy, it did not exude even a hint of inner conflict.

"If you ever want a peaceful place away from the crowds of the city, Madivitra falls and the vale are always open to you."

"It's pretty there, Raen," Iriscendra said. "But even if I wanted to go back, I know I couldn't stay."

Raen adjusted her chain belt and fidgeted with the clasp. "You're right. It's wrong for me to make you feel guilty about something completely beyond your control." She wrapped a hug around Iriscendra's neck. A stab of loss pierced Raen's heart.

"It's not just the weaving. There's important missions for dragons with V'yennel."

"There *are* important missions." Raen swallowed a lump in her throat. "Take care of Veranna for me, won't you?"

Iriscendra nodded. "So that little slip of paper—that's all the goodbye V'yennel gets?"

Raen glanced momentarily at the parchment, then propped a fist on her hip. "He wouldn't want some kind of messy, emotional goodbye."

"You sure?" The hatchling's stared pricked at Raen's skin and rose goose bumps all across her arms.

"Of course I'm sure. Now, quit making this harder than it already is. I have to get back to the nest—those eggs could hatch any day, if they haven't already. I have a lifetime obligation ahead of me that I have to see through."

Iriscendra sat up from her naptime curl. "But you don't have to keep them there. Not really. V'yennel says magic around the elf city would keep them safe."

"I've already thought all this through. Mythrenese absolutely abhors the idea of city dwelling. He misses home."

Iriscendra blinked slowly. "You hiding . . .you're hiding behind him."

Raen folded her arms and scoffed. "I am not. What if *I* don't like the idea of being surrounded by so many—"

The tent flap flipped aside, and Vinyanel ducked in. When he saw Raen standing in the center of the tent, he stopped short. Private Asmenius halted mid-stride behind him.

Vinyanel grinned. "To what do I owe this pleasure?"

Raen wrung her cloak. From the corner of her eye, she caught Iriscendra's smirk. The hatchling nestled back down in her corner.

That little stinker.

After a moment of observing Raen's posture and expression, Vinyanel's countenance fell. He said over his shoulder, "Private, if you would not mind waiting outside?"

"Sir, yes, sir," Asmenius said. He pivoted and put his back to the tent.

"Raen, is something amiss?" Vinyanel said.

"No, nothing," Raen said. *I wish I had pushed that parchment a little further under the blanket.* "But don't let me keep you from your business with Asmenius. I'll get out of your way."

"This better not be another attempt at spiriting Iriscendra away." Vinyanel's smile returned. "But even if you were, you would suffer no more harsh handling from me. Speaking of which, what report on the wrist?"

Raen turned part way from Vinyanel. "It will be fine in another fortnight. Then I—the cast can come off."

"Then I . . .? You mean to take the cast off yourself, then. Back to your life in the mountains."

Vinyanel's expression was inscrutable. The easy cast of his mouth, the unfurrowed brow all said the idea had no impact on him. But within the amethyst depths of his eyes, something more tumultuous churned. Raen tore her glance away and stared at the woven mat covering the floor.

A measured step drew Vinyanel within half a pace of Raen. He reached toward her and pushed the lock of hair that hung over her face back over her ear. "That *is* what you want, correct?"

Raen's muscles tensed. Her cheeks flushed. "It's what needs to be done."

"A sense of duty is something I can thoroughly understand."

He stood so close. All six-foot-two of him, made to seem even larger by the black lacquered plate mail, now healed of all its hurts. And for once, he even smelled good—like strong soap and warm vitality against the cold of the mountain air. Raen raised her eyes to his. Her heart thundered, and for an eternal moment, she stood transfixed by the power of his will. She drew a shuddering breath.

His lips landed upon hers without any hint of hesitation. Firm, earnest, and full of consuming warmth. Dizziness swept over Raen, and her limbs threatened to cast her to the floor, but Vinyanel's assured hold on the back of her head and around her waist drew her deeper into his kiss. Here dwelt bliss and confusion and emotions so wild no mere intention of hers could tame them. Too soon, however, he drew away.

"I will commission Asmenius to see you safely home, then," he whispered.

Raen swung her arm around and belted Vinyanel across the face.

"What?" she cried. "Are you trying to be funny? Because if you are, stick to being a jerk. You're much better at it."

Vinyanel blinked and put a gauntleted hand to the angry welt already rising on his face. "But I thought . . . frankly, I am surprised . . ." He abandoned both half-formed sentiments, and his features hardened. "Take the escort or do not. It is clear I waste my time by trying to help or understand you." He turned on his heel and flung the tent flap aside, then stormed out.

"Help? You insufferable—" An outburst of tears robbed Raen of further words. She cast Iriscendra one last, tortured look, then burst from the tent and ran, unslackening, to where Mythrenese waited on the southern edge of camp.

44

FUTURE PATHS

"*Y*ou have been awfully quiet during this ride, my friend," Majestrin said.

I clenched my fists around the handholds on my saddle. For the first time since I had ridden the wind, it had no power to sooth my seething nerves. "If I open my mouth, I fear I would say nothing that would later be to my credit."

Majestrin laughed. "I'm used to insightful nuggets flowing through, nestled in the rest. If you want to sort what's troubling you, we've many hours before we reach Delsinon."

What was there to sort? I was on my way back to the life I wanted. The outgrowth of one I had chosen. By the means Creo had ordained. A life with no room for emotional entanglements. My bride would forever be the weapontake, for it does not weep when its groom comes home only for his burial.

I scoffed. "Why did Creo make maidens at once so difficult to ignore and impossible to understand?"

"You're this annoyed about Raen's note?" Majestrin said. "I told her she was better off skipping it altogether."

"You knew about the note?" I squashed the self-conscious sensation of having been made a fool. "Then perhaps someday, when I am not in such a foul temper, I will ask you what it said."

"You didn't read it?"

"I threw it into the fire when I found it." I glared into the distance.

Majestrin turned his head back to me. "That, you will have to ask her yourself, if you truly wish to know. She did not tell me what it would say, except that it would explain her sudden departure. If you didn't read it, then what ails you?"

A sigh loosened my rigid posture. "We spoke before she left. The conversation made my head spin. Nearly literally. It seemed to me she sought a farewell, and when I offered her some measure of safety on her way, she exploded like a vial of alchemist's fire."

"Does it not occur to you that perhaps she was seeking in you a firm reason to change her plans?"

I swallowed. "Actually, not for a moment. If that is the case, then I suppose I earned the welt I received." In an intervening moment where I contemplated Majestrin's estimation, my shoulders wound back into knots. "I cannot give her what she seeks. Not and fulfill the destiny Creo sets before me."

"Are you so sure?" Majestrin lifted a brow. "You are young in Creo's statutes to proclaim such an exclusionary absolute. Besides, isn't Veranna the one in charge of prophesying?"

We banked to the southwest, and the warm, fragrant breeze of my homeland stirred my hair back from my face in a whispering caress.

I rubbed the back of my neck. "It seems I have an apology to formulate, should our paths cross again."

Majestrin smiled, then turned his head back to the front.

"It is an unlikelihood that such an occasion would ever arise, though," I added.

Iriscendra zipped across our flight path. She circled Majestrin's neck, then nearly grazed the top of my head as she shot past, off to invent more maneuvers.

Majestrin continued forward, the steady rhythm of his slow wing beats unaltered by the hatchling's antics. "One can never tell where the unexpected might lead you, young Windrider."

ABOUT THE AUTHOR

Rebecca P. Minor can't help but tell stories, whether that's in the form of animation, illustration, novels, or really long retellings of weird things that happened when she was a carriage driver. Her favorite stories, however, involve dragons, elves, sword fights, and magic, all of which you'll find in her written work.

You can news and updates on her creative endeavors at http://www.rebeccapminor.com, where she muses on anything from fantasy reading and writing, to making artwork, to the life of mother and wife.

Because all of this hasn't driven her crazy yet, Rebecca is also the conference director of Realm Makers, an annual symposium for people of faith who write science fiction and fantasy. (http://www.RealmMakers.net)

Rebecca resides outside Philadelphia, PA with her husband three sons, some fancy rats, cats, and dogs. Unicorns aren't allowed according to the regulations of the borough.

ALSO BY REBECCA P. MINOR

Curse Bearer, The Risen Age Archive:Book 1

Divine Summons,The Windrider Saga: Book 1

A Greater Strength, The Windrider Saga: Book 2

Beyond Price, a short story: The Windrider Canticles

www.ingramcontent.com/pod-product-compliance
Lightning Source LLC
Chambersburg PA
CBHW051210120726
47905CB00004B/1054